for

—enjoy—

2-29-2012
Vic Edwards

HANGER

By Vic Edwards

Copyright © 2011 by Victor W. Edwards

All rights reserved.

No part of this book may be reproduced, scanned, or distributed in any printed or electronic form without permission.

Please do not participate in or encourage piracy of copyrighted materials in violation of the authors' rights. Purchase only authorized editions.

This is a work of fiction. Names, characters, places, products, and incidents either are the product of the author's imagination or are used fictitiously, and any resemblance to actual persons, living or dead, businesses, companies, events, or locales is entirely coincidental.

ISBN:1463527659
ISBN-13:978-1463527655

DEDICATION

To Mrs. Obra Simpson,
my English teacher at Garden High School,
Oakwood (Hanger), VA.

To Sue Coleman Edwards,
my wife and my first editor.

To Charlotte Edwards Duty,
my sister and my second editor.

CONTENTS

Acknowledgments　　　　　　　　　　i

Prologue
- 1　1930's
- 2　Graduation Nears
- 3　Looking Back
- 4　The '57 Flood
- 5　Decisions
- 6　A Leave of Absence
- 7　Discoveries
- 8　Aunt Paula
- 9　Brett
- 10　Washington, D.C.
- 11　The Wrong Turn
- 12　The Investigation Begins
- 13　Rufus
- 14　Alma the Detective
- 15　Aunt Paula-Aunt Ellie
- 16　Bed-n-Breakfast
- 17　Alma One-Ups Brett
- 18　Alma Moves Home
- 19　Alma Finds Diary
- 20　ROMEO Club
- 21　Christmas
- 22　New Year's at Brett's
- 23　Log House
- 24　The Cistern
- 25　Jill
- 26　Detective Rife
- 27　Krista

28 The Rest of the Journal
29 Alma's Revelations
30 Open House
31 Finally
32 Alma Looks Back
33 Railroad Right-of-Way
34 Leroy

ACKNOWLEDGMENTS

Many thanks and love to my wife Sue, as my first editor, for her many readings and superb guidance. Thanks to my sister Charlotte, as my second editor, for her insightful editorial skills.

Prologue

Hanger, VA 1937

The month of May was the one everyone was looking for. Then the leaves would start coming out on the numerous hardwood trees and by the end of the month the camouflage would be nearly complete. Although you couldn't get anyone to say it publicly, since the bread on the table and the roof over their heads depended on the coal being extracted from the ground, they hated to see the end of October when all the foliage, although beautiful with the reds and oranges of autumn, had fallen to the ground and exposed the scars of the mountainsides.

But now it was midsummer, and Leroy had to mop the sweat and dust from his forehead as he walked down the tracks, sometimes walking a rail for a ways, then stepping from tie to tie. He could run a rail for maybe a quarter of a mile before falling off, but today he was too tired. He removed the hardhat with the headlamp on top and mopped his face and neck with the stained red bandana from his back pocket. He stopped after a ways and sat on the rail as he took the lid off his lunch pail, a two-pound lard bucket, and took out the tin of tobacco and the paper to wrap his cigarette. He was lucky he was working outside now and could be one of the few men allowed to indulge in a smoke when he had a break or opportunity. As he rolled the cigarette and licked the paper edges to hold it together, he watched the trickle of water flow down the river. It was the same in West Virginia. In the dry months the fish had a hard time finding a puddle deep enough to survive in, and when the rains came they had to find a rock to hide under to keep from being swept downstream in the torrential flood sweeping down the steep mountainsides. Shortly, he rolled over onto one knee and pushed up to his feet. Just a few years ago he could have taken his break by resting on his haunches in a squat. When he was ready to go again he would just spring up to his feet and probably trot down the rail a few yards. Now he was tired. He just wanted to get home, a little roofing-tin shack some fisherman had abandoned on the bank of the Levisa River near Garden Creek, and rest a bit. It was about a two-mile walk and it would be pushing dark when he got there. His day had started before daylight around 5:00 and it would be nearly 8:00 that night before he lay down on his blanket stretched over a pile of pine straw.

Leroy "Gator" Stuart was only 28 years old, but he carried the look of a man that was much older and carrying a heavy load. He had a fourth-grade education and could read and write and figure his time and paycheck. He reckoned a person didn't need much more than that. The men at the Mingo mine had given him his nickname because he could fight like an alligator and would use his teeth if he had to save his skin in a deadly match. One time he had bitten off a big white man's earlobe to break a choke hold because it was the only thing available. Leroy had never seen a gator.

He hoped the men at this job wouldn't find out about his past. None of it. He had been through a violent young life but he didn't consider himself a violent person. The fights, and his scars as results, just meant he was a survivor. He wasn't going to take a bunch of shit from anyone, white or black. He would work hard for a small wage, but the days of slave labor were over with the end of the Civil War, and the last fight had been over collecting his wages for a week's work from a black mine foreman at the Mingo mine. The son-of-a-bitch had pocketed Leroy's paycheck, forged his name, and cashed it at the company store. The Superintendent had just shrugged his shoulders and said he had a canceled check. The black foreman lost his job anyway, when he stole from a white miner. That's when Lenny was hired. Leroy had liked working for Lenny Jackson, but the mine closed and Lenny moved on.

Now he had a new job and his wife Nikki and his four kids were his life. He had worked since he was twelve, and most of it had been in the coal mines of West Virginia. Most of his wages had disappeared in a bottle of liquor, store-bought or moonshine, or on gambling on dog fights in the hollows of Mingo County. He figured he could have done better with cards, but the white folks wouldn't let a black man in the game. Most of his day was spent working alongside white men with black faces and most of his night getting cheated or fighting black men that had nothing to lose. Leroy was young and strong. He had once set the record for loading coal in a 12-hour day. He liked the work. He liked the solitude, the darkness, and the cool temperature on a hot day. He didn't need much, and saving his small wages for a rainy day required long-range plans he didn't have. Then along came Nikki.

He had skipped work on his eighteenth birthday, bought a gallon of moonshine from his cousin Anthony, stole an inner tube from the trunk of a car sitting up on blocks, bought three cigars at the service station, stripped off his clothes and tied them and the jug to the tube, and was floating down the Tug Fork River. Nikki was fishing with a hickory pole for catfish for the family supper. Neither had seen the other until it was too late. Rounding a bend in the river with his head downstream, Leroy was only twenty feet away when he heard her scream and saw her turn away. Nikki had seen too much. He rolled off the tube, breaking the gallon jug floating behind him, and tried to place the tube between himself and the girl. When he was out of sight, he put on his clothes, turned the tube loose and hiked back upstream. He helped Nikki catch enough fish for a meal. In six months they were married and he was a new man. Plans for the future looked good if they could just get through this Depression.

He knew he shouldn't stay. Only two days on the job and he had been warned, threatened, and promised "the sun won't shine on your ass a week in Buchanan County." As far as he knew and from what the boss had told him, he was the first and only black man to take a job working in the coalfields of Southwest Virginia. He had no choice. His wife and four young children were just barely getting by on handouts from the local church in West Virginia. He'd had no job since the coal mine worked out and closed two years ago in Mingo County and his boss Lenny Jackson moved his family and took the foreman's job at Red Jacket Coal Company in Keen Mountain, Virginia. His family starving wasn't an option. Dying while trying to save them might be.

Leroy trudged on down the tracks. He looked over the twenty-foot bank of limestone railroad rock at the Levisa. You could almost step over the river in some places. On down below, where Garden Creek and Dismal Creek dumped in, the town of Grundy, the county seat of Buchanan, would sometimes be under water during a flood. Buchanan County was a scary place for Leroy. He had ridden through the county back in February when Lenny had come over to scout out a job. With no leaves on the trees, you could see deep into the hollows as you rode along narrow curvy roads with high banks and no guardrails. There were some yards on the north sides of the steep hills that still had snow from the month before because the sun never reached the ground. Sharp rocky cliffs hugged the edges of the road, and strangers kept a wary eye out for loose boulders that could as easily crush you as a roof fall deep inside the mine.

Today, in the middle of the summer, he looked up from the railroad bed towards the milky blue sky and the heavy green foliage of the trees. He could not see the stark roughness he knew lay underneath. He was sure the locals considered it one of the most beautiful spots under the heavens. Leroy knew the only way you could get into this hole near Hanger was to descend some mountain, unless you came up the Levisa River from Kentucky, and the only way out was to climb back up again. His only wish was to have the energy, time, and transportation to carry his paycheck to Nikki and the four girls on Sunday.

Lenny said that years back the only jobs available in the county were logging the steep hills for Ritter Logging Company. Now, coal mining and the railroad were the only jobs hiring in the whole Appalachian Mountains. Buchanan County was the best opportunity after Red Jacket moved in and set up a camp of houses and a company store at Keen Mountain. Leroy couldn't afford a company house, not that the company would rent him one anyway. He would just live in his little shack down the river below Hanger and leave his family in Mingo County, West Virginia where he would hitchhike a ride to on Sundays, his only day off.

Lenny had been his foreman in West Virginia over a crew of twelve men with Leroy being one of three blacks on the job. Leroy's job at the Mingo mine had been setting timbers to hold up the mine roof or loading coal. Lenny was the fire boss at that mine and also here at Red Jacket. He was the first man to enter the mine and he checked for unsafe conditions like rock falls or buildup of gas in the mine. Here, Lenny had him on the outside of the mine picking rock and slate out of the coal.

"Give you a chance to run if you have to," Lenny had said. If he worked inside he could have been trapped if trouble came. Let the men get to know him a little first, then they would try for a more skilled job at the face.

Leroy looked down the track to where a railroad crew was pouring the last cubic yards of concrete to build the trestle support over Garden

Creek. Two men were working around a large bucket and a third was climbing down a ladder to help. Norfolk and Western Railroad was putting in a new spur to run up to the Page mine. The rest of the country was still struggling from the economic collapse of 1929, but Buchanan County was climbing out of the Great Depression with the help and necessity of coal. Coal mining had replaced logging operations and the bigger mines required more railroad lines. A lot of starving people could be well-fed with backbreaking work in the coalfields of the Appalachians. Leroy hoped they wouldn't notice the color of his skin with all the black faces heading home at the end of the day.

As he got closer to the work site, Leroy noticed another man approaching from the Garden Creek road with a camera strapped around his neck and a notepad swinging from his hand as he walked the foot log across the creek. The man walked up to the workers who were pouring the last of the wet cement into the huge iron bucket to be hoisted up to the top to cap the concrete pier. The man with the camera waved him over.

Leroy shook his head and continued walking down the tracks above the Levisa River.

The man hollered at him to "come over here" and the other men were waving for him to join them. Leroy was used to following orders, especially when given by white men, and now might not be a good time to draw attention to himself. He crossed the foot log.

"I'm doing an article for the <u>Bluefield Daily Telegraph</u> on this new railroad being built and that big coal mine they're opening up at Page. I want a picture of men working to show how times are changing here in Buchanan County. Now, stand over there with them other fellers and put your hand on the bucket like you're helping. I'll step back across the creek so I can get you all in the shot."

The man with the camera walked back across the creek, took the picture, threw up his arm and waved, then walked on down the road. Leroy started to follow him, but the bigger man of the crew took hold of his arm and turned him back around.

"Now, boy, you wouldn't mind giving us a hand here with this bucket and rope would you?"

Lenny Jackson waited three days before he turned in Leroy's time card to the superintendent at Red Jacket Coal Company. He wasn't surprised that Leroy hadn't shown up to work. He didn't ask any questions, didn't go down to the shack on the Levisa River to check it out, and he didn't make a call to his brother in Mingo County to see if Leroy showed up back home. He didn't want to know. Lenny just did his job and was glad to have it.

1

1930's

  The Great Depression had taken its toll on the people of the Appalachian Mountains. They didn't have the skyscrapers to jump out of, but when the logging jobs left, they were hopeful to hold onto the milk cow and the hillside garden. Then the railroad came. Well, they had kind of a railroad before that, to haul the timber from the lumber company out of the county when the river wasn't running deep enough to float the logs. But in the '30s coal and coalmining were the big hope for the people, or at least for the owners of the coal rights that were acquired during the Depression years. With the opening of the big mine, the railroad was ready with new lines and plenty of coal cars and smoking locomotives.
  Most of the logging jobs were lost, and farming the steep hillsides and bartering their goods

and services kept them hanging on. Then came a deal they couldn't turn down.

The old Ford jalopy came bouncing up the rutted-out road of the hollow, stirring up dust and scattering the groundhogs and chipmunks back over the creek bank or into their holes in the hillside. The driver parked at the gate and opened it enough to slip inside and walk up the worn footpath to the front porch. The rugged-looking farmer in his bibs, with a dirty white t-shirt underneath, and his wife with two hair curlers still showing above her forehead sat on the wooden bench in the shade of the porch. Four children, a teenage boy and two younger girls loitered on the steps below, while an older girl, maybe 17 years of age, was peeling potatoes and dropping them into a bucket of water near her chair on the other end of the porch.

"Good morning, folks. Ah, make that afternoon. The day has already slipped by the dinner hour, hasn't it? Hope you can spare me a minute of your time and maybe a cool glass of water?"

"Ike, go fetch the man a chair and a glass of water." The man and wife kept their seats on the bench and she wiped her forehead with the end of her apron, as she waved the girls inside. The visitor looked like he could eat more potatoes than were in the pot.

"You looking for someone in particular, Mister, or are you just looking for a shady spot, like a sheep, to put your head under?"

The newcomer chuckled a little and loosened his tie around his neck. "I guess a little bit of both.

I'm looking for the Baileys, and was told they live up in this hollow."

"We're Baileys."

"Well, I was wondering if you all are having it as rough as other folks in the county. I got something to talk to you about that might give you a little relief."

"We ain't interested in buying nothing, Mister."

"Nothing to sell. If you'll hear me out, there might be a way for you to get your hands on a little money and you don't really give up anything. How about that?"

The farmer and his wife looked at each other. The man in the tie leaned his chair back against the wall and took a long swig of the water. Mention money and you always had their attention.

"Boy, go in the house and fetch my gun."

As the teenager jumped to his feet and banged through the screen door, the man sloshed his water out of the glass as his chair hit the floor.

"Now wait a minute! You haven't heard what I've got to say. This could be cash in your pocket, like it has happened for a lot of your neighbors. If you don't like what I'm proposing, you can just tell me and I'll be on my way. No hard feelings."

The boy handed the single-barrel shotgun to his father and reclaimed his seat on the steps with his back to a post. The farmer placed it across his lap with the end of the barrel pointed towards the other end of the porch.

"What's your name and where you from, in case this don't go well, and we have to notify somebody?"

"My name is John and I'm working for them lawyers Steel and Leggel down at the county seat. You know of a few coal mines that have opened up around the county, don't you?"

"Yeah, I've heard of a few. Can't get a job there, though. They only have a few men working and they're mostly kin. What's your point?"

"Well, we're not hiring men to work. We're just trying to give people a little money for rights to the coal that might or might not be under the ground they own. Now, take you. You got a few acres of land, and if, mind you a big IF, there's coal underneath, we're willing to gamble and pay you so much for each acre you own to mine that coal."

"How do you know there's coal on my land?"

"We don't. Might not be. It might cost us too much to get it out if you do. We're just willing to take the chance and pay you now, per acre, for something that might not be there and might not happen. You still own the land and can do anything you want with it, including sell it to somebody else. It could be years or maybe never, before we find out you do have, or don't have, a little coal on your land. You can't lose. You get our money and get to keep the land."

"What about the fellow that might buy my farm? What's he getting?"

"He don't get anything except the farm. He gets everything you got, except the coal, if there is any."

"That don't make sense. Why'd you buy a pig in a poke?"

"I agree, it's a gamble. But some folks, like these lawyers, have a little extra money and they're willing to share it with some of the folks that don't and are hurting a lot in these times. They can't just give it away, but they're willing to bet that times will get better and that coal might be available here in the county. They might be able to afford to put in a small mine and put some of their neighbors, maybe you and the boy there, to work and maybe make a little money on their investment. Now what's wrong with that?"

The farmer shook his head and looked over at his wife again. She didn't look back, but fiddled with the apron strings in her lap.

"Tell you what, you folks think it over and if you're a mind to make a little money fer nothing, then come into the office and those lawyers will explain it better to you. They can have you sign a piece of paper and write you a check the same day. You got a way to town?"

"I reckon if we're a mind to do it, we'd find a ride to town. We had to sell the old truck last year, but we got good neighbors."

"Well, thanks for the shade and the water. You all must have spring water up here. Most of the water I'm offered ain't fit to drink."

He lowered the chair to the floor and tightened up his tie and reached his hand towards Mr. Bailey.

"I've got to call on a few of your neighbors over in the next hollow today. So you folks have a good day and let's all hope times get better soon."

He walked off the porch and down the path and through the gate to his car. After he turned around, he left it running as he got out and came back to latch the gate he had failed to do, on his way through.

"Hey, Mister. How much you think they'd pay?"

"How many acres you own?"

"A couple hundred, give or take."

"I'd guess you could get more'n a hundred dollars, if you strike a hard bargain."

The Baileys sat in their seats without saying anything for a long spell. The man got out his twist of tobacco and cut off a piece and placed it in his jaw. In a little while he just got up, spit into the yard, and walked towards the barn.

He didn't come in for supper. His wife fed the kids some brown beans, fried potatoes, and some milk and bread. Afterwards, the girls washed up the dishes and they all gathered around the radio to listen to some live bluegrass music from Bristol. Finally, she shooed the kids up to the loft to bed or to read a book, and she went to the chair on the porch and rocked back and forth, on the two back legs, while she listened to the night sounds of the hollow.

Later she heard the creak of the gate and he came lumbering up the path and took a seat on the top step and leaned back against the post.

"Guess we got to do it?"

"I guess." She couldn't see his face, but she could sense the clinched jaw and the frown over the brow.

"The store said they would have to cut us off if we didn't pay a little something on the account."

"I know. We hardly buy anything now. A little seasoning, some flour and sugar, and some seeds in the springtime. We do need to buy the kids some shoes come school time."

"We got the sow and the milk cow. Maybe we could raise a few pigs and a calf and sell them until me and the boy can get a job."

"Maybe. Where we gonna get milk while the calf is nursing? And we need to butcher that hog to get through the winter. If we don't pay the taxes this year, we might not have anything to sell and we'd need a place to stay."

"I know. It's like cutting off an arm or a leg. We sold off the timber two years ago and it got us through until now. I guess this could buy us another year or two."

"I guess."

They heard a hoot owl down the hollow. He looked up at the dark sky and the many bright stars twinkling through the treetop branches. She glanced towards the upstairs window as she heard it squeak closed. Maybe Elaine could sleep now.

About Twenty Years Later-Late 1950'S

2

Graduation Nears

She moved slowly up the dirt road, crisscrossing from shoulder to ditch line. She bent over and broke off a stickweed near the root dug into the black soil of the bank. She peeled off the lower leaves of the stick and left the ones on the end and it reminded her of a feather duster her grandmother had once used on the furniture. As she trudged up the hollow, she swirled the green-tipped duster in the dirt at her feet. She was barefooted and the cool packed dirt of the road felt good on her feet. Her mother had told her to put on her shoes before she went up the hollow to find the milk cow, but this was one little rebellion she could get away with. What did it matter if she had on shoes or not? It wasn't like adding shoes with a homemade dress was going to make her into some kind of fashion model.

She swung her stick at a butterfly fluttering over a white bloom on another weed and broke off her green duster. One of these days she would come back and introduce the word 'fashion' to this family. She was about to heave the three-foot skinny stick into the creek when the thought occurred to her she might need it when she found the cow, to drive the animal back to the house for milking.

She heard the humming of a gospel song coming from around the curve just ahead. She knew it would be Bobby long before she could see him. When she rounded the curve, there was the shabby overweight man-child sitting on a rock tossing gravel from the road into the creek and humming his heart out. He sat with legs spread wide; resting his head on one fist with the elbow perched on his kneecap. Bobby had noticed her coming out of the corner of his eye. He now turned his head sideways and peered from underneath dark bushy eyebrows and through gnarly, long black hair at Alma's approach, as though he were looking underneath his armpit. Alma's intention was to slide by the boy with little more than a smile and be on her way.

"Where you going?"

"Hi, Bobby. Just going to get the cow."

"Where's your shoes?"

"I left them home this time. Where's yours?"

"You know I don't wear shoes 'cept in the wintertime. Why you carrying that switch?"

"I might need it to drive the cow home. Ain't it about time you got back home for supper, Bobby?"

"Hit don't matter. I reckon if I don't show up by dark, someone'll come lookin' fer me. Haint never tried that though. Could be they wouldn't. Scared of the dark though, so I guess I'll be edging on down the road."

"You do that, Bobby. Tell you what, if I have to go as far as the old Martin place to find that stupid cow, I'll fetch you an apple from that broken-down tree and leave it on the fence post by your front gate."

Bobby smiled at her through yellow stained teeth as he rolled off the rock and struggled to right himself. Alma was afraid he might try to hug her so she scurried on up the road a bit to get out of his way. She had heard the poor guy had lice sometimes and, by looks of the knotted hair, she wasn't taking any chances.

Alma watched him waddle down the road much as a drunk might. She had no doubt that Bobby would find his way home. This was rather routine for him. His parents, now senior citizens, with only Bobby left at home out of eight children, had given him freedom for years to walk up the dirt road of the hollow, but not down the road below the house towards the highway. As far as Alma knew, Bobby didn't go anywhere except to church on Wednesday and Sunday nights. He had never been to school. The nice people called him 'slow', but the kids up the hollow and some of the grown men at church called him a 'retard'.

Alma always spoke to Bobby and gave him a minute when she ran into him on the way searching for the cow or when Alma's mother sent her up to Bobby's house with some food or a Christmas gift. She once sat on that same rock with him for several minutes talking and hoping to make the man smile. She had asked Bobby if he liked going to church.

"Of course I do, Alma. I'm a Christian. I sometimes get so happy I get up and shout like some of those women do."

"What makes you so happy?" Alma had asked.

"Cause Jesus loves me. Don't you get happy when you go to church, Alma?"

"I don't go to church unless they make me. I don't think Jesus knows me."

Bobby's face was not smiling. He took hold of Alma's shoulders and shook her a little. "You gotta go to church or you'll go to hell."

Alma had smiled and promised Bobby she would. She wasn't afraid of him, although he was overweight and strong as a mule. Bobby was probably in his mid-thirties, going on six years of age and she had never heard of him hurting a fly. What she had wanted to tell him, but she knew it would be the same as talking to the rock, was that she didn't have a lot of faith in churches run by men for the benefit of mankind. Not 'peoplekind' or 'womenkind', just 'mankind'.

She watched Bobby walk around the curve and out of sight and she turned up the hollow to find the cow. Sure enough the cow was chomping away at some weeds and grass on the hillside of the old abandoned Martin farm up the left fork of the road where she usually found her this time of evening. Alma picked an apple for Bobby and one for herself from the old tree and, with the switch, headed the cow down the hollow towards home. Getting late as it was, she would probably have to hold a lantern for her mother to see by as she milked the cow.

Early Saturday morning, she climbed in the back of her Uncle Bert's old beat-up and faded-out grassy green Chevy pickup truck. She and William joined their three cousins Bob, Billie, and Bo in the truck bed and her mother rode up front in the cab with her uncle and Aunt Molly. They were going up to the old family farm, that was now not part of the family since everyone had abandoned it years ago, to pick cherries from the few remaining trees that had not been cut down, blown over, or rotted away. She didn't want to go, but she couldn't blame her mother for seizing the opportunity to visit the place where she grew up and bringing home enough fruit, which they couldn't afford to buy, to bake a few pies and maybe can some for the winter.

The 200-acres, more or less, mountaintop farm still had some fruit trees on the high ridges, although most of the timber and coal rights had been sold off years ago by her grandfather. Alma couldn't remember anything but steep hills and deep hollows, but she had been told of the flowering orchard and bountiful garden that had sustained the large family of ten through good times and bad. What she found hard to believe were the tales of acres of corn and hay growing on the steep sides of the hollows that now contained brush and small trees and lots of rocks. Her mother had told of milking two cows and her dad and brothers killing a beef and three hogs every year. They had even sold excess produce and milk for spending money along with the cash crop allotment of tobacco. People from all over the county would haul off sacks of apples on horseback in the fall.

Alma didn't know how it could have been that good. Some of the family should have stayed on the mountain and kept that wonderful farm going. They would have certainly been better off than the Woodsons had been during the Depression. Alma was just glad it was over before she got here.

Her mother could have at least left William home. He was always showing off with brave boy stuff, like now hanging over the edge of the truck bed, just waiting to be bounced off when they hit the next rock or tree branch hiding in the dusty road. When they came to the third switch-back there was a blind curve with the sharp edge of a boulder hanging over part of the road. Uncle Bert laid on the horn to warn a possible vehicle coming down the mountain and William reach up and patted the rock with his hand as they crept by.

It was a long day for Alma. She didn't like the outdoors with the sweat bees taking a bite out of her every few minutes, trying to sidestep the poison ivy clinging to the base of every tree, and being on the lookout for snakes. She had to admit that William added a little sport and fun to the outing. While Uncle Bert took a long ladder and climbed to the tops of the blackhart cherry trees, William crawled out on the red cherry tree limbs and bent them down, so the girls could reach and pick the bright red cherries standing on the ground. He ate more cherries than he put in his bucket and spit the seeds down on the tops of their heads. Of course her bucket was mostly empty, also, as she had thrown a majority of them at

William or bounced them out on the ground while she was swinging on the branch he was riding, trying to knock him out of the tree on his head.

After half the day was gone and her mother had filled all the containers she had brought, she came to the tree Alma and William were working on and helped them finish filling their buckets.

"Come on, Alma. Let's walk a bit while William helps his cousins finish up here. We'll have a bite to eat when we get back."

"Where are we going?"

"Just around the ridge a little, to the cemetery. I want to clean up a little around your grandpa's grave. Don't know when I might get back up here again."

"Can't I just help Aunt Molly get lunch ready?"

"Ain't much to do there."

They walked a half-mile around the ridge to the overgrown cemetery. There had once been a fence surrounding the graves, but now there was only brush and shrubs marking where the row used to be. If you raked your shoes through the layer of leaves and twigs you might find a strand of rusted out barbwire or a hunk of decaying post. She stood with her arms crossed watching her mother on her knees pulling weeds and vines and raking out decay from the engravings in the small stone marking the head of the grave.

"This is your grandpa, Isaac Bailey's, grave. You were just a child when he passed. Don't guess you even remember what he looked like."

"I've seen pictures."

"Over there is your great-grandpa Jacob's grave with the bigger stone. It looks like it's about to tumble over. Could you straighten it up a bit? Maybe wedge some rocks in at the base to hold it sturdy."

She kept her arms crossed as she shuffled over to the tilted marker. She didn't notice her mother watching her. Hesitating to even touch the stone, she eventually stooped down to where she could read the faded-out inscription a little. She could read his name and the date of birth looked like 1830s something. She scratched through the leaves and found a small sharp piece of shale rock and began scraping at the numbers and lettering.

Jacob Hasting Bailey
1830 – 1882
A Farmer

She was still scraping on the headstone when her mother knelt down beside her with several small rocks cradled in her ever-present apron. They both looked at the marker a few more minutes. Then her mother stood up and pushed it back into its indention in the ground. Silently, Alma began wedging the small rocks in around the base.

After several minutes of pulling weeds and vines off the grave, they walked back to join the others in the orchard. Aunt Molly had spread the lunch out on the tailgate of the truck. Alma only ate one of the fried apple pies and drank one of the orange sodas Uncle Bert had bought as a treat for the kids.

The next day she was in the garden. Alma hated it! She hated her life. She had decided when she was only in the tenth grade that just as soon as she graduated from dear old Garden High School she was out of here.

She worked in the garden, a relatively flat spot on the hill above her house, supposedly hoeing potatoes. She hacked a few weeds down but probably cut more potatoes hiding under the hill than she had weeds. She spent most of the time cursing to herself, because her dad would have cut a switch off the mulberry tree and thrashed her a few licks if he heard any 'bad' words or saw her throwing rocks at her brother at the other end of the row. She hated hoeing in the garden. Her mother always said she had enough help in the house with her older sister Janice and made Alma go with her dad. The real reason Krista, her younger sister, had said was because Alma picked on the younger ones and kept an uproar going in the house. Well, this family didn't know what uproar was. She gave another vicious blow with her hoe and when she pried it out of the dirt, a small seed potato was wedged on the end of it.

"Alma, why don't you go up there and move those rocks, under that walnut tree, over to the edge of the woods. When I get through here, we'll plant a patch of strawberries in that spot."

"Aw, Dad. I moved that rock-pile from this potato patch last summer."

"Well, we should have put them out of the way, somewhere. Bert brought me a hundred strawberry plants the other day and we got to get them in the ground. That's the only cleared ground left to plant them."

"Can't William move those rocks? I've already got a blister handling this da…hoe."

"Stuttering there a bit, ain't you, girl. William's not slicing up potatoes and you'll both get a lot more done if you get on those rocks. If you get us a spot cleaned out before dark, I'll let you carry the water for the plants and have William dig up the ground. That ought to save those blisters."

Hooray! She now had the honor of carrying gallons of water from the creek up the hill so those precious strawberry plants could have a decent chance of surviving. She'd had to do it before for the sweet potato plants and the tomato plants and the pepper plants and every other damn plant in the damn garden. She was sick of it.

She picked up a small rock and carried it over to the edge of the woods. Just beyond was a huge poplar tree. She glanced back at her father and brother and saw their heads down concentrating on their work. She eased over and peeped once again from behind the big tree. They hadn't noticed. She smoothed out a pile of leaves and sat down looking down the hollow and over the ridges beyond Route 460. That would be the road out of here. One of these days.

The only good things to happen in her life had been making the basketball team and getting to spend a night once in a while with her friend Joalean. Being on the team meant she could go somewhere two nights a week and wear something besides her homemade dresses. Her mother wouldn't go to any more of her games, after the one she had attended and saw her daughter dressed very inappropriately in a pair of tight short shorts. Janice and Alma had laughed many times about their parents arguing whether Alma should go out for the basketball team.

"Dad, Mom says I can't go out for the basketball team. She says decent girls shouldn't go parading around in public wearing a pair of shorts. Does she think we can play basketball in a dress? Now that would be indecent, when you go tumbling and your dress tail goes flying up over your rear."

"Settle down, honey. I'll have a talk with your mother. You might be able to help your case some by helping her out a little more with all this housework and canning."

"I do my fair share. The others can help out, too. It seems all we do up here in the hollow is go to school and work. Well, I'd like to add a little fun to that. When William graduates, he's probably going to join the Army and be off to see the world. What are us girls supposed to do? Marry some local redneck and settle down in one of these dark lonesome

hollows? I don't see why we can't join the Army, too."

"Thank God you can't," he thought. He did sympathize with her, though.

"Elaine, girls don't get a fair shake. Girls only have the one sport they can play in high school, and that is basketball. That gives some of them their only chance to get out of the county and meet and compete with someone who isn't their neighbor and see more than the steep hillsides of Southwest Virginia. For most of them, it is the only time they have the opportunity to eat in a restaurant, wear something that isn't homemade, or shed some of their frustrations by beating a basketball onto the floor and maybe holding their hands up over their heads in victory. Winning at something is good."

Alma stomped out and his wife shook her head, stiffened her back and her upper lip.

"I don't care what she needs. She needs to be a lady. A good Christian woman doesn't go around half-naked for the world to see. Why can't you get her to take some home economic classes instead of another year of shorthand and typing? If she wants to work instead of getting

married and raising a family, she could get a job at the hospital or the school cafeteria and maybe help someone that needs it."

"That's you, what you would do. I couldn't imagine you in a short dress, much less short shorts, even though I've told you often you have the prettiest legs I've ever seen."

"They'd better be the only legs you have seen."

"Of course they are. She's not like the other children. When she graduates she is going to be leaving the county and she needs to be able to take care of herself. There's nothing to hold her here. She wants to see the world."

"Well, you saw the world and came back here. Why wouldn't she?"

"Yeah, but I came back because my heart was here. You were here. The world would be a small place if everyone stayed where they came from. The best chance we have for her coming back is to support her in leaving. I won't oppose you on this, but I suggest we let her play basketball and visit her few friends outside the county. In a couple of years the decision won't be ours to make."

She slumped a little in her chair and the upper lip eased into a half-smile. She got up and walked over and laid her head on his shoulder.

"I know you're right. I just don't want to see them grow up and move away. I also don't know what to say if someone in church sees her in a pair of those shorts."

"Nobody that goes to our church goes to a basketball game. If you hear a comment about her showing off her legs, just say 'ain't they pretty'."

Spending a night with Joalean was a real treat. They had an indoor bathroom and a tub/shower you could bathe in forever, except Joalean would yell for you to get out and not use all the hot water. They had a television and she and her friend would stay up all night watching if Mrs. Huffman didn't come in and turn it off so "somebody in the house could get some sleep." They would go to Joalean's bedroom; she had one all to herself, and giggle as quietly as possible over all the things they thought were hilarious in school and in their families. A few times Mrs. Huffman had persuaded Alma's mom to let her go with Joalean to Roanoke to visit or stay overnight at her mother's house.

That was Heaven! Joalean's grandparents were different from any grandparents Alma had ever known. Not only did they live in a big brick house in the city, but they also owned two cars and her grandfather worked on the railroad. He would take them down to the rail station and let them visit a short time on the train. Sometimes he would take them up to the engine and let them sit in the seat he used as an engineer and blow the steam whistle.

Joalean's mother would take them to the theater while they were in Roanoke, and that's where Alma saw GONE WITH THE WIND for the first time. She didn't like the war much and all the killings, but she fell in love with Atlanta and the fabulous plantations and the beautiful gowns the ladies got to wear to the parties. The slaves working and waiting on the rich folks didn't bother her much because they were so well taken care of. She would have gladly fed and housed a few if they would hoe the garden and pile the rocks and tend to the noisy little ones running around the house.

Joalean's grandfather took them to the Riverside Amusement Park one afternoon and she got to ride a Ferris Wheel higher than any building she had ever been in, which was probably Garden High School. They rode the roller coaster at speeds that would take your breath away. She ate cotton candy and caramel candy apples for the first time. She was given money to play games and ride the bumper cars. She and Joalean laughed and squealed as they tried to knock each other out of the cars. They later ate at a restaurant and Alma tried and loved the taste of shrimp. The only seafood she had ever eaten wasn't really seafood. It had been trout or bass or catfish her uncles caught in a stream or lake.

On the ride home down Route 460, Alma and Joalean would hold their heads out the open windows and let the breeze blow their hair. Sometimes they wouldn't speak for long periods of time as they closed their eyes and relived the past day and all they had experienced. Joalean was pretty much like Alma and couldn't wait to escape the hills of Buchanan County. The only difference was she wanted to marry a rich man and have some children she could spoil, and live in a city much bigger than Roanoke. Alma would never settle for Roanoke, either, but she wasn't looking for a husband. She wanted to see the world and experience all it had to offer. No man would ever allow his wife to seek her fortune and fame. She would just have to put that on the back burner.

When she came home from one of her outings with Joalean, she would spend days telling her siblings all she had done. They would sit around her, captivated by all they heard and awed by her bravery to ride a roller coaster or Ferris Wheel. This would just be the beginning of things to come. Famous places and famous people would be the stories she would bring home. Not news of how many gallons of blackberries you were able to pick or how many jars of beans you canned this morning or whose kid had the measles or chickenpox or why so-and-so doesn't come to church anymore.

Alma's brief outings were always over way too soon. She would find herself back in the house or up in the garden yelling at someone or having somebody yelling at her. The little ones were cute sometimes, but they got on her nerves. Janice did most of the caring and wiping noses and such. Alma just tried to stay out of the way and get her share at the table before it was all gone. It seemed they lived on beans and potatoes and cornbread. Sometimes they would have fried chicken or chicken and dumplings on Sunday, especially if some of the church people were coming for dinner. Her parents went to the Old Primitive Baptist Church, and when it was time for church to be held at Garden Creek they would often have preachers or members staying over for the night. It wasn't like the family had enough to eat, but when you had guests you gave your best and made do the rest of the week.

Alma was tough. You had to be to survive in Buchanan County. She could hold her own with anyone in the family and would hold her tongue only when her dad looked at the switch hanging over the picture, in an oval frame, of his parents. Her family had never owned an automobile but they usually got rides in one belonging to a relative or a neighbor. From the pictures she had seen of her grandparents, there had always been a horse or mule nearby. She guessed they were really tough.

She remembered living in at least a half dozen houses growing up. The next one had always been a little bit better than the last one. But not one had ever had an indoor bath or running water. She had to carry a lot of the water, from the well out in the yard for drinking and cooking and from the creek to wash clothes. It was a wonder all the family hadn't died from drinking after one another from the dipper floating in the water bucket. She hated using the outdoor toilet, but she hated even more taking a bath in the tub or taking time to heat up enough water on the woodstove to wash with. The first thing she was going to buy the family when she got a job was a bathroom and a sink with running water to wash dishes in. The next thing might be an electric stove for her mother to use. She really thought these people didn't know what was out there. They had done it this way all their lives.

Of course, the family income could have something to do with it. Her dad was the only wage earner in the family, and he only taught school and did a little work for the newspaper once in a while. She didn't know for sure, but she didn't think he made more than two thousand dollars a year. She guessed that wouldn't go too far in providing for six people. No wonder they didn't have a car. It would probably cost that much to run the damn thing.

HANGER

The girls' basketball team wasn't nearly as good as the boys'. She couldn't imagine girls running the whole length of the court for the duration of a game. While she was on the team there were six girls from each team on the floor at the same time. Three played offense on one end of the court, and three played defense on the other end. When the defense could get a rebound or steal the ball they would pass it across the half court line to the offense to try to make a basket. Alma played mostly defense because the coach thought she was tough. She wasn't that tough. An elbow in the ribs hurt, but she always gave a few more than she received. Twice she was called for unnecessary roughness and ejected once. Her sister said she played like she was mad at someone. She wasn't angry at anybody; just life in general.

The boys' team was very good. Her junior year they played for the State Championship and won it. She only got to go to a few of the boys' games. She especially enjoyed watching Brett Parker play. He was Garden's star player and usually led the team in scoring. Harold Shortridge was pretty good, too, but he was shorter and it appeared to be his role to get the ball to Brett. Brett and Harold both came to watch the girls play. Krista always said it was because they liked to look at the girls' legs in those short shorts. Alma threatened her that if she told their mother that, she would pull her hair out.

Brett did tell her once, "Good game". He also asked her why she didn't come to more of the boys' games. Alma couldn't tell him it was because she didn't have the money or that her mother wouldn't let her, so she just said she was too busy to spend her time watching a bunch of greedy boys hogging the ball and showing off.

Brett also asked her to dance one time in gym class. Every Thursday the PE teachers made the boys' and girls' classes join together to learn how to dance. Alma hated it. It would be years later before she would appreciate what the class was doing for her ability to waltz with a man at a social function or a Presidential Ball and not stumble all over herself or step on her partner's toes. But dancing with Brett was like an elementary kid dancing with a ballet instructor. He was so tall and could dance like he played basketball. His expertise showed in both. She usually grabbed

Wallace for a partner in class. He was a little clumsy and shy. He wasn't about to hold a girl close enough to squeeze the breath out of her like Brett would.

Brett never asked her to dance again, and he seldom spoke or looked her way in the hallway between classes. In fact, he usually was carrying one of the cute cheerleader's books or getting her to giggle over one of his stupid jokes. That was alright with Alma. One of these days she would be dining with a Congressman or an airline pilot at a fancy restaurant in New York City while he and his cheerleader wife were trying to figure out what to serve their bunch of kids for supper on a coalminer's wages.

"Alma! Alma! Alma, supper's ready. You'd better get to the house."

She jumped up and looked around the tree. William was standing at the top of the hill at the edge of the garden hollering his head off. She looked back towards where the sun should be closing in on the ridgeline and realized it was already gone. She was in the shadow of the hills now. It would be dark in an hour. How long had she sat there? The rock pile was still there. Her dad was going to be furious.

3

Looking Back

Alma's father wasn't furious, but he was determined that his children know and appreciate the value of hard work and hard times. He called Janice, Alma, William, and Krista into the living room and had them sit on the floor at his feet, as he rocked back and forth in the old squeaky rocking chair. More than once, he had let his children know he wasn't just a teacher when he was in the classroom. This time he told them how it was back when the men wished they had a job and could work, and how they later fought a war so families like theirs could own a small piece of land and plant things like potatoes and strawberries. Sometimes they had to move the rocks, first.

The man was the man of the house. He was the wage earner and he put the roof over their heads and food on the table. As he struggled, the family struggled. Not just the Woodsons or the Baileys, but also the Matneys, Hageys, Meadows, and even Joey

HANGER

Thornton. The last few years had not been good. First, he had lost his job and had to beg, borrow, or steal to do his job. As the Great Depression ended, the Great War came. He wasn't home, but the family had enough money to keep the farm until he got back from the war.

Joey was one of the lucky few that did make it back, although he saw the horrors of the war and watched many of his buddies die in the ditches, or on the beaches of another country, or, even worse, in his arms, before it was over. He killed as many men, who looked just like him and probably had families somewhere to get back to, as he could. It wasn't a choice. He had a family back in the Appalachian Mountains of Southwest Virginia who had fought their own war for the last ten years and had survived. The sooner he could end this nightmare the better for everyone.

The hero's welcome back in New York City lasted too long, but at long last he walked up the hollow to the only welcome that mattered, into the arms of the only ones that knew him. His wife gave him a hug and a kiss and held to his arm as she opened the gate and let the kids swarm over him. The smallest girl he held in his arms, he had never seen except in a picture he carried taped to the inside of his helmet. They all walked to the porch, where he dropped his duffel bag and sat on the bench beside his wife and sipped a cold glass of spring water. There were smiles and tears and more smiles, except from the four-year old he still held in his arms, who was still trying to figure out why she should love him, too.

Shortly, he got up and they all walked to the barn. He had yet to step inside the house. He stroked the milk cow on the head and tossed a couple ears of corn to the two hogs in the pen. They walked to the garden and he picked a ripe red tomato from the vine. As he bit into it, the juice ran down his chin and stained the uniform he had guarded so closely the past few years. It didn't matter now. The stain was the most enduring medal he wore.

The next few years were the same all over the country. The men had to secure a wage-earning job, make some repairs on the house and barns, and get a crop in the field. He seldom turned the radio on or bought a newspaper. Topics of conversation were turned in the middle of a sentence to the crop yield or the weather forecast. What was done was done. His pride turned to the new acreage he had bought, or addition to the herd, or the new wing on the back of the house, or the new machines that were making his power bill go up. His back stooped a little as he watched his oldest son walk down the hollow to register for the draft.

Alma hated she had brought a lecture on her siblings. She hadn't gotten to be a senior in high school without learning about the Great Depression and World War II. Her father was right about 'his time', but 'her time' was different. She thought about her generation and their migration to the cities. Josh told her about his father's reaction to his choice to go to Ohio.

The exodus from the hollows of the Appalachian Mountains was nothing compared to the rest of the country. The Cold War was in full swing between the Communism and Capitalism rages of the world. Boys, like her cousin Josh, were drafted or volunteered for the war in Korea, or swelled the college ranks. The girls made their way to Washington, D.C., New York, and California to work the switchboards or the typewriters. Elvis, Chuck Berry, Little Richard, and Jerry Lee Lewis pushed up the pulse rate and the tempo beat to the Rock and Roll music of choice. The ropes of social restraint that had held the young and restless to a rigid culture broke and the dash to individual freedom swept over the country, much as the flood waters of the mountain rivers washed over their only towns.

When they returned from the war, serving their country in other countries, the young men were somewhat confused and frustrated about why they were fighting. There were no glorious celebrations on their return home. They were not hungry to put in a crop or mend any fences. They shunned the solitude of the hollows and the mountain farms. Their pulse was racing with the beat of the time and they were impatient to join the frantic surge to the cities and the large factories to earn their fortune.

"The auto factories in Ohio are paying good wages for workers, Dad."

"So I've heard."

"Jack and I thought we'd head up there next month and see if we could get one of those jobs."

"That so? Josh, you know you're the oldest and I always figured you'd want to take over here someday."

"I know, Dad. But, I don't have a lost love living down the hollow or the longing to see what the land will yield to my careful and backbreaking cultivation of its rich soil. I don't want to work the mines or teach the kids or coach the teams or write for the newspaper. I'm not sure I'm as religious as you and Mom, and I don't have an inclination to join those in the pulpit. I would like to have the chance to make my fortune and if I should eventually choose farming, I would much prefer it be a large ranch out in Montana or somewhere."

"You'd be pulling up your roots, son."

"I know, but I'll put them back down sometime and somewhere. I just don't believe anymore that these mountains are my destiny."

"Have you told your mother?"

"Not yet. I'll find the nerve to tell her in a few days. You and Mom have done great here, and built all this into a good home, and I don't know of any family more loved or happier. I just can't see settling down here to wait for the trees to grow into timber or hope for a coal mine to open and provide for me and a family. Can you see where I'm coming from, Dad?"

"Much to your surprise I suppose, I do. Times are a lot different now. Your mom and I don't feel the urge to run with you kids. We're contented with what we have and we cherish the peace and love of our neighbors and the church. The place will be here and it's paid for. One of these days one of you

kids might want to revisit and, if not, it might help out on a ranch out west or something."

The young man and the old man stood in the garden leaning on the hoe in their hands and smiled at each other. The young man fought back a tear forming in the back of his eyes. He bent over and laid his hoe on the plowed earth. As he passed by the old man, he placed his hand gently on the stooped shoulders and gave him a soft pat.

The old man dug up another weed from the hill of potatoes. He turned and watched his son disappear over the edge of the hillside garden, then took the red bandana out of his rear pocket, wiped his brow, and blew his nose.

Oakwood, VA – 1957

4

The '57 Flood

In her last year of high school, Alma began working hard on her sister Janice. She made fun of her begging for a ride to the Dime Store to work all day for four dollars. She told how, when she graduated, they could go to D.C. and get their own apartment and get a job with the Federal Government making enough money to get a television and maybe even a car. Janice was having none of that. She had graduated last year and had already saved enough money to buy them both a new dress. She told Alma they would be killed or raped or something in a big city like Washington without anybody else around to even know who they were. Realizing how scared Janice was, Alma promised to get some other girls to go with them. Janice was still saying "no" right up to the end.

At supper one evening, just before Christmas of her senior year, Alma broke the news to the rest of her family.

"Dad. Mom. You know what I would like to have for Christmas this year? You can make it a graduation present, too."

"I bet she wants pierced ears." William was grinning over his dish of apple cobbler.

Krista and Janice just smiled and leaned back in their chairs. They knew what was coming. Her mom and dad put down their forks and put their elbows on the table with their heads in their hands, waiting.

"I would like a bus ticket to Washington, D.C."

Her parents waited. They turned their heads, still in their hands, to look at each other. Finally, her mother straightened up and wiped her hands on her apron and continued to wring the rag in her lap as she took another look at her husband.

"Now, Alma, I don't know where that came from, but I don't think we can afford that much this year. A trip to Washington would also mean money for a hotel room and food and, of course, a ticket back home. What about the rest of the chi…?"

"Just one ticket. I'm not coming back home. At least not for a while. I'm going to get a job with the government, and I'm going to room with some other girls that are going. I want Janice to go, too, but she doesn't know yet. We can't stay here, Mom. There's nothing to do and you can make several times more money working as a secretary in D.C. We could send some money home and help the rest of the family out."

"We're doing just fine."

"I know. I know you're doing just fine. I don't want to upset you or be disrespectable, but I don't know what would be wrong if you had an electric stove, a new washer, and an indoor bathroom with running water."

"I'd like to get those things for your mother, too, Alma, but until you kids get educated, I reckon we'll just do the best we can."

"I'm sorry, Dad. I should have kept my big mouth shut. Mom's right. We have done just fine. But now that I'm graduating I want to do more and see more than I can here in Buchanan County, and I want to help out if I can."

Her mother got up from the table and walked over to the stove to put some water on to heat for washing the dishes. She started clearing plates from the table. Even though William wasn't through, he didn't say anything when she scraped his plate into the trash and piled it on the end of the table with the other dirty dishes. Janice left the table with her hands over her eyes and headed for their bedroom upstairs. Alma wanted to crawl under the floor boards, but now was the time to see this thing through. If she didn't finish and win her argument tonight, she might never have the nerve to try again. She knew that someday she would leave and she didn't want to just disappear. It would mean the world to have their blessings.

The more Alma slumped down into her chair the straighter her dad sat in his. He looked at her for a long time and then glanced over at her mother.

"Will, why don't you go out and chop up enough wood for tomorrow. Krista, you can help him."

"Aw, Dad, I've stacked enough wood under the porch to do a week. Besides, I want to hear you tell Alma she ain't going anywhere. If you ask me, she's getting a little too big for her britches."

Her dad just looked at him for a minute before William and Krista got up and walked out the back door, letting the screen shut a little too loud. He waited until they could hear the ax falling on the chop block, which took a while.

"Elaine, why don't you leave those dishes be for a bit and join us here at the table. I could use a cup of that coffee if you don't mind pouring us both a cup."

Alma could see her mother's shoulders rise as she took in a long breath of air. She tilted her head back and took two cups off the shelf.

Her father didn't talk to Alma, only looked her way once in a while.

"Alma and her siblings were born here in Buchanan County, and as much as we love it here and wish they could settle here and raise a family as special as ours, I don't reckon it's too much of a surprise that some of them might not. Elaine, just as we did, when they graduate and reach adulthood they can and will go their own way. We're not in control any more. The good Lord will watch over them and bring them back home. The only way to get them back is to let them go. Maybe they will return with some grandchildren we can spoil. We've been fortunate they stayed in school and excelled to the point of having opportunities available to them. Let's hope Krista and William do the same."

This brought a slight smile to her mother's face. She reached over and patted his hand.

"I've sold a few more articles and photographs to the paper, and I'm thinking maybe we ought to give Alma her Christmas and Graduation present. Janice, too, if she wants to go. Maybe we could throw in some luggage and a month's rent. If things go well for the girls maybe we could go visit sometime and they could show us around our nation's capital. Maybe walk through the White House."

Alma started to jump out of her chair and run around the table to give her dad a big hug, but he held up a hand to seal her to her seat. He was looking into his wife's eyes and giving her room to object.

Her mother wiped a tear from the corner of her eye with the tail of her apron and surrendered a weak smile to her husband.

"I just knew this day would come. That girl has never been satisfied with just good enough. She enjoyed going to Roanoke with her friend better than going to the county fair with us. Nothing would do except put on those shorts and go out for the basketball team, and made the team, too. You can't get a decent home cooked meal or a clean house out of her. And she won't let the other children be satisfied with living in the hills, but stirs them up with all these stories from the city and how grand it is to get out of Buchanan County."

Alma had her mouth open and was staring at her mother. She had never heard her talk like this. She would never agree to let her go.

Just then, her mother looked her way and reached out her hand. When Alma took it, she gave it a good squeeze and smiled at her.

"I agree with your dad, Alma. I think you should go if that's what you really want to do. You'll never be happy here, and you're right about your chances. I'm proud of you and all the children. You've done well with very little to do with, and you'll do even better when opportunity comes your way. I only ask you to let Janice make her own choice. And when you become rich and famous, I expect to see that bathroom. And a new stove would be nice, too."

This time there was no hand to stop her. With tears streaming down her face, she almost knocked her mother out of her chair as she jumped into her arms. Her dad got up from the table and came around to wrap them both in a big hug.

"Now, go tell Janice before she cries her heart out. I've got to get to work on another article for the paper. Maybe two, with the way expenses are mounting around this place."

Then the rains came. For two days Alma and Janice and Krista lay across their bed upstairs and watched and listened to the rain hit the roof. She had always enjoyed the sound of the bubbling creek as she was lying in bed reading or dreaming of when she was old enough to make her own choices. But when she woke up and heard the roaring, instead of bubbling, she knew there would be no school and that some bridges might get washed out.

When she got downstairs, her mother was serving her dad sausage, eggs, and gravy and her homemade biscuits. He was tying up his boots and she saw his raincoat and hat on the floor next to his camera wrapped in a plastic bag near the door.

"Where are you going, Dad? The creek is up near the top of the bridge."

"I know. The radio said we've had several inches of rain already and it's expected to last the rest of the day. I've got to get out before the bridge goes, and to Grundy, or at least to Route 460 and the Levisa River, and get some pictures of the damage being done. This flood may be the worst we've had for twenty years. You all stay put. You'll be all right in the house, as high as we are on the hill, but the road might get washed out. If the bridge goes out you can watch it from the front porch. When I come back I'll try to bring some groceries from the store, but I may have to walk around the side of the hill above the creek if the road and bridges are gone."

"But Dad, what if the Garden Creek bridge gets washed out? You could get trapped on the other side of the river."

"No, I won't. I can always walk across the footbridge at the high school and across the railroad trestle. Both are high enough the water won't take them out. Now help your mother and keep the other kids inside. Read a book or something. I might have some interesting pictures to show you when I get back."

With a last bite of eggs and a gulp of coffee, he walked out the door. Alma could tell her mother was worried, but she didn't make a fuss. She got more breakfast ready for the rest of her family and probably said a silent prayer for her husband.

For the next couple of hours they listened to the rain beat down on the roof of their house and watched the water rise over the top of the bridge just fifty yards down the road. With a loud crack, the lower end of the bridge broke loose and flopped in the raging stream like a fish on a tight line trying to throw the hook. Within minutes, the guts came out as the bridge broke apart. Beams and boards battled each other on their race downstream.

It was a long and unusually quiet day in the Woodson home, with Janice not able to go to work and the children home from school. Even Alma and William hesitated to stir up an argument or bicker over something trivial. Her mother did a load of wash even though it wasn't her regular wash day, and Alma didn't have to carry the water. They just set buckets underneath the eaves of the house and caught the rainwater off the roof. The children spent most of the day between the porch and their room, reading a book, listening to a little 'rock and roll' on the radio even though Janice didn't want to do the 'jitterbug', and watching the rise of the creek. About mid-afternoon, the rain slowed and then stopped altogether. Almost immediately Alma got sent to her room as William sat in the corner of the couch crying and rubbing a red mark above his left ear.

About two hours after dark they all ran to the door as they heard the stomping of feet on the back porch. Their dad threw off his raingear and pulled off his boots and slumped into a chair by the kitchen table as their mother hastened to put the coffee pot on the stove. They milled around, or took a chair at the table, or sat on the floor near their dad, and waited.

He smiled at them and held up one finger, then got up out of his chair, and walked back to his bedroom. In a moment, he returned with a clean and dry shirt and pants on, and his old winter house shoes. As their mother handed him a hot cup of coffee, he took a large envelope out of a plastic bag and removed a handful of pictures.

"I made it all the way to Grundy. The local paper was kind enough to let me use their darkroom to print out two rolls of film. I'm sure my agreeing to share copies with them had something to do with it. I had to stop at Aunt Gracie's house down the hollow to leave my camera and borrow a flashlight, as I knew I would have trouble negotiating that hillside between here and where the second bridge was washed out down the hollow. You kids are going to be out of school at least a week while they build back some bridges."

William and Krista flashed each other a smile. Janice seemed worried.

"What about Grundy? Did the stores flood?"

"Route 460 is open, but in places only one lane. The river road in Grundy overflowed and the ground floors of most of the businesses were flooded on the river side. Your store is going to be closed for a while, Janice, for cleanup. I talked to Mr. Ratcliffe and he said he would call you when he needed you to come back in. Here, let me show you all some pictures and then let's go to bed. It's been a long day."

The pictures were exciting, but terrifying. The water was at the top of the banks, if not in the road, in lots of the pictures. Half of the Tookland Bridge was torn out. Logs, trees, outbuildings, and two houses were pictured floating down the Levisa River. The overflow bridge at Garden High School was several feet underwater. Water was flowing in the road, beneath the railroad bridge, going up Garden Creek. There were pictures of people standing along the road in raingear or holding umbrellas just looking at the raging river, or wading in the edges trying to retrieve some objects of value.

Alma looked through the pictures again after all the others went to bed. How much more could the people of Buchanan County take? Well, she'd had enough long before this awful flood. She wasn't going to take it anymore. It was time to move on.

What changed Janice's mind was the flood. The big flood of 1957 washed out Janice's job at the Dime Store. That flood, and a few more almost as bad, is what did the town of Grundy in. The riverbanks couldn't hold all the water rushing down the mountainsides and all the streams flowing into the Levisa. By the time the rising water reached Grundy, it was bringing with it most of the bridges and a few houses from Oakwood on, downstream. Alma's father had taken a lot of pictures, and she found a few more in his files years later.

The Dime Store and most of the other stores had to close for weeks as they tried to clean up and salvage some of the merchandise from the parts of the businesses located on the river road. Anyhow, Janice lost her job. Alma did get two other girls, which were just as fed up with Buchanan County as she was, to agree to leave the week after graduation. Janice came on board the night of graduation after sitting with the girls and listening to all the things they were going to do once they got a good job and a place to live. Pamela promised to get her cousin Louise to pick them up at the Greyhound Bus Station and said that Louise wanted them to stay at her place until they all found jobs and a place of their own. She said Louise had only been up there two years and was already making three dollars an hour and had married a soldier stationed at an Army base in Arlington. According to Pamela, they would all be rich or married, or both, in less than three years.

Only Janice promised, as they got on the bus in Grundy, that she would be back home in a month if she hadn't found a job. She also promised to send some money home when she got her first paycheck. Alma didn't promise anything. She just gave everyone a quick hug and took Janice's arm and dragged her towards the bus. Janice was crying. Alma was all smiles.

Oakwood, VA – many years later

5

Decisions

  They sat at the kitchen table, sipping coffee, looking at each other, and occasionally through the screen door at the white flowers of the hydrangea bush off the back deck. Their mother had been the one with the green thumb. Red paintbrush, green boxwoods, white dogwoods, yellow tulips, and much more bordered the small patches of grass on the hillside yard. Since her death two years ago, the place was run down and neglected. Only occasionally would her sister bring their dad back to spend a night at the house. Now it would all have to be sold.

  All of the siblings but Krista, had left at midmorning. Her sister Janice and family were on their way home to Ohio with a stopover in Knoxville, and two hours ago her brother and family left for their home in Roanoke, Virginia.

"Have you ever seen so much food? What in the world are we going to do with all this?" Alma wished she was the one on the road.

"It will keep you alive while you are sorting through all the stuff and selling the place." Krista couldn't hide the smile as she took another sip of coffee. Thank God for the good old Baptist Church members. She and the rest of the Woodson family had been served and waited on during the very stressful and sorrowful time of their father's funeral.

"Knock it off, Krista! I've told you and all the rest of the family, I'm not taking charge of this. I've got to get back to D.C. I only took off work for a week. I've got a delegation coming in from Germany on Monday and I have to be there to set up their tour."

A tear slid down her cheek as Alma sat up taller and tilted her head back and glared down her nose at her sister. She'd be dammed if she'd let her family railroad her into giving up one minute of her time to settle the family business. What business anyhow? There wasn't anything here worth a dime. The house, thirty acres of a steep mountainside, and a bunch of useless junk collected over sixty years of a life-and-death struggle.

Two days ago they had buried their father. The three sisters and their brother had huddled together in the small living room of the old home place and relived the life that once was. They hugged and cried. They laughed and slapped each other on the back as they told their tales. Stories they no longer knew what parts were true. The three girls once again slept in the lumpy bed in the room they had claimed as their own. William had made a bed on the couch as nobody wanted to sleep in their parents' bed. The spouses and children were put up at the Comfort Inn in Grundy. It was their time. A time to re-bond once again. To feel their parents' blood flow through their veins and know that part of each of them was the same as the others.

Never again would it be the same. To be one, inseparable, and part of a whole. Within a few days, they knew, the knot would come undone, the strands separate, and each would go their own way. Janice and hers to Dayton, Alma would leave tomorrow for Washington D.C. and Krista and her family would follow William and his family to Roanoke. A reunion next summer was promised.

"I was just kidding about the food, Sis. Aunt Paula said she would be here in the morning and pack up anything left over."

"Tell her to pack up everything and haul it away. Hey, Krista, that's it! We let Aunt Paula take all this stuff and she can get in touch with a realtor to sell the house. I bet Aunt Ellie would help."

"Listen to you, Alma. Both of our aunts are pushing eighty and Aunt Paula shouldn't be driving a car. This stuff isn't just 'stuff'. Our whole history is back in those rooms. All of us would like some things that would be personal and valuable to us or our children. Dad made you the executor, and it's you who will decide what goes where and what's sold according to his will."

"I'm not doing it. Dad made a mistake. He should have known I'm too busy---I live too far away. We'll just name a new executor. How about you,

Krista? You or William live close enough to handle this and deal with a realtor."

"Not this time, Alma. For the first time since you left home, after graduating from high school, you have the responsibility to do something for the family."

"What are you talking about? I've done plenty for this family. Janice and I bought the first TV you and William ever had, right after we got a job in D.C. Then she got married and moved to Ohio. Why, that dining room and this kitchen we're sitting in are mine. I sent Dad a check to pay for having it built, and the bathroom, too. You ought to be thankful for everything I've done for this family. You and William could've grown up using the outhouse like Janice and I did, and taking a bath in the wash tub."

"William and I are thankful for the money you sent home, Alma, and the things you bought. You made Mom's life a lot easier. I believe you also bought the first washer and dryer. Remember how we had to carry water in a bucket up from the creek to fill the old wringer washer on the back porch? Hung the clothes to dry on the line on the front porch? Who misses those good old days? Wonder what the restrictions in your neighborhood would have to say about that?"

"Yeah!" Alma smiled a little.

"No, Sis. I didn't mean to sound ungrateful. I guess I'm just sore at your not being here. It seems like it has been William or I to do the things needed doing for a very long time. I know, we live closer, just down the road until a few years ago. With no car in the family and Dad not knowing how to drive, not to mention never having a license, either we or the neighbors had to drive them places."

"Well, Janice and I never had a car, either."

"I know, but then you were gone. You never had to cancel plans because Dad needed a ride to pick up sweet potato plants some guy from church over in Dickenson County promised him, if he would come and get them. I think I lost my religion after about a million trips to a Primitive Baptist Church meeting at Vansant one weekend, Garden Creek the next, or Sandlick the next, and so on. Thank goodness their groceries were delivered. There were just lots of places they needed to go, even if they didn't have a car."

"Krista, you sound bitter."

"I know, and it eats the hell out of me. I volunteered to take Dad in to live with us after Mom died. None of you demanded or pressured me to do that because I lived closer and could make his life near normal. I wanted to, and I'm glad I did. It was hard sometimes but I got a lot of help and support from my good husband Jack and the kids. William helped some, too. Two years, my family and I have already given, Alma. William has also, and he has a business to run. Janice lives farther away than you do and she has a family to care for."

"Well, I'm busy, too. I don't have a family to take care of but I do have a career. I can't just walk away and pop down the road every time a closet needs cleaning out, a roof leaks, or a paper has to be signed. I'll hire a lawyer and he can take care of everything."

"You are the only one that can do this, Alma. A lawyer won't take care of the papers, letters, pictures, report cards, hair locks, etc. locked up in those file cabinets and closets in there. Dad didn't just teach school for forty-two years. He also wrote articles for a newspaper in his younger years. He has taken pictures and interviewed people all over this county, and a lot from horseback. You have to protect our family treasure."

"I'm telling you, Krista, I don't have the time for this."

"Make time, Alma. You have worked since you were 18 years old. You're old enough to retire."

"Retire! Are you crazy! I've got the best job I ever had with the State Department and you want me to give all that up for who knows what in the back rooms?"

"Yes, Alma. I do."

"Why, for God's sakes! I've finally gotten near the top, own two homes in Alexandria, and I don't owe a cent to anyone. You must be out of your ever-loving mind to want me to give up everything and move here, and do what?"

"Trace your roots, Alma. Maybe find what you have searched for your whole life. You've done it all and been everywhere. You're a Republican, but even Dad didn't hold that against you. I guess volunteering and getting Ronald Reagan elected Governor of California got you hooked. You've met and have pictures and autographs of a lot of famous people including the presidents Eisenhower, Reagan, and the Bushes, and Neil Armstrong, the man who walked on the moon. You have traveled all over the world from the Great Wall of China to the Alps of Switzerland. You have lived in Hawaii and Belgium. You even rode a mule down from the rim of the Grand Canyon to the edge of the Colorado River. What you've not done is spend more than a few days in Buchanan County since you turned 18 years old."

"And today has been one too many. I'm getting on that plane at Tri-Cities airport tomorrow and I don't know if I'll ever be back. I'll take care of this damn business one way or another, since it's my turn and my responsibility and I don't have a family to take care of, but don't think for a minute I care anything about what's in this house or the good old days or who gets what. If any of you want anything, you better come and get it."

Alma shattered her coffee cup in the sink, with some pieces falling on the floor, slammed the screen door and walked across the yard and up the road. Krista let her go. She knew she would be back in a few minutes. The deep dark hollows of Oakwood, Virginia, a barking dog, or a tobacco-chewing, shirtless, off-duty coal miner with a beer in his hand would quickly remind Alma she wasn't strolling down a sidewalk in Alexandria, Virginia, just outside the nation's Capital.

> *She hadn't been the only one to leave the hollows in the mountains of the coalfields. Her cousins over at Drill had left, too. Her cousin Josh would rather build cars than dig for coal.*

She had watched the Cold War end and the terrorist wars begin. World tensions eased, but the people in the cities and the airports started losing their confidence in the security that had enabled them to go where, when, and however they chose. Freedoms were lost as the lines got longer and the searches more invasive. Big Brother was showing up on every street corner. With video cameras, cell phone cameras, camcorders, and street light camera, traffic violators, street crimes, and even police officers abusing their authority and the rights of individuals could be caught in action. To catch an hour flight to a nearby city meant arriving at the airport two hours early and having your body and your luggage searched. Visits home were less frequent, but lasted longer. The peace, quiet, and security of the home in the hollow became more appealing to those weary of the rat race they had endured too long.

She couldn't wait to leave the hollow and join her lifelong friends in their venture for freedom, equality, and prosperity. Josh wanted more than a hillside farm or crawling on his knees digging black, dirty coal out of a hole deep inside the mountains.

HANGER

Building cars coming down an assembly line and earning union wages would be a big step forward.

She remembered getting off the metro bus at the corner stop, just down the street from their apartment building, with Lonnie, who had made the move out of the hollows with her to D.C. She was carrying a bag with takeout from the Chinese restaurant next to her office building, and Lonnie carried a bag with milk, bread, eggs, and cereal from the Quick Stop Store near her office.

"What do you mean you're getting married and moving to Wyoming? We just got here. I just got a new job making twice as much. Well, go on then. Linda and I will toast you a drink when we're lying on the beach in California or Hawaii and maybe send you a postcard you can read to the cowboys around the campfire."

Josh had told her about the day when he closed up his lunch bucket as he watched his buddy eat around the edges of his sandwich and then pop the middle of it into his mouth in one big bite. They were eating their lunch just outside the shop floor, which they usually did in warm weather, so they could watch the horseshoe pitching taking place between their factory and the fence separating them from the six-lane highway.

"When did you hear that?"

"It's been flying around all week. They're closing this place and building a new factory in Detroit. It's going to be high tech with robots and computerized everything. Some of the guys have already been offered a job there if they're willing to go back to school or take night classes."

"I ain't going. We almost got our house paid for and the kids are about to graduate and they can't leave their school and friends."

"I gotta go if they offer me the opportunity. I got too much paid into the pension and only have five more years till I can retire."

"I may just move back home and try to get one of those jobs operating a mining machine in one of those big shaft mines they've opened up, or maybe start up my own business."

"What about the house and kids?"

"If I lose my job I'll probably lose the house, too. And if I have to

uproot the kids, I might as well get out of this rat race."

She thought about her friend Patty and how she and her daughter had the big row over her child leaving home. The mother knew something was going on when her oldest daughter came in from school, threw her backpack on the kitchen counter, and sat down on a barstool, instead of stomping off to her room to get on the computer to chat with her friends.
"Rough day, dear?"
"Just the usual boring routine we go through every day. I hate school and can't wait until I graduate in a couple of months."
"Then it'll be back to the same old boring routine in college."
"It won't be the same. I'll at least have choices of classes and teachers. That's what I wanted to talk to you about, Mom. I got my letter of acceptance today from USC."
"But I thought you were going to UVA. Your father and I were so happy you were going to be close to home."
"That's part of the problem. It's too close and it's so uppity. I think it's time for me to find out if I can make it on my own, with your support

of course. I also would like to change my major from Law to Computer Science and maybe get a job with IBM or Intel out in California. That's where it's happening, Mom, and technology is the big thing."

"Have you told your father this?"

"Well, not yet. I just got the letter today. Could you tell him for me, please, Mom?"

"Not a chance. Finding out if you can make it on your own starts with you talking to your father."

"But it's no different than when you and Dad left home and moved here to the city."

"It's different, but I won't argue that point with you. I had no chances where I grew up, but you have a world of opportunities here. Talk to your father."

Alma turned at the forks of the road and headed back down the hollow. It was time to get back to Washington. This place would drive her mad.

6

A Leave of Absence

The alarm clock went off and Alma rolled over and punched the snooze button. She didn't go back to sleep, however. Her brain kicked into gear and her mind started spinning the black hole that would drag the bits and pieces of her thoughts of the past week into the deepest cavity of her being. Krista had left her and her luggage at the airport yesterday morning with a hug and an unwelcome promise to pick her up again soon. That girl was persistent – wrong, but persistent. It had been raining when she got off the plane at Reagan International Airport, but thank goodness she had only one bag and there were always plenty of cabs waiting. She was bone-tired and she hadn't slept well last night. Well, it was Sunday so she would eat a bowl of Honey-Nut Cheerios, take a long hot bath, plan for her delegation coming into town tomorrow, and maybe get in a good walk through the neighborhood and a nap in the afternoon.

By 6:00 that evening, Alma was a total wreck. She couldn't get her plans for the up-coming week organized. Damn it, organization was her forte. That particular skill had gotten her where she was today. She picked up the phone and called Steve, her trusted assistant. He could handle tomorrow and maybe she would have her act together by Tuesday. They had taken care of multiple delegations before. Most of the leg work was done weeks in advance with hotel reservations and historical tour schedules.

Why couldn't she get her mind off her father's death and the revelation that she was now the family senior member in charge of settling the estate? Her dad had lived to the ripe old age of 92 and never had to spend a day in the insanity ward or a nursing home as he so feared. Thanks to Krista. He had kept his mind and his checkbook right up to the end. He did his exercise routines every hour on the hour, even after he broke his hip, using a walker through the house for his legs and circulation, and arm stretching with cans of vegetables for his upper body. He had always liked a good debate on politics or religion. He had been proud of his children. All of them.

The funeral had been sad and long, keeping with Primitive Baptist tradition of several preachers and long drawn out hymns. Alma smiled as she thought of her church lining out a gospel song. The dozen or more preachers and deacons and their wives crowded the pulpit and would sing the line of a song after the preacher recited it from the only hymn book in the congregation. There were no musical instruments or thought of carrying a tune. The talent seemed to be how long you could drag out the words one letter at a time. Alma thought of it as more wailing than singing. She dropped her head to folded arms on the table and cried again. She was probably going to hell for having such thoughts of nice, honest, and faithful people. A minute later she was up and out the door. A few laps around the playground track of the elementary school, that was only two blocks from her home, would do her good. She had to get her act together.

Three days later she was again walking the track about sundown. She had not been in to work and Steve had called a couple of times each day. The last call he informed her that Mr. Warner, their supervisor and Assistant Secretary of State, wanted to see her in his office at 9:00 Friday morning. Would he fire her? Surely not. She had worked there longer than Mr. R. Stanley Warner and she had plenty of sick leave built up. Being an emotional mental case should be legal sick leave. Maybe she would tell him where to stick this job and see if he could manage a delegation of greedy spoiled foreigners himself. Maybe Krista was right. It might be a good time to get out of this rat race, pack a bag, and go lie on a sandy beach in the sunny southern Pacific somewhere. She picked up her pace.

She had worked under five different Presidents and had her picture made alongside each of them. She knew some of the FBI and Secret Service men personally after arranging so many interviews and national security clearances. She had worked in the offices of NATO in Belgium and would have stayed over there a couple of years if it hadn't rained so damn much. She knew how to find her way around inside the Beltway. And she especially knew her way from the Capitol to the White House, and how to deliver a memo to a senator or house member without having to ask for directions. After thirty-plus years, she had seen all the memorials, statues, and Smithsonian exhibits she cared to see. What more did Washington have to offer her? What difference would another year or five make? Had she hung on the past few years because she didn't have anything else to do?

Friday morning she walked into Mr. Warner's office and handed him a leave-of-absence form for a two-month leave. After spending some quality time with him explaining her state of mind and the burdens placed on her and the fact that she was contemplating retirement and that she had earned this time to consider her destiny, she walked out the door. She caught a cab for the airport with her one piece of luggage and called Krista from her cell phone.

"You can wipe that silly smile off your face, Krista. I'm just taking a short vacation. I'm sick and tired of D.C. right now and you got my curiosity up about what mom and dad might have saved over the years. I thought it might be fun sleeping in instead of getting up before daylight to catch the bus into the District. And I might turn up something interesting, shuffling through all that stuff at the house, like my tenth-grade yearbook that Brett signed."

"I remember that yearbook. We thought that he was the one and only until you met that cowboy from Montana. Where is the rest of your luggage?"

"This is it. I'll go shopping when I get to Grundy tomorrow. The clothes I own won't wear well in Buchanan County. I also need to buy a good, cheap, used car. If you will take me to the Comfort Inn in Grundy, I will buy your gas from Roanoke and back again."

"You're not staying at the house?"

"Are you kidding? I would be scared shitless to spend a night alone in that house up in that dark hollow. I'll work up there during the day, after I get my car, when I feel like it and read some good books in my hotel room when I don't."

"One thing, Alma. You have got to clean up your language. Folks down here won't look kindly on a beautiful middle-age lady with a trashy mouth. It might reflect back on Mom and Dad."

"Oh, shit. I'll be damned. What the hell are you saying now? How I look. How I talk. How I act is going to be judged by some rednecks from Oakwood, Virginia? There! I've said all the bad words I know so you just try to wash my mouth out with some lye soap."

Krista smiled. "Whatever happened to that cowboy, anyway?"

"Well, to be honest, I once thought he might be the one, too. But after a six-month fling in Washington, I flew back to his 4,000-acre ranch with him after his discharge from the army. In two weeks, I found out that life on a cattle ranch in Montana wasn't like the movies. His mother was the matriarch of the ponderosa and she let me know right quick that I would be expected to help run the household. I was to be up before daylight fixing breakfast for the men, canning and freezing meat and vegetables, washing their smelly clothes, and listening to their tales on the range. And their diet didn't consist of Honey-Nut Cheerios."

Krista hooted. She laughed so hard, tears slid down her cheeks. "I can see where that wouldn't do at all."

The next day Krista did deliver Alma to the hotel in Grundy and refused the gas money offered. She was so happy that Alma was making the effort, and she knew how apprehensive her sister was. Oakwood would be like the other side of the world to Alma now. Maybe like a third world country. Krista would be there to help when and where she could, but she would make Alma call her. This was unlike any federal project the girl had undertaken. She knew that Alma would organize, categorize, and prioritize everything before she attempted to settle the estate. It could turn out to be the best experience of her life. Rediscovering family and roots could save her soul.

Alma didn't attempt to leave the hotel the next morning, except to walk over to the Huddle House for breakfast, until she had jotted down the agenda for the day. First on the list was to get a car. She had noticed on the way in yesterday a car lot just up the street about a mile from the hotel. The walk would do her good and help shed the pancakes and bacon. Next would be clothes and she could surely find a K-Mart or Wal-Mart within driving distance. She didn't intend to stand out in any way and she would dress as country as the average Joe in this county. Next, she would find a supply store, or maybe the same Wal-Mart, and buy some writing tablets, pens, filing folders, and a laptop computer. If she was going to do this she would need a word processor and a spreadsheet to record everything correctly. After that she would make a trial run up to the house and record how long it would take her in travel time. She was certain she would not be caught out after dark. Of course, she would plug in the sheriff's number and the judge's, who she had to check with for executor's instructions, as contacts in her cell phone. She also needed to change her ICE number from her friend across the street to Krista.

Alma looked over the cars on the front row of the lot before she saw the salesman meander her way. Half the automobiles were pickup trucks. She ought to buy a truck, cut her hair short, and buy a baseball cap like the one the salesman was wearing backwards. He smiled at her and extended his hand.

"Hi. I'm Harold Shortridge. Could I help you with a great deal today?"

Alma thought 'great deal my a…butt!' His greedy hands probably started itching as soon as he saw a woman walk on the lot.

"Alma Woodson." She shook his hand, but reminded herself to dig the sanitizer out of her purse as soon as she left the lot. "I'm looking for something like a Honda Civic with low mileage and in good condition."

"Sure, I bet we got something like that. How about a Volkswagen Jetta? Got one in yesterday on a trade, two years old with only 26,000 miles, right back there near the office." He started walking away and Alma followed.

"Alma Woodson? You didn't happen to graduate from Garden High School in 1957, did you?"

"Now, Mr. Shortridge, you wouldn't be trying to guess my age, would you?"

"Lord, no, Ms. Woodson. I guess that was a personal question, but I graduated in '57 and there was an Alma Woodson in my class. I'm sure you would've been a few years behind me and I'm sure your name wouldn't still be Woodson. Name just rung a bell with me. By the way, call me Harold. My dad was Mr. Shortridge."

"Ok, Harold, you got me. I did graduate from Garden in 1957 and I do remember you. You played basketball with Brett Parker that year and the Dragons went on to win the state championship."

Harold slapped the cap off his head. "I'll be damned, Alma. Where in the world have you been?" He was all smiles now, and Alma was afraid he was going to hug her or something.

"Pretty much all over it."

"I'll bet! Wait 'till I tell Brett who stopped in on the lot today. He still stops in once in a while when he's in the county. You know he made his fortune in the coal business and spends most of his time at his mansion on South Holston Lake or on one of his golf courses. What are you doing here anyhow? I haven't seen you since high school."

"Business. My parents have died—Dad only a couple of weeks ago. I'm trying to settle up things. Know anyone that would like to buy a house?"

"Oh, I'm so sorry, Alma." The pleasant smile left his face. "Everyone loved your parents. I guess your dad taught almost all of us in elementary school. I still can't believe he taught all seven grades in a one-room school-house at Grimsleyville."

Alma didn't want to go there. "Is that the blue one?"

"Oh, yeah. The Jetta. Want to take her for a spin? I'll go in and figure the best deal I can, Alma. I promise you it will be a lot less than I had in mind when I came out to meet you."

"It had better be. I could see the dollar signs in your eyes when you shook my hand."

Harold smiled and gave her the key. "Tell you what. Stop at some garage and have a mechanic go over it while you're out. It's a good car. I would buy it for my granddaughter if she was old enough to drive."

Alma knew she would pay no more than $13,000. She had driven straight back to the hotel lobby and pulled up the Bluebook price on the hotel computer. She didn't bother with having it checked out, since he had suggested it. It looked good and she liked the color.

Harold met her on the lot. "Drives like new, doesn't it?"

Alma didn't smile. "What is the bottom line? I don't intend to hassle over a used car."

"How about $12,200? That's only a hundred bucks for the company. I really want you to stop back in. I'll handle the registration, tags, and all you have to do is call your insurance company."

"Deal. What time do you close? I would like to have the car today."

"I'll be here until 7:00 tonight. You can drive it off the lot as soon as my secretary gets the paper work done if you want. Do you want us to arrange financing?"

"No. It will be cash, if you will take a check." She saw the eyebrows go up, but there were no questions.

They chatted a few more minutes, she signed the papers and an hour later drove back to the hotel.

It took the rest of the day to do the other things on her list. She had a nice visit with the judge. He was gentle in giving her the key to the house and instructions for executing the will. He did let her know there would be strict scrutiny in the keeping of records towards her duty. The will was pretty simple. Sell the house and property and divide the cash assets, after paying any debts, equally among the children. All personal items and furniture were to be given to those that wanted them or to charity at the discretion of the executor. She was sad, but relieved to have the judge at her back if she needed him.

She hoped to brighten her day a little, buying clothes. Krista had told her to check at Marie's Fashions. She finally found it on the outer western edge of town located in a double-wide trailer with a hand painted sign on a sheet of plywood that advertised 'MARIE'S FASHIONS – Flamboyant Frocks & Finery'. If she hadn't told Krista she would check it out, she would have just kept driving.

The lady Alma assumed was Marie, was stocking the racks. She glanced up over the reading glasses perched on the end of her nose at the tinkling of the tiny bell over the door. Alma was surprised at the size of the woman. Marie looked six-foot-two weighing over three hundred pounds. However, she moved lightly on her feet between the racks and looked lovely in her Isabella Carter skirt and blouse, with an Annie Lewis jacket. When she cleared the aisle, Alma raised an eyebrow and smiled at the MoovBoots she wore.

"Look around, honey and if you see anything you want, give me a yell. I'm by myself today, but it has been slow. Dressing room is in the back."

"Thanks." Alma couldn't believe her eyes. There were designer clothes you should only find in a large city, some by Oilily, Reverie, Pencey and Grafea. De Line shoes; and jeans by Stich, Dylan George, Faith, and Tavernifi. She picked up a pair of Brooke's priced at $198, on sale for $68. She had never had a fancy pair of jeans before, but she couldn't resist these. She walked back to the dressing room and tried them on. They looked and felt great.

"Where do you find such lovely clothes?"

"Oh, honey, I take a long weekend once a month and drive my van up to New York City. Been doing this for about seven years and got some good contacts now. Those big fancy shops have to turn over their inventory every little bit and they like to dump their goods down south away from the competition. Find something you like?"

"If you'll take a check?"

"Well, honey I will if you are from around here. I don't recall seeing you in here before."

"I haven't lived in Buchanan County for many years, but my parents lived up at Oakwood until recently. My dad was Elmer Woodson."

"I remember Mr. Woodson. He was my mom's teacher in the 5th grade at Garden. You go right ahead and write that check."

"What was your mom's name?"

"Marie Sutherland. This store is hers. I'm Maxine, her daughter. Mom is semi-retired and I pretty much run the place now."

"Good to meet you, Maxine. My name is Alma. I just assumed you were Marie. These jeans are great, but I'll have to save them for special occasions. Have you got some Levi's or Wrangler's, or could you direct me to a store with cheaper clothing and shoes?"

"Oh, honey, with my prices you can work in good clothes." Maxine gave off a belly laugh that even made Alma smile.

"I know, but it would destroy my conscience. By the way, do you think your mother would mind if I stopped in to visit someday, soon? I would love to talk with some of Dad's former students."

"Mom would like that. It'll surprise her to death to know you are here. I think the last of the children she has seen in years was Krista when she took your father to church. You can find about anything or everything you want at Magic Mart up there above Tookland."

"Thanks, Maxine. If I get invited to a party somewhere I'll stop back in to see you."

"You do that. People around here don't go anywhere much, but when they do they like to doll up as much as the city folks. That's why Mom and I can eat and have a nice roof over our heads."

Alma felt good when she left. She had been in town only a day and already met two people that made her feel like kin. She had lived in D.C., or thereabouts, for thirty years and she didn't know if there were two people that cared if she stopped back in to just chat.

At Magic Mart, she got some work and casual clothes and a pair of New Balance tennis shoes. She would have to drive to Richlands to find office supplies and a laptop. The clerk in Magic Mart gave her directions to the new Wal-Mart and Home and Office Supply at Claypool Hill. Alma checked her watch and the speedometer on the car, and then headed towards Oakwood. She would have time to drive up to the house and have dinner somewhere and still be back at the hotel before dark.

Twenty-two minutes and 16 miles later, she turned in the driveway without even walking up to the porch or deck. She would try to get her courage up by tomorrow to walk into the house alone for probably the first time in her life. Now she wasn't going to think about it. She would stop at The Black Stallion Café beside Oakwood General Store for dinner, then head back to Grundy for a good night's rest. The journey could begin early the next morning.

The sign at the entrance said to seat yourself, so Alma picked a booth about halfway back. It would be a good place to see anyone who came in and to be seen in case anyone might recognize her as a Woodson. After all she hadn't changed much since she graduated. She was only six pounds heavier at

142 and her hair was the same color, thanks to her hairdresser. She glanced at the menu lying on the table and decided she would go for the fish and chips with a Pepsi.

"My name is Lori and I'll be taking care of you. Could I get you something to drink while you look over the menu?"

"I'll have water with lemon."

The waitress had stepped away when she called to her. "I think I'll change that to a Pepsi."

"Sure."

When the drink was delivered, Alma smiled at Lori and asked, "What would you recommend?"

"I like the roast beef sandwich with mashed potatoes. We get a lot of requests for the hamburger steak and fries."

"No, that sounds like too much fat," ignoring the fading smile on the heavier waitress's face. "Do you serve breakfast all day or just the mornings?"

"From 6:00 to 10:00 in the morning."

"Some places like Cracker Barrel serve breakfast all day long. Do you have fresh fruit?"

"No, ma'am, we do have fresh salads."

"Do you make your own dressing?"

"No, but we have most of the standard ones served in most restaurants."

"I'll have one with Ranch, please. Is the chicken fried or grilled?"

"Either way. You can also get it as a salad if you wish."

"Oh, no. I like my salad separate, and could you bring it with my meal instead of early?"

"Certainly."

"I think I'll have a cup of coffee, also. Only half of a cup. I like to sip it hot, and sometimes a whole cup gets cold before I finish."

"Would you like that now or with your meal?"

"With my meal would be fine."

"And that would be…?" The shifting from one foot to the other by the waitress didn't register with Alma as frustration.

"The fish and chips sound good. I think I'll have that." She handed the menu to the girl.

"The menus stay on the table. Just return it to the rack behind the salt and pepper."

Alma sipped on her Pepsi while she waited. She noticed a man in a cowboy hat, black silk shirt, and blue jeans smiling in her direction several times while she was placing her order. She would look away or search her purse again before she let her eyes meander back his way. Again, he smiled and touched his hat. Again, she looked away without smiling. You couldn't encourage a stranger or, for that matter, someone like Harold. It wasn't always used cars they tried to sell or buy.

7

Discoveries

Alma walked through the house, found the breaker box in the hallway, and threw the switch. The house had a stuffy smell to it. Everything was quiet. She found the radio and turned it on. The station was country. That would do. She opened the windows on the first floor. Thank goodness, the screens were still in place. She didn't want to deal with wasps, bees, or flies. She walked back to the kitchen table and opened her briefcase. The morning was mostly shot, but the trip to Richlands was time well spent. The case held everything she needed – her laptop, two yellow legal pads, pens, clips, and index cards. She took a pen and a legal pad and started her inventory.

The stove and refrigerator would go with the house. She listed them anyhow. When she opened the door to the fridge, she smiled and gave silent thanks to Krista or Aunt Paula. It was empty and clean. It must be 40 or 50 years old, because it was the only one she ever remembered. Mom always called it the Frigidaire, and sure enough, there was the name in the upper right corner. Alma just shook her head. She knew she had bought at least four refrigerators since she had left home.

    She opened the kitchen cabinets and listed the dishes and the pots and pans. She didn't count all of the place settings or silverware; she just jotted the items down to let whoever have a list of what was there for the taking. Alma walked through the house again and made a note of all the pictures or paintings hanging on the walls. She was a little less nervous now and the music helped.

    She moved from room to room and made a note of each piece of furniture, lamp, rug, and whatnot displayed on the tables. She opened drawers in the dressers and chests and spread everything on the beds along with clothes from the closets. She found some of her mother's jewelry, and small items that had belonged to her dad and put them in an old pocketbook and placed them near her briefcase on the table. They might be valuable and were small enough to be picked up and carried off without anyone noticing. She noted some things she thought might be antique on a separate page. She remembered the gold pocket watch with the gold chain as one her father had worn sometimes when she was a little girl. And there was the shaving mug and brush he continued to use even after one of the kids had bought him an electric razor for Christmas.

    Alma heard the news come on the radio and stopped to check her watch. It would be dark in a couple of hours and she still had to eat dinner before checking back in at the hotel. She decided to wrap it up for the day. She made one last trip through the house and closed all the windows. She turned off the radio, gathered the snacks and drinks she had bought at the convenience store, and forgotten to eat, and put them in the Frigidaire. She picked up the briefcase and pocketbook with the valuables and locked the door. Tomorrow, she would be back and, to her surprise, she was looking forward to it. When she was through with the house, she might take one day and walk up through the garden and orchard.

When she walked through the door of the Black Stallion Café she saw the same guy talking with Lori, the waitress, at a booth near the front, the same one he had been sitting in yesterday. She took the same booth she had before, near the middle. He was dressed in bright green pants and a white pull-over shirt with a golfing hat lying on the table beside him. He again nodded his head at her as she passed. Lori finally broke away from the conversation and walked back to Alma.

"Could I get you a drink while you look over the menu?"

"Water, please. What do you recommend today?"

"I don't. You have all the choices on the menu." Lori walked away to get her drink.

Well, Alma thought, that was rather rude. I guess she has never been trained how to treat a customer. Her tip just got smaller.

Alma decided on the grilled chicken and steamed vegetables and placed her order when the waitress returned with her drink. Today might not be the time to make the girl earn her wages.

"Who is the golfer in the booth up front? He seems to be a regular here."

"Oh, that's Brett Parker. He is a regular when he's in the county. His company is probably the biggest employer in Buchanan. He is over this way often checking up on things, but spends most of his time at the headquarters in Bristol."

"Bit of a flirt, isn't he?"

"Oh, no. That's just Brett. I shouldn't have said that much. I don't like to gossip."

I'll bet. Probably a requirement of the job. She let the waitress leave without additional inquiry and took the notes from her purse to review the progress she had made. It only took a minute for Lori to make her way back to Brett's table.

Alma looked up when she felt his presence. She remained sitting erect and glanced at him over the rim of her eyeglasses.

"Hi, Alma Woodson. I guess I don't need to introduce myself as Lori has already done more than an adequate job, I suppose."

"Hello, Brett. I guess the question is, how did either of you know my name? I'm sure you don't recall all your classmates from years ago."

"Age of information and technology. As most people do now days, you used your credit card to pay for dinner last night and again for breakfast this morning. Lori has an excellent memory. Mind if I join you until your dinner arrives?"

"Of course. As dad would have said, 'have a seat and take a load off'. Maybe that waitress would bring you a cup of coffee if you ask politely. She can be quite rude."

"Not Lori. You two just got off on the wrong foot. She is one of the most friendly and efficient waitresses around these parts. Speaking of your dad, I'm truly sorry to hear. He and your mother were very close with my mother and father."

"I know. You lost your parents a few years before we lost Mom, didn't you? I guess that makes us the older generation now, doesn't it?"

"You could say that, but you don't look like an older generation. Life seems to have been kind to you. No gray around the temples and a very beautiful young woman."

"You can stop that right now, Brett. Remember, I knew you back in high school. You can save all that charm until you get back to the wife and kids."

"Ouch! Still got the bite, don't you? You'll enjoy coming back in here to eat if you apologize to Lori for the way you harassed her on your order yesterday, and for sending your eggs back twice this morning and how you don't like greasy bacon, but prefer it crisp."

"That girl has probably never heard of client confidentiality. And she has a thing or two to learn about waiting on customers. I would have fired her long ago if I ran this restaurant. I don't think I have an appetite any longer, and I'm sure there are other eating establishments that would appreciate my business!" Alma was furious and was preparing to leave.

"Cool down, Alma. This is the best you are going to get in Buchanan County. I wouldn't have mentioned it except I do want you to enjoy your visit and, believe me, Lori is the best. Speaking of wife and kids—two wives and two divorces. No kids. How about you?"

Alma slid back into the booth and dropped her shoulders a little. She had been a little too demanding of the waitress. Just a habit of hers, she guessed. Eating out was usually an adventure for her, and she enjoyed retelling the experience to her friends in Alexandria. Dining here was probably just a necessity and no one cared about drawing attention to minor details. Did he say no wife or kids?

"My name is still Woodson, as you so cleverly discovered. I haven't had time for that game."

Brett laughed loudly. "I bet you haven't. I used to be able to keep up with you through your mother. She was so proud of you and all your experiences and travel."

"I would figure you didn't have time for much socializing with my family after you became rich and famous."

"We always had time for your mom and dad. I don't know of anyone that my dad would rather visit than your dad. They would talk for hours about the old days. Sometimes looking at pictures or old news articles. Your mom, however, just wanted to chat over a cup of coffee or iced tea and catch up on the gossip. Often, you had to walk with her through the flowers and take time to smell the roses or take a clipping home with you."

Alma could feel her eyes filling. "You should have taken time to visit with her. After all, she washed your underwear for years and helped your mother clean house as well as laundry."

"I remember that. Mrs. Woodson would walk the mile between our houses about twice a week and carry the laundry in a straw basket. She always took time to tell Charlie and me a story or fix us a snack. We didn't have a lot back then, either. The money came later. If she was with us today, I would make sure she never cooked or cleaned or did laundry another day of her life, unless she wanted to fix me one of her famous chocolate pies."

Alma and Brett talked on through her meal and a couple of cups of coffee. She turned down his offer to buy her breakfast tomorrow and his invitation to the Country Club dance on Saturday night. She explained she had work to do and a short time to get it done, and even though it was good seeing him, she wasn't interested in developing any kind of a relationship.

Brett hung his head and pouted like a stood-up teenager. They both laughed at his antics. She accepted his card and promised to call him if she needed help with any legal or labor problems in selling the house.

Alma slept well. She got up early, worked hard, and made sure she was back at the hotel before dark. She talked to Krista and Aunt Paula almost daily. She arranged a meeting with a realtor and showed the house and property. After being reassured that the realtor could take care of everything involved in selling except the signature at closing, Alma pushed herself to getting the house cleaned out of furniture and personal belongings. When the inventory was completed and the safe deposit box emptied, Krista would get the family together to distribute the family inheritance. The final act of executing the will would be a year from now to disburse the cash assets. There wasn't much, and no one was holding their breath or making grand plans. It was just all sad and necessary for closure.

Alma looked around the house again with her inventory list in hand. The only thing she hadn't tackled was the two filing cabinets. She opened the top drawer and the files inside were hanging nicely from file holders and labeled. She remembered helping her dad about three years ago, placing the hanging file racks and choosing the files to go in the first drawer. Before, some of the files had been pushed and stacked and bent until items were falling out of the files into the drawer below. Now, they looked so neat. A tear slid into the corner of her eye as she visualized the endless task of sorting all his records and the dedication he would have given to a new project.

She quickly scanned some of the labeled folders and found pictures by the year of their travels, high school photos of the kids, report cards of each child, saved letters and cards from relatives or friends. One folder contained envelopes with her and her siblings' names. She opened hers and clasped her hand over her mouth as she poured the contents onto the bed. There was a small baby tooth, a clip of blond hair, and a small wooden comb. She remembered getting the comb from her grandfather when she was five or six years old. She would spend hours combing her and her sisters' hair, and even the cats. She eased the items back into the envelope. Lots of time would be needed to carefully scrutinize the many files in the two cabinets.

Alma opened each drawer and quickly scanned the folder labels. When she got to the middle drawer of the second cabinet, she found it locked. Puzzled, she jerked on the handle again in case the drawer was simply stuck. When she failed to open it, she checked the bottom drawer and found it opened easily and no surprises inside. What was so important in the locked box? Where could the key be? She remembered the door key she had obtained from the judge and that the ring did have more than one key on it. She found her purse and the key ring inside. Sure enough, there were three keys on the ring. One had the name Yale on it and she assumed it fit the padlock on the shed in the back yard. The other key was smaller and very well could be the key to the file cabinet. When she inserted it into the lock and turned, the lock popped out and she opened the drawer.

Again Alma found labeled folders. One with 'DEED' written in her father's handwriting, another marked 'BILLS', several labeled 'CHECKS' with the year following, and one marked 'WILL'. She knew then there would not be a safe deposit box at the bank. She also realized she had not found a deposit box key on the ring.

She pulled a folder labeled 'RED JACKET MINE DISASTER – 1938' and sat down in a chair at the dining room table. In the folder, she found the newspaper article from the *Bluefield Daily Telegraph* and a picture. The article was a detailed account of the explosion of the Red Jacket Mine on Friday, April 22, 1938, which claimed the lives of 45 coal miners. It was a gruesome article describing the explosion as a jarring roar and gusts of black clouds spurting out of the main entrance of the mine and decapitated men being hurled down the side of the mountain.

Alma placed the article to the side and picked up the picture. She took a sip from her Pepsi to help settle the bile forcing its way from her stomach. The picture was old, ragged around the edges from the many hands that had tugged at the why and how such a scene could have developed in the midst of such God-fearing people of their community. Yellow from age, with a few wrinkles down the face, it appeared too brittle to be picked up again. Alma handled it with care and stared at the many bodies covered with once-white sheets. Spectators stood along the bank of a river in the background. She turned the picture over and read her father's note on the back: 'Red Jacket mine explosion – 45 killed – Hanger, VA – April 22, 1938"

Did he take the picture? Did he write the article? Alma knew some of the stories her father had written for a newspaper, before she had left home, and that he had been a part-time photographer. She had just yesterday found his old camera, the size of a shoe box, in the bottom of the cedar wardrobe. She gingerly placed the folder back into the file and removed another simply marked 'HANGER – 1937'

The only item in the folder was another old photograph of four men standing beside a huge bucket tied to the end of a long rope hanging from the top of what appeared to be a concrete pillar. A creek or river flowed around the man-made island the men and structure stood on. Alma read on the back: 'Grady Bracken, Jackson Mullins, Thomas Wills, '?' – Hanger, VA 1937'

She turned the picture to look at the photo again. Four men and only three names. She looked closer and the only thing that stood out was the three men in the back row were white and the single man up front was black. She wondered if maybe the black man was the '?'. There was nothing in the folder to indicate why this picture was important or why her father had saved it over hundreds he must have taken. Alma placed the pictures into a clean white envelope and slipped it into her purse.

She heard a truck stop near the house. When she looked outside, there were three men unloading lawn mowers, weedeaters, and leaf blowers from a trailer hooked to the back of the truck. A huge, shiny black Hummer pulled up behind the trailer. She recognized Brett in his cowboy hat, but she couldn't understand the instructions he was apparently giving the men. She picked up her cup of coffee, even though it was now cold, and walked out on the porch. Brett waved to her and strolled up towards the house.

"What's going on here, Mr. Parker?"

"Hi to you, too, Alma."

"What do those men think they are doing? I never called for lawn service, and the realtor has not said anything about hiring any. Do you also own a landscaping business?"

"No. These men work for me. I'm just trying to pay back a little on a huge debt I owe. I drove up here yesterday, just to see the place after about forty years, and I noticed the weeds need to be cut and bushes trimmed if you expect to get anything out of this sale."

"Well, I'm not paying for the labor of three men. I will get to cutting the grass maybe next week. I still have things inside that need attention."

"You don't have to pay for this, Alma. Remember, I said I was paying on a debt. My treat. They should be finished in a couple of hours, but I could use a cold cola, or just water, if it was offered to me."

"Sorry. Come on up and have a seat. I'll go and get you a drink. How about iced tea? I brought a jug with me this morning."

"That would be great."

Alma brought them both a glass of tea, and they sat and watched the work and talked a little louder over the noise of the machines. Occasionally, Brett would get up and point out a place one of the men had missed.

"You didn't have to do this Brett, but it's awfully nice of you."

"My pleasure, Alma. Really, it's for your mom. She always kept the place looking nice, and I guess it just makes me feel a little better to do something. Soon, there will be someone else living here that we don't know and have no connections to. I once had connections here and a few other places around here. I'm just now beginning to miss that. I've been too busy making my way to notice the little nicks and scars appearing on the horse I rode in on."

"It looks more like a tank than a horse. How much did that black beauty in the driveway set you back?"

"Oh, that's my workhorse. That would run you about $72,000, with all the extras I have on it. Want to go for a ride? I could take that machine right up the side of that hill and through the garden."

"Maybe some other time. I'm about finished up here, and I think everyone is coming in next weekend to empty out the house. I need to get back to D.C. and see if I still have a job."

"Did you find any surprises, cleaning out?"

"Not really. Some sentimental items, but most of the stuff is just everyday household things you need to get by. I still have a couple of files to go through. By the way, do you remember anything about a mine explosion at a Red Jacket coal mine up near Keen Mountain that killed about fifty people?"

"That happened about the time we were born, Alma. No, I don't remember it, but I do remember Dad talking about it and showing me some newspaper articles. It left a lot of single mothers around Oakwood. Why?"

"I found a picture with bodies lying on the ground and a newspaper article telling about the disaster. It must have been horrible, Brett."

"I'm sure it was. We have not had an accident like that, since. Once in a while, we have someone killed in a coal mine, but mostly it is just that – an accident. Like someone careless in operating machinery or maybe a rock fall that should have been detected before it fell. With all the union, state, and federal safety regulations, a coal mine is about as safe as any other industry."

"So you say. Do you really go a mile or more back under hundreds of feet of mountain over your head? Wouldn't that develop some kind of phobia, or something?"

"Well, I don't go in the mine often, anymore. Somebody has to keep pushing the pencil, and I'm on the road a lot. I could arrange a trip into a mine for you if you want to see first-hand how it works."

"Not on your life. Just talking about it reminds me why I couldn't wait to get away from this place. I don't see why our parents didn't move somewhere else when they got married. Maybe they were born here, but they didn't have to stay. Thank God, I didn't see the tragedy and face the hardships they suffered most of their lives."

"Alma, aren't you going a little overboard after only seeing a picture? Most of the guys your father's age served in a war. Don't you think they saw much worse than the Red Jacket mine explosion? Besides, today people can leave and work wherever they want, and they still choose to live and work and raise their families in Buchanan County. You remind me about the boy in the song from Indiana who wanted to 'go where the corn don't grow'."

Alma smiled. Maybe she was one of those that searched for the greener grass on the other side of the fence. She and Brett talked on until the work was done and the men loaded up the mowers. He asked if she would have dinner with him or let him take her for a boat ride Saturday on South Holston Lake. Again, she declined. She was planning on spending time with Aunt Paula, and she and Krista had to get together to finalize the division of property.

After the guys left, Alma checked the files, made sure the drawer was locked, closed the windows, and locked the door. If Brett offered again to be of assistance, maybe she would have him deliver the file cabinets to her hotel room. There was little left to do at the house, but lots of files to look through. If there was any treasure here, that would be where she would find it.

8

Aunt Paula

The next day was Saturday. Alma decided she was going to take the weekend off. She got up early, ate a hearty breakfast at the Huddle House, and packed a small cooler with drinks and snacks. First was Aunt Paula, if she could find her. Alma remembered going to her house when she had lived at Page, but now she lived somewhere near Marvin. Uncle Jake had built her a nice two-story home after he retired, and then he died a year later. Three children and their families lived nearby, but they couldn't badger Aunt Paula enough to get her to move in with one of them or to an assisted-living home. She was 81-years old, a good cook, still driving the '68 Chrysler, and tended a large vegetable garden.

Alma smiled and shook her head. What was it about these mountain people that they had to die with their hands in the soil and their backs bent with the sacrifice they gave daily to God, country, and family?

Why couldn't they set aside one glorious day for themselves? Attend a magnificent performance at the Kennedy Center, walk the streets of London, sip a glass of wine at a sidewalk café in Paris, or gaze at the famous dome frescoes of St. Charles Cathedral in Vienna.

Gabby, Alma's name for her GPS navigation system, told her to take the next right off Route 460. She did so and recognized the road as the one leading to Lane School where her dad had taught when she was about ten. Talk about sacrificing! How did anyone learn anything in a one-room schoolhouse, with one teacher and about 70 students in seven grades? Her dad had also been the custodian, who built the fires and swept the floors.

"Take the next left, go .7 of a mile and your destination will be on your right."

Yes, Gabby, I gotcha.

Aunt Paula didn't answer the door when she rang the bell or when she knocked on the jam. The door was open and Alma's heart gave a twitter as she let herself in.

"Aunt Paula! It's me, Alma! Where are you?"

No reply. Alma called as she walked through the house to the kitchen. A pot was boiling on the stove and Alma raised the lid to see brown pinto beans cooking. Aunt Paula wouldn't be opening a store-bought can. These would be from scratch from a sack. And there would be cornbread warming in the oven. In spite of herself, Alma relished the thought that some things never change.

When she looked through the screendoor, she spotted Aunt Paula bent over a row of potatoes in the garden on the hillside above the outdoor toilet, or outhouse, as it was known around here. She had three and a half baths in the house, but Uncle Jake had insisted on the outhouse 'just in case', and Aunt Paula refused to let it be torn down after he died.

Alma gave a yell, as she didn't want to climb up that steep hill. Aunt Paula gave a start and clutched her chest as she turned and waved her dirty hand. When she stepped up on the back porch, she had a bucket full of new potatoes she had graveled. A bucket of potatoes would have lasted a month or more at Alma's house, but, knowing Aunt Paula, they would be gone by the weekend with dishes to the church or a potluck dinner somewhere in the neighborhood.

"I'd give you a hug, Alma, but I might mess up that pretty red blouse with these muddy hands. Go on in and help yourself to a cup of coffee, and I'll wash up here on the back porch and be right with you."

"Can I help?"

"No, child. You just give me a minute and I'll fix you something to eat, and we'll get to catching up on all you've been doing the past week or two. I'll bet Elmer and Elaine's house don't look the same since you took over." Aunt Paula smiled, as though that could have been a compliment.

Alma shuddered a little as she turned back to the kitchen. Aunt Paula looked forty years older without her teeth. Alma had forgotten that her aunt usually went without her set of false teeth when she was home alone. You couldn't catch her dead without them out in public. Alma decided right then she would have the rest of her teeth capped as soon as she got back to civilized society, even if it meant root canals.

Alma poured them both a cup of coffee and placed the cups on the end of the snack bar. Unlike the bar at her house, this one was squeaky clean. She wondered if Aunt Paula ever used it. Snack bars and kitchen counters were not part of the older folks' kitchens. They had been lucky to have a sink with running water. When Aunt Paula came in, all washed up and house shoes on, instead of the garden boots, and a mouth full of teeth, Alma helped her peel the potatoes and chop up the other vegetables for the stew. They got caught up on recent events, including what Brett Parker was still doing in these parts.

"Well, honey, Brett still has family living in Buchanan County. He probably is the biggest employer in all of Southwest Virginia. His brother and uncle are big politicians as members of the Board of Supervisors and School Board. Brett would rather make money than be a government server. He still does a lot for the folks back here and helped to get the coal severance tax established so we could have more money for education, roads, and water. He married and lives somewhere over near Bristol, but still shows up to eat at the Black Stallion Café, occasionally."

"Not married. Divorced. Twice."

"Is that right? Now, I didn't know that. Guess he doesn't have time for family. How did you find out that little nugget of information?"

"Ran into him at the café. Still a good looking feller, don't you think?"

"Wouldn't know about that. I haven't seen him since he was a young'un'. Don't you go falling for any of that smooth talking. Twice divorced, you say?"

"Oh, Aunt Paula, I was just leading you on. I've got to get this house cleaned out and sold and get back to my job in D.C. Let's refill our cups, now that dinner is on, and go sit on the swing out on the front porch."

Aunt Paula's feet didn't touch the floor, but Alma kept them swinging slowly so they wouldn't spill their coffee. It was beautiful up in this hollow, at least in the summer time. Flowers blooming, birds singing, and the trees so close you took deep breaths just to fill your lungs with the oxygen. Neither of them spoke as they enjoyed the aroma of their coffee and the peace and quiet. Maybe Aunt Paula didn't need assisted living just yet. She was strong, agile, and sharp as a tack.

"We are going to clean out the house next weekend, Aunt Paula. Is there anything you want before the rest of the family gets here and picks over everything?"

"No, child. All that is for you kids. Besides, I've got enough junk around here for my children to fuss over when it's time to do just what you've been doing. I'll just do what Elmer and Elaine are doing now – look down and smile as the kids make their choices, and wonder why that particular item made any difference."

"I don't want to sound unappreciative, but there's not anything I want to take back with me except maybe some of the pictures and records stored in the filing cabinets. I need more time to go through the files, and I may ship them back to D.C."

"The pictures will mean a lot to you, Alma. Some of the family and some of neighbors you don't remember. But your dad took a lot of pictures of history. I look back at the times Elaine and I would sort through some of his black and white photos: of the railroad steam locomotives; of teams of horses pulling logs out of the mountains; of preachers dipping a convert out of the waters of the Levisa; or that river flooding in '57, about the time you graduated and moved on. There should be some precious stuff in those folders."

"I've found a couple already. Do you remember much about the Red Jacket mine explosion?"

"Like a nightmare, Alma. I was just a teenager then, but I'll never forget the number of grieving families lined up along the banks of the river trying to see and turning away from bodies lying on the ground. We lost some relatives, too. Your uncle Robert, married to your daddy's sister Laura, was one of those killed. He was only 24, and poor Laura never remarried and died when she was only in her forties."

"Why did they, do they, do it, Aunt Paula? Why work in the mines and risk such horrible injuries and death? Why not move away to Cleveland and build cars, or Washington and work for the government?"

"Some did. A lot moved away when they were young and moved back again when they started a family. It's just different here, Alma. You love it or you hate it. It's a simple life. We only want an honest day's work, love of our neighbors, to hear the gospel from a preacher blessed with the spirit of the Lord, to hunt and fish when and where we want, and a good belly laugh at least once a week. We want success for our children, peace in our heart, and a chance to pay back those that lent us a hand. Kinda boring, ain't it?"

"You make it sound simple, Aunt Paula, but I believe it's mostly fear. Fear of the unknown, of change, of falling off the end of the earth."

Aunt Paula didn't smile or attempt to argue the point. Like most of her kind, she let others find their way, hopefully with the help of the Lord, and she didn't want to be pushed out of the bed she had made for herself. Even though Alma was nearly a senior, she was still young and the world revolved around her.

"I've got a picture I want to show you, Aunt Paula." Alma dug the photo of the workers on the railroad out of her purse and handed it to her aunt.

"I've never seen this picture, Alma. Was it among your father's possessions?"

"Yes. The names are on the back?"

Aunt Paula turned the picture over and read the names and turned it back again to study the faces. She repeated the action a couple more times.

"I do know these men, except for the black man in the front. Grady, Jackson, and Thomas were all first cousins and born and bred up at Deskins near the old Poor House. First time I knew they ever held a job. The whole clan up there mostly ran moonshine and would work in the fields or cut timber for a few days at a time. I guess this was one of their temporary jobs, building the railroad. That picture was taken just down the road here at Oakwood. I recognize where Garden Creek flows into the Levisa, and that's the railroad spur they're building that runs up to Page."

"The picture says 'Hanger, Virginia'"

"Yeah, that's what Oakwood was called before they built a new post office across the river and up 460 a little ways."

"Why did they call it Hanger, Aunt Paula?"

"Who knows? The story goes that more than one hanging took place from a big sycamore tree that stood on the bank near the fork of the river. Now, I don't know if there is a shred of truth to that, child, but I'm glad they changed the name. Who in their right mind would want to be born in a place called Hanger?"

Alma smiled. "Not me. Do you know who the black man is?"

"No idea, but the daughters of those other men might. Jill, Thomas's daughter, goes to church where I do, up on Prater. She'll probably be there tomorrow. You want to take me to church?" Aunt Paula looked over the edges of her eyeglasses and gave that 'gotcha' smile.

"I don't know about that, Aunt Paula. Couldn't we just go by her house and visit for a while? I feel like I have had enough religion in the past few weeks to last me a good long time."

"You can't ever have enough religion, dear. You just ain't heard the right preacher or had the spirit to move you. No, I wouldn't feel right just dropping in. It's best to be invited, and the best place to get invited is at church. We might not want to visit in her home 'cause the rest of her family is a lot redneck. You might get all the information you want right after church."

After dinner the two of them took a walk up the road to the end of the hollow. There were only three houses above Aunt Paula's home and they were anywhere from a quarter to a half-mile apart. Only within the past five years had the road been paved with asphalt. Before that, a lot of the roads were gravel, and dusty. Thanks to the coal severance tax, many rural roads were no longer dirt roads, and most of the county now had public water from Flanagan Lake, over in Dickenson County. The sulfur-laden water from the hand-dug or drilled wells had always tasted bad, and smelled worse, and added another chore to the housecleaning trying to get rid of the rusty stain.

There was little traffic above Aunt Paula's, therefore the peace and quiet. Only one vehicle passed them on their mile-and-a-half walk. Aunt Paula asked her to spend the night so they wouldn't have to rush getting ready for church. Alma was thinking about it. It wouldn't take more than an hour to run to Grundy and pick up an overnight bag and a dress for church. She really did want to meet some more of the locals, especially the daughter of the man in the picture.

The next morning Alma woke to the smell of breakfast cooking and fresh coffee. When she made her way to the kitchen, she found Aunt Paula stirring a black cast-iron skillet of red-eye gravy. Part of the ingredients for the red eye were the leftovers from the country-fried ham in a platter on the snack bar, along with scrambled eggs, homemade biscuits, fried apples, blackberry jam, fresh square of butter, probably from the milk cow they had passed on their walk yesterday, and two glasses of orange juice. Alma was relieved not to see a jug of milk. She would absolutely refuse to drink it unless she personally pulled off the seal from a container marked with a grocery label.

"What in the world are you doing, Aunt Paula?"

"Cooking breakfast. You better eat up, too. It's hard to tell when dinner will come. It all depends on how many preachers feel blessed to say a few words. Or, maybe, a lot of words." She smiled as she handed Alma an empty plate.

"Aunt Paula, you ought to weigh 400 pounds. How can you eat all this food? How can you live to be 81, if you do?"

"Well, child, you have to keep your energy up if you're going to climb that hill to the garden a couple of times a day, or walk to the head of the hollow to pick blackberries, or dig a little ginseng, or carry a sack of groceries from Joe's Convenience Store down the road. By the way, I don't want to slow down my walk the next time we go. It breaks my stride. With those long legs of yours, you ought to be able to keep up and pull a little oxygen into your lungs."

"Why would you walk and carry groceries? You have a car."

"I do, but it eats gas and gas costs money. It's only a mile down to the main road and Joe's store. I ride when I can't walk. Now, eat your breakfast and we'll get ready."

Alma knew better than to push this conversation. She ate a small bite of everything and it did taste delicious. They got ready and left a little early, so they could have some visiting time before the service started. It seemed that going to church was something more than an obligation to Aunt Paula.

There were about 35 people at church. They stood around in the church yard and parking lot, shaking hands, inquiring about each other's health, and issuing invitations to come by or get together soon. Aunt Paula introduced Alma to all they met. By the time church started, Alma had shaken hands with everyone there, including Jill. She was now waiting for an appropriate time to go to the restroom and wash her hands, or pull out the bottle of sanitizer she carried in her purse. She had not shaken that many hands since the Republican Convention.

When she started to pull out the picture to show to Jill, Aunt Paula shook her head and whispered "wait until after church." This would probably be a long service, but, whatever. Alma would have to be patient. As they filed into church, about a third of the people climbed up into the pulpit, including women who retrieved hymn books from their purse. When the singing started, Alma soon found herself joining in. She had never participated in singing at her church, afraid her shrieking voice would bring the roof in, but here she somehow felt comfortable repeating the lines called out by the lead singer. Aunt Paula smiled at her and raised her voice another level. Alma smiled back and likewise increased the volume. The competition continued throughout the service.

Between preachers, the congregation would often extend a handshake or a hug as they walked around the church and sang the selected song. Alma was amazed at the emotion and love displayed in the eyes of those that approached Aunt Paula. Some of the men had apparently been in love with her from her younger days. When she jokingly asked her aunt after the service, she got a curt reply.

"Don't be ridiculous, Alma. The feelings we share for one another come from the Lord and long acquaintance. I've known most of these people since they were children. Some of those men have not always been godly souls. Take Preacher Jimmy. When he was a teenager and his father was the preacher, he would often play with the other boys in the church yard during service. He also liked to pull pranks on his elders."

"What kind of pranks?"

"Well, we do foot washing about once a month. You probably never saw that when your daddy was going to church because you were one of those kids playing outside or chasing some boy around the church house. But we get down on our knees and, using a wash basin and clear water, wash the feet of the member sitting next to us." Aunt Paula laughed as she recalled the prank.

"Well, what happened?"

"Preacher Jimmy, mind you he was just a kid then, knew that his father laid out his church clothes the night before, including his socks and his newly-shined shoes. Well, he sneaks in after his father had gone to sleep and takes his socks back into the living room and rakes some black soot out of the stove pipe and dusts the insides of his father's socks. The next day was one of the Sundays when we had the footwashing."

Alma busted out laughing. "What happened?"

"What do you think? When the water turned black, Sister Rachel, who was washing the preacher's feet, gave a scream and fainted right there in the floor. Everyone rushed over thinking she had just caught the spirit and was shouting to the Lord, but it took a few minutes for her to regain consciousness. We couldn't find out what had caused her to faint until a few weeks later. The next person in line did notice the black water and, thinking it might need changing after several feet had been washed, simply got up, emptied the basin and refilled it."

Alma was still clutching her side and shaking with laughter when Jill walked over to say her goodbye. Alma quickly got herself together and gave her a hug.

"It was so good to meet you, Jill. Before you go, could I show you a picture my father took years ago and see if you could tell me anything about it?"

"Sure. My dad told me once your father used to take pictures for the newspaper."

"He did? This one was taken about the time I was born." She handed the picture to Jill.

"Oh, yes. I have seen this picture before. That is Dad and his two cousins, Jackson and Grady. I found this picture when I was sorting through Dad's things after he died. It was included in a newspaper article about building a railroad up Garden Creek to Page. Jackson's oldest girl and Grady's only son also have this picture. We were comparing family photos at our reunion a couple of summers ago."

"Would you know who the black man in the front is? Dad wrote your father and cousins' names and the date on the back, but he didn't write the name of the other man."

"Sorry, Alma, I don't know. I'll ask my cousins if they know, if it is important to you. There weren't many black people around here back then. I don't recall ever hearing anyone bring up who that fellow might be."

"Thanks, Jill. If you don't mind, check with your cousins. I don't know that it matters, or is important. It just seems strange that Dad would take a picture and write an article and not mention everyone in the picture."

Later, as they were driving back to Aunt Paula's house, Alma asked her why she and others had never seen the picture, but the people in the picture would keep a copy until the day they died?

"Well, honey, if your dad took the picture, he probably kept it among hundreds of others. As far as

Jill's cousins, most people keep newspaper articles that are about themselves or have their picture in it."

"I guess, but this picture chills my spine for some reason. I think I'll check the rest of the files and see what I find."

Alma had lunch with Aunt Paula and told her how much she had enjoyed the weekend. She drove back to her room at the hotel, took a long bath, dressed in her pajamas, poured herself a glass of red wine, and settled in with a copy of a fashion magazine she had picked up in the hotel lobby. Tomorrow, she would check in with Steve and see if Mr. Warner was still okay with her leave.

9

Brett

The next morning, she stopped in at the Black Stallion Café for breakfast. Lori seated her at her table and brought her a steaming cup of coffee. Since Alma had learned to order from the menu and take without complaining what was brought to her and to leave Lori a twenty percent tip, the waitress had become prompt and very efficient.

Halfway through her breakfast, Brett strolled in and came directly to her table. Without asking, he sat down opposite, took off his cowboy hat, and smiled at Lori, who immediately brought his coffee.

"Good morning to you, too, Brett."

"Hi. You are up and at it early. It's been almost two weeks and I thought you would be about finished with the house."

"I am. I'm just going through some files. I may just box them up and have them shipped to my home in D.C. Steve, my assistant, says if I don't show up for work by Monday he is going to get a promotion. I'm tempted to go in and tell Mr. Warner what to do with the job and go on a long vacation. What are you doing in here today? I thought you only got over this way once a month or so? Lately, you have been a regular at the Black Stallion."

"Ah, some times are more demanding than others. Why don't you retire and move back here? You could travel the world from here as well as D.C. You told me you have over thirty years with Uncle Sam. Instead of fighting the traffic up there, you could start a personal project back here like fixing up your parents' old place. Think what it would mean to your siblings and your nieces and nephews to come back home once in a while."

"Ha! You are a good one to talk about moving back home. I understand you haven't lived in Buchanan County for years. Even though your work and employees are underground here, your headquarters and fancy homes are elsewhere. I couldn't wait to get out of here and I'm certainly not homesick. Fix up your own birthplace."

"I just might. Been thinking about it. Since I don't need the money and I've lost my appetite for the work, I've been kinda looking for a hobby and something that might leave my mark on somebody. Rebuilding the old home place might be the thing. If I can do it right, keep the outside looks but make it much larger, I could make it into a daycare center for senior citizens and name it after my dad."

"You're serious, aren't you?"

"Really thinking about it. You could do a new small scale of your parents' house and use it for a summer home or a get-a-way. You never know, the

IRS may catch up with you one day and you'll need a hiding place."

Alma laughed. "You can't hide from the IRS. They can find a worm under a rock. Just ask Al Capone."

"Getting back to your problem, why don't I go back to D.C. with you? While you're setting your boss straight, or getting fired, I'll check out the Smithsonian. I haven't seen those museums since I was on our senior trip in high school."

Alma blushed and dropped her head for a minute. This was totally unexpected. Was he hitting on her, or did he just want to help out? She knew Brett was wealthy and had traveled all over the world the past few years, and he could see or buy a museum if he wanted. But it might be fun to have some company on the road, and she could show him the side of the federal government he couldn't even read about. Money he had, but she had contacts. She had better talk to Krista.

"Tell you what, cowboy. You buy me that dinner tomorrow night, which you have been promising, and I will tell you what I've decided to do. I am going to D.C. this week, but I'm not sure if you are tagging along."

"I never tag along. I was thinking, instead of driving eight to ten hours one way, I would fly you up in my jet. Then, I could stay at the Hays-Adams Hotel and walk across to the Washington Mall while you take care of business."

Wow! Did he bring her down a notch or two!

"For someone eating breakfast at the Black Stallion Café, I wouldn't have thought you'd be interested in spending $500-plus per night on a five-star hotel room. Why don't you just get one of the White House Secret Service guys to show you around?"

"I might do that. One of the guys I play golf with at The Virginian has a son that is CIA and works his dog at the White House, sniffing out explosive substance."

Alma quit trying to one-up Brett. He was getting to be more interesting each time they met. She pushed back her plate and reached for her purse.

"I gotta go. I'll call you about that dinner when I'm sure I can make it."

"You have my card. Just give me a couple of hours' notice in case I'm not in the county." His smile reminded her of a cat with claws already pressing down on the captured prey.

Alma set her jaw, placed a twenty-dollar bill on the table, which included a fifty percent tip, strung the purse straps over her right shoulder, and gave her hips an extra twist as she headed for the door.

Krista held her hand over her mouth as she struggled to hold back the laughter. Alma was getting steamed. She had driven three hours to visit Krista in Roanoke, so she could look in her sister's eyes as she tried to explain everything that had and was happening to her.

"Cut it out, Krista! I'm being serious here and you think it's funny. I don't know where the hell Brett is coming from, or what his intentions are. I don't plan to travel alone with him to D.C., but I don't know how to get out of it without being cruel."

"Well now, Alma, I never knew that to be a problem for you before. You didn't hesitate to be cruel, rude, or downright dangerous when dealing with me or one of your other siblings. But, I'll take it seriously. It sounds like Brett has run into you on the rebound and you are a different spark than he is accustomed to. You have spiked his interest. You are still a good-looking woman. He feels a little nostalgia flowing through his blood and at his age, and yours, he wants to get his hands on something honest, good, and rewarding to the soul. To leave behind his wealth may or may not be beneficial to his heirs. Sometimes, unearned riches lead to more greed and corruption. It sounds like Brett is yearning to make another mark that history will record as a worthwhile contribution from his life. He already has wings on hospitals and college buildings named after him, you know. I don't see why the both of you could not rebuild your home places and be honored by your families, if not history."

"Well, there you go again, Krista. I don't think you have heard a thing I've said. I'm not worried about history and rebuilding a shack on Garden Creek. I want to know what I should do about letting Brett tag along to Washington with me."

"He can go wherever he wants, with or without you. I think it's great he even spoke to you. You would be crazy not to grab his hand and drag him with you. Besides, riding in that Falcon 10 would be a lifetime thrill for me. We saw it parked at the Tri-Cities Airport when Jack and I flew back from Ohio, after visiting Janice."

"I don't care about flying in his silly little plane. I have flown in Air Force One, thank you, when I flew with the Secretary of State from Belgium back to Washington. If you think he should go, he can ride in my car. I just thought you might help me decide if I should waste anymore of my time letting him barge in here and there. I told you he mowed the yard. Now, he wants to take me out to dinner and try to convince me to give up my career and become a contractor, or something. I may come back for a week or two and finish going through Dad's files, but then I'm out of here."

Krista smiled and reached over to pat Alma's hand before she jerked it away. Krista knew if she came back it wouldn't be for the files, which she could easily take with her. She felt like Alma had gotten her appetite whetted with an adventure unlike any she had undertaken before.

They spent a couple more hours talking, looking over the pictures Alma had brought, including the four railroad workers and the Red Jacket coal disaster, and eating a hamburger lunch at Fuddruckers. Krista wished she could be a fly in the car, or on the plane, to witness the next few days, or weeks, that were unfolding. The dynamic duo would surely plunge down the mountainside they were climbing, like an avalanche.

Alma stopped in Pembroke, a small town on Route 460, to get some gas and a coke to help settle her stomach. She couldn't figure out why she was so unsettled and queasy. The whole day had been a rush, starting with breakfast at the café and Brett pushing to go to Washington with her, and now Krista taking his side. She picked up a flyer from the countertop and read about the waterfalls just up the road from the convenience store where she was sipping her coke. She put the flyer in her purse as she paid for the drink and the gas. She rolled the windows down in the car and turned right out of the parking lot onto the side road leading towards the park.

The parking lot only had six automobiles, including four pickup trucks. She could hear the roaring creek before she could see it, as she followed the signs to the walking trail. It appeared you could take either of two different paths to the Cascades, as the falls were called. The one to the right followed the creek. The other was a wider trail along the hillside for rescue vehicles and a shorter trip out of the mountain. Alma picked the crooked trail along the creek.

The sign said the waterfall was a two-mile hike. She probably wouldn't go the whole way, but she felt like stretching her legs. The rumble of the creek was soothing to her troubled mind. For some reason, the isolation and wilderness didn't seem to bother her. A week ago, this city girl would not have dared to brave the Appalachian trails alone. She took deep breaths of the mountain air, stopped to dangle her fingers in the ice-cold water of the rushing stream, and smelled the leftover blooms of the mountain laurel. She rubbed the shiny green leaves and pictured the ancient Greek gods with wreaths of the greenery upon their heads. She climbed some of the huge limestone boulders, which had been pushed down the mountainside by the flood waters of another time, and soaked in the quiet that only the birds, squirrels, and chipmunks interrupted. Unaware of the time, she rounded a bend in the creek to the deafening roar of water crashing into a churning pool of the Cascades. She stopped in her tracks to just watch. The falls must be nearly a hundred feet high. The water poured over a ledge onto a bench about a third of the way down before plunging into whitecaps in the pool. It was absolutely beautiful!

Alma was alone at the Cascades. The people that had occupied the vehicles in the parking lot must have passed her on the opposite trail leading back to the park. She slipped off her shoes and waded in the edge of the pool. In just a short time, she could not feel her toes. The water was so cold it numbed her feet. She left them in a while longer, anyway, and splashed some water on the back of her neck. The walk up the trail had left her hot and dry. Foolishly, she had failed to bring a bottle of drinking water. Something she would never have done in Washington, she lay down flat on her stomach on a wide slick rock and sipped out of the stream. What dead animal might be decomposing in the creek above the falls didn't enter her mind. She knew from reading the pamphlet that she was in the Jefferson National Forest, and that it included thousands of acres to the top of the mountains and beyond. The water tasted delicious.

She lingered by the pool and explored the trail leading up to the top of the falls, but decided she didn't have the nerve to climb to the ledge. When she noticed the shade covering three quarters of the creek and looked up to see the sun was slowly setting in the west among the tall hardwood trees, she put her shoes back on and meandered down the trail. Before she rounded the bend, she turned for one last look at the falls.

On the way back to Grundy, she felt revived and energized. She wondered if Brett would enjoy a hike to the Cascades. Probably not. Even though he was rich, he still had a fortune to make and a cause to conquer. She punched in his number on her cell phone.

"Hi, Alma."

"I see you have caller ID, Brett."

"Yeah, and I'm sure you do, too. That's why you didn't answer the last two hours I have tried to reach you."

"No, I didn't get your calls until I got a missed-call ring in Bluefield. I was in a no-service area for a while. Sorry about that."

"Well, I got this crazy idea. Why don't you pack a bag for tomorrow night and spend a day in Abingdon? Now, before you go off on me, I thought you would enjoy, in addition to dinner, a play at the Barter Theatre, the State Theater of Virginia, and a night at the historic Martha Washington Inn. Don't worry; I will be spending the night at my house. But, I would like to show you the highlights of our area, and it will be too late for you to drive back to Grundy after dinner."

Alma was quiet for so long that Brett thought he had lost the connection.

"Brett, I don't know about this. But, I have to admit it sounds better than another night at the Comfort Inn and breakfast at the Huddle House."

"Tell you what. I'll pick you up about 3:00 tomorrow evening, and if it is only dinner, then it's only dinner. No pressure."

"I would still like to eat at the Martha Washington and see the play, even if I drive back to Grundy for the night. How about I meet you somewhere in Abingdon around 5:00?"

"That works for me. Let's meet at the Inn. It's right across the street from the Barter Theatre."

"Sounds good. See you tomorrow, Brett." Alma hung up.

The next day, Alma struggled with her decision. She didn't dare call Krista or Aunt Paula. She knew they would only encourage her. She was afraid to tell Aunt Paula much about Brett or any other guy. The elderly lady was still strong enough to load cupid arrows in her bow.

At last she was on her way, and she did have a bag packed. In fact, she had loaded her luggage and her computer and checked out of the Comfort Inn. She had decided to head to Washington after a night in Abingdon. What she didn't know was whether she was driving or flying. It would probably be driving, as the short notice wouldn't give Brett enough time to get things arranged and packed for the trip.

She was wrong. Brett had everything arranged, and he was packed. They had enjoyed a great dinner at the Inn complete with a lobster salad, prime rib, roasted pineapple, cheese and red wine.

They spent two hours in front row seats at the Barter Theatre and laughed and applauded the characters as they did an excellent performance of the origins of country music representing the Carter Family. Alma had no idea that Bristol was considered the birthplace of country music. She and most Americans thought it was Nashville, Tennessee. After the play, Brett rented a horse and carriage, and they rode through the historical part of the town. Abingdon had many old houses, and they put on one great festival each summer that lasted two weeks. You would think it was Brett's home town the way he showed it off. Alma was impressed with all the famous actors and actresses that got their start at the Barter Theatre. When they were through for the evening, she checked into her room. It was already prepared, with the bed turned down and a yellow rose on her pillow. She smiled, but was relieved that Brett had gone on, with the promise to pick her up at ten the next morning.

Alma was ready and sitting in one of the many rocking chairs on the wide, front porch of the Martha Washington Inn when Brett pulled up in his Hummer.

"Don't you own a car?"

"Four, in fact. Two are classic Ford Thunderbirds, a '55 and a '57. I also have a new Lincoln Town Car and a modest Toyota min-van. But since you refused a ride in my work truck, I thought I would bring it to drive to the airport."

"You need a ladder to just get in this thing."

"You do not. There is a step bar. If you need more help with those long legs of yours, you can push this button and an additional lower step will pop out." He pushed the button and it did.

It was a nice ride with all the extras and Brett showed them off. Alma had expected lots of road noise and bounces, but it was smooth and quiet. She could have been happy to ride the Hummer all the way to Washington.

That was until she got on the plane. The Falcon 10 was spacious, with four passenger seats facing each other, that would recline or swivel, and a bar area that Brett called a refreshment center. The co-pilot also served as the steward. Within 90 minutes after taking off from Tri-Cities Airport, they were landing at Reagan National Airport. It was the most pleasurable flight Alma had ever taken, with no other passengers to compete with.

10

Washington, D.C.

Brett did indeed have reservations at the Hays-Adams Hotel. Alma continued with the cab to her house in Alexandria, after agreeing to meet Brett each evening at five to dine, until they flew back to Southwest Virginia. Alma couldn't tell him how long she would need in D.C., but she supposed a couple of days would do. Brett assured her he was in no hurry to return and was looking forward to his time as a regular sightseer.

Alma pushed her luggage into a corner of the bedroom, took a warm bath, changed into her pajamas, and crashed in her own bed with her head on her own pillow. During the couple of weeks sleeping on a strange bed, she had not slept well. There were a few things she needed to do in her house but they could wait until tomorrow. If at all possible, she wanted to be functioning at 100 percent the next few days and that meant a rested body and a rested mind.

Twelve hours later the alarm went off at 5:00 A.M. It was still dark outside and daybreak would be seeping through the curtains in about an hour. Alma took the subway and arrived at her office by 7:00. She logged into her computer and began selecting names, addresses, and phone numbers from her database. If she was going to be away from the city again for an extended period of time, she wanted to have certain people and information at her fingertips. As the printer spit out the pages, she pulled up the word processor and typed a long, but appreciative, letter of thanks and resignation to her boss, Mr. Warner. Just in case she got what she wanted from the FBI, and just in case she would rather be in Oakwood than Washington, D.C.

When Steve walked in, right on time, they gave each other a loud yell and a tight hug. He seemed genuinely glad to see her and not the least perturbed about losing out on a promotion.

"Alma, I'm so glad to see you back! This place is going to hell-in-a-hand-basket, and quickly."

"Good to see you, too, Steve. You'll know in a couple of days if I'm back. I'm checking on a few things from back home, and I may be winding it up here and turning it all over to you. I'm sure Mr. Warner will be happy to see you step in, and he has probably been searching for ways to ease me out the back door, anyway."

"No way, Alma. I can't fill your shoes, and I don't know anyone that can. You have got to stay and get all our lives back to normal."

"We'll see. Right now, I would like for you to get Brian Winehouser on the phone for me, or better yet, see if he can come see me today sometime."

"You mean Winehouser, the FBI field commander that coordinates federal security with the White House? What's up? Is that why you popped back into town without notice? Did Mr. Warner call you directly? He never mentioned anything to me."

Alma laughed and grabbed Steve's arm. "Slow down, Steve. This has nothing to do with the White House, security, or Mr. Warner. Brian and I go a long way back. He has already notified his department of his retirement soon, and I plan on being here at his party to help send him out in style. I would like to see him for lunch and catch his thoughts on retiring, and see if he has any pointers for me. But if it bothers you to talk with the FBI, I can make the call myself."

"Nah, it don't bother me. I've talked with Mr. Winehouser several times in the past few months. You just had me going there for a minute. With you out of town and me trying to cover the bases, I thought I had just missed something. See why we need you here? You stay cool when the rest of us go off half-cocked."

Alma patted him on the shoulder. Moving over to the printer, she placed the pages in a folder and into her briefcase. A short time later, Steve informed her that Brian was on his way over. He had a meeting in the building at noon, but would swing by her office first. They might have time to slip down to the cafeteria for a cup of coffee.

Alma decided to meet in her office, so she had Steve send someone down to bring up a fresh pot of coffee and some cups. She could have made the coffee in her office, but that in the cafeteria tasted a lot better. When Brian arrived, they took the comfortable seats next to each other instead of the chair behind her desk. They indeed talked about retirement and the possibilities of life without work.

"My sister retired two years ago from teaching elementary school and she highly recommends it," Brian said.

"If I tried to teach eight to ten-year olds, I think I would look forward to retiring, too."

"Well, tomorrow is my last official day on the job. That's why I'm in town instead of dealing with some drug smuggling or terrorist's threat in Miami, or Arizona, or somewhere. The Bureau is throwing me a big party tomorrow night at headquarters, in the main conference room. You coming?"

"I wouldn't miss it. I hate to see you go, but I may not be far behind you. Are you moving back to North Carolina?"

"Yeah. Barb and I decided a long time ago that when the kids were grown and gone and we retired, we were going to buy a small farm near Charlotte and have a couple of horses, dogs, and maybe some chickens for fresh eggs, and take it easy."

"Won't you miss Washington and all the buzz going on here? Don't you think you ought to rent a retirement place first to see if you are going to like the area and the lifestyle?"

"Nope. If you're not working in D.C., you are mostly holed up in your small overpriced apartment watching CNN and envying the people getting interviewed and having all the action. You are afraid to venture out into the stop-and-go traffic or ride the subway into the District. It's safer watching history being made on TV than fighting the hordes of tourists wanting their picture made with a marble, twenty-foot-tall Abraham Lincoln. By the time we are ready to retire, we have seen everything the Nation's Capital offers. We take short trips to the grocery store or to church on Sunday, and look forward to the more and more frequent trips out of here. I compare it to a bee living in a beehive. They spend all their time in the hive traffic trying to get to see the Queen and then make a dash for the fresh air and a chance to smell a rose, sip some sweet nectar, and visit a few fruit blossoms. I want to spend the rest of my days somewhere I want to be and enjoy, and not sitting around in some city planning when and how I'm going to get there. Peace, nature, and low adrenalin I say, Alma."

Alma smiled. "You may be right, Brian. Keep me posted. I want to know how it's going."

Alma dug out the two pictures, which she had kept in her purse since the day she found them, to show Brian. He studied them for several minutes and spent more time with the one of all the bodies of the mine disaster.

"I take it that these mean something to you, but you will have to explain. Especially, this massacre on the riverbank."

Alma tried to summarize, since time was limited. She told Brian about her parents' deaths and being named executor after her father died. She didn't go into details about the battle between her and Krista about who was responsible for settling the affairs of the estate, but she did explain how she had found the pictures while going through some of her father's papers and files. She pointed out the notations on the back of the pictures. She described a little of her home place and how the coal mine was only a few miles from there. In addition to neighbors, she may have had relatives killed in the explosion. The fact that it all happened about the time she was born was probably the reason for her ignorance. But now that she had found the pictures, and they had evidently meant a great deal to her father, she wanted to know the rest of the story.

"I'm sure you can search the internet and get the old news articles."

"I did, and it was a gruesome account of a coal mine explosion. I didn't find anything about the other picture. They both are history, and I may find more when I have had a chance to look through the rest of Dad's files and talk to some of the older generation still living down there."

Brian laughed. "Older generation! Do you realize how close we are to being the Older Generation?"

Alma laughed along with him. "It's scary, isn't it?"

"Yeah. I got a feeling you called me to meet you for reasons other than talking about retirement and looking at seventy-year-old pictures. Is there something you think I can help you with? By the way, is there a place called Hanger?"

"Yes, there is. Or rather there was. It is now called Oakwood, Virginia. But the time these pictures were taken, and when I was born, it was called Hanger, Virginia. The name is on old maps and was mentioned in the newspaper article about the mine explosion. I'll fill you in on the history of Buchanan County some other time. Just look at the picture of the four construction workers and read the caption on the back, again."

Brian did. He turned the picture over a couple of times.

"I don't see anything unusual except the name of the black man is missing. Whoever took the picture evidently didn't know his name for some reason."

"My dad took the picture. I'll fill you in on him also, later. Is there any way of finding out the black man's name?"

"Well, I'm sure there is. If you have the resources and time, you can find out about anything. The man may be dead by now. If the date on the back is correct and looking at this picture, I would guess all of them in the photo would be pushing a hundred. Why is it important to you? Are they relatives of yours – I mean the other guys, of course?"

Alma smiled. "Right. No, I don't know them, but I now know the daughter of the big guy there. I don't know if it is important. I just have a feeling. I can't explain, but I have an urge to trace this story back and see where it leads. Crazy, huh?"

"Maybe. I don't know what I can do, but let me study it a while. After tomorrow, I have no authority to push many buttons, but I still have contacts and favors owed me, so we could get lucky. Can you print me a copy of these pictures? You just want a name for the black man?"

"And last-known address. That's all, to start." Alma gave her sweetest smile.

Brian got up to go. "You better plan on retiring if you want to play detective, Alma. I'll help where I can, but I'm serious about becoming a farmer."

She ran the pictures through the copier in her office and handed him the copies. They gave each other a hug, and Alma promised to be at his retirement sendoff. She gave Steve a few more instructions, and then called for a cab to take her to the National Mall. She would try to surprise Brett, but if all else failed, she would call his cell and arrange a meeting place. There was a bounce in her step as she contemplated the next few days.

She found him in the History Museum and sneaked up behind him and gently tapped him on the shoulder. He jumped and spilled the bag of peanuts he was munching all over the floor as he threw his hands in the air.

"What the hell are you doing? You almost gave me a heart attack. This place is scary enough without you sneaking up and attacking me."

Alma laughed. "Attacking you? That was hardly a peck. I first thought you would be over at the Air and Space Museum, then I said 'nope, that would be the younger Brett'. The older Brett is more interested in his past than the jet age and moon missions. Having fun yet?"

"I was until my heart stopped. Did you see that Mammoth with the long, curved tusks when you entered this place? Talk about an oversized elephant! And the Indian displays are fascinating. I can't believe how they were such survivors until the white man showed up. When I come back in another life, I want to be an Indian before the white man. Clean air and water, a good wife to cook and serve me, no work, no money, and no taxes. Just a good horse, hunt all day and have sex all night."

Alma smiled. "I don't think it works that way, cowboy. When you come back, it's in the future, not in the past. You'll probably be a little green Martian with one big eye and pointed ears and webbed feet."

Brett gagged and took her arm to move on to another exhibit. They spent another hour in the museum, and then got a cab to Georgetown. Alma wanted Brett to experience good food and some fine wine that was a step up from the Black Stallion Café. Thank goodness, they were both dressed appropriately.

The maitre d' Jardin Latermer at the University Club smiled at Alma as he checked his reservation list. She was not going to tell Brett that she was close friends and went to church with his mother. Not finding her name, he handed her a red tag.

"Ms. Woodson, I can have you a table in about 15 minutes. If you and your guest would like to have a glass of wine on the house, you can wait in our lounge."

"That would be fine, Jardin."

Alma gave the tag to the waiter and ordered a glass of Corton-Charlemagne for each of them as they settled into soft, white, leather lounge chairs.

"Ms. Woodson has been here before, I presume. How do you get a table in a joint like this without reservations?"

"First of all, you don't call it a joint. It is one of the finest restaurants in the Washington area. I'm just glad you had a tie in your pocket and were carrying a blazer. Wait until you see the menu. They have a first, second, and main course, plus dessert."

"I think I had better have you order for me. Just don't slap my hand if I use the wrong fork or something."

Brett was teasing. Not only did he use the correct silverware, he had his cloth napkin properly across his knee. Alma ordered the brook trout caviar, buttered brioche toast, Thel Pine Farm radishes, baby arugula and lemon vinaigrette for the first course. They ate slowly and rehashed the day Brett had sightseeing. For the second course, she ordered Maine scallops, baby beets, blue-foot mushrooms and Bronte pistachios. She let Brett choose from a couple of her favorites for the main course, and he picked Carolina Red Grouper, fresh garbanzo bean puree, cherry tomato comfit, pickled pearl onions and house-cured bacon.

They were slowing down considerably before the main course was consumed. Brett wanted to know about her day, and if she had filed her retirement papers.

"Of course not! I have several things to consider before I make that jump. I did have an interesting conversation with an old friend who is retiring tomorrow. You and I are invited to his retirement party tomorrow night at the FBI headquarters."

"FBI? I don't know if I should show up there. Do the Feds get drunk and out of control at their own party?"

"I don't think so. You aren't afraid one of them will recognize one of your old wanted posters, are you?"

"Funny. All they could get on me is being a redneck hillbilly from the Appalachians. Do you deal with these guys a lot?"

"Only occasionally, and they're not all guys, you know. I am long-time friends with Brian, the guy I met today, who is retiring, and his wife. I just wanted to show him the old pictures I found in Dad's file to see if it was possible to identify the construction crew on that railroad job."

"I thought you or your aunt Paula knew those guys."

"Not the black man."

"Why do you care? They're all dead by now. I'm sure there are many photos in your dad's files of people you will never identify. He was a newspaper photographer and, if he were still alive, he probably wouldn't know some of them."

"You're wrong there. Not only would Dad identify the people, he would tell you the story behind the picture, even if it were a lost and forgotten story written years ago. I just have a feeling about this one. And it was locked in a box, in a sealed envelope. No harm in checking it out, even if it doesn't go anywhere. Tell you the truth, I can't wait to get back and finish going through the rest of his records."

"Want to leave tomorrow?"

"I might. Let me sleep on it tonight. I still have to show up for work tomorrow and settle things with Mr. Warner. Oh, and we have a party to go to tomorrow night."

Brett groaned. "You know, this is possibly the most elaborate place I've ever eaten in and the best food I can remember. But I still wouldn't trade it for the Black Stallion. Jardin is very professional, but Lori would have been by my table a dozen times by now. And I would know what has happened in Buchanan County in the last week. That girl has prevented more than one walkout at my mines. She lets me know what the miners are thinking and unhappy with. Sometimes, I'm able to head off trouble before it happens. And the food's not bad, either. Beats cooking for yourself."

"You homesick, Brett? How about ordering dessert before you head back to the Black Stallion for a banana split?"

"I'm stuffed, but you order and get us a cup of coffee. If I don't switch off this wine, you may have to walk me up to my room."

Alma checked the menu and ordered the coffee and a dark chocolate black mission fig brownie with vanilla bean ice cream, honeycomb, and Bartlett pear cream with Marcona almonds. Brett listened to the order and dropped his head to the table. When the dessert arrived, they spent another 45 minutes savoring the sweetness and sipping two cups of coffee. This time, Brett saw her to her home and kept the cab for his trip back to his hotel.

Alma had a hard time sleeping. Since she had been to Oakwood, she had difficulty sleeping in her own bed. She even said a little prayer. Not like the ones she had memorized and repeated before, but a down and out talk with God with a plea to show her the way. What she was supposed to do about retiring, selling the house or fixing it up for her summer home, tracking down the black man or letting sleeping dogs lie, was Brett just a friend, did she want to find her roots, and the list went on. Later, she thought about Aunt Paula. She loved the old woman and she was fun to be with, in spite of the difference in their ages, but maybe she had better slow down on taking her to church. She didn't know where that prayer had come from. But it did feel good to get some of that off her chest. Soon, she was asleep.

The next day she met Mr. Warner as he got off the elevator and invited herself to his office after he had settled in and had his cup of coffee. She was all smiles, but professional, as she handed him her letter of resignation. He made a weak attempt to talk her out of it. They sat and talked a short while about the years and experiences they had shared. She ended up informing him that today would be her last day, and the vacation days she had built up would serve as her two-week notice. He acted a little upset, but they both agreed that Steve would do nicely until a permanent replacement could be found. They also agreed that would probably be Steve. Alma hugged him, promised to stay in touch, and spent the remainder of her time cleaning out her desk and closet and saying tearful goodbyes to Steve and the rest of the staff in her office suite.

That night, Brett rented a tux and Alma dressed in her favorite gown. They attended the retirement party for Brian for a couple of hours. She made sure Brian had her cell phone number and her e-mail address. He informed her he was already in contact with the agent in Beckley, West Virginia, who had agreed to start the probe in Southwest Virginia, as well as adjoining parts of West Virginia and Kentucky. He couldn't promise her anything on such a cold case, but she would know when he knew. That was more than she had hoped for. It was probably all for naught, but the Federal Government had spent more time and money on less causes.

Noticing Brett's restlessness, she wished Brian and his lovely wife an early goodnight and said goodbye. She promised to check in when she was back in Washington, which would probably be in a couple of weeks. Then, she and Brett made a hasty retreat and stopped at a swinging nightclub she knew of in Old Alexandria. About midnight, Brett dropped her off, after they agreed to meet at the airport at ten the next morning.

11

The Wrong Turn

Before they were in the air, Alma realized that, for the first time since she had left Buchanan County as an eighteen-year-old graduate, she was excited to be going home. To her childhood home that she had been so impatient to leave. This time, she vowed to stay at the house and not rent a motel room. She would have to buy a bed and a few other things since her siblings had cleaned out the place. Thank goodness, the stove and fridge were still there. They were so old nobody wanted them, but they still worked.

Brett suggested they fly in to Lynchburg on the way home and tour the battlegrounds at Appomattox Court House. Alma quickly agreed. She had never been there, even though she had driven close by on her way from Oakwood to D.C. They rented a car in Lynchburg and, in less than an hour, they pulled into the parking lot of the Appomattox Court House National Historic Park. They walked into the McLean House and looked into the parlor where General Robert E. Lee, of the Confederate Army, surrendered to Lt. General Ulysses S. Grant, of the Union Army, to mark the end of the Civil War, on April 9, 1865. They looked at the slave quarters, the tavern, and the storehouse. There was even a Woodson Law Office building.

"Relatives of yours, Alma?"

"Maybe so. I'll have to do some research on that." Alma laughed.

They got a snack and drink from the vending machines and strolled over the grounds. They walked through the woods and over some battlefields where hundreds had been killed just days before the surrender. Alma became melancholy, and a short time later asked Brett if they could leave. They were back in the air before she began to feel better. Brett had the pilot fly low over the Shenandoah Valley, hoping it would lift her spirits.

Alma was nearly her old self as they flew over Lexington and followed Interstate 81 several miles. She had ridden on that road many times but had never realized the magnitude of President Eisenhower's greatest achievement. Now, she could believe the Interstate system in the United States could rival the Great Wall of China.

"I'm sorry, Brett. It was weak of me to spoil your tour of the battlefields."

"No problem, Alma. I had seen enough. It was my first time there. It's amazing how just standing where so many died, and history was made, gives you a touch of the struggle that went on in that tragic war."

"And slavery was ended."

"That, too. Oh, what a price we pay for wrong choices."

"But for so many, Brett, it wasn't their choice. How many boys from the mountains of Southwest Virginia died, whose family never owned a slave or, for that matter, had never seen a black man?"

"Causes of war are seldom those of the soldiers doing the fighting, Alma. In this case, I believe it was probably the slave owners that pressured the politicians to spin the case for states' rights. The soldiers fell into the patriotic trap, and some were redneck enough to fight instead of bending to the will of the Feds or letting any outsider tell them what they had to do."

"Well, I just think it was an unnecessary, terrible thing that happened. Once it started, I'm glad President Lincoln fought on until he won, or we wouldn't be the United States of America. We would be two or more countries. I wouldn't want to grow up in a country that allowed slavery. I had a great-grandmother who lived to be 104 years old, and she remembered parts of the Civil War. She used to say that folks just wanted to kill some 'damn Yankees'."

"How old were you when your great-grandmother died?"

"Oh, I was probably ten, or twelve. I remember her smoking a pipe and sitting in a rocking chair on the porch. I believe she, and many others back then, would feel different now about slavery and the difficulties black people still suffer. We have been a racist country in the past, haven't we, Brett?"

"Some of us still are. Don't you know people today who are prejudiced?"

"Yeah, but not like before. I think we will one day have a black president, don't you?"

"Maybe. But we will probably have a woman president first, and neither of us will live long enough to see either."

When they landed at Tri-Cities Airport, Brett retrieved the Hummer and delivered Alma to the Martha Washington Inn. He hinted about staying over with her, but she pushed him out and told him to go earn some money. She might need a loan now that she was retired. She also wanted to check on some furniture before she headed back to Buchanan County.

After Alma dumped her bags and freshened up a bit, she walked over to the Barter's outdoor café and had a sandwich and a coke. She got her car and drove down the street to Kingston's Furniture. In about an hour, she had purchased a bed with a good mattress, a chest of drawers, a small dining table with four chairs, and a long leather couch. She made arrangements for delivery the next morning, then drove to Wal-Mart for bedclothes, a coffee pot, and some items of dinnerware. It might not be much more than camping out, but she was ready to make a start on a new life. She would add to her collections as the need arose. That might include a fellow. She wasn't sure how long she could live on Garden Creek without having someone get her out to civilization again. Aunt Paula she was not.

The next day, the guys that delivered the furniture also set it up for her. She chose the largest bedroom on the first floor next to the bathroom, and while they were putting her bed together, she loaded the new bedclothes into the washing machine. She intended to hang them out on a line on the front porch to see if she could recapture the fresh smell she remembered as a teenager. After the delivery men left, she walked through the house again and decided she could survive temporarily, after making a trip to the grocery store for supplies.

Alma bought enough groceries to last a couple of people for a week, including a few items that were not available at the local store. She solved that by making a trip on to Grundy to the only state ABC store in the county. She got her favorite wine and a bottle of Jack Daniels, which she seldom consumed, but visitors might, if she ever had any.

After she had restocked the cabinets and fridge, she poured herself a glass of wine and picked a file at random out of the locked drawer of the cabinet and settled into a lounge chair on the front porch for some exploratory time of her father's memories. The first article she found was on the TMI, Triangular Mountain Institute, a school started and built by the Methodist Church at the forks of Garden Creek. Alma remembered her mother had walked from the family farm on top of the mountain to attend TMI. She finished the article and looked at the picture of the Methodist Church.

There was an article about the early history of Buchanan County land grants, the arrival of the railroad, and even Indian exploration into the county. It appeared the Indians had little use for the steep hills and deep hollows and only traveled through to hunt and fish and returned to Tazewell or Russell counties.

Some of these articles were researched and written by others and her dad had secured or made copies because of his interest. Two that were interesting to Alma were about the Melungeons, an ethnic group of people who were a mixed race of black, white, and Indian, that settled in the Appalachian wilderness. One article supported the idea of the Melungeons, but the other dismissed the idea as folklore, mythology, and hearsay.

One article described how Daniel Boone had traveled through Buchanan County and discovered, what is now, the Breaks Interstate Park. Another told of the lost Swift's Silver Mine and how vast sums of silver had been hidden in several locations before Swift and his partners were killed by Indians. Alma's father had written about how two of the Harrison brothers near Drill had supposedly found one of these caches of lost silver while hunting. But they were never able to return to it because, failing to make a map, they could never remember the number of ridges and hollows they crossed on their way home to tell members of the family. Alma smiled as she laid the article aside. This was one she would show Brett. With his skill in finding money, they could explore and see how many pieces of silver they could find.

She read several more articles and finished the folder with one about the hanging of John Hardin in Grundy for killing a man, in 1897. It seemed the murder occurred in September, and he was hanged in December. Alma thought about the years it would take now for the family of the victim to see justice done. She closed up the folder and locked it back in the file drawer. After a small snack, she took a warm bath and turned in for the night with her CD player playing classical music. Tomorrow, she wanted to check some more files, but also needed to decide what to do about renovating the house.

Alma spent the next few days searching through the files and picking out old pictures she wanted to put into a scrapbook, reading the comment sections of old report cards – hers and those of her siblings, and putting together a graphic family tree. Sitting in the old swing on the front porch with a glass of wine, she wondered why she was so interested in the family thing. Before, she had wanted to reach out to the horizon and see and experience what was waiting for her.

After a few hours of searching through the folders, she decided to take a walk up the road. Now, there were only two families living up the hollow above the house. She could remember when there had been about ten. The homes had either burned or been torn down. Only the flat surface leveled out of the steep hillside, filled with weeds and briars, would indicate where they had stood. She traveled old logging roads and a couple of graveled roads that had once led to a drift coal mine, and saw the rotting timbers of a temporary tipple. She marveled at the greenery of the poplar, oak, and maple trees that covered the mountainsides. She now remembered how beautiful the colors were in October and looked forward to being here during that time of the year. She also remembered how she had been fascinated by the wide openness of Arizona and the bald rock formations. She didn't think she could now ever live anywhere without green grass and trees. These steep mountains and deep hollows were suddenly cuddling her as a protective mother would her very young. She smiled as she thought about how impossible it would be for a jetliner to crash into her house down the road.

Alma took several walks up the hill behind the house through the old garden and orchard. Here, about two acres were nearly as flat and level as where the house was located. Most of the old fruit trees needed pruning, or were broken and dying. She followed a deer trail through the woods and around the hill to the top of the ridge. She thought about the first television her family had after she left home. Krista and William had to run the TV line to the antenna on top of the ridge almost weekly to clear fallen branches off the line so they could get a signal. It was beautiful up there. You could see a good way towards Garden Creek and Route 460, but you couldn't see houses, roads, or rivers because the trees and foliage hooded everything below.

When she came back through the garden, she stopped and looked around. She walked off the footage of what she imagined a house would look like in certain locations. It was just far enough off the road to give peace and quiet and a pretty view. Maybe she would think about buying out the other kids, and maybe she would build a vacation home up here. Maybe!

The next morning, Alma heard the hoot owl before daylight. She rolled over onto her back and, with her arms behind her head and her hands touching the wall, she eased into a full stretch. The muscles in her legs and upper body were urging her to get up and move, but her eye lids pleaded to sleep on. After hearing a few more hoots, she opened her eyes, found her robe and slippers, and padded into the kitchen to turn on the coffee she had prepared the night before.

After a few minutes in the bathroom and a splash of cold water on her face to smooth out a few wrinkles, she poured herself a cup of caffeine. Wrapped in the blanket from her bed, she moved to the rocker on the back deck to watch the brilliant starlight seep into the blackness of the hollow. As daybreak approached, the eyes of Heaven closed their lids while objects on earth formed their shape.

Alma found the owl just before it gave one last hoot and took flight from the top branch of the tall blue spruce near the road. She could hear the beat of its large wings as it lifted into the lightening sky.

She took the last sip of her now-cool coffee and a long breath of fresh air and made her way back to the kitchen to fix herself a breakfast of toast and oatmeal. She thought she might just take a long walk after the sun came up and before her shower and the day began. With Brett out of town on business, it would be a good time to do some thinking about her long-term plans.

Alma stopped at the fork in the road about a half-mile up the hollow from the house. Her intentions had been to walk the mile up to the old Duncan place. She looked again at the left fork. She knew there were no houses this way, but there was a narrow trail where the road used to be. She thought of the times she and Janice had traveled this road looking for the milk cow before she was even a teenager. She decided on the left track. She would listen for the cow bell again and see if the blackberry fields were still there.

After a quarter-mile, she stopped. There were no cows, no bells, and no fields. There was only brush and young trees and a path that was now not much more than a game trail. She had just turned around when the shot rang out. She dived towards the boulder at the edge of the road.

Oh shit! What a headache! Alma tried to open her eyes, but there was only blackness. Her eyes and forehead felt cold and wet. She reached her right hand up to her face and pulled off the damp cloth covering her eyes and looked around.

The small room was dim, but she could see and feel the dark green army blanket covering her. There was a small window over a make-shift table and a seat made from a cut-off log. Startled, and scared, she rolled her head to look back into the room when she heard a light scraping sound behind her.

The sudden jerk of her head and the desperate effort to rise swiftly brought on the darkness that squelched her scream. Fighting unconsciousness, she lowered her head and closed her eyes for a second. When she tilted her head on the pillow and opened her eyes again, he was still there.

She thrust the wet cloth she still held in her hand over her mouth to keep from screaming out. The man, who had his back to her, bent slightly over a bench working on something in a bucket. Sensing her, he turned his head and looked over his shoulder at her. His dark brown hair was long and hung over the collar of his camouflage green jacket. She stared at his face. She was sure she had never seen this man before in her life and would probably never forget that look, if she lived to tell about it. He didn't smile or speak to her, but instead glared as though he was angry. Finally, he turned back to his chore.

Alma looked around slowly, not daring to raise her head again and bring back the darkness. She spotted her bright yellow wind jacket hanging on a nail beside the open door. Quickly, she reached under the blanket to feel for the cotton cloth of her pants and upward to assure herself the white T-shirt was still in place. He hadn't undressed her—at least not yet.

She looked back at the jacket. Something was different about it? Lots of things were coming back to her quickly now. The hike up the road, taking the left fork, turning to head back, then the gun shot and … Oh, my God! He shot me! That's blood on the back of my jacket!

This time, she did scream. He turned quickly in her direction, and she saw the bloody knife in his hand. She screamed again and tried to get up and run. He placed a hand on her shoulder just as the spinning room crashed in on her.

Alma felt him rubbing her hand as she woke up. When she jerked her hand as she opened her eyes, he released her hand, and this time he smiled.

"You had better not try to get up again. You'll just pass out and do more damage."

"Who the hell are you? Why did you shoot me?"

He laughed out loud. "My name is Rufus, and I didn't shoot you."

"The hell you didn't! My head feels like it's been blown off my shoulders. And what do you think that is on my jacket?"

"Blood."

"I knew it! You son-of-a-bitch! Are you going to finish the job with that knife?" Alma heard herself screaming and felt tears streaming down her cheeks. She pulled the blanket up under her chin to try to ease the shivering and chills.

"You had better calm down, lady, or you may go into shock. I wasn't the dumb ass that drove his head into a rock and probably got a concussion. That blood on your jacket is from a squirrel. I didn't see you coming up the trail until I shot the squirrel out of the top of a hickory tree. I heard you scream and saw you dive head-first into that boulder. The dead squirrel fell out of the tree and landed on your back while you were lying there, knocked out from diving head-first into a rock."

Alma could feel the heat from the blanket warming her. The shaking had stopped. She didn't know whether to believe this story or not, but she reached her hand up to discover the goose-egg-size knot just above the hairline on top of her head.

"What about that bloody knife?"

"Weren't any use in a good fox squirrel going to waste. I skinned it out, and it's boiling in that pot over there. In a few more minutes, I'll pour you a little cup of broth and, maybe before dark, you can get the hell out of my hollow."

"I ain't eating any squirrel stuff!"

"You want to spend the night on that bunk, be my guest."

Alma looked around. It was the only bed in the room. In fact, this 10x12-foot room appeared to be a house, or cabin, or whatever it was. He had this bed, the bench he had used to clean the squirrel, the table consisting of two wide boards nailed to four small poles, the stump to sit on, and what looked like a small homemade stove with a flat piece of metal as the stovetop. Surely, it was just his hunting cabin.

"It's not hunting season. Why are you shooting squirrels?"

"There ain't no season, lady, when you are hungry."

He poured a cup of the broth and handed it to her. She had already thrown off the blanket, but the warm cup felt good in her hands. She looked at the broth and could see tiny pieces of what she assumed to be meat from the squirrel floating around. She hesitated.

"It's all I got, lady. If you want to get your blood flowing again and get rid of that headache, you'd better drink up."

"My name is Alma. Alma Woodson."

She took a sip. It wasn't bad. He had seasoned it with some kind of herbs, or something. She noticed two rough-looking cabinets nailed to the wall and several cans stacked on one end of the bench.

"Rufus, do you come up here often to go hunting?"

"This is my home, and I don't take kindly to folks trespassing."

"Then your last name must be Martin. I know this is the Martin place, and it's been tied up for years in probate court. The family, wherever they are, own the whole side of this mountain."

"I'm not a Martin, but I'm telling you this is my place, and I don't want anyone coming up here messing with me. I don't bother you, and you don't bother me. Now, let's see if you can stand up."

Alma let him help as she stood. She could feel the energy returning to her limbs and the headache was no longer throbbing.

"Now let's see how you do taking a few steps."

She walked to the open door and looked out. He was still holding to her elbow. She gasped when she saw the shack was perched just a few feet away from the edge of a high cliff. She could see over the treetops all the way down the hollow to the forks, where she had made the wrong decision this morning. She could barely see the trail and boulder underneath, through the heavy foliage.

"How did I get up here?" A really dumb question.

"The same way you are going back down. If I can get you back to fairly level ground, we'll see if you can walk to the forks of the road. Then, we can go our separate ways."

"You're a real friendly fella, Rufus. I'm sorry I've messed up your day."

"Let's not drag this out. I carried you up here in my arms, like a baby. You want to go back the same way, or do you think you can piggyback down the side of this hill?"

"I can ride on your back, but I must warn you. If you drop me over the edge, I've got a big tough boyfriend that'll be looking for you."

"And I've got a gun."

Rufus squatted down enough for her to climb onto his back. She wrapped both arms around his neck as he locked her knees inside his elbows. Alma grabbed her jacket off the nail as they passed through the doorway and headed down the mountain.

It was farther down to the boulder where she hit her head than she would have thought. The ride down was smooth. She knew he had gone slower and more cautious to prevent rattling her brain any more than necessary. For a mountain man, or hermit, or homeless person, or whatever he was, she was surprised to find he smelled pretty good. He was clean-shaven, except for the Clark Gable mustache, and his clothes, although worn and a tear here or there, held only a slight touch of his body odor. His hair, which was practically in her face, smelled a little like some kind of mint.

He eased her off his back by the boulder, a quarter-mile or more from the shack. He didn't seem to be even breathing hard after lugging another 140 pounds down the trail. Without speaking, he motioned her on down the road. Several times, she glanced back to find him only a step behind her. If he followed her all the way home, she hoped she would have the energy to fix him a huge dinner. It was hard to tell when he had last eaten a decent meal. He had nearly killed her, but then he had saved her life. She didn't think she could do it, but she might get Brett to kill and dress out a squirrel once in a while for a late evening snack.

When she arrived at the forks of the road, she turned to ask him if he had a squirrel recipe. He wasn't there. She looked back up to the bend in the trail, and he was nowhere to be seen. She called his name, but knew he wouldn't answer. With a smile, she blew him a kiss and headed down the road to home.

"Mr. Rufus, I will find out more about you, and I will see you again."

12

The Investigation Begins

Two days later, Alma walked into the sheriff's office located just behind the courthouse in Grundy. The town was going down fast. Only part of the dozen or so buildings on the river side were now occupied. Floods of the Levisa River in years past had all but wiped out any hope the businesses could survive. With only a half-dozen cars challenging her for a parking space, Alma felt the town was already dead.

Brett had said no. Big things were planned for Grundy. According to him, the Army Corps of Engineers was going to dig out several acres from the mountain on the other side of the river and move the town. A four lane highway would be built where the buildings were now. Only the courthouse side of Main Street would be left.

Before Alma went to see the Sheriff, she had walked the river road and the half-mile of Main

Street. This was the town of Grundy. The only town in Buchanan County. She just couldn't picture it. Had a town ever been moved before? There was only a small strip of land on the other side of the river where the train depot used to be. Grundy wasn't that small.

Well, what they say is going to happen doesn't mean it will. She had been in politics for over thirty years and knew how that ball bounced.

"Hi!" She gave her best smile to the deputy behind the desk. "Are you the sheriff?"

"No. I'm Deputy Harmon. Can I help you?"

"I need to see the sheriff."

"Well, if you want to give me your name and tell me why you want to see Sheriff Tabor, I might be able to see if he's in."

"My name is Alma Woodson. My business with the sheriff is none of yours. Now, can he, or can he not, speak with me?"

"Just a minute." The look from the deputy was cold.

Alma smiled behind the officer's back. The sheriff was in, and he would see her. If for no other reason, to see what woman could have dared to piss off one of the county's finest.

"Ms. Woodson, Sheriff Tabor. How can I help you?"

"Don't you have an office, Sheriff?"

Without hesitation, the sheriff turned to the deputy and spoke calmly.

"Search her and her bag. When you are satisfied she is clean, show her into my office."

"Yes, Sir!"

"Sheriff, you can't do that! You have no reason…"

The sheriff had already closed the door.

Alma clutched her purse close to her chest and glared at the deputy.

"Your choice, ma'am. If you want to see the sheriff, I have to search you." The deputy was smiling now.

"This is ridiculous! If you touch me, I'll have the State Police in here and have you arrested for sexual assault."

"I only need to look in your handbag. The way you are dressed, I'm sure there's nowhere you could conceal a weapon."

Alma opened her mouth and then slowly closed it. She handed over her purse to the smiling deputy. She was now glad she had placed her Sig 9mm Luger in the glovebox of her car before she came in. She was wearing a tight, yellow, cotton short-sleeved blouse over mint green capris with beige sandals. She guessed any weapon would have been detected if she had been carrying one. No use wasting any more time with this grinning idiot, anyway. The sheriff would probably be just as useless.

She was seated opposite the desk where the sheriff appeared to be working on a huge folder. After a couple of minutes passed, he stuffed some pages back into the folder and looked across the desk at her.

Alma took the picture out of her purse and slid it across the desk. It appeared professionalism was finally at hand. She needed help, and he was here to serve the people.

"This picture was taken by my father, Elmer Woodson, long ago. I recently found it among his belongings after he died. As you can see on the back, he has identified the three white men and left a question mark for the black man. I would like for you to help me identify him. Maybe you have a cold case from the late 1930's or 40's of an unsolved death, or missing person's record, on file for a black man. I imagine it would be kinda rare in Buchanan County."

"Sorry about the death of your father, Ms. Woodson. Elmer was well-known and respected throughout the county."

"Thank you. Please call me Alma."

"Alma, I've never seen this picture, or recall hearing of a black man dying or missing. I'm going to call my top detective in to meet with you. He is a good man and has worked for about five different sheriffs in this county. Please get off to a good start with him and watch your mouth. We may look like a hick town and a hillbilly police force to a lot of city folks, but you should know better. Elmer was very proud of you and his whole family."

"I'm sorry about my rude entrance, Sheriff. Thanks for your help."

When the detective walked in, Alma rolled her eyes and then caught herself. Here was an old man, five foot six, wearing a flannel-checkered shirt, patched blue jeans, and dirty white sneakers. He had a two-week beard and long grey hair tied in back with a red bandana. He did look trim and fit, though.

The sheriff laughed. "I'm sorry, Alma, but the look on your face... Alma Woodson, this is Detective Ronnie Rife."

The detective held out his hand and Alma shook the strong grip.

"I'm sorry, Detective, but you just don't look like any law enforcement men I've ever met."

"It helps to blend in with the criminals passing through. Doesn't help much with the locals. They all know me, anyway. Looking like this, I can be a bum, a redneck, or a drug-pusher. Dressed up in my Sunday best, I can sit in on the board of directors meeting. It also helps to keep my wife riled up, which is not always a good thing."

"Show him the picture and tell him what you know, Alma." The sheriff had returned to his seat.

She handed over the picture and told the detective what little she knew.

"My question is why? Why do you want to find out who this guy is? Why should you care? All these men would be dead by now. I agree, it is unusual to have a black man in the picture, but the railroad brought in all kinds to work at different times."

"I don't know why I feel the need to know who this guy is. It's a puzzle to me. Why did my dad keep this picture? In a safe place, by the way. Did he find out something later, or did he file a report with the sheriff's office when he couldn't find the man to write up his report to the paper? The other men in the picture kept a copy of this picture and passed it down to their families. Or, at least, left it to be found after their deaths. Why? Is it so hard to find one man?

Maybe his family never got this picture and would like to know their father, or grandfather, worked on the railroad. Maybe he ended up owning the railroad. Hell, I don't know. But I want to know why it was important enough for my dad to lock it up and leave it for me to find."

"Ok, Alma. I'll go through our files and see what I can find. Don't hold your breath though. Not many people know that Oakwood used to be Hanger. I suspect the guy did his job and moved on, or back home. Not many hung around in Buchanan County back then."

"You could watch your choice of words, Detective. I appreciate your effort."

"How did you get that bump on your head?"

"I told you he was a good detective, Alma." The sheriff looked at her head and said something about running into a door wouldn't cause that kind of injury.

"Oh, I almost forgot. There is something else I wanted to ask. Ronnie, I'm glad you are here. Do either of you know a guy, a hermit, living in the woods up on Garden Creek who goes by the name of Rufus?"

The sheriff shook his head no. The detective gave a slow grin.

"Did he do that to you?" the sheriff asked.

"No! No, I fell into a rock hiking up the trail in the hollow above the house. But I ran into Rufus, and he is a weird one."

"You got that right, Alma," the detective said. "I've known of Rufus for over thirty years. Few people get to lay eyes on him. I'm surprised you 'ran' into him."

"What can you tell me about him? I didn't get much in the way of answers for my questions, and he seemed in a hurry to get rid of me."

"Well, his name is actually Rayvar Jeeter. He is from the area around Red Jacket, West Virginia, about our age, maybe a little older."

"Just a minute! I'm not about your age."

"Sorry. I wrongly assumed you to be at least forty. Bad mistake. A guy should never try to guess a woman's age, especially if they are still young and beautiful."

"Nice recovery, Detective. We won't talk about age, but you are impressing me as a detective. Now, what about Rufus, or Rayvar?"

The sheriff covered his mouth to hide his smile. Detective Rife went on revealing his knowledge of the hermit.

"He is a Korean veteran, actually wounded while serving in the war in the early 50's. Divorced shortly after returning from the war. He took up what he called homesteading on the old Martin property up the left branch of Little Garden Creek. Nobody knows where the Martin family is, or if they still own the property, so we let him be until we get a complaint. He kills a squirrel or turkey out of season once in a while but doesn't seem a threat to anyone. The owner of Garden Supply says he delivers a box of groceries to a spot in the forks of the road once a month and picks up a check, nailed to a tree by the side of the road, for last month's supplies. Several of us, and a few hunters, have attempted to find him and talk, or just see if he needs help, but nobody besides you has seen him in over five years. What did he look like?"

"Better than you." Alma smiled as she said it. "He was clean-shaven, clean but ragged clothes, and had little to say."

"How did you find him?"

"Actually, he found me. When he shot a squirrel out of a tree, and it landed on me, I dived for a boulder beside the road and knocked myself unconscious. He carried me to his lookout high on the cliff and made me some squirrel broth after I came to. Scared me shitless, until I found out what happened. Please don't bother him on my account. I hope to see him again. I think he needs a friend, in case of an emergency."

"I don't think you have to worry about anyone bothering him. Nobody can find him."

The sheriff and detective promised to get in touch with her if they discovered anything that might be related to the picture. After giving them her phone number and address, she shook their hands and apologized for her awkward introduction. They both smiled and said it was nice meeting her.

On her way home, she thought a little about how she must come across to these people she seemed to have little in common with. She didn't want to tell Brett about this episode or about meeting up with Rufus, but she knew she would. He would probably tell her it was time to get off her high horse and join the real people.

Alma had not heard from Brett since they returned from Washington. After a few times in the Black Stallion Café, she asked Lori if he had been around. Lori hadn't seen him for a couple of weeks. Oh, well, he probably had more business out of the area to attend to. He certainly had more important things to do than watch over her. He had been a big help, though, and she would miss him if he didn't show up again.

At the end of the second week back, she got a call from Brian Winehouser. After several inquiries about her health and happiness and his retirement and family, he got down to the reason for the call.

"There were no black families living in Buchanan County at the time that picture was taken, Alma."

"Well, maybe not, but there was a black man in Buchanan County when that picture was taken. The railroad bridge is still standing in that same location, Brian."

He laughed. "The obvious, Alma. That is why we moved to the second picture. Because of the number of deaths and the mystery of the explosion of the Red Jacket Mine, the federal government got involved in the investigation. Records were searched ten years back from that time and a list compiled of all employees that had worked there. Guess what?"

"A black man worked at Red Jacket."

"Yes, but only one. According to the employment record, he was employed for only three days. We searched the records for the railroad company, also. They did employ some black men during that time, and sometimes they would work a train traveling through. They were all accounted for, up to transfers, or resigning their jobs. However, the one at Red Jacket just failed to show up one day after the brief employment. The company is no longer in existence, and, of course, there is no one still around that worked there at that time, being they would be nearing a hundred years of age."

"A name, Brian! Give me a name."

"For whatever good it will do you, Alma, his name was Leroy Stuart."

"And address?"

"Well, he didn't record an address in Buchanan County. He did give an address in Mingo County, West Virginia, as a home address."

"And?"

"You are not going to believe this, Alma. It was Rt. 2, Red Jacket, West Virginia. Evidently, that community, or at least the post office, was named after the coal company. Or the company took its name from that community."

"Did you find any Stuarts living in Mingo County?"

"No. We checked, but there are no black families with that name registered in Mingo or the surrounding counties across the river in Kentucky."

"They just vanished then. Where do we look now?"

"I don't know, Alma. If there were a Stuart family there at that time, they could have moved to California, as far as we know. Remember, it was during or just after the Great Depression, and people moved all over this country searching for work."

"I know, Brian. Just hoping for more. I don't even know why I want to know. I appreciate all you have done. I hope I didn't get you into any trouble working on a case after you have retired."

"No problem, Alma. Sorry, there was no more information, but if I can help somewhere in the future, just give me a call."

"You would be the first, and you are the best, Brian."

After they hung up, Alma poured herself a small drink of Jack and water and curled up in the swing on the porch. She didn't know why she was disappointed with Brian's news. It should have been expected. It was none of her business, anyhow. It was just a picture her dad had taken. But why did he keep it sealed and locked away? And why did the other men in the picture keep a copy to be discovered by their descendants? If Leroy's family could be found, would they have a copy of the picture?

13

Rufus

Alma put some food - a 16 oz. steak, fried potatoes, and corn on-the-cob in a carry out, hot-pouch she used occasionally to help Aunt Paula with a meal at the church. To be sure Rufus got the food, she watched for the Garden Supply delivery truck to go up the hollow. The owner of the store, George Forster, had told her the day of the month and approximately the time he personally made the delivery.

"The guy served his country, and I'm not about to sit by and wait for him to starve himself to death just because he's given up on the human race. I take him a box of groceries once a month, always on the third Monday about 5:00 in the evening. I also take the money he leaves because, if I didn't, the next box would just sit there until some hungry animal came by to help himself. The man has pride and won't accept a handout."

She waited until the truck came back down the hollow and backtracked it to the forks of the road, where she had made her wrong turn a few days before. She left her meal beside the grocery box and walked back home. The next day she walked by the drop-off spot, a few yards up the left fork, and there was her carry out pouch. She picked it up, looked around, and called out his name. Getting no response, she carried it home and set the container on the kitchen table. When she opened it, she found the dish, washed clean, and a ten-dollar bill tucked inside.

She shook her head, but also smiled. He was an independent hermit.

She waited two days. She cooked up a crockpot of chili, ate a small dish of it, and put the rest in a cooking pot with a lid. It could be heated up when one felt like a hot ready-to-eat meal.

She drove her car up to the forks of the road to ease the burden of carrying the chili all the way. She tugged the pot up the trail and up the mountain side to the shack perched on the cliff. If she hadn't been to his house before, she was sure she would never have found it. It sat in a thicket of mountain laurel, far enough back from the edge of the cliff to be hidden from the trail below.

Alma put the pot down on the bench, looked around and found everything the same as she remembered. She didn't shout out his name this time. She reckoned she had been watched ever since she had entered the trail. He would come in when he wanted. She was in no hurry.

She sat on a log near the edge of the cliff, where he probably spent many hours of his day, and looked out over the hollow. She couldn't see her house or any other houses, but she could place about where it would be by the ridges running along the tops of deep hollows. Hers would be three ridges down, to the right of the forks.

Later, she moved back a little to lean against the base of a large oak tree. She watched two squirrels chase each other through the branches of a hickory tree just below her and near the trail. Maybe this was where Rufus had been sitting when he shot the squirrel that had fallen on her, before she crashed her head into that boulder.

She saw four turkeys scratching through the leaves searching for acorns underneath the many oak trees. So this was what it was like to be a modern-day hunter. Find yourself a nice soft pile of leaves under a huge tree and wait with a high-powered rifle, or shotgun, until some hungry unsuspecting animal came walking by.

To Alma, it didn't seem as sporting as shooting at a target on a firing range.

She lost track of time. She must have sat outside the cabin for several hours. A lot of the time she spent thinking about Rufus and what he must have gone through in the war and his marriage. She thought about Leroy. Where was Red Jacket, West Virginia? Could Rufus have known any of Leroy's family?

Just about dark, she went into the cabin and fixed herself a bowl of the chili. She found a clean blanket and tucked herself in on the cot. Surely Rufus was too much of a gentleman to intrude on her in the middle of the night. She was probably as crazy as he was just to take the chance. Brett would be furious if he knew.

She listened to the night sounds as darkness faded out the images in the room. What was wrong with her? A month ago, she would have been terrified out of her mind to be alone in the middle of the wilderness, surrounded by wild beasts, or worse, wild humans. As Rufus said, she did have a gun. She touched the pistol under her pillow.

Alma smelled the coffee before she opened her eyes. She rolled her head away from the wall to see him sitting on the stump stool by the table, with a metal cup of steaming coffee in his hand. He had a red bandana wrapped around the handle of the cup to keep from burning his hand. He just stared at her.

"Good morning, Rufus. You got any more of that coffee?"

"What the hell are you doing in my house?"

"Well, I figured you weren't using it, and I felt like camping out. I brought you some chili."

"Yeah, I know. If your trespassing on my property is going to cost me, you can just take it back."

"Now don't get mean, Rufus. I just wanted to talk with you, and the only way I could figure out how to do that was to bring you a token of goodwill and camp out here until you decided to come in. Where did you sleep last night?"

"I've got places. What do you want to talk about? I don't have all day to sit around chatting with some crazy woman. I don't want any of your goodwill gifts, either."

Alma figured if she didn't get to the point and bring up a topic worth his time, he just might tie her up and deposit her back down by the road.

"Can I have a cup of coffee first?"

He handed her his cup. "There's more in the pot on the stove."

She helped herself. Evidently, he only had one cup. She pulled the picture out of the pocket of her cargo pants. She had found the pants worked great on her walks, when she didn't want to carry her purse. The pockets also made a good holster for her pistol.

"Is that gun loaded?"

She looked at the cot and the pillow. There was no way he could see her pistol under the pillow.

"What gun?"

"If you want to talk, you ought to start by being honest. I found it while you were sleeping. I don't know why you bother carrying it, if you're going to sleep like a bear."

Alma walked over and got the gun and put it in her pocket. She handed him the picture.

"Do you know any of these men?"

He took the picture and looked it over, front and back.

"All but the black man. The big guy on the left is Grady Bracken, the one in the middle is Jackson Mullins, and the one on the end is Thomas Wills." He handed the picture back to her.

"How did you know them? And what do you know about them?"

"I don't know anything about them, but their names are on the back."

He didn't smile, but Alma did. He was witted.

"My dad took this picture many years ago, and I found it after he died. I'm trying to find out who the black man is, and if there is a story to this picture."

"Why?"

"Because I don't have anything else to do. Seriously, I have just retired from my government job in Washington, D.C. I'm trying to sort through the things our parents left, and I'm trying to decide if I really want to come home again. I found out you once lived in Red Jacket, West Virginia, and that the black man in this picture might be Leroy Stuart, who may have had a family living in Red Jacket. I thought you might possibly shed a little light on my investigation."

She saw his head come up and a frown crease his brow when she mentioned Red Jacket.

"Are you a cop? Why are you investigating me?"

"You're not listening, Rufus. I'm not a cop. I'm trying to find out why my father took, and kept this picture. If this is Leroy, why didn't my father know his name? Did something happen after this picture was made? Why did the white men in the picture keep a copy and pass it on to their children? Just a mystery, Rufus. Like I said, I don't have anything else to do but bug you."

"If I tell you what I know, will you leave me alone?"

"Probably not. Tell me anyway."

"I grew up in Red Jacket. I didn't know anybody named Leroy, but I did know a colored family named Stuart. A woman with four girls. They ought to be about our age now. That's all I know."

Our age! He had to be at least ten years older than she was. Alma got up and refilled the coffee cup. She offered it to him, but he refused. She told him about her family and was surprised to find he knew her dad. Despite refusing her father an interview, he allowed him to squirrel hunt up in his hollow. Her father bought him a jug of whiskey, occasionally, and persuaded Rufus to let him open a checking account for his military pension. He admitted it had been a help, since he could leave a check for his groceries and not take a chance of being hunted down and robbed for the cash he had kept hidden in a can under a rock. He still kept a little and the preacher down at the church at the mouth of the creek was his friend, as well as her father's, and now helped him with business after her dad died.

Alma got more information than she would have guessed when she started. Not much on the Stuarts or Red Jacket, but a little of Rufus and his wish to live alone and not be bothered. He did admit to being in the Korean War, but didn't mention being wounded and she didn't bring it up. He had been married, but for only a few years, and had no kids. He didn't seem impressed by her occupational history, or her extensive travels, or the famous people she knew personally. Well, except for being in the army and seeing the war end of one country, he probably had not been out of the Appalachian Mountains. She might bring him a few books and show him some of her pictures the next time she visited, and maybe he could develop an interest in something besides shooting animals and living off the land.

14

Alma the Detective

The next morning Alma decided on the Black Stallion for breakfast instead of the usual Honey-Nut Cheerios. She had just ordered a stack of pancakes, a large orange juice, and coffee when she saw Brett walk through the door. He spotted her and walked straight to her table and slid into the booth beside her instead of the opposite side. He smiled and leaned over towards her until their shoulders touched. She leaned back and eased her hand over to cover his.

"Did you miss me?"

"A little. Where have you been for the past month or so?"

"Ah, Alma, it's only been a couple of weeks. I had to fly out to Wyoming for a little business. I knew you were going to be busy yourself, so I thought I would give you a little room and bug the hell out of you when I got back."

"Well, I have been busy. I've got enough furniture to camp out at the house, and I've made great progress archiving Dad's records. I've found Leroy; or rather Brian has found him."

"Who's Leroy?"

"The black man in the picture I showed you."

"Well, where is he, and how did Brian find a hundred-year-old man?"

"We didn't actually find him, Brett. We think we know his name and where he lived, before he came to Buchanan County."

"That doesn't sound like much. Maybe it was him, and maybe not. Where do you go from here?"

"I don't know. I just thought it was exciting to put a name to a question mark. Maybe."

He smiled at her and shook his head. Their breakfast arrived with Lori bringing him his usual country ham and eggs and coffee, without asking. As they ate, Alma could feel his knee brushing up against hers, and she didn't resist.

When they walked out to their vehicles, Alma asked Brett if he would have time to come by the house for a few minutes. When he smiled, and too quickly agreed, she told him to cool off a little. It wasn't to be that kind of rendezvous. She laughed as she took his hand again and explained she needed some advice, and she wanted him to look at some real estate.

"Ah, shucks! I should have known you were just teasing me. Sure, I've got time, and, sooner or later, you will, too."

Alma led the way with a warm fuzzy feeling in her veins. She showed him the garden spot and asked him what he thought. Could she build a small house up here? What might it cost? Brett walked off the foundation as she described it, checked the angle for a winding driveway, and took in the view.

"It could be beautiful, Alma. It's a much better site than where the house now sits. It's almost out of sight of the road and away from the noise. All the trees give it a peaceful and pretty setting this time of year, and even more so in the fall. I like it. When do we start?"

"Not so fast, cowboy. First of all, it's not 'we'. If I can buy out the others' shares, I want this to be my project. I've never designed anything before, but I have ideas. I might be able to use your help though in picking out a contractor, since you seem to know everyone in Buchanan County."

"Fine. I'll just be an observer and be at your beck and call. Don't be blaming me when the roof falls in on your head."

"That shouldn't happen with a reputable contractor." Alma laughed as she took his hand, and they walked back to the house for a glass of iced tea.

"Brett, I'm not going to do you like you did me, so I'm telling you. I'll be gone a few days. I plan to leave tomorrow, but I should be back in a week, and I want a picnic at the Breaks before the weather gets colder. Do you think you could schedule a date with me?"

"Just give me a day and time. Where are you going?"

"I'm not sure. I plan to start over in Red Jacket, West Virginia, but I don't know where that might lead me. That was the last known address for Leroy Stuart, the man in the picture, and I want to see if there is anyone there who might remember him. I know, it's crazy, but let me have my little adventure here and play detective."

"At least, let me go with you. That is not the civilized world of Washington, D.C., or even Oakwood, Virginia."

"No, Brett. This is something I want to do myself, but I'll have my cell phone with me at all times."

"That may not do you any good over there. A lot of places won't have reception."

"If it will make you feel any better, I'll call in every evening from some phone or other."

When he got ready to leave, she walked him down to his Hummer. After opening his door, he turned and took her in his arms and gave her a rousing kiss. With a 'be careful' and 'if I don't hear from you every day, I'll be in Red Jacket the next', he drove out of sight.

Alma spent the rest of the evening after Brett left studying roadmaps on her computer. She went to bed just after dark and got up early the next morning. She spent most of her time making notes to herself of what, where, and how she was going to proceed. She left about midday and drove to Pikeville, Kentucky. After checking the map, she figured she had a better chance of getting a motel room in Kentucky than she did across the Tug Fork River in West Virginia. She checked into the Sleep Inn and smiled at the friendly clerk behind the counter. There was little chance she would be sleeping in tomorrow. She had some investigating to do, and she had no idea where to start.

She bought a bacon, egg, and cheese biscuit at Hardee's the next morning and checking the map and her handwritten directions, she drove to Red Jacket. After driving up and down the road a few times, she finally realized that the old abandoned mining community now consisted of less than a dozen occupied homes.

A few miles away, she found a larger settlement with a country store and a couple of fast-food restaurants. She decided on the country store. Inside, she found an elderly lady stacking cans of food on a shelf. The woman, with her gray hair tied up in a bun on the back of her head, was dressed in a long granny gown and a full-length, dirty white apron. Alma chose a bottle of water from the cooler and a bag of chips and waited at the counter. Eventually, the little old lady noticed her. Wiping her hands on her apron, she moved behind the counter near the outdated cash register.

"Would that be all, Miss?"

"Yes, thank you. I'm just traveling through, and I got hot and thirsty for a cold bottle of water. You just can't get a cold bottle in the Dairy Queen."

"That's the truth. You know I sell more water than I do pop these days. I never thought I'd see the day when people would pay for drinking water. Of course around these parts, the bought water is the only kind fit to drink. All the rest have sulfur and it tastes as bad as it smells."

"If you don't mind me asking, have you lived around here long?"

"All my life. I grew up at Red Jacket, but hardly anyone lives there anymore. My husband bought this store after he got crippled in the mine. He died about ten years ago with the black-lung disease. I get by selling odds and ends to the folks that don't want to drive to Williamson."

"I drove through Red Jacket a little while ago. It does look deserted."

"I thought you said you were just driving through? People 'driving through' don't drive through Red Jacket. I figured you were driving Route 119 or 52. You would have to be looking for Red Jacket to find it."

"My name is Alma Woodson." Alma held out her hand.

"I'm Marge. Glad to make your acquaintance, Alma. Not many outsiders stop, and most don't want to talk."

"Well, Marge, to be honest, I was looking for Red Jacket. I'm from over the mountains in Virginia, near Grundy. My parents passed away, and when my dad died I was put in charge of settling his will and clearing out the house. I discovered a picture of a mining accident where a lot of men were killed and found out that there was a place in West Virginia with the same name as the coal mine they died in. So, I decided I would try to find the place."

"Well, a lot of men were killed in this Red Jacket, too."

"Would you like to see the picture?"

"Sure."

HANGER

When Alma handed her the picture, the woman studied it for several minutes, turning it over to read the name and date on the back.

"Is there a place called Hanger, Alma?"

"It's now called Oakwood. But back when the accident happened, Hanger was the place down the road where they brought the bodies."

"Coal mining is a bad business. Most of the menfolk in my family were killed or badly crippled in the coal mines."

"Would you mind looking at another picture, Marge?"

"Why, no, honey. I got nothing much else to do today. You open that bottle of water and show me all the pictures you want. I just hope they are a little more pleasant than that one."

Alma handed her the picture of the railroad crew. Again, Marge looked it over closely and read the names and date on the back.

"Looks like this was taken about the same time and the same place. I'm glad they changed the name of that place. Guess whoever took the picture didn't know the name of the black man."

"I think my dad took the picture. I found it among his records, along with the other picture that had a newspaper article attached to it. It was a gruesome story. Anyway, I think I know the name of the black man, and, if my information is correct, he once lived in Mingo County and probably at Red Jacket."

"Well, that could be. There were a few black families living in Red Jacket when I was a young girl. You say you have a name?"

"Leroy Stuart. Do you recall any Stuarts living anywhere in Mingo County?"

"We moved out of Red Jacket after Billy and I got married, but he drove back there to work in the mines. I started working part-time in this store for the Daltons. They got old, and Billy got hurt, so we bought them out about twenty years ago. Anyway, Stuart rings a bell with me. Seems like a black woman, named Nikki, raised four girls over at Red Jacket by herself. I never seen her man. Don't know if she was married or not. If so, he must have been lazy and a run-around, because you only saw her and the girls. She came in here a few times, right after we bought the store, and got some things for the girls on credit. Billy said we would never see the money, but it wasn't much. About two weeks later, she came in and paid us several dollars, in change. The last time I saw her, she stopped in to buy a coke and wait on the bus. She said she was going to live with her daughter in Kentucky."

"Did you say her last name was Stuart, Marge?"

"Well, I don't remember if she ever said, but I'm thinking that's how she signed the bill that time she bought on credit. They are probably not the ones you're looking for. Like I said, I don't even know if she had a man. If she did, I doubt if he ever worked a day for the railroad."

"You wouldn't know where, in Kentucky, Nikki's daughter lived, would you, Marge?"

"We used to sell the bus tickets right here in the store. I'm thinking maybe it was Pikeville, but that could be wrong. It was a long time ago."

"Marge, it has been a great pleasure talking to you. I'm going to head on home. I don't need to buy anything more, but, if you will let me, I want to leave you some money to help pay for a few necessities someone might need when they don't have the money."

"Honey, Nikki ain't never coming back into this store."

"I know, but there might be another single mother trying to get by. You can't give everyone credit."

Alma placed two one-hundred dollar bills on the counter, gave Marge a small hug and left. There were tears edging out of the corner of her eyes as she crossed the Tug Fork River and drove down Route 119 to her motel in Pikeville. She had checked her cell phone while on the road in Red Jacket and Brett was right, there was no service. She would call him from her room tonight. She had a lot to tell him.

The next day Alma stopped and tried to have conversation with dozens of people. She asked at the motel desk if they had a black employee that worked there with the last name of Stuart. The clerk called the manager over, and he told her he had several black employees, but none by that name. Alma realized how lucky she was that he would even give her personal information. It wouldn't happen in Washington. She stopped at the post office, and again, they listened to her story and said they had two families of Stuarts getting mail there, but both were white families. She found the pastors of three churches in their offices, and they informed her there was no one in their congregation with that last name.

She bought a small pizza and drink from Pizza Hut, then drove out to Fishtrap Lake and ate, perched on top of a small boulder along the shore. She rolled her pants legs up and soaked in some sun, as she pondered what to do and where to go next. Large Canadian geese flew in a v-formation across the water. She was surprised to see a few sea gulls this far from the ocean, circling in search of food. The scenery was beautiful, and it was quiet and peaceful. She was tempted to spend the rest of the afternoon here, but she had work to do.

That night, she soaked her feet in ice water, as she sat on the side of the bathtub and talked to Brett.

"I'm so tired, Brett. I have walked a hundred miles and talked to every store and motel manager in this town. I think they have more churches here than they do in Alexandria."

"Churches and banks. Every town has a few. You are in the Bible belt, you know."

"I only found six families named Stuart, and they were all white."

"Maybe the ones you are looking for aren't Stuarts."

"Why not? That's the only name I have to go on."

"Well, the mother has surely died by now, and the daughters could have easily married, with a different last name, of course."

"Of course. Well, cowboy, what do you suggest?"

"I suggest you come on home, and I'll rub your feet."

"Don't tempt me. I'll give it another day, or two. I should have thought about them being married. I have wasted a day."

"Not exactly. All those people you talked to will remember that you are trying to find someone named Stuart, or used to be, and they are black. Somebody may have known the mother, or you may run into someone who knows a daughter well enough to know she used to be a Stuart, or lived in Mingo County."

"Right. I'll give it tomorrow, and maybe the next day. If I don't have any luck, I'll just come home and probably forget about it. If Brian couldn't find Leroy or his family, I don't know why I should expect to."

"But Brian isn't the hound you are. I have a feeling once you smell blood, the victim doesn't have a chance."

When Alma hung up, she eased into bed and set the clock for ten the next morning. She needed her rest, and most people wouldn't appreciate being bothered early, anyway.

The next day, Alma walked the streets and checked the stores and business offices until noon. She got in her car and drove west on Route 460, to the edge of town. On her way back, she saw a sign for Pikeville College. This might be her last stop in Pikeville.

She found the personnel office listed on the directory in the main lobby of the administration building. The student assistant behind the desk led her into the office of the personnel director, where she quickly explained who she was looking for and why, including showing the picture. The director turned to her computer and appeared to be searching a database. In a few minutes, she copied something down on a post-it-note and handed it to Alma.

"We have several Stuarts at this campus, but only one female listed with the maiden name of Stuart and African-American. I may get into trouble for giving you this information, but, after listening to your story, I think Professor Pruitt would want to talk to you. You will find her, after her class ends at 3:00, in her office in the history department at Swanson Hall. I have written some directions and her office number on that note. Good luck, Alma."

Alma thanked her and looked at her watch as she left the building. She had over two hours to kill, and she was starving. She walked over the campus and asked two female students in faded jeans and cutoff T-shirts, with heavy backpacks hanging off their shoulders, if they could direct her to the student union. It had been years since she had ventured this route, and she knew she would be in for loud voices and even louder music.

She ordered a cheeseburger basket, which included fries and coleslaw, and a vanilla milkshake. She found an empty table in the back, out of the way of foot traffic. She was amused at the difference in the student body today compared to when she was at Georgetown University. Of course, she had not been a full-time student, nor did she live in a dorm on campus. She earned her degree in business the hard way, while she worked for the Federal Government and going to school evenings and nights. These students would be out of here in three to five years and looking for a job. She had a job, and it had taken her seven-and-a-half years to get that piece of paper.

Alma finished her meal and sat back in her chair, sipping on the shake and tapping her foot to the loud music. She watched the chaotic coming and going of the students and glanced often at her watch. Was this Professor going to be the one? What if she felt this was an invasion of her privacy? What if she had the campus police escort her off the property? Alma looked at her note again. Dr. Leslie S. Pruitt. Well, Dr. Pruitt, did you grow up in Red Jacket, West Virginia? It could be as simple, and short, as that.

At 3:00 sharp, Alma walked into the office of Dr. Pruitt and gave her secretary the brief explanation of why she wanted to see the professor. It would only take a few minutes. She had been directed to Dr. Pruitt's office by the personnel department. She would like to ask for any information the professor might have to offer on the settlement and the people along the Tug Fork River. That was enough to get her admitted to the professor's office. The secretary returned after a short consultation and introduced Alma to Dr. Pruitt.

"Have a seat, Ms. Woodson. I only have a few minutes, and I'm not sure I'm the one with any useful information of the Tug. I might be able to refer you to some history buffs we have here, with loads of local knowledge."

"Thanks for seeing me, Dr. Pruitt. I won't waste your time, and this may be very short. I really only need an answer to one question and that may, or may not, lead to a longer discussion, solely at your discretion. Please pardon me if it seems personal, and give me a chance to explain."

By the frown and the way she leaned back in her chair and pulled the half-glasses down on her nose, Alma could tell instantly that the professor was taken aback.

"Dr. Pruitt, did you grow up in Red Jacket, West Virginia?"

"Ms. Woodson, I do believe you are getting personal. Before I answer that, I think you had better take your one chance of explaining."

"Fair enough. After my father passed away earlier this year, I discovered, among his records, a picture he had taken of some men working on building a railroad in Buchanan County, Virginia. One of the men, an African-American, was not identified. I know he may not be living now, as he would be pushing a hundred years old. But, I have learned his name was Leroy Stuart and he once lived in Red Jacket."

Alma handed her the picture and took a deep breath. The professor pushed her glasses back into place and took a long look at the four men. She pulled a small magnifying glass from the desk drawer and looked closer.

"Alma, I think I'll drop the proper and formal protocol. How did you find me? Why do you think I might be the person you seek? I think I might be entitled to file a complaint against you for violating my privacy."

"Oh, please don't, Dr. Pruitt. I don't want to get anyone in trouble, and I don't want you to consider this another minute if I'm out of bounds. I really don't know why it's important to me, or why I have this urge to track down someone that knew, or was related to, this man. It just seemed to be important to my dad. He kept this picture sealed and locked in a file drawer for years for no apparent reason. It's just a mystery that I thought I'd solve since I recently retired from working in the Federal Government, and I don't have much to do. We can forget the whole thing."

Dr. Pruitt looked up over the top of her glasses and actually smiled.

"Calm down, Alma. If you will swear to me that you are not a reporter, or investigator of some type, from some big city, looking to harass some poor mountain folks to make a buck, or a name for yourself, I might give you a minute to see if there is a mystery, or reason, for you to continue your search."

"I swear, Dr. Pruitt, I don't know why I'm tracking something my dad started. I don't work for any publication nor serve any investigating role for any legal or law enforcement organizations. I'm just serving my own curiosity, without a reason, as far as I know."

"Your minute is up, Alma. I …"

"But, Dr. Pruitt, I get a sense you know something, and I haven't said the right things to make you trust me, and…"

"Alma, if you will let me finish. I was going to say I don't have any more time now, but you have raised my curiosity enough to hear you out. If you will have dinner with me this evening at the Peking Restaurant going east on Route 460, we can explore your little project a bit more. If you don't like Chinese food, we could eat at Jerry's or some other restaurant."

Alma stood quickly and smiled a sigh of relief.

"I love Chinese food. In fact, there was a Peking restaurant only blocks from my home in Washington, D.C that I ate at frequently, but I'll tell you about that later. I won't take another minute of your time now, but thanks so much for seeing me later. What time?"

"Let's make it 6:00." The professor held out her hand and Alma grasped it firmly. She backed up to the door, looking into Dr. Pruitt's eyes as though the good doctor would disappear if she blinked. When she was safely out into the hallway, Alma found a water fountain, then rushed to a restroom. She was as nervous as a whore in church, as Brett would say. Although she had been sitting for the last several minutes, she felt that her legs would collapse if she didn't find a place to sit down.

Alma arrived early at the restaurant. She waited in her car until she spotted Dr. Pruitt pulling into a parking space, right at 6:00. She gave the professor enough time to be seated in case she had a preferred table at the restaurant. The hostess took her back to join Dr. Pruitt at a small table in the back of the dining room near a gas-fed fireplace. A small flame was burning, even though it was still in the eighties outside. Dr. Pruitt had already pulled out a notepad and was jotting down something as Alma approached. Dr. Pruitt motioned her to the opposite chair and when she had finished her note, she put the pad away and smiled at Alma.

"I see you found the place."

"Yes, it's very nice. I'm pleasantly surprised to find a Chinese restaurant in the middle of the Appalachian Mountains."

"Well, as they say, 'build it and they will come'. I don't think you will find any people who will work harder to be successful, and give you good, quality food. Would you like a glass of wine before we order?"

Dr. Pruitt ordered each of them a glass of Chardonnay, and then asked to see the picture again. Alma handed it over and watched as the professor studied the photo front and back.

"I have never heard of a place called Hanger."

"It's now called Oakwood. It's a small community located about twelve miles east of Grundy, Virginia, probably about fifty five miles from here. There was a terrible explosion a year or so after this picture was taken that killed more than three dozen miners at a mine called Red Jacket, near Oakwood. They took the bodies to a place down the river called Hanger, now Oakwood, to be identified and transported."

"Is that how you found me? A connection between a coal mine and a place with the same name! And, of course, you were looking for a black person. There is a question mark for the man. How did you know to look for a Stuart?"

"I didn't. I have a retired friend who works for law enforcement, and he traced the name from employment records at the Red Jacket Coal Mine.

There weren't many, if any, black men working or living in Buchanan County at that time. Leroy Stuart's name came up in the search, and his only known address was Red Jacket, West Virginia."

"Well, Alma, do you mind if I call you Alma? And please call me Leslie. I get enough of this Dr. Pruitt stuff in class and on campus."

"I don't mind at all, Leslie." Alma smiled.

"My father's name was Leroy Stuart. I was raised over in Red Jacket, West Virginia, and I do believe this is a picture of him. I was only ten years old when he disappeared. My mother raised my three sisters and me by herself, with the help of the church and the work she could get in the community doing laundry and cleaning houses. She thought, and told us girls later, that our father had gone off to get work somewhere, after the mine he worked at in West Virginia closed. She told us that he was going to come back and move us there when he had made enough money. Mommy said he must not have made enough money. Like so many men back during the Depression, especially black men, he just left. Mommy didn't seem to dwell on it, and my sisters and I were too young to know we should have a father taking care of us and buying us things. We made do with what we had, and our mother made sure we studied hard and got a good education.

"If this is him, it looks like he had a job working on that railroad, or, as your search revealed, a job at the Red Jacket coal mine. Now, I wonder why he never came back for us?"

"Maybe, Leslie, he didn't just leave. According to the records, he only worked at Red

Jacket for three days. I don't want to speculate too much, but I want to follow this trail a little bit further, if you don't object, because I think there is more to this picture."

"I don't object, Alma. I'm retiring after this year. I'll be sixty-five, and I can leave with full benefits and health care. My kids are grown, and my husband and I plan on traveling a little and seeing more of the country than the Appalachians. Maybe I can help you investigate this story, which should be my story. Most of what I'm telling you, Alma, is not common knowledge around here. Not that I'm ashamed of my past, just the opposite. I'm rather proud of what I've accomplished. It's just that I don't want, or need, the sympathy. I would appreciate your confidentiality."

"Of course. I promise to run anything I find by you. It's just a puzzle I happened to run across, and I want to find the pieces. If there is a story, or more to the story, I expect it will mean more to you and your sisters than anyone else."

"I will call each of my sisters tomorrow and tell them about you and your dad's picture. I know they'll feel the same as I. This is the part of our history that we thought was lost, and that we desperately tried to forget, but may now be with us again. Alma, I don't mean to sound heartless, but I kind of wish you had not found your father's picture, or found me. We have lived for years hating him and what he did to our mother, when we thought of him at all, and now we may have to discover a man we never knew."

"I'm sorry to think I may have brought you pain, Leslie. I beg you and your sisters to keep an open mind. All we know is Leroy was at this place at this time. Your mother has got to be one of the saints of the world. I can't wait to hear more about her. But, as you said, you never knew your dad. You could be surprised to find he was a good, honest, hard-working man who loved his four little girls and their mother and wanted to do his best to take care of them."

"Or, find he was exactly what we feared. That he was selfish, and he ran away from his responsibility to his family and died in some city in California, gambling away money that could have put shoes on his little girls' feet."

"I'm betting on my version, Leslie. Would you mind giving me your sisters' telephone numbers and addresses? I'll give you my number and address, and I'll wait to hear from you before I contact them. I want you to have some time to talk about the possibilities before I get too much in the picture."

Leslie laughed and said she didn't want to hear any more about pictures. They had finished their meal long ago, but yet they sat, sipped their wine, and told each other about their lives.

It was nearly midnight when Alma crawled into bed. She had called Brett, but she was too drained to display any of the enthusiasm and excitement that had occupied her for most of the day. She simply told him she was coming home tomorrow, and, if he wanted the rest of the story, he would have to buy her dinner at the Black Stallion Café. He should probably come prepared to spend the night because she didn't think she could cover all the details over dinner. When she didn't get any pressure to cough up the story instantly, she knew his mind was on the possibility of spending the night, and the hell with any old picture or long-forgotten revelations.

15

Aunt Paula-Aunt Ellie

Revived, Alma checked out of the motel early the next morning. She stopped in Grundy at the Huddle House for a bite of breakfast and hurried on home. She knew Brett would be calling by noon, and she needed some time to straighten up a bit and take a long warm bath. She hoped he would be as excited as she was about finding Leroy's family. She intended to talk to Leslie's sisters soon and maybe get another piece to the puzzle. She resented the fact she had no idea what the next step would be, or what she hoped to accomplish, even if she found out where Leroy had gone after the picture was taken. Leslie could be right and he had hopped a train and headed west.

She was still daydreaming when she rounded the curve to her house. She almost drove into the ditch when she saw Brett's big black Hummer in the driveway. What the hell was he doing here already? Why was she asking herself that question? She knew why he was here. And she was glad. Alma had pushed away the urges and warm fuzzy feelings she had experienced ever since they had run into each other again in the Black Stallion Café. She whipped her car in behind the Hummer and rushed to leap into his arms as he sprang out of the swing on the front porch. It was a strong hug and a longer kiss, as they gave in to the inevitable. Neither of them wanted to keep the barrier up any longer. Maybe keep enough of a spark for a good fight, but nothing to put real distance between them. She had known for some time that the enchantment he had placed over her in high school was still there. She knew he was no prince, but she might as well give him that kiss that might keep the fairy tale going a little bit longer.

He took her hand and led her up onto the porch. She expected to sit in the swing and begin the story of her adventure, but he continued on into the kitchen and sat her down by the small dining table. He unloaded a takeout bag from the Lone Star Steakhouse and placed it in front of her.

"Hold on a minute, Brett. What have you done? I couldn't possibly eat anything right now. I just ate breakfast in Grundy. I thought we were going out for dinner."

"I brought you some lunch. How the hell was I supposed to know you would stop for a decent breakfast? You eat like a bird, and I figured you hadn't had much more than the usual bowl of Honey-Nut Cheerios. I'll just put this in the fridge, and we can heat it up for later."

"What did you get, anyhow? That looks like enough to feed a family." Alma reached for the box.

She found a twelve ounce prime rib, a sweet potato, and a salad. It smelled delicious!

"Well, maybe we could eat a little of it now. I bet you haven't eaten."

"You know better than that. I had a decent breakfast about 6:00 this morning, and I'm starved."

They ate. She ate a little, and he ate all of his. He had brought both cold drinks and large coffees. She drank her coffee and listened as he told her some about his week. Most of all, she liked the mention of how much he had missed her.

After they had finished eating, they pushed back their chairs, sipped their coffee, and sat looking at each other as though they were waiting to see who made the first move. Alma moved. She walked over, straddled his lap, placed her arms around his neck, and whispered in his ear.

"Want to hear about my trip?"

"Not just now."

"You have something else in mind?"

He pulled her head down and smothered her lips with his, as his hands eased up under the loose polo shirt she was wearing. When she began to lose control and could feel the excitement rising underneath her, she eased off his lap, took his hand, and led him to the bedroom. In frantic moments, they had removed each other's clothes, with Brett popping buttons on her shirt and nearly tearing an earlobe off when the shirt caught on a dangling earring. Realizing no great harm had been done, he lifted her in his arms and applied soft kisses to her nose, neck, lips, and beyond. Gently, he laid her down on the cool, silky comforter and started massaging her from her feet to her temples. Alma had almost forgotten she had such sensitive arousing parts to stimulate. He was quite the titillator! In slow tender motions, he took her to heights she had not experienced in years. Maybe never! Lost hours, or minutes later, she drifted back from dreamland, cuddled in his arms, exhausted, and tingling to the tips of her toes. Their bodies glistened with perspiration and the comforter was damp and rumpled. He gently rubbed a fingertip along her eyebrow, down the bridge of her nose, and over bruised, but smiling, lips. Alma wished she could capture the satisfaction and the smile on his face. Waking up beside such a hunk for the remainder of her life wouldn't be so terrible.

"You know, Brett, this would not have happened when we were in high school."

"I don't see why not? Maybe it would have, if only I could have gotten you to look my way once in a while."

"No. Back then it was quite a curse. Besides, you were so into sports and chasing anything that wore a skirt. We good girls had to avoid creatures like you."

"Well, now, I'm kinda glad you did. Back then, I admit to being carefree, reckless, and unappreciative of what I had, or could get. After so many failures in my life, I want to gather what's real and good."

"You are rich, famous, and still have your good looks."

"Let's throw something on, grab a glass of something intoxicating, go sit in the swing, and you tell me all about your trip. I have a feeling you were quite successful."

"Let's go!"

While they were just a swinging, with a glass of white wine for her and a Jack and water for him, she spilled the whole story.

Brett listened attentively and interrupted only occasionally. When she had finished the story about the dinner and being allowed to call a professor by her first name, he told her she should try her hand in Las Vegas with her luck.

"I can't believe the great FBI detective in our nation's capital can't find Leroy's family, but you wander down to the coalfields of West Virginia and Kentucky, and they invite you out for Chinese food."

"Well, Brian did find out Leroy's name and his last address. Can I help it if I have such an honest face that people just open up to me?"

"What are you going to do now? What's your next step?"

"I'll give Leslie and her sisters a week or two to sort through all this. Then, if I don't hear from them, I'll call one of the sisters, since she gave me their telephone numbers, and see if she will talk with me. Tomorrow, I'm going to pick up Aunt Ellie and Aunt Paula and take them to church. If I remember correctly, this weekend they meet over at Frying Pan."

"You know you have come around almost 180 degrees. Remember when you couldn't wait to get away from here? You just wanted to fly all over the world and worry about nobody but Alma. Now, you are back to taking elderly family members to a church you thought came over with the pilgrims, thinking about rebuilding the family home, and sticking your nose into other people's business with a mystery that can't be solved. I think I like the Alma that cares about her family and her roots better than the one who tries to make Lori earn her tip."

Alma smiled. She let him know that without people like her, the help would get sloppy with their work. What was the point of tipping at all, if you couldn't demand quality service? They walked up to the old garden and looked over the stakes Brett had driven into the ground as the temporary foundation for the house. She told him she had about decided on a log house with a full front porch and lots of bedrooms and baths. He took a card from his wallet and gave it to her. He told her the guy was the best he knew with log homes, but he worked out of Abingdon and might not want to take on a project this far away. When she frowned, he tried to reassure her he would apply some pressure if she and the contractor could settle on a plan.

Alma thought it might be time to tell Brett about Rufus. The bruise on top of her head was about gone, and she had cleverly disguised it with her hair.

"Do you know a guy named Rayvar Jeeter that goes by the name of Rufus?"

"Kinda. But you don't want to know him. Crazy. Seems to be a war vet that got wounded, left his wife, and is holed up somewhere in these mountains."

"But I already know him. At least, I have met him."

"Come on! Nobody meets Rufus. The law can't even find him when they want to question him about deer poaching or the location of Jake Harris's latest still. Tell me you're just kidding."

Alma smiled as she saw the serious and concerned look creep over Brett's face. She told him about her encounter with the mountain man.

"Alma, you could have been killed by that crazy hermit."

"But I wasn't. In fact, he saved my life. It was my entire fault for invading his space. He was just shooting some food."

"It's not his space, or his land. The fool is homesteading or, at least, trespassing. I think I'll give Ronnie Rife a call."

"You'll do no such thing. Rufus is harmless. If anything, he could use a friend or two. Besides, Detective Rife already knows about Rufus and the whole story of me banging my head against a rock."

"You have already met Rife?"

"And the Sheriff and his silly Deputy Harmon."

"I wouldn't call Tim silly to his face. He would just as soon lock your ass up for the night than take bad mouthing from a Yankee."

"I'm not a Yankee. I'm a born and bred Buchanan countian. Deputy Harmon and I are now friends."

"Getting back to Rufus, I don't think you ought to walk up the hollow near his territory alone, again. Next time he might…"

"There's already been a next time. Don't even think about telling me what I ought not to do, Mr. Parker."

"What do you mean, there's already been a next time?"

"I spent the night in his cabin just a few days after the accident."

Alma smiled, but Brett clenched his teeth and walked back to the house. Alma found him, a couple of minutes later, slugging down a beer on the back deck. She walked up behind him and put her arms around his waist.

"I don't remember the last time I've had a man be jealous over me. I love it. But, Brett, you've got to learn to listen better. I said I spent the night in his cabin. I didn't say he was there. I wanted to talk to him, maybe find out if he knew my dad, which he did, or if he knew the men in the picture, or why he didn't want to be part of the human race, or just about anything he would reveal. But he wouldn't come in or show himself, so I decided to spend the night and wait him out. He showed up the next day and surrendered. When I got all the information I figured I would get, I released him back to the wild and left."

Brett handed her the rest of the beer.

"Alma, you are amazing. You scare the hell out of me, but you've got more guts, or lack of sense, than anyone I know. I think I'll advise the sheriff to fire Ronnie and hire a real detective, like you."

"Rufus once lived in Red Jacket."

"And I guess he knew Leroy?"

"No. But he remembered a Stuart woman with four girls."

After Brett left, Alma sat on the porch with a legal pad and pencil and began sketching out house plans. When she met with the contractor, she had to be sure of what she wanted. He could build it, but this was to be her first real house, and she was determined to design every detail herself.

The next morning she picked up Aunt Ellie first, then drove up to Aunt Paula's house and blew the horn. She had called both ladies the night before and arranged times. Each of her aunts wanted to go to her own church, but would let Alma decide for the group. Alma felt out of place, dressed in her best pantsuit she had worn to the office, compared to the two women with full-length dresses, stockings, light shawls, and small hats perched on top of their heads. They did look elegant. As she drove down the road, Alma kept an eye on the rear view mirror and Aunt Paula in the back seat. The show was about to begin, and she intended to enjoy every minute of it.

"I think we should go to my church. It doesn't start until 11:00 and will be over around noon. We could have lunch at the Black Stallion Café before we go home." Aunt Ellie said, as she straightened her shoulders in the front passenger seat.

"That ain't church. That's a small group calling themselves a choir singing a couple of songs off-key. And a preacher reading verses out of the Bible and keeping his other eye on his watch, so he won't make anybody mad for going overtime."

"I want you to know the Methodist is a church. They do a lot of Christian good for everybody. In fact, they started the first high school on Garden Creek when they built the old TMI School. Just because they act like a civilized organization that preaches from the Bible, instead of scaring a body with all that hell-fire and damnation, don't mean they are less a church than the Old Primitive Baptist. I don't know how you can talk, Paula, about off-key singing, after listening to you joining in with the whole church reciting one line of a song at a time."

"What do you think, Alma? Which one do you like the best, and think is a real church?"

"I don't think you want to get me in on this. I went to a huge church in Alexandria that had thousands in their membership. They had a hundred in their choir and a dozen in a live band. The preacher read scripture from the Bible, but he added in current events with a little humor. It was a lot different than either of yours."

"I'd call that a rock concert, if you ask me." Aunt Paula was glaring from the back seat.

"Well you ain't never been to a rock concert, Paula."

"I've seen them on TV. I believe Elvis could have had a large church if he'd added a sermon with some Bible reading."

Alma laughed. The two aunts argued back and forth. Aunt Ellie liked her Methodist Church and the laid-back, no-pressure style. Aunt Paula thought the only true religion was the Primitive Baptist, with emotion and connecting with the Lord. Occasionally, Alma would butt in with some neutral conversation to take the edge off.

"Ladies, I don't think it matters. We agreed to go to Aunt Paula's church today and to Aunt Ellie's the next time, and we are almost there."

They all settled down to their own thoughts until Alma parked the car. There were maybe thirty automobiles in the graveled parking lot. There would be a good crowd today.

They were early, as usual, and everyone visited with each other either in the parking lot or inside the church. Aunt Ellie seemed to know as many of the congregation as Aunt Paula. Alma looked around for Jill, but never located her. As the time drew near to 10:00, the small crowd began to find their seats among the preachers on the pulpit or the hard, wooden benches. Alma seated herself between her two aunts. She hoped to squelch any comment that might draw fire from Aunt Paula.

The singing was long, slooooow, and loud. Alma joined in from the beginning. She noticed after a verse or two that Aunt Ellie was also singing. Aunt Paula punched Alma in the ribs with an elbow, nodded her head at her sister and smiled.

Brother Jimmy gave a good sermon, but it was Brother Randy who had felt the spirit call him today. As he progressed from a low whisper to a ringing redemption from sin and the glorification of salvation, a few women in the pews were shouting out "Amen" and "Hallelujah", as tears ran down their cheeks. Alma was astonished to find Aunt Ellie was one of them. As Brother Randy came to a close, and his voice lowered back to an exhausted muttering, Aunt Paula, with tears seeping out of the corner of her eyes, crossed over in front of Alma to hug her sister. As others in the church were shaking hands and hugging each other, Alma felt a tug at her shoulder and turned to find Jill standing in the pew behind her with her hand outstretched. Alma clutched the hand in both of hers and gave Jill a warm smile.

After service, two-and-a-half hours after it had begun, the congregation moved into the small kitchen and larger eating area packed with folding tables and chairs and a couple of handmade wooden picnic tables. There was plenty of fried chicken, vegetables, breads, desserts, and, of course, Aunt Paula's chicken and dumplings. Aunt Ellie had brought a chocolate pie. Alma had brought nothing.

Jill carried a plate and came over to join Alma and her aunts at one of the folding tables. They welcomed her, and the conversation ranged from the weather, to gardening, to friends and neighbors. No one spoke of the service or the emotion Brother Randy had stirred up in church. That appeared to be church, and this was eating and visiting. Alma was somewhat puzzled that one minute the tears and shouting were flowing freely and the next there were only smiles, laughter, jokes, backslapping, and sometimes outright lies told around the tables. It was definitely different, but warm and soothing. Alma liked it.

Jill was the one who brought up the subject. She asked if Alma had had any luck in finding the name of the black man in the picture. Aunt Ellie wanted to know what black man and what picture. Aunt Paula leaned over and whispered that she would fill her in later. With a frown, Aunt Ellie leaned back in her chair and listened attentively to the others' conversation. Alma told Jill part of the story and how she had indeed traced the man to a small place in West Virginia and found out his name was Leroy Stuart.

"Good. I talked with my cousins and nobody knew the name or why the black man was in the picture. Hester told me that Grady Bracken's son Larkin, said that 'no one cared who he was, but one thing was sure, he didn't belong in the picture'. He said 'there was no way in hell that a black man would have been part of the crew working for the railroad. Not in Buchanan County'."

"Why not, Jill? I've seen plenty of black men working on the railroad, driving from here to northern Virginia."

"Don't get me wrong, Alma. Me nor my cousin Hester, Jackson Mullins' daughter, who has the same picture, have anything against African-Americans. But I can't say the same for Larkin. That picture was taken a long time ago. Most people don't feel the same way now as they did then, when there weren't any blacks living or working in the county. But Larkin and a few of his buddies still say harsh things and tell bad jokes about them. I don't think many people know, but Larkin's mother spent the last few years of her life in the mental hospital over at Marion. Some of my kin say she kinda went crazy, fighting and arguing with Grady and Larkin over something they wouldn't talk about with any of the rest of us."

"Did you ever talk with her much about Grady's work, Jill?"

"No. He never worked long at any one job. They all kept pretty much to themselves and lived way back up the hollow on a small, mountain farm. Aunt Betty hardly ever left the place, until she got sick and they had to put her in the State facility. Larkin quit school in the seventh grade and spent most of his time hunting or fishing or taking off with his daddy for days at a time after he got old enough."

"Where did they go?"

"I don't know it to be true, but the talk was that they would take a load of moonshine up to Pennsylvania, or somewhere. I do know that Aunt Betty would ask Mom and some of my other aunts to buy pounds of sugar for her. She said it was for making jelly and such, but often it would be at a time when no grapes or apples would be ripening. She said she didn't have the money to buy it herself and she would pay it back when she could. Mom always said she would bring the money only a few days after she picked up the sugar. Sounds fishy, doesn't it?"

"Could you go with me sometime, Jill, and talk with Larkin?"

"I don't even know where he is now that his parents have died. He moved off the mountain several years ago and nobody has bothered to find him."

"Would any of your other cousins know where to find him?"

"I doubt it, but if it means that much to you, I will ask around. I like you, Alma, and I love your two aunts here. They have always been so nice to me. But, Aunt Paula, if you don't quit bringing me all those vegetables and baking that delicious German Chocolate cake, I'm going to have to go on a diet."

They all laughed and gave her a hug. Unlike the other Sunday when Alma had met her, Jill hung around and talked for some time. Alma was anxious to gather more information from her, but didn't want to scare her off. The conversation never returned to the picture. On the way home, Alma handed it to Aunt Ellie while she and Aunt Paula filled her in with all the details. Neither of her aunts could explain why they had never seen the picture, or if it had any meaning other than one of hundreds Alma's father had taken in his career. Aunt Ellie threw out the possibility that Leroy had indeed gotten a job working for the railroad, regardless of what Larkin thought, and had quit Red Jacket after only three days on the job. Maybe the railroad had transferred him somewhere else, and maybe the professor was right about him just abandoning his family for selfish reasons and greener pastures. The ride home was short, with all the speculation of who Leroy really was and where and why he had disappeared.

16

Bed-n-Breakfast

Alma loved and, more importantly, enjoyed her two elderly aunts. She wondered why she had hardly known them when she was growing up. Looking back, she was worse than Brett. She had not been interested in anything to do with home or family after she became a teenager. Her total occupation was getting out of Buchanan County and becoming 'Someone'. Now, she knew she had been a dreamer as a teenager, and maybe it had served her well. With her classes as a model and a job that dressed her well, she had quickly climbed whatever ladder she was on and didn't hesitate to change ladders in the middle of the stream. Anyway, lately, she had not thought much about a career or what she owned, even though she owned enough to not have to worry about living comfortably for the rest of her life. She had no great urge to travel to the other side of the world or a longing to have her picture made with important or famous people. Right now, she was content.

She didn't mind going to a funeral in Buchanan County, anymore. The service for both her mother and her father had been sweet, personal, and consoling. The three preachers had known them all their lives and had many memories to share with the children. They left little doubt that her parents were in Heaven and were looking down, smiling and protecting them. Alma couldn't imagine having their funeral and burial in a place like Washington. She was beginning to think that when her time came, she wanted to be buried in these mountains where someone would stop by and maybe leave a flower or two, sometimes.

Weeks had passed since she found and talked with the professor. She had spent her time with Brett and her relatives and organized all the pictures into files or scrapbooks. The weather had turned cold. Early in the week, she had seen her first frost of the fall. The leaves were coloring and she knew in another month they would be gone. She probably ought to head back to Washington to spend the winter. This place would lose some of its new appeal after the trees were bare, and she could see the rugged outline of scars on the mountainsides caused by the huge dozers cutting roads and strip-mining the coal. She really hated that practice. She knew that coal fed the families still living in the county, even though it lavished money on the owners like Brett who didn't live in the county. But, she didn't understand why they couldn't have just dug holes in, or under the ground, instead of leveling whole mountaintops and cutting huge slices into her view.

She went to Roanoke and spent a weekend with her sister. She took along two full albums of pictures of Krista, Jack, their kids, or all of them together -- collected by their mother and father, and too precious to toss. They sat on Krista's bed until the wee hours of the morning looking at the pictures, recalling favorite memories, and crying over missed opportunities.

"Alma, this is soooo sweet of you! I figured you would eventually hand me a box of pictures and tell me to pick out what I wanted and pass the rest on to the others. I am truly appreciative and happy you took the time to pick out my family's and put them into albums for me."

"I did scrapbooks and albums for the others, also. They'll just have to wait until I get time to deliver them or else come and get what they want."

"I wouldn't hold my breath on any of them coming to Buchanan County any time soon. William is tied down right now trying to expand his business, and Janice lives so far away. I expect they would be happy if you sent them their pictures in a gift box and sold the place."

"Speaking of selling the place, how would you and William and Janice feel if I wanted to buy you out? I've kinda gotten attached, and I hate to see it go to some stranger."

"Oh, Alma! That would be wonderful! Wait. Are you just pulling my chain? You hate it. You never wanted to visit. Why would you now want to live there?"

"Who said anything about living there? I just mentioned buying the place. Maybe fix up a summer home."

"But why buy us out? We all would love for you to stay there as long as you want and do whatever you feel like in fixing it up."

"No, that wouldn't work. I don't intend to spend a dime on the place, or stay any longer than necessary, if it's not mine. I don't like loose strings. The will says to sell the property and divide the money. The other two might need the cash more than you or I do. Take William. I bet he's sinking a fortune in that business."

"You're right, Alma. I can see where problems could develop. I guess that's why it's called 'settling the estate'. Let me talk to our brother and sister. I'm sure we'll all be delighted that you want the place."

"Let me know soon, Krista. You know me. I could change my mind before I get back to Hanger. Why do you think they called it Hanger?"

Krista laughed. "I have no idea. I don't think I would have ever known that if Dad hadn't left the articles for you to find."

Alma took her time driving back home. Why was it beginning to feel like home? Would the peace and contentment last? Were her aunts, Brett, and even Rufus, enough? Wasn't that more than she had anywhere else in the world?

As the car topped over Short Gap Mountain, entering Buchanan County, she smiled, and pushed the gas pedal towards the floor. The Jetta hung to the curves as she did imaginary shift changes, and the wind whipped her hair through the open window.

She just might ask Brett to take her to a NASCAR race over at Bristol. She could buy some Bluegrass CD's, some fried chicken, take a cooler of beer, and melt right into the landscape. And she fully intended to be at the Rhythm and Roots Festival next summer on State Street in Bristol. The poster she had seen at the Inn said there would be nearly a hundred and fifty bands playing at different locations all along the street dividing Virginia and Tennessee, with thousands of people and plenty of food.

Maybe Washington, D.C., was just a place she had visited.

She planned to leave for D.C. in a few days, but she needed to contact Dr. Pruitt again and she wanted to find out more about Jill's Aunt Betty. Also, the contractor was coming on Friday and she had several pages of drawings to show him. Her two aunts and her brother and sisters were so excited that she was buying out the rest of the family and planning to rebuild the home place. But, she didn't know if they would be so thrilled once they found out she planned on tearing the house down and building something new and completely different up in the garden. Aunt Paula would probably tell her in no uncertain terms that a house could be built anywhere, but the garden and orchard couldn't be replaced. Well, she didn't plan on being a gardener. She might raise a few tomatoes and have a couple of apple trees, but that would be the extent of her farming.

Sure enough, early Friday morning, Jeffrey Conners, the contractor, pulled into the driveway. Shortly after introductions and a few cups of coffee, he asked her what she had in mind. Before she showed him her drawings and got down to the paperwork, she took him up to the garden and showed him where she thought the house should sit and the stakes she and Brett had driven into the ground. She explained the view and the direction the front should face, and the fact that the house had to have a wide and long front porch. He smiled and agreed. Did she want the house on a level spot, or did she want to retain the flow of the land? If they leveled the site, they were sure to uncover some rocks, maybe some very large ones, and would she want them hauled away or kept for landscaping?

"Well, I'm not sure now, until I see them. I guess you would haul away most of them, but if you discover a couple of nice, unique ones, I might want to keep them for the kids to climb on, or something."

"I thought Brett told me you were single and didn't have any kids."

"Brett has a big mouth. I was talking about my nieces and nephews. I'm not a hermit, and if you call me an old maid, you can just pack up your stuff and leave before you even start."

Jeffrey didn't smile, but turned a little red around the collar of his shirt. He would have to be careful with this one. Brett had warned him.

"Brett does have a big mouth. You can be sure I won't call you anything but Ms. Woodson, unless you instruct me otherwise."

"Alma will do nicely. I have some drawings, back in the house, of what I have in mind if you would like to see them. And I would like to see some house designs if you have them available. I don't have much experience with log homes. In fact, I have never been in one of the new ones. I thought log cabins went out with the pioneers and my grandparents."

"I don't think you will compare these homes to log cabins. Some are more expensive than a brick house, and more elegant."

"I'm anxious to see some plans. I'm not interested in elegant, but more on the comfortable and rustic side."

They walked back to the kitchen table. Alma refilled their coffee cups. Jeffrey spread out his house plans, and she handed him her notebook of drawings. Several minutes passed before either of them spoke.

"I think I like this one," Alma said.

She had picked a design that was 102 foot long and 28 foot wide. It had an A-roof and a three-quarter, covered front porch. The windows were small and few. Maybe that could be changed. The roof was metal and hunter-green in color. She liked that. She had not slept under a tin roof since she visited her grandparents as a child, but she still remembered the rhythmic sound of the rain on the metal.

"If I understand these drawings, Ms. Woodson, you are dividing the house into halves down the length, with the front being one big room with a large stone fireplace in the middle surrounded by a living space. A dining area and kitchen on one end and a family, library, recreation combination room on the other end."

"It's Alma! Can you do that?"

"You can do anything you want on the inside as long as you leave supports in place to hold up the roof and walls. I just never saw a residential house with so much open space. That front room will not have a divider except the area around the kitchen."

"I know. That's the way I would like it to be, if it's possible. I don't know why the women have to be isolated in the kitchen and dining area while the men put their boots up on the furniture, sip their beer, and watch some ball game. If I have company, I want everyone to mingle and be able to have a conversation, even if they have to yell to the other end of the house."

"Interesting. How about these bedrooms in the other half of the house? Aren't they pretty small, and a lot of them?"

"Another concept of mine. You don't need a bedroom to hold more than a bed, a chest of drawers or a dresser, and a nightstand. Make them small and people will have privacy enough to sleep and whatever, but not comfortable enough to hide out in all day. Put a small bathroom with a shower, commode, washbasin and mirror between two bedrooms, with adjoining doors that can be locked from either entrance. Then, everyone has a private bedroom and bath for themselves, including children."

"So, on that side of the house, you will have the kitchen, six bedrooms, and three baths?"

"Can you manage that?"

"Of course, I can. I'm just making sure I understand what you want, Alma."

"Oh, I hope I'm not coming across as uncooperative or unappreciative, Jeffrey. I just don't know if what I imagined and tried to draw out is possible, or not. Thanks for taking time to go over it with me. Feel free to tell me changes that have to be made."

"I like it. Unusual, but I like what you have done. It will add a lot to put in a dormer window opposite the fireplace, since you have an open space from floor to ceiling. You have a forty-foot loft on each end of the room, with a staircase leading to each, so that leaves you with a twenty-foot-wide open space to the ceiling. I suggest you put in a walkway between the two lofts and underneath the window."

"I like that, Jeffrey. I was going to ask you about more and bigger windows."

"We can do about whatever you want, as long as we include it in the design before the logs are cut."

They talked and planned for another hour or so before Jeffrey gathered up his materials and left. He told her he would have preliminary blueprints to her by the end of October, and they would make whatever changes and get the final ones by Thanksgiving. Meanwhile, she should study and make decisions on the lot and landscaping details. He wouldn't commit on the cost, but said he thought he could keep it under $400,000 and that his estimate would be in with the blueprints.

After he left, Alma poured herself a double Jack and water. What was she getting into? That amount of money for a summer home was ridiculous. Spending nearly half a million dollars would put a big dent in her reserves, even though that house would sell for well over a million in the Washington suburbs. She might have to sell her house or her condo, which she had thought about doing anyhow, because of the maintenance and headaches of renting. But to invest that much money in Buchanan County, well off the only four-lane highway, was bound to be a loser. She needed to talk with Brett and see if he had changed his mind about doing the same thing with his parents' place.

Speaking of the devil, she heard and then saw him pull in at the house. Brett had been coming over two or three days a week. Sometimes only for dinner at the Black Stallion or stopping by on his way from a business trip to Grundy or Pikeville. Or, if the mood was right, and it most often was, for a good romp in the bed. Evidently, she turned him on, and she was charmed by his chivalry and wit. Not too many men had made her laugh or tolerated her independence in the past few years. Besides, she was now retired and had no worries of gossip or damage to her reputation. If her aunts or Krista thought she was fooling around with Brett, they would just urge her on. It wasn't like they were going to marry. She was well past the age of needing a man to control her life or, for that matter, interfering in her life. If she wanted to build a damn mansion on Garden Creek, then she would.

"Hi, beautiful!"

"Hi, yourself. What brings you to the back woods? You run out of ways to make money or spend it? If you stopped by for a little pleasure, then you came to the wrong place, because I'm not about to be charmed by your wit or good looks today. I don't see why you are interested in me anyway; it ain't like it's going anywhere, permanently."

"Whoa there! What the hell has gotten into you? I just stopped by to tell you that you are beautiful, and that I'm hungry and maybe willing to buy your dinner."

"Well, I'm not hungry, and I think it's time I started packing for the trip back home."

Brett could feel the cold and the fear spilling out of her pores. Now was not the time for bantering with her. He held out his arms, and she wilted into them. When the tears started, he gently squeezed her tighter and stroked her hair. After a while, she sniffed and turned away to wipe the tears.

"I'm sorry about that. I don't know what has come over me today. I hate winter, even in the city. I need to get out of here before all the leaves fall and depression sets in."

"The leaves will fall, but depression doesn't visit here any more than other places. Tell me about your day. Did Jeffrey come by?"

"Yes, and I wish he hadn't. Do you know this project could cost me nearly half a million dollars?"

"It doesn't have to. You can spend as much or as little as you want. You can put a new roof on this place and stay right here."

"You know what I mean. I have already bought out the rest of the family, and if I continue with this project, I want to do it my way. I showed you the plans. Don't you think that would be the way to go?"

"I do, but then I'm not the one crying over spending a few dollars."

"I guess it would be a few dollars to you. What happens when I don't come here anymore and the rest of the family don't want to, or have time, to visit the 'old home place'? It doesn't make any sense to spend that much and let it just rot away. This is Buchanan County, Brett! Nobody would pay that much to buy the place when I decided it was time to sell. Are you still going ahead with rebuilding your parents' place?"

"I started the grade work last week. I bet you I finish my house before you do. Pour us a glass of wine and let's talk about this. You have just let Jeffrey scare you off. I told him not to mention money, yet."

Taking their drinks, they walked up to the garden and looked over the house site and the view down the gorge between the mountains. There were lots of Poplar-yellow, Maple-orange, and Oak-red leaves showing now. It was beautiful being enclosed by all that color. They sipped their wine and looked around for several silent minutes. Brett told her if, and when, she got tired of the place, he would buy it for ten-percent more than she had invested in it.

"Now, why would you do that, Brett? I know you are a darling, but you don't have to feel obligated to protect me and take care of me. I won't have that. I can take care of myself, and I don't want, or need, your sympathy. I'm not trying to be mean, Brett. I just could not let you take a fall for some mistake I might make."

"You are talking to Brett Parker, my dear. If you knew me at all, you would know that I never take a fall intentionally in a financial deal. If you build it and promise to keep it for five years, because that's how long you should give any venture to see if it will succeed, then I'll take it off your hands when you want to give it up. And I'll make a profit out of the deal."

"You're crazy! How could you make a profit up in this hollow?"

"This location is only a mile-and-a-half off Route 460, the one and only four-lane road going through Buchanan County. It is on a paved road with good public water, and it's about fifteen miles from Grundy which has only one decent motel. Dozens of businessmen visit this county every week, and some stay for days at a time, dealing mostly in mining sales and service. A bed-and-breakfast with as many bedrooms as you are planning, plus a few more built in the lofts, would be a gold mine."

"You are a Midas, aren't you, Brett?"

Laughing, he took her hand and led her back to the house. She was all smiles and relaxed now. She almost loved the man. With his confidence and analytical mind, he was handy to have around. Maybe there was time left in the afternoon for pleasure. What did she know? He placed the glasses in the sink, gave her a kiss, and left. She felt like he was manipulating her again, just by easing her mind and then leaving her alone to stew over whether he was worth having around. Well, she wasn't going to stew over anything but the plans for the house and when to call Leslie and her sisters.

Alma got a call through to Dr. Pruitt in her office at Pikeville College the next morning. Leslie apologized for not getting back to her first. She had talked to her sisters. One of them wanted to meet with Alma, but the other two did not. Leslie had been busy trying to talk them into forgiving and forgetting, without much success. Kathy, the oldest sister, who still lived near Red Jacket, in a town called Williamson, West Virginia, didn't want to see the picture or hear the bastard's name mentioned. Tonya, the youngest sister, who also lived in Williamson, didn't care one way or the other. She had been too young to remember Leroy when he left. The other sister, Shirley, who lived in Blountville, Tennessee, was excited about seeing the picture and hearing what Alma had to tell. They talked on for a while and agreed to meet at the Chinese restaurant in Pikeville on Wednesday evening at 5:00. Again, Leslie said she wasn't sure if all her sisters would show up, but the ones that did could have their say.

After she hung up, Alma thought about calling the Southwestern State Hospital. She finally found the number, but the place was now called Southwestern Virginia Mental Health Institute. First, she called Jill and asked her if she had ever been to the State Hospital to see her Aunt Betty. Jill told her she had been the only relative to visit Betty during the last year of her life. Larkin never visited, and his dad had died the year before his wife. Alma wanted to know if Jill thought the people at the hospital would talk with her, if she called. Jill told her probably not, but she had an authorization form to pick up and deliver items to her Aunt Betty. If Alma wanted to come by and get the paper, it might get her in the door to talk to somebody. So, instead of calling, Alma decided to take a shower, then drive over to Marion and take her chances on getting in to see the administrator. She would stop by and get the form from Jill on the way.

When she picked up the paper, it read, but in more legal terms, that Betty Bracken gave permission for her niece, Jill Wills Casey, to receive medical information and to pick up and return personal items belonging to Betty. Alma was glad this was Southwest Virginia, instead of Washington, D.C., where privacy policies had not yet become such a vital part of patient's security. She would attempt to pass as Jill, and hoped they didn't ask for a picture ID.

Alma drove Route 460 over Short Gap to Caypool Hill, and then turned right towards Abingdon. She had considered driving through Tazewell, taking Route 16 across the mountains into Marion, but she remembered the road being so crooked. She had been car sick traveling that road, when her senior class had gone to Hungry Mother Park. Whether she would drive back tonight, or spend another night at the Martha Washington Inn in Abingdon, depended on how long she spent at the Institute.

She noticed the razor wire along the top of the fence as she drove into the parking lot. That must be there to keep the patients, or were they called 'inmates', in instead of keeping other people out.

"Dr. Anderson, I'm Jill and I've come to pick up any belongings of my aunt, Betty Bracken, that might have been saved when she passed away in your Institute." Alma handed him the paper Jill had given her.

The administrator looked at the paper and then at Alma.

"It took me a minute to place Betty Bracken. She died shortly after I took over here three years ago. This form would not be issued now at this Institute, but I guess I have to honor it. May I ask why it has taken three years for you to come by and collect her things?"

He went over to a cabinet, pulled out a file, and sat down at his desk to browse through it. He never invited Alma to sit.

"I now live in northern Virginia. I thought Larkin, the son, would have taken care of everything after the funeral, but I've just recently been informed that he moved out of state after his mother died. So, I thought I would check to see if there was any unfinished business to take care of and pick up personal items that had been left behind."

"Well, Mrs. Casey, it looks like you are a little late. This file has been closed, with the state writing off any cost not covered. Larkin did indeed come by and retrieved a small box of belongings. It seems that included mostly pictures, a Bible, and a diary she kept with the help of one of the counselors, who is no longer with us. Sorry, it doesn't seem like I'm going to be of much help."

"I guess things were taken care of, then. I'm sorry to have bothered you, Dr. Anderson, but I do appreciate your taking time to see me and for checking her file. Larkin, or his father, was never one to spend much time looking after her. I'm surprised they didn't just kick her out on the street somewhere when she got sick. That's what happens to a lot of mental cases today, don't you think? The state used to take them in and give them treatment and guidance, and sometimes they recovered enough to go back home and lead near-normal lives. Now, it seems like most of them are left to be homeless on the street. They could be cared for by family or be receiving treatment in an Institution like this. I tried to do the best I could."

"We also do the best we can, Mrs. Casey. We don't turn away anyone we can treat."

"Then, why did you care for about 1,500 patients back in the '60's and now you have probably less than 500?"

"I don't know where you got your information, but times have changed and for the better. I don't think I care to discuss the health care, provided by our state, with you."

"I'm sure you don't. Well, I'll bid you good-day, and thank you that my aunt was one that did receive treatment."

Alma turned and walked out without offering to shake his hand. She mumbled as she stepped through the door, "It was probably the only way Grady Bracken had to lock up his wife".

She was too upset to attempt the drive back home, so she drove the short distance down to Abingdon and got a room at the Inn. She took in the play, <u>Of Mice and Men</u>, at the Barter Theatre, to boot.

More so than ever, she would now have to track down Larkin Bracken. If there was a diary, and if he hadn't destroyed it, there might also be answers to a lot of questions.

The next evening, she sat in the parking lot of the Peking Restaurant and waited until she saw Dr. Pruitt and three other ladies walk in. They all did come, then! Leslie must have convinced them to seek out the truth of their father, if at all possible. It could be a disappointing evening for all of them. There was not much information to go on, but a lot of speculation.

When Alma walked up to the table, Dr. Pruitt stood and shook hands with her. She turned to her sisters and introduced each of them to Alma. They all ordered drinks and chose to eat from the buffet bar. Leslie asked Alma if she could see the picture again. When Alma gave it to her, she studied it for a few minutes and, with Alma's approval, passed it on to the sisters. There was mostly silence around the table as the picture moved from one to another. Tonya was the first to bring up the subject.

"I don't remember him. But that looks a lot like a picture Mommy showed me of Leroy, taken when he was coming home from work at a mine in Red Jacket. Don't you all think it quite funny that he once worked at a coal mine in Red Jacket, West Virginia, and this picture was taken when he supposedly worked at a Red Jacket coal mine in Virginia?"

"Strange, yes, Tonya," Leslie said.

"I guess you find it strange, Alma, that we call him Leroy instead of Dad, or something? Well, I do remember him, probably not as well as Leslie, and he was fun to have around. He always saved something from his lunch and gave it to us when he got home from work. We went fishing on the Tug Fork River and he told us that was the way he met Mommy, fishing. We floated in inner tubes and he told funny stories." Shirley wiped a tear from her cheek.

Kathy didn't say anything, but she was still holding the picture. Alma couldn't get a read on her and held back from asking direct questions. Leslie spoke up again.

"Alma, where do you think we go from here? Do you still plan to find out what happened to him? We all know he is surely dead by now. But speaking for myself, I would like to know if he did abandon us, or did he have an accident and maybe died trying to provide for us."

"It's family and history for you ladies. It is a puzzle my dad left for me. They are quite different objectives for us. While I really want to solve this case, it's more like a detective trying to tie up loose ends or a reporter finding the end of her story, which I again assure you I'm neither. But for you, the results could prove very painful, or could help you come to terms with your father and lay to rest all questions and suspicions that have burdened you for so long."

Alma told them she didn't have much to go on. But, she did know about the other men in the picture, their names and members of their families who were still alive. She wanted to explore that avenue, but she didn't want to cause any more pain to

Leroy's family. She had the sisters' telephone numbers and addresses and could let them know if she learned anything new, if they so wanted. They all said they wanted to know if she found out anything. They talked and finally began to smile, and then laugh a little at some of the things that happened back when they were growing up in the coalfields of West Virginia. All the girls had married and raised a family of their own. Kathy was the only one that had not been employed in the work force. She had raised five children and each of them had gone on to college. Her husband still worked for a mining equipment company in Williamson. All three of the other girls had become teachers, although Leslie was the only one to become a professor in a college. Alma was amused by the way the sisters teased Leslie and referred to her as the 'Doc'.

Everyone gave Alma a hug and walked her to her car when she got ready to leave. Kathy asked for her address so she could send her a Christmas card. Alma was touched and, biting her lip, she jotted down her address on post-it-notes for all of them. As she drove back up Route 460 towards Grundy, she tried to think if there ever had been a time in her life when she cared about what happened to other people and their families, of course, with the exception of her immediate family and relatives. Her heart ached for this family. She wanted more than anything to find Leroy and bridge this gap in their lives. This was now more than a puzzle.

17

Alma One-Ups Brett

The next day Alma sat down in her father's old recliner, the electric lift chair he had bought after falling and breaking his hip. During his last few years, it had been a great help to him in trying to get up and down. The old sofa was too low, and the hard straight-back chairs were not comfortable for an extended stay to watch TV or review his files. She leaned her head back against the head rest and closed her eyes for a while. She could feel the slight dip in the seat where he had worn it down over many hours of use.

She opened a file marked 'For future stories'. The folder she removed was labeled 'Maxwell'. She began to read.

> *This is the story that Maxwell Shoemaker told me about his friendship with one of our legends. According to Max, Charlie could have been the first professional football*

player to ever come out of Buchanan County.

Max said that Charlie Newberry was a tough old nut. Always had been. When he was in high school he liked to run. They didn't have anything like a track team back in those days. But they had a football team, and he wanted to be in shape when practice started. So he ran to school in the morning and back home afterwards. That was about three miles down the mountain from the family farm and three miles back. He knew the run back up the mountain was what built the strong legs and lungs. He expected to be the fastest and strongest player on the team. And he was.

Garden High School didn't win anything like a state championship, but Virginia Tech heard about him and offered him a scholarship. He went one year. He didn't get to play any, but they promised him if he would just be patient and learn, that next year he would be the starting tailback. He did. But then during the summer break his dad let Jake, the mule, kick him in the head while he was tying the harness on Jake to do the plowing.

That's how he became a farmer instead of something else. His dad stayed in bed most of the time, but occasionally, would sit on the porch in the sunshine on a pretty day. Charlie's mother would take care of him. That included feeding his dad and helping him sit on the pot several times a day and night. Charlie inherited the farm that summer because the rest of the kids wanted nothing to do with it and had married and moved away to Ohio where they could make real money.

Charlie's mom was good to his dad that first year. She doted on him and his many needs. She seldom went anywhere, not even to church, although Charlie told her he would look after his dad. All that began to change the next year when Charlie finally persuaded his high school sweetheart Jeri to marry him. After they were married, he moved his wife into the house and things began to tumble. His mother retreated into the back bedroom with his dad, or would work hours in the garden. She seldom initiated conversation and gave short answers to questions.

Seeing the confusion and turmoil caused by two families trying to live together under one roof, Charlie offered to sell the farm and move his mother and dad into a smaller place in town. His mother wanted none of that. She told him this was now his farm and he could push his parents out if he wanted to, but she would rather die than see Charlie's dad forced out of his home and off the farm he had built and where he had buried Charlie's grandparents.

Five years later he buried his parents in the family plot. His mother died 21 days after his father.

Charlie and Jeri had four children, three boys and a girl. The farm served them well. With the cattle and the orchard, he was able to send them all through college. With pride, he and Jeri watched them graduate, marry, and start their own families. His oldest boy Bobby and his family lived the closest, about a hundred and fifty miles east in a college town called Radford.

After the kids left, he and Jeri settled comfortably into middle and then old age. He bought his first tractor when he was about fifty and switched over from square bales of hay to round ones when he was about seventy. He could take care of the farm pretty much by himself except when the apples needed picking. Then he hired some migrant workers for about six weeks.

HANGER

The one guy he could count on to help out, even if he didn't ask, was Max. He was a coal miner, but Max loved to work on the farm. If Charlie and Jeri needed to go visit the children or something, he would feed the cows or get some help and bale some hay. Charlie always shared a hog with him at killing time and gave him permission to hunt on the farm.

The good life ended when Jeri began to get sick. Charlie had noticed it for some time but thought she was just getting old. Both of them were pushing eighty. Jeri had always volunteered at church, cooking for the sick or for families after a funeral. She was the head cook at the new school. She loved to sew and had made most of the kids' clothes until they got older and demanded store-bought.

But then she started forgetting things. It started with the food. Sometimes she would forget to put in the seasoning or sometimes put salt in twice because she didn't remember adding it the first time. Then she quit sewing. A quilt she had started for one of the grandkids was only half done. The bubbly conversation at dinner got quieter.

One day he came in for lunch as he always did, and the pot of beans on the stove had burnt and was smoking and smelling up the whole house. She was talking on the phone to their daughter in Cleveland and hadn't noticed until he took the lid off the pot and started opening windows. Jeri hung up the phone without saying goodbye and covered her eyes with her hands. Charlie had to explain everything to their daughter when she called back.

The next year was filled with stress and tension. The children started coming in regularly, sometimes staying for several days at a time. They would often find their dad somewhere on the farm and ask endless questions about their mother. They first implied that maybe he should stick a little closer to the house. Then they insisted he rent out the farm or consider selling and moving to town. When he balked, they reminded him how their mother had devoted her whole life to him and his farm, and it was time he gave back.

Over time, they wore him down. He wanted to, and would, take care of Jeri. Children that only came in once in a while couldn't see how the farm was going down because he was spending most of his time watching over his wife. He wouldn't agree to sell, but he finally agreed to try an assisted living arrangement nearby. He could still check on the farm.

That lasted three days. They both hated it. He moved Jeri back and called the kids and told them he would stay in the house and rent out the farm.

They were back, more often than ever. 'He wasn't cooking very good meals'. 'They were eating too much cereal or sandwiches'. They took their mother for more tests.

After months of trying to reason with the children, Charlie moved into a nearby nursing home with his wife. The home assured the kids that their parents would have a room to themselves and that all their needs would be taken care of. Charlie wasn't taking but a couple of prescription pills a day when he moved into the place, but then he started having trouble sleeping. The staff and the doctor insisted on him taking a sleeping pill to help.

By the time Max saw him for the last time, Charlie wouldn't talk to him. He would only sit and stare out the window, or at the wall, if they had him sitting in the hallway, while they

*cleaned his room, so he could socialize
with the other residents of the home.*

That was it, but there was a picture. The wide-angle picture showed a group of elderly guys sitting at tables and booths in what appeared to be a restaurant. Alma turned the picture over, but there were no names or dates on the back. Evidently, her father had intended to do a story on either Charlie or the group of men gathered in the restaurant. She hated there was no more. She wondered if Charlie was still alive. Probably not.

She put the file beside the chair when she heard an automobile pull in and cut the engine. She had told her aunts, Krista, and Brett that she was going back to Washington any day now, but one thing led to another, and the days got shorter and the leaves all fell, and she was still here. Brett came over regularly, and now he shows up pulling a trailer with two 4-wheelers on it. It seemed he was now mostly retired instead of partly. He kept telling her 'his people' were taking care of this or that. If she had as many 'people' as he did, she would have retired a long time ago. She put on a button-up sweater and met him at the truck.

"What in the world have you here?"

"We're going 4-wheeling. You need to get out of the house for a while and have some fun instead of stressing out over something you can't do anything about."

"I'm not getting on one of those things. I would freeze to death for one thing and probably fall off, or wreck and kill myself. Is this what rednecks do for fun back here in the mountains?"

"Yes, you are, and yes, it will be fun. You won't get cold. I brought you a hooded sweatshirt, a down vest, and a pair of boots. You do have a pair of blue jeans, don't you?"

"Yes, I have blue jeans, but I'm still not riding one of those monsters. I don't know how to drive a straight-stick pickup truck, much less something like that."

"It's easier than driving your car. Listen, we'll take a trial run up the road here. You can drive, and I'll sit right behind you to help if you should need me. But you won't."

Brett unhooked and backed one of the vehicles off the trailer. He reached inside the cab and pulled a red vest out of a bag and a pink helmet. She put them on while he started the engine.

"What's the helmet for, if it is so easy and safe?"

"It's the law for 4-wheelers and motorcycles, mostly to protect the makers from lawsuits. I don't like wearing them, but I figured you to be one to follow the rules. Hop on, and let's go try this baby out."

"It doesn't look like a baby to me, or sound like one either. Brett, I've done told my aunts that if you hurt me in any way, they are to get dad's old shotgun and blow a hole in you. So, you had better make sure I get back here in one piece. I don't even have my blue jeans or boots on."

"That's for later. This is just a short learning session up the road and back. You'll need to pack us a lunch before you put your boots on, for we are going on an all-day excursion."

In spite of herself and all her reservations about a fifty-five-year-old lady straddling a seat like she was riding a horse, she enjoyed the short ride up the hollow to the end of the paved road. With Brett's arms around her and his body close to her back and rump, she somehow managed to concentrate on operating the loud machine between her legs. The wind in her face turned her eyes watery and her cheeks rosy red. It was easier than operating a car. All she had to do was twist her wrist to give it gas, squeeze the lever at her fingertips to brake, and turn the wheels like turning the handlebars on her bicycle. By the time they got back to the truck and the other 4-wheeler, Brett was encouraging her to slow down and occasionally reaching around her to squeeze the brake lever.

She was all giggly and rosy when they got off and shut down the engine. She told Brett she would run in and make the lunch and change into her jeans and boots, while he unloaded the other 4-wheeler. When she got back fifteen minutes later, he had stored water and cola into compartments on the side of the vehicles, into which went the lunches, also. He also had stored an air pump and a tire-plugging kit in case they needed to repair one of the tires. He knew from experience that sharp rocks or pointed tree stumps could mean a long walk out of the mountains. He also put in his 4-wheeler two handguns and ammunition. If she would try, he wanted to teach her how to load and shoot a pistol for her own protection. Living in Buchanan County was in itself a lot safer than Washington, D.C., but a woman living by herself, that far off the road and not within sight of a neighbor, had made Brett uneasy from the start.

He made sure she was buckled in on the 4-wheeler and told her they would go into no more than third gear and to be sure she did not attempt to pass him. No matter how comfortable she became with operating the vehicle, they were out to enjoy the scenery, get some fresh air, and have some fun, but no foolishness or taking chances. Alma smiled. It looked like he was having second thoughts about turning his expensive toys over to this wild woman.

They drove to the end of the road. Brett slowed down and eased into an old logging road off to the right and leading uphill between two ridges. In a short while, they looped left in a turn-about and climbed to the top of the hill. From a narrow, rutted path they emerged onto a wide, level cut in the mountainside that resembled a construction site for an eight lane highway. The high wall on the mountain side of the cut was about forty to sixty feet tall. The dirt and rock from the cut had been pushed over the side of the mountain, and the fill was almost as tall but sloping to the battered trees below. Alma wondered how wildlife could navigate up and down the mountain. She guessed they had to go around the high wall, but she could see no end in sight in either direction.

Brett explained this was a mined-out and abandoned strip mine. All the coal was long gone, but it made a nice trail to go 4-wheeling or for dirt bike rides. They headed out to the left slowly, but still going faster than on the logging road.

Occasionally, they had to dodge stray cedar bushes or fallen rock, but, for the most part, the ride was smooth and the view over the valleys and tree tops was enjoyable. Although the leaves were gone, the small trees were thick and gave the ridges and hill sides a brownish grey color to contrast against the Carolina blue sky.

They stopped often. Sometimes, Brett would point out a red-headed woodpecker, a hawk perched in the peak of a large pine tree, numerous squirrels, and chipmunks. Once, they rounded a curve, and he pointed to a red fox hurrying down the high wall side of the road. The small animal would dart halfway across the road before figuring his chances of beating the 4-wheelers were slim and scurrying back to the barrier of the wall. After a short run, Brett eased back on the gas and gave the animal plenty of room to cross over and down the bank on the other side.

Later into the ride, he pulled over near a huge boulder that had been dozed to the side and looked ready to topple on down the mountain. There was a flat spot on top of the rock about the size of a large dining room table which was washed clean of dirt by many rains. With hesitation from Alma and encouragement and assurance from Brett, they walked out to stand and view the mountains off in the distance. They could see over smaller hills and ridges and hollows to taller mountains several miles away. The view reminded Alma of stopping and looking over the hills at selected spots on the Blue Ridge Parkway. It was peaceful and quiet. She could not hear anything but the chirping of squirrels and the singing of birds. There were not even the sounds of automobiles or airplanes. She didn't know how far away from civilization they were, but the solitude was a bit daunting to a self-made city girl now used to high-rise apartment buildings, eight-lane freeways, and helicopters and passenger jets flying overhead. A couple of months ago, she had loved being surrounded by the bustling of a large city, and she had hated the teenage memories of suffocation of steep mountains and deep hollows. She smiled as she recalled one of her father's sayings that everything that goes around, comes around.

Brett asked her if she was ready for a bite of lunch, and she agreed that it was time. They brought the bagged lunches that Alma had prepared and a Pepsi and leaned back on the tabletop boulder, with Alma propped up against Brett's knee. She told him about the file she was reading just before he arrived and showed him the group picture.

"I don't know if Charlie is still alive, or not. The stories I've heard are all about what a great football player he was. Max is still living, though. He lives down there somewhere close to where those men in the picture you have with Leroy lived. That group in the picture meets every Wednesday down at Grundy at the Dairy Queen for breakfast. Some of them call it the ROMEO Club."

"ROMEO. Ain't that a bit sissy for a bunch of guys?"

"Retired Old Men Eating Out. I think it's kinda clever."

Soon they were finished with the meal.

"Alma, I've got something I want you to try, and this is the perfect place. I know it probably goes against your usually sound judgment, but it would relieve me to know you are capable of taking care of yourself and your property."

"Try what, Brett?"

"Learn how to shoot a gun. I've brought along two pistols and ammunition to do some target shooting. Once you get over your fear of guns and the loud sound, it can actually be a lot of fun to practice target shooting."

"I don't know about this, Brett. Isn't it against the law to discharge firearms?"

"Only in a city. We do it all the time back here in the sticks. Come over here and lay your vest over the front of the 4-wheeler for a cushion, and to steady your aim, and I'll show you how to load and handle a gun. We'll shoot at that stump over there against the high wall. It's about twenty yards away, and we won't have to worry about a stray bullet. In reality, if you are facing someone dangerous, and he is farther away than that, it would be better to run as fast as you can to get away."

Alma did as she was instructed. When Brett brought the pistol he wanted her to try, he painstakingly showed her how to push the lever to open the cylinder of the revolver and how to insert the bullets one at a time as she rotated the cylinder. When the gun was loaded, he showed her where the safety was and how to set and release it. He told her to cover her ears for the first shot. Afterwards, she would know how loud it was and could decide for herself whether to cover her ears. She smiled, and he agreed it would be difficult to shoot a gun and cover your ears at the same time. He leaned across the 4-

wheeler, rested his elbows on the vest, gripped the pistol with both hands, and fired at a tree stump near the high wall.

"You missed. Now, it's my turn."

"Give me just a minute, and I'll put up a target on that stump using our lunch bag."

He walked over with the bag and a piece of furnace tape he had taken out of one of the saddlebags. Alma wondered what all he carried in those compartments. He also carried the handgun with him. Maybe he didn't trust her to hold it while he put up the target. When he returned, he handed her the gun and gave additional instructions.

Alma leaned across the 4-wheeler and took her position just like he had done. Listening to his advice, she kept her trigger finger outside the guard until she was ready to fire. She supported the short pistol with her left hand. Just before she made the move to fire, he quickly, but cautiously, removed her hand from the gun. Puzzled, Alma looked over at him.

"Why did you do that? I was ready to shoot."

"Yeah! Ready to shoot your finger off. Alma, didn't you notice that you had placed your first finger over the end of the barrel?"

"No, I was just trying to steady the gun with my other hand. You're kidding, aren't you?"

Brett took the gun and showed her how she had held it. He was having second thoughts about this whole episode. Having a gun around Alma might be more dangerous than living alone with no protection. He handed the gun back to her and watched closely as she again got ready to shoot at the target. Instead of hitting the target, or the stump, she chipped the bark off a tree on top of the high wall.

"Wow! Did I hit the target, Brett?"

"Not bad. I think you need a little more practice, though."

"Why don't you get your gun and we can have a little contest. Maybe, if we put a little money on each shot, you would shoot a little better."

Brett laughed. He took her gun and walked over to get his out of the 4-wheeler. He would place a dollar bet on the shots just to humor her, and maybe she would get a little better before they ran out of ammunition.

"O.K. Load up, and we'll call it a dollar a shot, okay?"

"You have got to be kidding. How about a hundred dollars a shot? Or, are you scared to tell your friends how much money you lost to a city girl?"

"Okay, a hundred per shot, and we're keeping score."

He watched her reload. She flipped the cylinder open and spun it around before quickly loading .357 bullets into the revolver. Without pushing the cylinder back into place, she gave a flick of her wrist and it popped back with a click. She turned and fired at the target without balancing herself across the vehicle or steadying with the opposite hand. Brett's eyes widened and his mouth dropped open as he saw the paper target flinch.

"You want me to load that Sig Sauer 9mm Luger for you, or are you going to stand there with your mouth open? It's your turn."

"I think I've just been conned." Brett smiled anyway, loaded his gun and took his shot. The bark flew from the stump just inches underneath the target.

"How did you know I was shooting a Sig 9mm? As far as that goes, how about I just give you a thousand dollars and we head back home."

Alma laughed. "You're giving up that easy? I say we shoot ten shots each and let me earn my bet and ease your concerns about me protecting myself in the bargain."

"Okay, it will still be fun, and I might get in a lucky shot."

While they were shooting, Alma explained about her experience on a firing range with the FBI agent, Brian Winehouser, as her instructor. She also informed Brett she had a LaserMay Laser Sight Sig P226 9mm Luger in her purse and kept it in a drawer by her bed when she was alone. She had obtained a concealed weapons permit a few years ago, again with Brian's help. She had never had a reason to pull the gun out of her purse and hoped she'd never have to. She didn't know if she could fire it at a living thing, even if it appeared necessary.

Brett was happy to hand over the thousand dollars, but was surprised when she took it. He would rest easier now, but he would make sure he announced himself before he sneaked up on her. They drove slowly off the mountain. Alma helped him load the 4-wheelers onto the trailer before they went into the house. They were both covered in trail dust, so Alma suggested he spend the night and offered him the shower first.

"I would love to spend the night. How about I just move in here with you and help build that log cabin? You may owe me more than a night after working that con job and embarrassing me with your skill, to boot."

"One night, if you're clean. I don't want my aunts to lecture me, and I don't want you taking credit for building my log house, not a log cabin."

Alma thanked him for a great day. She still couldn't believe she, fifty-five years old, would climb on a 4-wheeler and race through the mountains. She gave him a hug and a long satisfying kiss, helped him out of his clothes, and patted his fanny towards the shower with instructions not to use all the hot water.

She was still in Oakwood in late October when Jeffrey came by with the house plans. They sat down at the kitchen table with cups of coffee while he went over each detail. He thought she should level only enough for a nice front yard, but leave the slope of the land for the house. That would give her first floor entry on the upper level, but allow for a walk-in basement on the lower. The basement could be finished, if she wanted, and sliding glass doors installed. Either way, it would come in handy for the heating and plumbing and storage.

She liked the idea and the detail the blueprints provided. She asked him how much more it would be to install similar bedrooms upstairs on one level and a large bedroom suite on the other level. She also wanted more and bigger windows on the main level in the living section and a small deck outside the large bedroom upstairs. He showed her the current estimate of $248,000 and began to do more figuring. After a bit, he pushed the paper over to her. For $298,000 he could do what she asked. It would only mean adding more partitions and extra plumbing for the bathrooms, and more for the extra windows and deck. Alma was rather pleased with the cost. She had been expecting at least the mid $300,000 range and wouldn't have been shocked if it had hit the $400,000 price. Maybe she had lived in D.C. too long. Confident in what Brett had told her, and his promise to take it if things didn't work out, had her anxious to begin. She asked Jeffrey when he could start. He informed her that building in the wintertime was always problematic, but he could order the plan and start the grade work at least by the first of the year, and maybe a little sooner. It could be spring before the logs arrived, but the work would go quickly once they did.

  She signed the contract he placed in front of her and urged him to start as soon as he could. Living in the old home place was just getting by. She hadn't liked it much when she was growing up, but then again, it was full of kids and no bathroom. He promised to put her at the top of the priority list, but repeated the custom-made logs would be the holdup. If he were building her a frame or brick home, he could probably complete it in about four months.

  After Jeffrey left, she called Brett and told him about signing the contract and she hoped to be in her new house by summer. He seemed pleased and excited. When she told him about the additions, he asked where she had come up with that idea.

"You know where, and I thank you. By the end of summer, I will be busting at the seams with guests in the only B&B in Oakwood, maybe in the whole county."

"I thought you were retired."

"I am, but if I'm going to go head-over-heels in debt, I'll need to supplement my income some way. I will have all the living space and privacy I need in the loft on the left side and my own private entrance. I'm looking forward to having a house full of men visiting me every day."

"That won't last long with you cooking and keeping house. I hope Lori tells all of them how you treated her when you ordered at the Black Stallion and to give you a little of the same."

"But I changed. She is one of my best friends, now. Besides, I'm not cooking or cleaning. I'm the host. I intend to hire a cook and a desk clerk that will double as housekeeper."

Brett laughed. "You'll do fine, Alma. I'm excited for you. Does this mean you are going to stay?"

"Maybe. We'll see how it goes. I'll still have a place in Washington if this place stops being fun and interesting. Six months ago, I was not thinking of even retiring or visiting this place. Now that I've quit work, I don't seem to know anyone of consequence in D.C. I love being around Krista and my two aunts, and even you. I like going to church now, instead of making the required appearance on Sunday and shaking only the preacher's hand and buying a chance for heaven. I know, Brett, this county probably has the dirtiest air and water in the whole state. But I feel like I can breathe, the simple food tastes better, I want to know everyone I meet, I laugh and sing from the pit of my stomach and don't care who hears me. And, I haven't had a stressful headache since I retired."

"Be careful, now! You sound like you may be heading towards becoming a hillbilly."

"Well, I probably can outshoot most of these mountain men. And, if I can keep Krista off my back, I probably can cuss as well. Just don't expect me to take up chewing tobacco or dipping Skoal."

"Congratulations on the contract. I can't wait to see the cabin going up. How about tomorrow I come over and we celebrate?"

"That would be lovely, but I can't. That's really why I called you tonight. Tomorrow, I'm going to drive back to my house in Alexandria and organize and pick up some things. I may spend a few days since things are quiet here, but I will call and keep in touch and let you know when I head back this way."

"Well, I'll go with you. We could fly up again, and if I have to be back here for something, I'll come back to get you when you're ready."

"Not this time, Brett. You make me want to rush things, and I want to take my time. I'm going to rent a van from our good friend and car salesman, Harold Shortridge, down at Grundy, and I'll probably pack it to the gills when I head back here. Unless I find some handsome dude that wants to sail away with me down the Potomac, I'll be back by Christmas."

She could tell he was disappointed. It made her heart swell to think he would miss her, even for a few days. They talked on for a while, but she wouldn't let him change her mind about him tagging along. When she hung up, she wasn't sad about leaving him or this house for a spell. She would be back. She now had a plan and pieces were falling into place. She smiled as the thought occurred to her; she had probably never had a plan before, but had just taken a day at a time and hoped she didn't fall on her face.

18

Alma Moves Home

Harold rented her a minivan and took all the back seats out to give her more loading room. She was on the road by 10:00 and was grateful to see Interstate 81 a little over two and a half hours later. Driving Route 460 through Richlands, Tazewell, Princeton, and Pearisburg brought back old memories when she had begged a ride back home for Christmas, arriving in the wee hours of the morning. Most of the few times she made the trip, she flew into Bluefield or Tri-Cities and had a relative pick her up. She had claimed it was too far to drive by herself, and getting out of D.C. on the beltway was too dangerous. And that was when she was younger. Now look at her - almost a senior citizen and driving back along the same road, but now more crowded and much more dangerous with all the big rigs on the road.

When she got to Harrisonburg, she realized how tired and hungry she was. She decided to make this a two-day trip and checked in at a Holiday Inn.

After checking her room out and dragging in a bag, she drove across the street and filled the van up with gas and grabbed a chicken sandwich at McDonalds. She walked around the parking lot at the motel a few times to get the kinks out of her legs and back, went to her room, took a long hot shower, and crashed for the night.

Alma got to her home in Old Alexandria before noon the next day. She pulled the van into the garage and unloaded the only bag she had brought. After taking time to check out the house and finding everything in order, she also found it dusty and stuffy. She immediately set in to dusting and opening windows. She would save the vacuuming for tomorrow. An hour later, she took a large glass of ice water out to the deck and sat for a while watching the squirrels play among the large maples in the common area. Besides packing up a few boxes and choosing some small pieces of furniture to take back to Oakwood, what was she going to do for the next few weeks?

She did pack a lot of boxes. Over the next several days she went through her own files and photos. Not being able to decide which she should take or leave behind, she decided to take one whole file cabinet, and some extra files were added to a box. There was only one small display table she had bought in Italy that she thought couldn't be replaced, so she set it aside to be loaded in the van. When she had finished going through her closets, she only had two boxes of clothes she wanted to take. Most of the office clothes she left hanging, and the thirty boxes of shoes were restacked in the corner of the closet. Most all her paintings and framed family pictures were boxed up, and she carefully wrapped her china and silverware in old newspapers and placed them in boxes and stuffed more newspapers in around them. She only had small jewelry boxes. Even though most of them were crammed with gold and white-gold chains, she had some small, elegant earrings to big dangling ones. She wrapped the boxes and placed them in bigger cardboard boxes.

When Alma had done all the packing she thought she should, she didn't know if it would all fit in the van. She would save the loading until the last day, but didn't know exactly when that would be. She had been home for more than a week and had not gone out of the house except to buy some groceries, or to the library to return some books for which she had to pay late fines. If there were nothing else left to do, she might as well head on back to Oakwood. At least Brett and her two aunts would find something to occupy her time. But first, she had one more thing to do.

She called Brian Winehouser's home number and talked to his wife Jetta. After identifying herself and asking how Brian's retirement was going and if he was driving Jetta crazy lying around the house all day, she was informed he played golf three times a week and spent most of the rest of the week working out in the gym or jogging to fight back a beer belly that looked almost six months along. They both laughed and Jetta said she would put him on the phone but he was presently on the golf course, or so he said. She would have him call Alma tonight at home.

Brian called a little after eight just as she was getting interested in a serial killer crime investigation that she hated. If you have seen one of those CSI shows, you have seen them all.

"Well, how was the golf game?"

"It sucked. Just like all the rest of these pickup retirement activities I have tried. As soon as I can convince Jetta to move out of the Washington area, I'm going to settle down on a small farm, buy a tractor, and grow sweet potatoes."

Alma laughed. "I can see you in bibbed overalls and a straw hat, perched up on a big, green John Deere tractor plowing a few rows of rich farmland. Why don't you pick up some part-time consultant work or start a private investigation service? You would make a great PI man and would have all the rich want-to-be divorcees swarming all over you."

"No way. I don't want to work, I want an interesting hobby. Speaking of interesting, I'm glad you called. I have been interested and anxious to find out how your own PI work has gone down in the coalfields."

"Well, that is why I called you. I have made some progress. I found Leroy's family and the names and families of the other men in the picture. But I need your help again."

"I'm retired, Alma. I'm losing my contacts, and I could get into legal trouble interfering in law enforcement work."

"I'm not asking you to arrest anyone, Brian. I just need to find one more person. His name is Larkin Bracken, the son of Grady and Betty Bracken.

Grady was one of the men in the picture. Larkin should be around fifty years old and has been in trouble before, mostly with his father dealing in illegal whiskey."

"Whoa, Alma. You're assuming I want to get involved and spitting out lots of information. Just wait a minute until I get a pen and some paper."

Alma smiled. She had a feeling Brian wouldn't turn down an opportunity to do a little nosing around. How much golf and jogging could an old FBI retiree do?

When he came back on the phone, she repeated the information, and they talked about the participants in her mystery. He was glad to hear some of Leroy's children had done well. He still didn't know how any discoveries could do any good after all this time and with all the original parties dead. He wished her luck, anyhow, and would get back to her if, and when, he found Larkin.

On Sunday, she went to church. Two women that usually sat in her pew came over to ask where she had been and if all was well. The choir sang for about half the service, and, again she was too ashamed of her voice to sing out. The pastor spoke for the remainder of the time. Alma walked out of the church, alone, and felt a little let down by the service. If this had been Aunt Paula's church, she would have been greeted by every member of the congregation. She would not have been able to just shake hands with the preacher and merely walk away, but would have been surrounded by others who wanted to get out of church mode, which they had been totally into, and back into their everyday happy gossipy mode. She wondered if she was a religious person or just an obedient member of a church.

On Monday, she was contemplating going to the library and checking out another book when the phone rang. It was Brian. Without too much chit chat, he told her the latest on his search.

"I'm sure we have found your man, Alma."

"Great! That was quick. I told you, you were too good to be retired. When and where?"

"Well, this one wasn't too difficult. I ran him through our database. Do you know where Keen Mountain, Virginia, is?"

"Of course, I know where Keen Mountain is. The picture I showed you of the coal mine explosion was taken near Keen Mountain. What has that got to do with Larkin? He left Buchanan County a few years ago, after his mother died."

"Well, he's in Buchanan County now. Did you know they have a prison located on top of a mountain at Oakwood, Virginia, called Keen Mountain Correctional Center?"

"Yes, I knew they had a prison there. It was built only a few years ago, and I understand it is a secured facility for long-term, bad guys. Are you telling me that Larkin is locked up there?"

"Yes. It seems he is serving his second term in prison for Interstate transportation of illegal whiskey, meaning 'moonshine' to the locals. He was caught once in Pennsylvania and locked up for two years. This time, the Feds caught him loading up his vehicle in Franklin County and tailed him to Pittsburg before arresting him. The judge gave him ten years and threatened to lock him up next time and throw away the key. He still has six years to serve on this sentence."

"Well, I'll be! He was right under my nose the whole time. His cousin Jill said he left about five years ago, after his dad died, and nobody had heard from him. She said he didn't even attend his mother's funeral. Maybe he was locked up then."

"All I can say is if you had planned to have him arrested for any plot in your investigation, you are too late."

"Funny, Brian! But you are the best. I owe you another one. You can get back to your golf now, but go easy on that beer. Overweight golfers could be flirting with a heart problem, and I might need you around."

He reminded her he was as fit as the day he retired. Besides, he was going to be a farmer and lead a stress-free life. When they hung up, she called her neighbor Henry, a retired teacher and football coach, and asked him if he would be willing to help her load some boxes in her van for a trip to Southwest Virginia.

The rest of the week, Alma piddled around, cleaned the house, took down the drapes and took them to the cleaners, shampooed the bedroom carpet, and polished the kitchen cabinets. She walked over to her friend's house two blocks away and took a pie she had bought at the Safeway grocery store. After an hour of visiting with Donna and listening to all the valuables she had discovered at flea markets and estate sales, she walked back home. Alma had tried to talk Donna into going to the Sandwich Shop in

Seven Corners and talking over old times with a glass of wine. Donna begged for a rain check. She was retired from the government just like Alma, but she was heavy into crafts, especially refinishing antique furniture. Today, she was elbow-deep into the last coat of stain on a 70-year-old corner cabinet.

Next, she called Pamela. Pam had come to D.C. with Alma, her sister Janice, and two other girls straight out of high school. Pam had vacationed with Alma in England, Scotland, and Switzerland. Of course Pam had nearly a free ride, as she was a stewardess for United Airlines, while Alma had to take out loans to pay for the trips.

That seemed so long ago. Janice had married an FBI agent and they moved to Dayton, Ohio. Lori married a soldier from Montana and, within two years, was living on a huge ranch with her husband's family and 12,000 sheep. Pamela never married, but her feet hardly ever hit the ground. She loved flying the friendly skies as an airline stewardess, and she came back to D.C. with tales of great cities all over the world. Within a few years, she and Alma flew to some of the same places. The only problem with Alma was she had a tendency to stay awhile in California, or Hawaii, or Brussels, Belgium. She was trained as a secretary and she could do that anywhere. After staying a couple of years in Hawaii, she moved to Los Angles and got a job working in the campaign of Ronald Reagan's bid to become governor of California. This was her introduction to politics, and there she found a home. To be in love with politics, you had to love the Nation's Capital. She left often to visit all over the world, but she made Washington, D.C., her home.

After graduating from Garden High School and leaving Buchanan County, Alma had done what she wanted to do. She always had a good paying job and the next one was always better. If she had an itch, she scratched it. It wasn't unusual for her to move upward in her occupation twice in a single year. Transfers to other cities, and, sometimes, other countries, were something she looked forward to. Others had families and ties that bind. Not Alma. If it was a promotion, then it was a good move.

Alma did find her way back to Buchanan County, occasionally. She did send money home so that William and Krista finally had a TV, although they had to run the antenna line all the way up to the top of the mountain and keep it cleared of tree branches, so they could get a signal. She had a wing built onto the house, and a bathroom and somewhat modern kitchen were installed. Her mother not only got her electric stove, but she also got an automatic washing machine to replace the old wringer type sitting on the back porch. With the new addition, she had the contractor add baseboard electric heaters to the other rooms in the house. It was funny to everybody but her, when her father refused to take out the old Warm Morning wood stove or to have the outhouse torn down. He reminded her that, in this part of the country, you could lose your electricity for days at a time and when company came you could always use an extra toilet.

Now, Janice had three children and five grandchildren to keep her busy. Alma had not heard from her sister since the funeral. Now, Pam was the only one of her pioneer friends left in the Washington area. Pam didn't answer the phone.

Alma decided to go alone down to Old Alexandria. She would grab a bite at one of the outdoor cafes and have a glass or two of wine and watch the tourists walk by.

As she was touching up her make-up, the tears started. She reached for a towel and dropped her head down on the edge of the sink.

Damn it! Now, she would have to start over with the eye shadow. What was wrong with her, anyway? This wasn't the first time, especially in the last couple of years, that everyone was too busy, or not available, to spend some time visiting or chatting over a glass of wine. Now, it seemed the only socializing she had was at work or at church. Neither of them was an appropriate place for building a relationship.

She decided to walk to Old Town. It would only be about a two-mile hike.

All her old friends had abandoned her. Most had gotten married and now had families. Only she and Pam and Donna were still single. Or, were they 'old maids', as her smart ass nephew Bobby had called her a few years ago at Christmas? Krista had laughed at the kid until Alma got up and left the room. Later, she had apologized and promised the children would not say it again.

She requested a table near the sidewalk with an opened umbrella. She ordered a BLT on toast, a wedge of Colby cheese and a glass of Chardonnay. When the waiter brought the wine, she asked him to leave the bottle. She was determined to relax and enjoy the afternoon.

She couldn't understand what Donna got out of fooling with antiques. Antiques were what Alma had grown up with and she would just as soon leave them in the past. If Donna wasn't working on a piece, she was at a yard sale buying something, or talking about it. It was like her siblings. If they weren't babysitting their grandchildren, they wanted to talk about them, or show you dozens of pictures.

Alma could remember a time, several years back, when her family and her friends wanted a piece of her time. They expected and got trips through the White House, to the National Zoo, through the museums at the Smithsonian, or a stroll around the Tidal Basin during cherry blossom time. She had spent valuable time showing them their Nation's Capital, or entertaining them with pictures and details of her latest trip to a foreign country or a photo opportunity with a famous person, like a President.

She ordered another bottle of wine and some pretzels.

So what, if she didn't have kids and a bunch of grandchildren to fuss over. She had a fantastic life. She had done what she wanted to do. Like she had told her high school friend, Ruby, no man was ever going to dominate her life and tell her what she could and couldn't do. She had made her own life and her own decisions. Most of them had been good ones. And she wasn't through yet. Maybe her friends and family had gone their own way and had no more time for her. Well, that was okay. There were roads yet to travel, and she was years away from needing a rocking chair and wasting her time with her nose stuck in a book, or some other foolishness they called a hobby.

Alma had been watching people go in and out of the library up the street. Her eyes kept coming back to the shingle above the door on a building halfway between her and the library. She could only read the larger red letters on the sign. REAL ESTATE.

She sipped the last of the wine from her glass and read the tab the waiter had left in a small silver tray on her table. She added a twenty-five percent tip, picked up her purse and walked out to the street.

When she got closer, she could read the names of the realtors and the office hours. They would be open for another hour. She walked into the office and interrupted an overweight white girl talking on her cell phone.

Thirty-five minutes later, she walked back to her condo with an appointment for 9:00 the following morning with a realtor named Douglas Fairbanks, from Fairbanks and Walters Realtors.

Before noon the next day, Alma had signed a contract to sell both her house and her condo, and notified her renter he had thirty days to move or deal with a new owner. That afternoon, she packed up the rest of what she owned, except the furniture and linens, and got Henry to help load them in the van with the ones he had already loaded. She was ready to head down the road early tomorrow morning to Oakwood, Virginia.

Alma was moving to Hanger.

By 6:00 the next morning, Alma was on the road. She had never completely emptied her luggage, and the rest of the clothes and personal items were stored in a box somewhere in the van. She couldn't drive all the way to Oakwood tonight, but she might stop in Roanoke and sponge off Krista for the night.

Krista was excited to see her and catch up on what was happening. They talked long after midnight. Krista was concerned that Alma might be carrying this Sherlock Holmes business a little too far. After all, now one of the suspects was in prison and evidently dangerous. Krista liked the juicy stuff about Alma and Brett. She repeated several times that Alma was crazy if she didn't get her hooks in him while the time was ripe. When Alma told her about the B&B, Krista screamed and lunged over the bed they were lying on to give her a hug. She reminded Alma of the battle they had suffered through when she forced the job of settling the estate on Alma and of her telling Alma then that it might be a good time to retire and search out her roots. Alma now had to agree that it had not been so bad and probably was a good thing to happen at this time in her life, although they both cried at the memory of losing their father and wishing there was no such thing as settling the estate.

19

Alma Finds Diary

Brett was waiting for her on the front porch when she pulled up. She had called him before leaving Roanoke and left a message on his answering machine of her ETA. After a long hug and a longer kiss, he picked her up and carried her into the house and seated her at the table in front of a hot cup of coffee. She protested that they had a van full of boxes to carry in, but he insisted on later. They had some catching up to do. Realizing she wouldn't get any help until he was satisfied he knew everything she did, she began giving him a rundown on her days away.

She sipped on the coffee a minute, then got up from the table and walked into the hallway beside the bathroom and searched behind the curtain that served as a door to the closet. She found one of the four bottles of wine she had stashed between some blankets, retrieved two glasses from the cabinet, and rejoined Brett at the table.

"I think we had better switch to something a little stronger, Brett. I've got some good news and some bad news. Which do you want first?"

"Oh, I don't know. The good news is you're back."

"And the bad news is, FOR GOOD! I put my house and condo and all the furniture up for sale. Everything I own is in boxes in that van out there."

"I think that's great news. What's the bad news?"

Alma told him all. That Brian had found Grady Bracken's son Larkin and she was planning to see him in the next few days.

After they got all the boxes carried in, Alma realized most of the things would have to stay in the boxes, as she lacked storage space. She had Brett help her string a clothesline in the back bedroom. She found some hangers in the pile of discards to be given away or dumped and hung up most of her clothes. Brett begged to spend the night, but Alma told him maybe later in the week because she wanted to contact Jill and see what they could do about visiting Larkin at the prison. She also needed to visit her aunts and get in touch with Jeffrey about the house. He reluctantly gave up his argument after she explained she had too much to do. When he was here she wanted to concentrate solely on him.

The next day she called Jill and surprised her with the information on Larkin. Jill didn't know he was in prison or that he had spent a couple of years locked up before. She was willing to go with Alma to see him. They both agreed that Jill should do most of the talking since she knew him better and he was a relative. Alma told Jill about her visit to Marion and the State Hospital. Since everything her Aunt Betty had owned had been picked up by Larkin, they needed to get Larkin to reveal what he had done with her belongings without giving away they knew about the diary. Jill thought for a minute and said she had a plan.

When they got to the prison about noon the next day, they had to fill out a request form to see the prisoner, and he had to agree before they would be admitted. They waited until Larkin signed the form for his cousin to visit with him and still had to wait in line to get into the visiting room. A guard led them to a table where a small long-haired man with a drooping handlebar mustache sat. His appearance caused Jill to turn to Alma with her hand over her mouth in shock.. She hesitated, in fear of meeting her cousin who was now a felon and a prisoner. Alma nudged her with an elbow and placed a hand on the small of her back for support.

"Well, well, if it's not my long-lost cuz, Jill Wills. But you married a Casey, didn't you? I guess Jill Casey sounds better than Jill Wills. I always thought that was a funny name. I reckon old Thomas couldn't come up with nothing else that would have made sense. I don't reckon him and Daddy and Jackson Mullins ever stayed sober long enough to give a second thought on what to name one of their brats. I can't say Larkin Bracken is anything to brag about. Well, don't just stand there. Have a seat and introduce me to your friend. Or, is she a lawyer?"

"Hi, Larkin. This is my friend Alma Woodson. She ain't no lawyer, but you might remember her folks, Elmer and Elaine Woodson, who lived over on Garden Creek. Her daddy used to teach school, and if you had gone on further than the fourth grade, you might have had him for a teacher when he was at Deskins. Our cousin Hester and I both had him for a teacher two years before he moved on to Marvin."

"Yeah, I remember her daddy. It wasn't because he was a teacher, but my daddy talked about him some and pointed him out to me once when I was about ten and we were at a coal miners' strike up at Keen Mountain trying to sell a little liquor. He was there taking pictures, and Daddy said he didn't want to be in any more pictures, and somebody ought to take that camera and throw it in the river. I sneaked up real close, but I never got the chance to grab the camera."

"I didn't know you were locked up until the other day. I went by to get your mother's things after she died, but they said you had already got them. How come you never came to your mother's funeral, Larkin?"

"Well, that's kinda hard to do when you're locked up in jail. Yeah, I was caught running moonshine, and now I won't get out for a few more years. How come you to go get Mommy's things?"

"I didn't go until after you skipped out of Dodge and nobody knew where you went or how to get in touch with you. I thought somebody ought to check and see if everything was all square with the hospital and your mother hadn't left anything personal to hand over to you."

"Hell, there weren't anything but a few items like clothes and her Bible that they took out of a box and threw into a plastic trash bag and gave me. I wouldn't have gone, but Daddy kept after me to go get her things before she died and somebody else got them. But I couldn't just steal them while she was still living. Too bad he kicked the bucket before she did. I guess he thought there might be some money or something valuable that somebody had given her while she was there. She was crazy, you know. I never went to see her but once when she was alive, and she wouldn't talk to me then."

"Would you like me to bring you her Bible, Larkin?"

"Hell, no! Why would I want her Bible? I threw the damn bag in the closet. I guess the rats have chewed it up by now."

"Would you mind giving me permission to go in the house and get a few of Aunt Betty's clothes? My mommy made a lot of her dresses. A few of the old ones were made from feed sacks and would be worth a little money now. I would like to keep some for old time's sake, but I could sell some and give you whatever they bring."

"I don't care what the shit you do with them. There's a key hid in a Skoal's tin over the rafter in the outhouse just to the right of the door, but you will have to feel for it cause you can't see it without climbing up on a ladder or something. And don't get bit by a snake or spider or something. Like I said, the rats or bugs have probably destroyed anything left in the house if it weren't stolen by kids or hunters trampling through the place. The house has been empty for years, Jill, and located up on that mountain, I'd be surprised if it hasn't been burnt to the ground."

"Do you still smoke, Larkin? I brought you some Camels if that's what you still smoke. I don't think anybody ought to smoke now they know it could kill them, but I remember you and your daddy always had one lit up."

"Yeah, I still smoke Camels when I can get them. Who cares what you think? You're gonna die from something. It might as well be something you enjoy. Like drinking. I ain't died yet from that, either. Although I have to admit this place has put a pretty big dent in my habit. How come your friend don't say anything? You scared, or cat got your tongue, Alma?"

"Neither. I just came along to keep Jill company. I figured you two had things to talk about, and it's really none of my business. She has never been in a prison to visit anyone before. Once she found out you were here, she thought she ought to check on you and see if there was anything she could do to help you. As far as me, I would let scum like you rot in hell before I would give you a cigarette to kill you."

"Whoa there, you bitch! Jill, get her out of here before I get another twenty years. Guard! This visit is over. Jill, don't ever bring her back here again. Where's them cigarettes?"

Jill threw them over the table to him and stood up quickly to go. Alma was already on her feet and headed towards the exit.

When they got outside, Jill took Alma's arm and began laughing. "Alma, you have to be the bravest woman I've ever known, or a little bit crazy. I wanted to say the same thing to him, but I would never have had the nerve."

"Jill, I love you, but I hate your uncles and cousin, and I don't really know why. I'm beginning to get the feeling they have been involved in more than running illegal whiskey across state lines. I hope you will help me find some answers, but I understand if you don't want to get involved. They are kin, and you have every right to stop right now."

Jill shook her head and said she was in for the long haul. Since meeting Alma, she now had excitement in her life and had a new friend. The others might be kin, but they weren't close relatives that she loved and cared about, and certainly were not friends. They agreed to meet at the Rainbow Restaurant the next morning for breakfast, then go up to the Bracken house and see what they could find.

"No, wait, Alma. I can't go tomorrow. I have to sub in the elementary school cafeteria. Let's make it the day after."

When she got home, she called Brett to report in. After listening to her story, he said he would be over early that morning and go with them. Alma told him not to come, that she and Jill could take care of it, and there probably wasn't anything to find anyhow.

"From what you have told me and what I know about these mountain homesteads, you may not be able to get to the house. I'll bring my 4-wheelers in case the roads have washed out so badly you can't drive a car up there."

"We can drive as far as we can and walk the rest of the way."

"I'm sure you can. How about snakes and bears?"

"Don't be silly, Brett. Buchanan County doesn't have any bears. Do they?"

He laughed. "No, I was just kidding about the bears, but the place is isolated and has been abandoned for years, and snakes and rats and who knows what could be using it for a den. I know you don't need protection, but I would feel better if I were there to watch you shoot off the head of a rattlesnake. Besides, you have gotten my interest up on this case and I would like to be a part of it."

"Okay, Brett. We are going to meet at the Rainbow at 8:30, day after tomorrow, for breakfast. If you aren't there when we get ready to leave, then you'll have to find your own way."

He was there, 4-wheelers and all, when she pulled into the parking lot of the restaurant. Alma introduced him to Jill. Of course, he charmed her socks off right away. After they ate and had an extra cup of coffee and Jill told him about how brave Alma had been at the prison, they all loaded up in the Hummer and headed up towards Deskins.

Sure enough, a few hundred yards past the last house in the hollow, the road was impassable. Brett left the Hummer parked in the road and unloaded the 4-wheelers. He let Jill double up with him, and they picked their way around fallen trees and large rocks and a couple of places where the bank had slid down to cover half the road. Small brush and scrubby trees were growing in scattered spots along the way, but the 4-wheelers rode them down. It was at least three-quarters of a mile from where they parked the truck to the house.

Surprisingly, the windows were still intact and the doors still on their hinges and locked. Brett pointed out several places on the roof where the rusty tin had blown away or bent back to expose rafters underneath. After walking around the house and checking for vandalism, Brett spotted the outhouse and went to retrieve the key. He found the door open and hanging by one hinge. Looking in, he spotted a hornet's nest in the corner near the roof, but there were none flying around. This time of year, it was too cold for bugs and snakes, but he wasn't going to tell Alma. He tested the floor with his foot before stepping in. A board cracked and part of it fell into the hole. Nobody should set foot into this pitfall, he decided. Walking to the upper side, he leaned into the building and felt it give, so he picked up a broken tree branch and pushed it over. With a loud crash, it tumbled to the ground and broke apart. In just a short time, he found the Skoal can underneath one of the broken boards. The can was so rusty he couldn't read the name of the tobacco that it once contained, and he couldn't twist the lid off. He shook the tin and could hear something rattle around inside, so he took his pocket knife and punched a hole in the lid and widened it enough that the key fell out. It, too, had deteriorated, but he thought with a little oil from the dipstick on the 4-wheeler, it might open the lock on the door of the house. He didn't know why it would matter; he could probably push in the door as easily as he had pushed over the outhouse. But then again, the key would eliminate charges of breaking and entering.

Alma and Jill had heard the crash of the outhouse and ran around from the front of the house to check on the cause. Alma was relieved that Brett was safe and sound and holding up the key. She was also glad he had talked her into letting him come along. With a little work on the key, Brett unlocked the front door and they entered the house.

The two women were close behind Brett as he made his way across rough and broken flooring. Again, he tested the boards before putting his full weight on them. Being under cover for the most part, and with the windows and doors closed, the floor was pretty stable. Small animals had been using the place. He spotted a couple of mice darting out of sight as they entered a bedroom. The whole house contained only three rooms on the first floor, with a living room, bedroom, and kitchen. The attic had been converted into a second bedroom, or, in this case, a mattress on the floor with wooden shelves nailed on the walls for storage.

Alma opened two folding wooden doors to reveal a small closet. There were a few shirts, pants, and homemade dresses hanging on a wooden rod and several bags piled on the floor. She picked up the only plastic trash bag and dumped the contents on the bed. There was the Bible, a few Christmas cards from the staff at the Institute, a few pieces of cheap jewelry and hair pins, a red sweater, two dresses, a robe, and a white towel with something wrapped up in it. With a quick look at Jill, Alma unwrapped the towel and found a small journal-type book with the letters BB written with black ink or markers.

Alma stepped back and looked at Jill and waited. After a moment of hesitation, Jill walked over and picked up the family Bible and the journal. She tucked the Bible underneath her arm, handed the journal to Alma, and placed all the other contents back into the bag and returned it to the closet. Without a word passing between them, they followed Jill out of the house, got on the 4-wheelers and let Brett lead them down the mountain.

After they dropped Jill off to get her car and she hugged each of them goodbye, Alma asked Brett if he would spend the night. She told him she wanted to dwell on the journal, but she was afraid to read it while alone. Of course he was happy to oblige. He had left a few clothes and toilet items weeks before and, not knowing if he was going to be invited to stay or forced to leave, he was always prepared. They stopped for dinner at the Black Stallion Café, and soon after they had gotten into the house, Alma changed into her pajamas and stretched out on the sofa next to Brett with the diary. He let her snuggle in close with her head resting on his chest and his arm around her shoulders. Alma read aloud for a while and then he took over for a few pages.

Betty Bracken revealed how she had started her journal three years after being admitted to the Institute, with the encouragement of her counselor Janice Atwater. They had written the first dozen or so pages together so Betty could get comfortable before making it a true diary and finishing it alone. As she was learning how to write down her life story, Betty described her growing up years in Kentucky and working on the family farm and helping to take care of six younger sisters and brothers. The generic terms and situations she wrote about could have been those of anyone growing up shortly after the Depression of the thirties. It wasn't until later in the book, and when she was obviously alone, that she revealed startling details about her own family, her husband Grady and her son Larkin.

      Betty's life changed rapidly after she met and married Grady Bracken. They moved from her family farm in Ivel, Kentucky, to the thirty-acre mountaintop plot at Deskins, Virginia. She had dreams as a teenage wife of raising a family and having a home of her own. Grady was twelve years older and she had accepted his assurance that he would take care of her and make her happy. Little did she know that her happy days were over? In less than a year, she had Larkin and found herself pretty much alone on the mountain trying to raise enough in a vegetable garden to feed the family and can up to get through the winter. Grady was seldom home, and, when he was, he was drinking and abusive. He worked for wages only a few weeks at a time. The only money he gave her was to buy sugar for his still and a little feed for the hog and milk cow. She was expected to make her and the family's clothes from the feed sacks and whatever she could barter for among the families down the hollow. Grady did let her take Larkin to church once a month until he got old enough to run with his daddy. That was where she met the only friends she had and where she found some peace and hope.

Grady let Larkin drop out of school when he was in the fourth grade. There was nothing Betty could do to change his mind. He insisted it was time the boy learned how to work and help the family make a living. Book work was not going to put food on the table. Someday, the boy would have to know how to take care of his own family. Betty got her face slapped and lost another tooth when she said the boy could take care of his own family a lot better if he got an education.

She left the family once and ran away. With no money, she walked almost to Grundy and stole a night in a barn, crying herself sick over her baby. The next day, she walked back home and Grady and Larkin never knew she had left. They were gone for almost a week before they came stomping into the house, waving fistfuls of money in her face, and declaring themselves rich. Betty knew it would all be gone in a few days, some for buying more ingredients for the still and some lost in gambling and buying drinks for his friends.

Alma let Brett read on for a while. She walked into the kitchen to make them a pot of coffee. She brought back a box of tissues. She tried not to think of Betty as someone she knew, but as a stranger going through hard times with an abusive husband, as many other wives had done before her and many would do as long as evil men were rulers and masters of their home. But Alma did know Betty, and she knew some of her family who were good, like Jill.

Alma's own father had once taken her husband's picture that might be proof of how evil the man had been. The woman had not been crazy. She had been shredded.

Once the coffee was ready, Alma got each of them a cup and put milk and two spoons of sugar in Brett's, just the way she knew he liked it. No wonder the man was always wired up and ready to go. It was well after midnight, as she noticed the time on the stove reading 1:22 AM. She placed his cup on the end table, retrieved the book from him, and picked up where he had left off.

Betty's story went on page after page after page. The tragic life she had lived with Grady and Larkin was detailed and exposed the slave-like treatment she had received from both of the men. Larkin had become almost as cruel to her as his father and would not hesitate to slap her around if he didn't get what he wanted. As time went on, she realized she could never leave the mountain and what little home she knew. Her own family had abandoned her when Grady had threatened to shoot them if they ever came back to see her. A few years later, her niece, Jill Wills, had told her about reading of her parents' death in the obituary column of the newspaper. Betty had received one last letter from her oldest sister telling how her parents had died about eight months apart of heart failure. All the children had sold their place and moved to Ohio to get jobs in the automobile industry.

All of her time was not unhappy on the mountain. Grady and Larkin were often gone for days at a time. She enjoyed working in the garden and tending to her flowers. The men did kill a hog and a cow every winter because they liked to eat when they were home, and she had a smokehouse with salted pork. Grady had arranged with Jackson Mullins down the hollow to store the beef in his freezer for half the meat. Jill would sneak books to her, which she had to keep hidden. Sometimes, she would take one to the overlook out on the ridge and read for hours when she knew she would have a day to herself.

Betty had learned to manage her days at the Institute, also. Grady and Larkin seldom came by, but when they did she would fake not being in the real world. She would sit in the rocker, wrapped in a blanket, and stare out the window. She refused to speak even when Grady would yell and curse her. Once he slapped her, but she never responded. When the caretaker came to tell them it was time to leave, she noticed the red mark on her cheek, and failing to get Grady to admit what had happened, she informed him that he would not be permitted to visit alone with Betty anymore. He never came back.

Jill and her counselor, Janice, were the only two people to whom Betty would open up. With Jill, she kept the conversation on books they were reading or the more pleasant memories of family relationships. She liked talking about Larkin as a baby or when the cow got out of the field and she had to chase it all over the mountain to get it penned back up before Grady got home. Early on, she would let Janice read what she had written in her diary and ask what she shouldn't have written or what she ought to mark out. When Janice told her to write whatever she wanted, and that nobody would be reading it unless she wanted them to, Betty got personal and detailed in her narrative. She wrote that if she died in the Institute she didn't care who read her diary, but she hoped someone would before Grady got hold of it and burned it.

Alma smiled, knowing that Grady had died before his wife and never knew of the book. Even Larkin never knew what he had. If either one of them had cared a little about Betty, they would have perhaps looked in the Bible to see if she had entered the baby's name and birthday as part of the family tree. Jill would now check that out and take care of the Bible as the only material thing left of Betty's life. Alma would do the same with the journal.

"SHIT!" Alma screamed as she frantically turned empty white pages in the book. Brett jumped when she yelled out and leaned over her shoulder to try to see what her problem was.

"Hold on there, Alma. Slow down a little or you're going to tear the pages out. What's wrong?"

"That's it, Brett. There are no more pages. She just quit right there. I can't believe she would go this far and just stop. She was on a roll, and she wanted to tell everything. I know she did."

Alma was trembling with rage and frustration. Tears were welling up in her eyes as she tore at the book. Brett held her tight with one arm as he eased the journal out of her hands. Caressing her shoulders with one hand, he turned to the empty pages with the other. After turning from written pages to empty ones several times, he discovered that pages were missing and Betty had not just quit writing.

"Look here, Alma. She didn't just quit. There are pages torn out. Look at the binding. There are ragged edges left where pages have been ripped out. Look back at the written ones and see how she had numbered the pages. The last page is numbered 27 and the first empty page is numbered 34. She must have filled the last page she wrote and had numbered the next page where she would pick up again later."

Alma grabbed the book and examined it closely. With a heavy sigh, she slammed it closed and leaned her head back into Brett's shoulder. Several minutes later, she wiped her eyes and looked into his.

"Larkin must have found the journal and tore out the pages. I'm sure he destroyed them, but somehow I'm going to make him tell me what she wrote. Can I take him to court for destruction of property and concealing evidence?"

"I doubt you would have a case, Alma. First of all, it would now be his property. We don't know if there was any evidence of criminal behavior in the journal unless it would be abusing his wife. And that would be Grady, not Larkin."

"Well, I'm going to find out, if I have to wait until the bastard serves his time and gets out of prison. Then, I'll grab him and torture him until I get the truth."

"That's what I would do, Alma. When you get your hands on him, he will wish he was back in prison."

She saw the twinkle in his eye. She smiled in spite of herself.

"Let's go to bed, Brett. I'm exhausted. I'll decide later what my next step will be. But first, I'm going to take my aunts to church tomorrow. Why don't you come along?"

"The roof would fall in if I stepped into the church. I think God wrote me off years ago as one of the lost. You go ahead, and tell Paula and Ellie I said, 'Hi'. Maybe we could meet up at the Black Stallion for lunch."

Alma could tell it would take desperate action to get him near organized religion. She had been much the same only a few years ago. She couldn't say she had ever been comfortable until recently, in Aunt Paula's church. She still thought they were old-fashioned, with prehistoric habits, but they were comfortable. She would have to put on her pity face.

"Brett, I really need you to be with me. You are the only other one who knows what I know, and I don't think I'm strong enough to handle this by myself just yet. Couldn't you stay a couple of days and hold me up when I fall apart? You could go with us and stay in the car and read a book, or make a few hundred of those phone calls you are plagued with."

He looked into those big chestnut brown eyes and knew he would go along. He just hoped she wouldn't make him sit through the service. Attending a funeral was almost more religion than he could take.

"Okay. If I can stay over. Do I have to go out and buy a suit and tie for this, even though I will sit in the car?"

"Of course not. Aunt Paula's church will take you as you come. I'll throw in a couple of Superman comic books for you to read. Dad kept a bunch, and I'll bet some of them are worth a lot of money."

"I'll buy them from you if you want to sell?"

"Just hold on. You wouldn't take advantage of an illiterate comic book owner, would you?" Alma took his hand and led him to bed. It had been a long night. With daylight seeping into the hollow, she thought they might now get a little sleep. After her adrenaline and blood pressure had returned to near normal, she felt very tired. She would leave getting him into church to her aunts. He didn't stand a chance.

20

ROMEO Club

      The next day, Sunday, Alma and Brett picked up her aunts and drove to the Big Prater Primitive Baptist Church. Alma had called the night before and Aunt Paula insisted they come early for breakfast. Alma thought it very unhealthy to eat all that fatty food, but Brett loved it. He chowed down on country ham, biscuits and gravy, and more buttered biscuits with homemade applesauce. He not only had coffee, orange juice, and a large glass of milk, but he tried a small glass of buttermilk. When Alma tasted it and gagged, he laughed and told her his favorite snack at his grandmother's had been a glass of buttermilk and cornbread with a big slice of onion. They finally got him away from the table. Alma loaded the dishes in the dishwasher while Aunt Paula pulled off her apron, touched up her hair, and put on her hat and coat. They picked up Aunt Ellie who was dressed equally as well as Aunt Paula. Alma whispered to Brett that old people still liked to dress up for Sunday service.

When they got to church, they visited a while and Alma introduced Brett around. Jill came running over and gave all of them a big hug. Aunt Paula had Brett carry her food basket into the kitchen. When he rejoined them in the parking lot, Alma took his arm and steered him back towards the church. He resisted and whispered to her that he was going back to read those comic books. She smiled, released his arm and walked towards the front door. She looked over her shoulder to find Aunt Paula on one of his arms and Aunt Ellie on the other. Both of them were talking to him in a low, but serious, tone. Alma seated herself halfway across the pew, allowing room for the others. She leaned across Aunt Ellie to smile at Brett and shrugged her shoulders as if to say it was out of her hands. His scowl said, 'I'll deal with you later'.

Alma noticed he didn't join in the singing as she now did, but he smiled when he shook hands with the congregation as they milled around during the singing. He escaped during the handshaking after the second preacher had finished. Alma felt pleased that he had stayed that long. Brother Myers, the third preacher, was just into his low 'finding-the-spirit warm–up' when Brett tiptoed back across the toes of the ladies on the outside of the bench and reclaimed his seat. Alma thought the preacher did a good job talking about the love of a father who gave his sons all he had. Even after one of them left to travel the world and wasted all he had been given, he returned to find his father welcoming him home with a feast fit for a king. The preacher spoke of the love of those that 'had', and their giving and caring for those that 'had not'. It was a touching sermon. When Brother

Myers got into the spirit and the tears started flowing, it seemed the whole congregation had their handkerchiefs or tissues pressed to their eyes and noses.

After the service, Brett didn't put up any resistance to being led by her aunts into the kitchen and dining area and filling his paper plate with huge helpings of fried chicken, country ham biscuits, potato salad, green beans, corn-on-the-cob, and banana pudding, and a large cup of iced tea. Alma and her aunts joined him at a rough, hand-made picnic table with much smaller plates.

Aunt Ellie asked him if he enjoyed the service and he replied he did.

"Where did you go during the service?" Alma couldn't resist asking.

"Well, if you must know, I had to go to the restroom."

"Well, if you hadn't drunk five glasses of beverages with your breakfast this morning, you might have made it through the whole service."

They all laughed at Brett's discomfort, but he kept right on eating. Several people came by to tell him how glad they were to see him and hoped he would come back again. While Alma and her aunts were helping to clean up and pack up, she noticed him standing off in the corner of the parking lot talking with a couple of other guys, and they were laughing good-naturedly about something. With this group, Alma was sure it was all about hunting or fishing or some male thing. They didn't usually loosen up that much if a woman was in the midst.

On the way home, Brett asked why the church didn't play musical instruments when singing.

Aunt Paula tried to explain, "It's just the way Primitive Baptists are, Brett. We don't sing for the enjoyment of others as much as to praise the Lord. Some of us probably shouldn't be singing at all with our voices. But, with the preacher lining the song and it being slow, all of us can join in, even the very old."

"Well, I rather liked it. I have heard them singing before, of course, at funerals, but I thought maybe at church they would have a piano or guitar or something. Why don't they pass a collection plate around?"

"Sometimes we pass a hat if there is something the church needs or one of the members is in a pinch. All our churches are small and are usually built and maintained by the members. Our preachers don't preach for a living. They have other jobs and this is a calling. Sometimes they don't preach, but sit in the pulpit and offer encouragement to the others or lead the songs."

"Well, I don't understand why you don't need bigger churches with the food you ladies bring."

They smiled and reached over the back of the seat to pat him on the shoulder as he drove them home.

Two weeks before Christmas, Alma woke to find the ground covered in snow. It was beautiful. She took a walk up the road with her camera to take pictures of pine tree branches, bending low towards the ground, laden with puffy white snow. The rocks in the creek above the water line had white caps that reminded her of the skull caps worn in certain religions, with their heads bowed in prayer. She walked to the end of the road, taking several pictures. She captured the brilliant red of a Cardinal perched on a green pine limb covered in snow. As she walked back down the hollow, she remembered the times she and her sisters and brother had ridden sleds and tubes down this road when there was a good snowfall, and how they sometimes ran into the creek, frozen into ice, if a vehicle should come along. She wondered if Brett came by and brought sleighs, would they still have the ability to ride down the hollow without breaking every bone in their bodies. She would probably risk hitting a car rather than turning over the bank into the creek.

    The next morning, while she was sitting at the table sipping her coffee and wondering if she ought to tackle her dad's files again, it hit her that today was Wednesday. Didn't Brett say that the 'whatchamacallit' club met on Wednesday mornings at the Dairy Queen near Grundy? She rushed to the bathroom with her cup of coffee and took a quick shower. She would let her hair finish drying on the way.

    It was a little after seven when she took her sausage biscuit and coffee to a booth near a table where three men were seated. They all looked to be from seventy years old and up. They were eating gravy and biscuits and drinking coffee. As she nibbled on her biscuit, she listened to them talk. Although her seat was several feet away, she could make out all of their conversation. A few minutes later two more, older gentlemen, came in, then another one shortly after that. It didn't take long before she knew each one's name. They would call one another by their first name as they asked a question, demanded their opinion on a specific point of view, or when a newcomer walked in.

"Hey, Max! Pull up a chair and take a load off." Larry kicked a chair out a little bit from the other side of the table. Max was carrying his coffee and a sausage biscuit on a tray and he had to put it on the table before he could grab the chair and sit down. Larry was a little bit younger than the rest of them, but he had the biggest mouth. Still, anybody over seventy ought to know when to keep his trap shut and let it rest awhile.

"What do you say, Max? Should the government run our health care and provide a public option for everybody? Or, do you agree with Carson over there who says the government can't run squat and we ought to kick the whole bunch out of office?"

"I didn't say kick them all out. If you do that you have to put somebody else in that makes up his mind how to vote, no matter what's right or wrong, before he's even sworn in. They don't vote on the issues. They vote with their party. When you're the man, then all the other side votes 'No'. When they're the man, you vote 'No'. Hell of a strategy for getting nothing done."

Alma learned later, after she had made friends with Maxwell Shoemaker and earned his trust a little bit, that Carson had retired as a teacher and football coach. "He was good, too. He only had two losing seasons in his thirty years of coaching. He's been out now nearly 15 years. The new group that has taken his place hasn't had two winning seasons. He was a tough nut. He believed in everyone on the team knowing what to do and then getting it done. He held his coaches meeting on the weekend, and nobody went home until they agreed on what and how the practice week was going to go. Another coach could vote *no* on his plan, but he'd *better* have a better one ready."

"Well, Larry, I don't know that I would vote against Carson here. His record is a little hard to question."
"Hell, I didn't say anything about voting, Max. We're just giving our opinion on this mess we're in."
"I kinda like the health care plan I have. Of course, it's a public option plan just like all the rest of you have. Now, I could say the rest of the country ain't entitled to it because they ain't earned it like we did. But I reckon most of the country is doing exactly what we did. They are working and paying their taxes and their social security, that may not be secured, and waiting until they retire and get on the public option."
"But the country is broke, Max. The Chinese owns us now, and I don't think they are going to pay for everyone's health care."
"They don't have to, Larry. Nobody pays for my car insurance. And I don't pay for theirs. Why can't health insurance be the same way?" Brody said.

Max later filled Alma in on Brody, too. "He's probably in his mid-eighties, but Brody drives his Cadillac down to the Dairy Queen every Wednesday morning. He had been a football coach, too. But only for a few years. He did the smart thing and got into coal mining and hired all his former players to run the mines. Nobody knew how much Brody was worth. But, except for the Caddie, he looks and talks like the rest of us."

"What are you talking about, Brody? We're talking about health insurance. Everybody that owns a car has to have insurance. That ain't true for health."

"I think that's what he is trying to tell you, Larry. Maybe if everyone paid for health insurance then it wouldn't cost so much for anyone. A lot of people have a public option. They just choose not to buy insurance and show up at the emergency room and let the public, the ones paying for insurance, foot the bill."

Max said that Tommy usually offered his two cents worth but you had to sometimes wait for it. "Tommy and Ed are two of them who worked for Brody. He's in his late sixties, but he wheezes and coughs a lot. He's been on Black Lung benefits for about ten years. Ed has only started joining us since his wife died a couple of months ago." Like most of the miners, Tommy didn't have to worry about health insurance. The union workers had the best coverage in the country, and the non-union workers had just as good because the owners didn't want a union vote as long as they could keep them out. The only problem now was all the coal companies didn't want to offer coverage to retirees and the union wasn't strong enough to hold that benefit.

"Well, I guess you're right, Tommy. If we all paid our share, then it shouldn't be so hard on any. But then you got the insurance companies that have to get rich and keep their million-dollar bonuses."

"Not if there is a public option with a lower premium. And if companies can't make a justifiable decision, that's where regulators come in."

"Well, I'm glad we got that all taken care of. How come you are late this morning, Max?"

"I was just watching over the house, Brody. I wanted to make sure it would still be there when I got back."

"Where's the damn thing going? Ain't it got a concrete foundation?"

Everyone laughed a little at Larry's wise-assed comment. Alma could tell that Max wished he was twenty years younger so he could just wade in and cut a little of that long tongue down to size.

"Well, I don't reckon it's going anywhere, Larry. But if I don't take good care of it and myself, I might."

"I thought you owned your house."

"I do. Have any of you been down to the home to see Charlie, recently?"

"What's the use? Charlie wouldn't know it if you did."

"I know, Carson. But my kids took me by last week, and you're right. Charlie doesn't know his ass from a hole in the ground. They didn't admit it, but I'm sure the sole reason for the trip was to introduce me to all the great advantages and benefits offered at the Grandeur."

"You ain't signed nothing or give up your checkbook yet, have you?"

"Hell, no, Larry! They haven't asked outright for anything. I just been getting this crazy feeling they want to take care of me and that means seeing that I'm taken care of."

"You got that right, Max. I think we're all doing a good job taking care of ourselves. If any one of us needed anything, all he'd need to do is give one or all of us a call, and we'd be there. You give up what's yours and you ain't nobody anymore."

"Take Charlie. Do you'all remember him from last summer?"

"Yeah!"

"Yeah, Ed."

"If he knows you, he won't acknowledge you. Now, I don't think he knows himself."

"Better watch out if you run into one of his kids on the street. They can't understand why you haven't been by to see him lately. Oh yeah, and this is the second time they have been in town in the last three months."

"I can't say you guys are doing a hell of a lot for my mood. I was just a little nervous after visiting Charlie, with my kids. They ain't going to do anything. At least not yet. They brag on me to most everyone we visit, on how much I do and how they

wished I would slow down a little. When I can't walk up the hollow twice a day, tend my garden, and get down here to be harassed by you guys, then one of you just hit me on the head with a hammer."

They all laughed and asked for the same good deed. Tommy got up to leave. The rest of them finished their coffee and followed suit.

Alma dumped the rest of her breakfast into the trash and caught up with Max as he was opening the door to his truck. Being Elmer Woodson's daughter might be just enough to get a word in.

"Hi. I'm sorry to bother you. I'm Elmer Woodson's daughter, and I wondered if you knew him?"

"Why, yes. I reckon about everybody knew Elmer. He used to come here once in awhile and join us for a cup of coffee. I'm glad we didn't talk about him today since you were listening in."

Alma blushed a little, but she extended her hand. These old codgers didn't miss much.

"I'm Alma Woodson. Would you mind if I asked you a few questions?"

"I'm Max. Are you a reporter or a cop, Ms. Woodson?"

"Oh, no! I'm neither. I am here to try to settle my father's estate. In going through his papers, I ran across a note about that Charlie you all were talking about, and your name was mentioned. I would just like to meet and talk a little with some of the people that knew my father."

"Well, I'll tell you what, Ms. Woodson. Next week, I'll sit with you and have my coffee, and we'll have a little chat. I don't know that any of my two cents worth is worth you wasting your time. Right now, I've got to get home. I'm a little tired, and I have a routine you know."

"That would be fine, Mr. Shoemaker. But I would hate to take up your time with your buddies on Wednesday morning. Do you know my Aunt Ellie?"

"Yeah, I know Ellie. Your dad once told me he and Elaine couldn't have raised you four kids if his wife's sisters hadn't pitched in and helped. But I don't recall me telling you my last name."

"Oh, I know your name from the article my dad wrote about Charlie. Would you rather I called you Max?"

"Please. It's been so long since I've been called Mr. Shoemaker, I might not realize someone is talking to me."

"Okay Max. I was just going to suggest I fix one of Aunt Ellie's recipes and bring it to your house for dinner. You know, sorta pay you back a little for sharing some information about my dad, when I wasn't around."

"I guess that would be alright. Tomorrow afternoon about 3:00. I don't like eating very late in the day. Just turn up Deskins. I'm in the white house with the green roof just after you cross the bridge."

Alma thanked him and promised to be there. She watched him start up his truck and look several times before he backed up slowly and pulled out of the parking lot. She hated to barge in on the ROMEO Club, but some of these guys would be close to her father's age and might have some valuable information. She was anxious to see how tomorrow would go.

Alma spent most of the next morning trying to decide what to fix for Max's dinner. She first brought out the recipe for baked spaghetti. After reading it over, she decided rich, spicy food might not go well for someone nearly ninety years old. Max might have acid reflux or stomach problems. She chose recipe after recipe and rejected them all. Finally, she settled on the Appalachian standard. She fixed a pot of pinto beans, adding two spoons of peanut butter, a skillet of cornbread, fried white sweet potatoes, corn on the cob, a small jar of sweet pickles, and a bowl of banana pudding. Max would have enough left over for a couple more meals if he wished.

When she knocked on his door, she was surprised to hear him holler "Come in" instead of opening the door for her. After all, she had her arms full. She managed the door and saw the kitchen table just beyond the living room, where he was sitting back in a recliner.

"Just put the food on the table in the kitchen, Alma."

Alma felt like tossing it in his lap. He obviously saw her, through the window, park her car and lug the box filled with pots and bowls up to the house. The least he could have done was open the door for her.

When she had deposited the food on the table, she made her way back to the living room and the sofa opposite his recliner. That's when she saw the bandage on his head and the ice pack he gingerly held to his head for a second or two at a time.

"Max! What has happened? Did you fall?"

"Oh, sit back down, Alma. I banged my head and the doctor said to hold this ice to the knot to help the swelling, but it freezes my brain."

"The doctor? Did you have to go to the doctor? Did they put stitches in? How bad, and how did you hurt your head?"

"If you'll calm down, I'll tell you all about it. I wrecked my truck on the way home yesterday from the Dairy Queen. If you're hungry you can go ahead and eat, but I think I'll just sit here a bit first."

"Oh, no, I'm not hungry. We can heat up a plate for you later when you're ready. Tell me what happened."

"I was about six miles from the restaurant towards my house. I was almost here when I saw the green Buick come around the curve on my side of the road. I blew my horn and moved over to the edge as close as I dared when the Buick struck the left side of my truck just about the rear wheel. I was already laying on the brake, but I couldn't hold it from slipping over the side of the embankment and coming to a sudden stop against a fallen tree about twenty feet down from the road.

"I remember striking my head against the door jamb and falling over in the seat, so I must not have blacked out. Anyway, the next thing I knew, there's this crazy woman standing up in the road screaming her head off."

"Mister! Hey, Mister! Are you alright? Can you hear me? I've called 911 and help is on the way."

HANGER

"She must have stopped the next vehicle coming by because in just a minute two young men were trying to open my door on the driver's side.

"I heard one of them say, *He's moving his head, Robert. I think he's alive and trying to sit up.*

"I said, *of course I'm alive*. I asked them if they could just move the seat back a little and help me out of there.

"The same one said, *I don't know, Mister. I don't think you ought to move until the rescue squad gets here. You might have something broken.*

"I told them there wasn't anything broken. That I had just banged my head a little, and to get me the hell out of there, and that the old truck might blow up any minute.

"Now there wasn't enough gas in the tank to blow out a candle, but it got them moving. In just a minute they had the seat moved back and was pulling me out through the driver's door.

"One of them said, *"Mister, you had better lie down here until help comes. There's blood on your face and hair and we don't know how bad you're hurt.*

"I reached up and felt the knot on my head. I felt the sticky gob in my hair, and when I pulled my hand away it was covered in blood. I reached around and dug my big red bandana out of my back pocket and pressed it to the sore spot on my head. After a few seconds, I pulled it away and found the bleeding had about stopped. I guess the blood that had dripped down on my face had scared them boys pretty good.

"I told them that I thought the bleeding had about stopped, and if they would help me up the hill, we'd see if that crazy woman was alright.

"The one called Robert said, *We ain't moving you anywhere until the rescue squad gets here. We may be in trouble already for moving you out of the truck.*

"It was only a few more minutes until I heard the sirens. A State Trooper and two county deputies scooted down the hill and started throwing out questions faster than firecrackers going off on the 4th of July. I explained I was alright and, if they would just help me up to the road, we could call a wrecker and get my truck pulled into a shop somewhere and get it fixed. They insisted I lie still until the paramedics arrived. Then they started checking out the damage to my truck.

"Don't you want something to drink, Alma?"
"No, thank you, Max. What happened next?"

"Well, to make a long story short, the police questioned the woman and found out she was talking on her cell phone when she crossed the line and hit me. The skid marks in the road proved I was in my lane and she had drifted over when her car struck my truck. I think they gave her a ticket, but she was a good-looking woman. Anyhow, she said her insurance would pay to get my truck fixed. They loaded me up in the ambulance and took me to the emergency room, where they sewed me up with seven stitches and released me."

"Seven Stitches! That wreck could have killed you, Max."

"Well, it didn't, and you're starting to sound a lot like Sally."

"Who's Sally?"

"She's my daughter. Anyway, Kenny, my son, and Sally came bursting into the hospital about the same time. At first, I thought they were concerned about my health. When they found out I was stitched up and all the blood was washed off my head and face, with just a bit still staining my shirt, they lit into me about driving every week down to that restaurant just to jaw with a bunch of guys.

"Sally said, *Dad, if you have to go down there, why don't you call me and I will drive you?*

"I told her the guys would laugh me out of the building. The only one that has to be driven in is poor old Tommy. He has to stay hooked up to his oxygen and he's not driven in a dozen years. I don't know if he still has a vehicle.

"She said, *I would think it would be better to be laughed at than having your head busted in a car wreck.*

"I told her that the wreck wasn't my fault. That the woman was charged with causing the accident.

"Sally said, *I don't care whose fault it was, Dad. You're almost ninety years old, and it's time to give up driving your old truck. You're going to kill yourself or somebody else. I promise to take you wherever you want to go. Please give me the keys.*

"I told her they were in the truck, and I would appreciate her crawling down that hill and getting them for me."

Alma smiled. She sat back on the couch. She was beginning to enjoy the story. Max had a way of telling a tale. He even sounded like a young agitated daughter trying to reason with her father when he quoted Sally.

"Kenny told me they'd already towed the truck to Mack's garage and I asked him to get them to tow it to his place. I think he can get it fixed up in no time. He's a real good mechanic. I wasn't going very fast and I think it just slid over the hill and into that log.
"He asked if I was ready to go and if I wanted to ride home with him or Sally?
"Sally said, *He's going home with me, Ken. I think it would be good if he were to lie down for a spell.*
"I told Kenny I'd ride with him. I didn't want to take another chance with a woman in an automobile, and I told her that. Imagine Sally talking about my driving. She's had three accidents in the last five years. I haven't had three accidents in the last fifty years.
"Sally stormed out of the hospital. I don't reckon I blame her. I didn't have to get so mean and say that about her driving. She's really a pretty good driver. I taught her myself. It's just, if you don't make them mad enough, they just keep coming on. I'm not worried about hurting myself, and if I thought

I would hurt somebody else, I would gladly give up the driving. I just think the short distance I drive I can handle just fine. I don't drive on the interstate or nothing. I just drive around here to the doctor, store, church, and the restaurant. I'd just give up buying groceries if I had to call Sally every time I needed something."

When Max finished telling about his accident, Alma went into the kitchen and heated a plate of food in the microwave and brought it to his chair on a tray. He put up a fuss and said he could walk to the table. She returned the food to the kitchen, and sure enough, he made it to his seat at the table without even the help of a cane. She was surprised at his agility and the fact the lick on the head didn't seem to be any more than what he had said; a cut with seven stitches and maybe a headache. That was also when he filled her in on some of the guys who met at the Dairy Queen. It appeared she had read Larry right, but Max and the others didn't mind his big mouth. It seemed Larry kept the pot boiling when the conversation got bogged down.

She told him she would stay and put away the remainder of the food and wash the dishes, but she would come back another day and let him fill her in on the life of her father. He agreed that might be good, but he was capable of cleaning up the table. He thanked her for the food and asked if it really was one of her Aunt Ellie's recipes. She smiled and said no, that it was just a meal she remembered eating when she was a young girl.

21

Christmas

A few days later, Brett did show up. He brought her a seven-foot Fraser Fir Christmas tree that barely fit under the ceiling. The smell of pine refreshed the aroma of a house long closed up, even though Alma had opened windows and doors on several occasions before the weather got cold.

They made a trip to Wal-Mart in Richlands and spent the day buying lights and ornaments for the tree, and gifts. Alma wanted to mail a Christmas gift to each of her siblings this year instead of mailing a small check as she had done in the past. Her excuse had been lack of time and not knowing what to get them. She still didn't know what they would want, but it didn't matter. She wanted the joy of choosing an individual gift for a special person in her life. There were cousins who still lived in Buchanan County and, of course, Aunt Paula and Aunt Ellie. She wanted to get Jill something, and Lori deserved more than just a tip when she ate at the Black

Stallion. She bought a gift each for Leslie and her sisters. After loading Brett up and sending him packing to the car one last time, she asked him to stay put and relax while she made one last stop for her aunts. She had already bought their gifts, so when he was out of sight she dashed across the street to a jewelry store she had noticed earlier. In thirty-five minutes, she left the store with the twenty-dollar gold piece from her collection mounted in a gold casing, engraved 'To Brett, the man who returned my life', hanging on an expensive eighteen-inch gold chain.

They ate at a steak house on the way home. While Brett pigged out, she had a grilled chicken salad and water. He reminded her to leave him home next Christmas. He was exhausted, but he liked the glow in her cheeks and the twinkle in her eyes. When they got home, it was too late to start on the tree or gift wrapping, so they poured a glass of wine, wrapped up in blankets, and took folding chairs out on the deck to do a little star gazing. It was pitch black and the stars were brilliant and hypnotic. Occasionally, they would spot a satellite slowly working its way across the southern sky. In Buchanan County, you had to lay your head back and look straight up as though looking up a chimney; otherwise, you would be looking into the side of a hill. Brett moved his chair close and let her lean her head back on his arm to take the stress off her neck. They didn't talk much. Shortly, Alma could feel the warmth and soothing effects of the wine. As she took in the wonders of the universe, she didn't think she was in Heaven, but maybe she could see it from here.

Brett tried to talk her into going to New York for Christmas and watching the ball fall in Times Square on New Year's Eve. She told him another time, another Christmas she would consider just that, but this year she wanted to spend it with what relatives and friends she had in, what might be, her new home. He reminded her, this was her old home, and her new one would be built up in the garden. She laughed. She told him about Max and his ROMEO Club meeting at the Dairy Queen down at Grundy. She got up from her chair and flipped on the outside light and showed him the picture her dad had made of the group and the article he had written about Charlie.

"I know this bunch of guys, Alma. In fact, I've drunk coffee with them at the DQ a few times. Charlie used to be there, too. I remember my dad talking about what a great football player he was."

"I'm going to meet Max again and try to squeeze his brain a little about the old days, especially anything involving my father."

She told him that tomorrow she was going to call Leslie and set up a meeting with her and her sisters. She wanted to give them their Christmas gifts and relay what she had learned about Leroy. The news wasn't much, except she now knew more about some of the people in the picture. Maybe the season would be the reason they could accept God's love and that of Leroy's to be genuine and everlasting.

Two days before Christmas, she drove into Pikeville. The appointment with Dr. Pruitt and her sisters was, again, at the Chinese restaurant at 6:00 in the evening. It would be dark this time, but it must be the standard appointment for the professor outside of college and business hours.

Alma told them about finding relatives of the men in the picture with Leroy. She didn't paint a true picture of Larkin but gave a loving account of Jill and her help in tracking down the information. She told the sisters about Grady being a bootlegger and him and his buddies making and transporting moonshine. She told them she had information he had abused his wife and that he and his son, and maybe one or more of his friends, had spent time in prison.

"I want you to know I think and feel in my heart that your father was a good and loving man. I can't prove, yet, that harm came to him and prevented him from returning to his family. But especially here at Christmas, I hope you can find good thoughts and believe he loved you. I'm not finished tracking my father's picture, and I hope to someday bring you news of your father."

The girls gave Alma a weak smile and looked at one another. Leslie started by remembering something silly Leroy had done on her birthday. Each one of the sisters contributed a memory of their dad or their mother. Kathy couldn't remember much about him, but she felt her mother really did love him.

When the conversation slowed, Alma asked them if it would be alright if she gave each of them a small Christmas present. They all smiled and nodded their heads. She handed out the gifts, wrapped in the same red paper with large green bows, and watched as they opened the token of her love and friendship. They apologized for not bringing her a gift and got out of their seats to come over and give her a hug.

Shortly, they began to collect their belongings and made their excuses to leave. Leslie hugged each of her sisters, and they all agreed to get together after New Year's. Leslie sat back down after her sisters left, so Alma reclaimed her seat.

"Are you okay, Dr. Pruitt?"

"Yes, Alma, I'm okay. I've been suspicious for a long time that our father may have met with foul play instead of running away. Look at the times we grew up in. Segregation and prejudice were abundant and just slightly less so, now. I also think our mother knew more than she told us. From little things she said, I now think, after you brought that picture and raised suspicions in our minds, she suspected that he had died or maybe been killed in an accident of some kind. I also think, Alma, that there are questions you would like to have answers to, but you are just too protective of us to ask."

"Like what, Dr. ….?"

"It's Leslie. Please don't call me doctor, or professor, Alma. After all you have done, and with all the healing that has gone on here tonight, I don't want us to be anything but the closest of friends. Being a history professor and considered an expert of Appalachian folklore, I should be the one to uncover the real truth about my own father. I don't know where I would have started, and evidently didn't want to, but you took an old picture and traced us all down."

"Leslie, I'm so sorry to have brought any of you pain. I had no right to interfere into your family affairs and bring back unpleasant memories or tragedies. Once I found you, I promised to tell you about anything I found, and that is why I came tonight. I think there is more to learn about Leroy, but I don't think there will be any justice for you or your sisters. I do have some gruesome suspicions that I will share with you later if I can prove any of it. Or, maybe if I come to the end of the road and just want you to know what I think. You can share with your sisters whatever part of it you wish. I don't think I can stand to see any more sorrow bestowed on any of you."

They talked on for a while, gave each other a goodbye hug and promised to call or visit at any time. Alma knew on the drive back into Buchanan County that it would be another sleepless night. The wheels were turning, and the road had many sharp curves and dangerous drop-offs.

Early on Christmas Eve, Alma trudged up the hollow with her gift for Rufus. She left just after breakfast. The temperature on the new atomic clock Brett had installed in the kitchen read 28 degrees. There was a slight breeze so the wind chill factor was probably in the low 20's. She would have waited until the sun had a chance to reach a little farther down in the hollows, but she figured Rufus would be invisible and she would have to wait him out again. Maybe the cold temperature would drive him indoors a little earlier.

She saw smoke spiraling above the treetops as she approached his cabin. Without bothering to knock, she raised the latch on the door and stepped inside.

He was sitting on the 'stump' stool beside the barrel stove drinking a cup of steaming coffee.

"Sorry, Rufus. I should have knocked, but I figured you had vanished once you saw me coming."

"Figured there was no use leaving. You would only be waiting here until I froze to death."

Alma smiled. "You're right. Can I have a sip of that coffee? It's cold as a witch's tit out there."

He handed her the coffee and she drained the cup.

"I don't know what you've got in that big box, but you can just turn around and pack it back down the hollow."

"You listen to me, Rayvar Jeeter. I ain't packing this Christmas gift another foot. It's Christmas, for Heaven's sake! The good Lord will be frowning down on you quite furiously if you can't accept a gift in honor of baby Jesus on the day of His birth."

"This ain't the day. That's tomorrow."

"Well, just wait until tomorrow to open it."

"And you can take them books back you left at the forks of the road last month."

"I don't want them back. I've already read them. They're used paperbacks, anyhow. If you don't want to read them, you can use them to wipe your butt."

"I did read them. You got poor taste in reading material to loan out to others."

"I don't see how you can say that. Every one of them was a classic."

"Maybe so. You just don't give WAR AND PEACE to a veteran who's been wounded in a war."

"You've read that already? Well, at least you didn't die in the war like thousands of those men did."

"Maybe I should have."

"Seems to me like a man who can run up and down these mountains and shoot helpless animals could do whatever he wanted to."

"Well, I can't. So take your gift and your ass out of here and leave me alone."

Alma thought she might have pushed too far. She could lighten up, but she couldn't leave. Not yet.

"I think I'll just stick around and watch you open your gift tomorrow. Unless you want to open it now."

Rufus threw the coffee cup into a bucket on the bench. His eyes were glaring as he walked towards her. Alma sat down on the edge of the cot and waited. She couldn't run, and she sure as hell couldn't stand.

He stood over her and took a couple of deep breaths. Alma stared him straight in the eyes. Whatever was coming, she was going to face it head on.

"You are one tough b...."

"If you say 'bitch', I'm going to harass your ass every day for the next year."

In spite of his anger, Rufus smiled.

"If I open the damn package, will you leave and not come back?"

"I'll leave. But I may come back. Occasionally. A lot depends on you and how cooperative you can be."

"Cooperative? You are trespassing and invading my privacy. All I want is to be left alone, and you want me to be cooperative? I think that takes more than one person, and I don't want any part of it. I ought to tie you up and feed you to the wolves."

"There ain't any wolves in these parts. Rufus, you helped me find Leroy's family in Red Jacket, and I may need your help again down the road. All I want to do is leave you some books, maybe an old radio, or some things at the drop area and not have you insult me with a check or money. If you don't pick it up, I'll be back."

He reached for the gift and ripped off the paper. The down sleeping bag was rolled up in a tight ball. He unrolled it and felt the softness inside the unzipped opening. He looked back at Alma. There was no longer any anger in his eyes.

"Say 'Thank you, Alma'."

"Thank you, Alma."

She put on her gloves and walked out of the cabin. When she looked back from some distance away, he was standing in the doorway.

Alma asked Brett if he wanted to spend Christmas with her.

"Alma, I would love to. I know Christmas is the time you want to spend with family and loved ones, but since I have no children and my brother Charlie and his family are spending the holidays in Las Vegas, I was dreading the thoughts of getting drunk on the shores of South Holston Lake by myself. We could still fly to New York, or Paris, for a couple of weeks."

"No, thanks. This is home, at least for now. I want to spend Christmas here and with family. We can have dinner with my aunts, and you and I can pretend we are roasting chestnuts on an open fire and open our gifts on Christmas Eve. You did buy me a gift, didn't you?"

"Oops! It's not Christmas, yet. I still have one more day. You know what I want for Christmas?"

"Don't tell me. With my limited imagination, I could guess. You'll just have to take what you get, and you'd better be happy with it."

They both laughed as he wrapped her up in a big hug. Before they left the Black Stallion Café after their breakfast, she filled him in on her trip to Pikeville and the visit with Leroy's daughters. He was surprised at her visit with Rufus. He laughed at her facing him down and admitted Rufus might be harmless after all. They both thought it was a shame about the missing pages of the journal, but it was possible they only contained more of the abuse that Betty suffered. They would still try to get to Larkin somehow and see if there was more he could reveal. But for now, they wanted to enjoy the holidays and each other.

Late in the afternoon on Christmas Eve, just when Alma was starting to worry that Brett wasn't going to show, he drove up in his Hummer with the tailgate down and the rear window up. She watched from the kitchen window as he pulled a two-wheeled dolly out of the back and placed a portable ramp up against the bumper. In a short while, he was wheeling a large container up to the back porch and into the kitchen as she held open the door.

"What in the world have you got there, Brett?"

"Just wait and see. How about moving the table over a little so I can get this thing into the living room? Move the recliner over to the other side of the room and take that picture off the wall covering the flue to the chimney."

He kept giving instructions until he had the crate into position. With her help, they got the box opened. He finished assembling a self-contained fireplace with enough black stovepipe to connect it to the flue and safely away from the walls. He left Alma standing there with her hands over an open mouth and tears in her eyes, as he marched back to the vehicle and brought up an armload of firewood and a paper bag.

"I'm afraid to ask what's in the bag." Alma stood behind him, with a huge smile and a pounding heart, as he placed the wood in the fireplace.

"Chestnuts, of course."

"Oh, you lovely man! There really is a Santa Claus." She grabbed him in a big hug and pulled him to the couch.

"Wait! I haven't started the fire, yet."

"Oh, that can wait. I just want to see how it's going to look from here. We need to move the couch over near the window and that table can be moved to the wall near the door. We need a rug in front of the fireplace. I know… I'll pull the comforter off the bed and we'll use the pillows as cushions."

"I brought a fireproof mat to place in front of the fireplace, so we can keep the doors open as we roast the chestnuts. To ease your mind, I also checked out the chimney and flue while you were in Pikeville, and they're still in good shape. Only needed cleaning out a bit."

"You have been busy. Had this planned out all along, I suppose?"

"Well, just in case. I try to be prepared. I was an Eagle Scout, you know. Anyway, I wasn't going to do anything until I got an invite."

"Prepared and a bit selfish, I'd say. Didn't it dawn on you I might enjoy this even if you weren't here? On second thought, it wouldn't be nearly as nice without you here. Oh, Brett, this is such a nice Christmas gift. As Aunt Ellie would say, 'you shouldn't have'."

"But it's not your Christmas gift. It's for us both. Remember, I waited until I got invited." He smiled as he held out his arms.

She melted into them and pulled his head down until she could weld her lips to his. The sun was long gone behind the mountain and the gray shadows were quickly turning into black. After a minute of ravishing his mouth, she pushed him away.

"Well, go get the mat and the matches. I'll round up some candles and pour us a glass of wine, and we'll get this party started."

Alma had all the things in place when she heard him stomping on the back porch. She rushed to the door after she realized she had cut off all the lights. She flipped on the kitchen and porch lights as she flung open the door. Brett stood there with the big mat over his head which he set down against the wall and grabbed her hand.

"Turn the flood lights on and come here. You won't believe this."

She turned on the lights and stepped onto the porch. Coming down in heavy quarter-size flakes was the prettiest, whitest snow Alma had ever seen. She walked out into the almost white grass in the yard with her arms outstretched and her face tilted up into the glare of the lights outlining each individual flake. Brett smiled as he watched her stick her tongue out to catch a disappearing flake. She twirled around and around and laughed as she bent over to gather enough in her hands to make a small snowball to launch towards Brett.

"Now, is that any way to treat someone who dragged you out here to witness one of Christmas' miracles? Wait until tomorrow when we have enough to have a real snowball fight."

"Oh, tomorrow, Brett, we can make snow angels. We'll make one for each of our parents."

"That will be fine. Right now, you better get back inside and let me start that fire. At least, go get a coat and put some shoes on. I don't think I have ever seen a city girl running around in the snow barefooted."

"I'm coming, Brett. Isn't it just perfect? If I didn't know this was a little beyond your awesome power, I would guess you arranged it all."

"Yeah, I'm pulling off a lot of wonders since you and your aunts dragged me into church last Sunday."

Laughing, she jumped into his arms. He carried her into the house and dumped her on the couch. He lit the fire, turned off the lights, picked up their glasses of wine from the table and joined her on the couch. Sipping their wine, they stared into the flames and said their private silent prayers.

Alma woke up freezing. As she tugged the half of the comforter partially covering her, she glanced at the window and saw daylight was pushing out the night. It took a minute to get her bearings. She now realized she was naked and lying on the floor with a man she hoped was Brett. She smiled as the previous hours came back to her.

They had sat on the couch, sipping wine, remembering their younger days, watching the flames from the fire lick at the wood, roasting chestnuts in an old black iron skillet she had found in the bottom of a kitchen cabinet, listening to the crackle and pop of the wood, and throwing the chestnut hulls back into the fire. They finally ended up on the comforter on the floor in front of the fireplace with Brett caressing her body and unbuttoning her clothes.

Now, she didn't have to feel under the cover to know that he was also naked, but she was going to take his part of the comforter to still her shivering body. She remembered him cutting off the baseboard heaters so they could better appreciate the fire. Now, the damn fire was only a few smoldering ambers. He could just wake up cold and turn the heaters back on or build up the fire and put some coffee on. She would just pretend to be sleeping.

It would seem that Brett knew the plan because it worked out just that way. When he returned from the kitchen with two cups of steaming coffee, she was tucked warmly in the corner of the couch wrapped in her robe. She did smile at him, and that made his efforts all the more worthwhile.

"I thought you would build up the fire, but you have turned the heaters on again."

"We have to be at your Aunt Ellie's for breakfast in two hours. I didn't think we would have time to enjoy a roaring fire."

"I guess you are right. Merry Christmas, Brett."

"Merry Christmas to you, Ms. Alma."

"This has been the best Christmas Eve ever. Did you like your gift?"

Brett smiled and pulled back his shirt to show the gold chain and coin hanging around his neck.

"I love the necklace, too."

Alma laughed and blushed from the tip of her ears down her neck to the collar of the robe. Brett took her coffee, set it on the table, and wrapped his arms around her.

"Did you like your gift?"

"I love the fireplace. If I were to never use it again, last night made it the best Christmas gift I could have wished for. But I will use it again. I'm going to have it installed in my bedroom in my new house."

"The fireplace was a gift, but not your Christmas gift. Have you not looked out in the yard?"

She screamed and dashed to the front door. Sitting just off the porch was a bright pink 4-wheeler with a big red ribbon tied across the handlebars. Alma jerked open the door and ran out in just her robe and straddled the seat.

"You had better get back in here before a neighbor drives by and sees a half-naked lady sitting on a 4-wheeler, or you catch your death from a cold."

"When did you put this out here?" She gave him a quick kiss as she darted back inside.

"While you were sleeping so peacefully by the fire, or passed out from the wine."

"Let's ride it to Aunt Ellie's house. It's only about five miles, and it will thrill her to death."

"More like shock her to death. They already think we are two senseless buttheads. Besides, we don't have enough clothes in the house to keep us warm for a five-mile ride in this weather. We'll park it in the empty room in the back until the weather is fit to ride."

They did make it to Aunt Ellie's house by 8:00, but barely. Alma had dashed back outside and insisted on making snow angels in the four-plus inches of snow. She peppered Brett with a few snowballs before she came in, to shower and get ready. The biscuits were coming out of the oven as they walked through the door.

Thanks to the snowball fight, Brett was hungry. He looked over the spread Aunt Ellie had put on the dining room table and could hardly wait for the ladies to be seated. Aunt Ellie said the prayer. Brett thanked the Lord again for it being short. After all, he had now been to an Old Baptist church meeting and understood what could be expected. He had a tall glass of orange juice and a mug of coffee sitting by his plate. Aunt Ellie informed them if they wanted water or milk, they could help themselves from the pitchers on the counter. She passed the biscuits first and advised them to butter them while they were hot. Brett loaded up on sausage and egg casserole, strips of bacon, homemade applesauce, blackberry jam, and a small bowl of fresh fruit. The apples and jam on buttered biscuits would melt in your mouth. Everything was delicious.

"Pass Brett some of that chocolate gravy, Alma."

"No, thanks, Aunt Ellie, I've got more now than I can eat."

"You don't like gravy?"

"Sure I do. But usually I have sausage gravy. I don't think I've ever had gravy with chocolate in it before. It looks pretty rich, and I'm about full."

"Brett, you've got to try a bite. All the kids and grandchildren beg for a big breakfast when they come to visit Aunt Ellie and that includes chocolate gravy. I think they would go on a hunger strike if she didn't make it at least once while they were here. If you don't want to fix your own, then try a bite of mine."

Brett could see that Alma was coming to her aunt's aid. He had to oblige, so he took his spoon and got a bite of buttered biscuit dripping in chocolate and placed it in his mouth. He reached for the orange juice to help wash it down. Maybe he wouldn't even taste it.

"Aunt Ellie, just put any leftovers in a bowl and I'll take it home with me. Add a few of those biscuits. I'll have a nice breakfast in the morning, while Brett chows down at the Black Stallion."

"Hey, wait a minute, Aunt Ellie. Don't go bagging up anything just yet. I've got a clean plate and I would like a couple of those biscuits. Would you pass that bowl of gravy this way?"

Alma and her aunt smiled and passed a wink between them as they sat back, sipped their coffee, and watched Brett finish off the bowl.

Alma loved her two aunts. Aunt Ellie was just so much different from Aunt Paula. You could find Paula dressed in work clothes, maybe bibs, bending over a hill of potatoes and getting her hands dirty graveling out some new ones to cook in a pot of stew; you'd never catch Ellie in anything that didn't look like church clothes. She was a proper lady through and through. Her house could be checked by a sergeant with a white glove, but he'd never find a speck of dust. This was saying something for Buchanan County where dust was plentiful. From dust blowing off the road or tumbling in from the tops of uncovered coal trucks to the pollen from the many trees covering the hillsides, dirt was a never-ending chore for all the women.

Aunt Ellie was a regular churchgoer, just like Aunt Paula. But, she preferred the sophistication of the Methodists over the Baptists. She couldn't see putting her hair up in a bun on top of her head. She always wore dresses, whereas you might see Aunt Paula go out occasionally in a nice pantsuit. Aunt Ellie was very polite and considerate of others, except for her sister. She would only take so much from Paula before slamming back. Alma remembered taking advantage of her cousins, yelling and screaming at them when she was losing while playing games so they would run to their mother crying. Aunt Ellie would not put up with such confrontation and arguing. The kids had to learn to let their actions speak for themselves, and they'd better be proper actions.

As they were putting on their coats to leave, Brett picked up Aunt Ellie in a big bear hug and thanked her for the best breakfast he had ever eaten. He asked for the recipe for the chocolate gravy. She went to the kitchen and came back with a printed copy.

"It's the most requested recipe people ask me for. Merry Christmas, Brett."

Alma drove the Hummer back to their house. They had a few hours before they were to be at Aunt Paula's for Christmas dinner. Brett was reading the recipe out loud, as though Alma had never heard of it before:

-CHOCOLATE GRAVY RECIPE-
1/3 cup all-purpose flour
1/2 cup sugar
1/4 cup Hershey's cocoa
2 cups milk
1 teaspoon vanilla
1 to 2 tablespoons butter

Combine dry ingredients; mix well. Add milk and cook over medium heat stirring constantly until thickened. Add vanilla and

butter; stir until melted. Serve on hot buttered biscuits.

"Alma, when we get back to your place we have to hike to the head of the hollow, or something. I don't think I will be ready to eat a Christmas goose at Aunt Paula's if we don't work off some of this breakfast."

"It's a wild turkey, not a goose, Brett. Aunt Paula always gets her neighbor Henry to kill her one every Christmas. She used to hunt her own, but has refused to fire a shotgun after she turned seventy. She can still handle that .22 rifle, though. You ought to see her pick off the groundhogs that occasionally creep into her garden."

Brett just grinned. He didn't doubt a word she was saying.

"The walk sounds good. I love walking in the snow, and we can sing some Christmas carols."

22

New Year's at Brett's

The day after Christmas, Brett took off to Kentucky for a three-day business trip. One of his mines was considering going union. He knew he couldn't stop it if the employees voted the union in, but he wanted to be in on the bargaining and lay out what he thought would be disadvantages if they did so. His policy had always been to offer as many, but different, benefits than the union. His pay scale was higher, full health care for employee and family, but not lifetime health care as the union offered, retirement earlier, and Christmas bonuses based on years of service. He had a personnel office with an open-door policy to hear suggestions or complaints and a slush fund to help with family emergencies. He felt he could take care of his own employees without the friction of a union.

Alma wasn't too sad to see him go. She needed a few days to get over the holiday. Past Christmases had been spent mostly by herself or maybe a dinner with a close friend. She wasn't used to having family smothering her. Although she dearly loved her aunts and enjoyed the time spent with Brett, she just wanted to slow down on the eating and find a corner of the couch with a good book and a blazing fire in the fireplace. She hoped to find time for a walk in the snow, before it was all gone, alone. There were things she wanted to run through her mind like her new house, Leroy's disappearance, his children and their happiness, and, most of all, her future. Was she really going to stay in Buchanan County? Was she in love or just having a hell of a good time? She might need more than a few days. Brett could fly to Times Square in New York for New Year's Eve if he wanted to. By himself!

    But he didn't. Satisfied with his trip to Kentucky, he asked her to spend the New Year's holiday with him at his home on South Holston Lake. When she balked, he whined and angrily accused her of being selfish. After all the time he had spent with her at her place and with her relatives, the least she could do was visit with him in his home. If she couldn't bear to spend the night, then he would bring her back whenever she asked.

    With head bowed and an apology on her lips, Alma relented and promised she would go. She would pack for an overnight stay, but he would have to give her the option of coming home. What she didn't tell him was that she had never spent a night with a man in his place since the visit to see the cowboy in Montana. Although his family had been at the ranch and nothing bad happened, she had not been in control of things. Alma liked to be in charge and in her space.

When they drove into the driveway at his house, her mouth dropped open and her eyes doubled in size. The driveway itself was magnificent!

Running nearly a quarter of a mile and ending in a circle surrounding a small garden filled with barberry bushes and holly and a lion's head fountain, the concrete drive was bordered with red paving brick, and Bradford Pear and Dogwood trees alternated every 14 feet along the side.

Brett pushed a button on the dash of the Hummer, and one of the doors to a three-bay garage opened. He smiled as he cut the engine. Alma didn't know whether to get out or crawl under the floor mat.

"Welcome to my home, Alma. Come in the kitchen and I'll pour you a glass of wine. You can browse around if you want."

"Don't you have a butler or someone to give a guided tour?"

"I do have an assistant that spends some nights in the guest house by the pool. He and his wife and little girl live in Abingdon, but have gone to Charlotte, N.C., to spend the holidays with her parents. I thought you might be more comfortable meandering around by yourself. I'll start the grill."

"What if I get lost?"

"Just push the button underneath the light switch in any room and I can talk to you. I can also see your location by the light on the display panel under that cabinet."

Alma shook her head, took her glass of wine and eased out the glass French doors to the patio. She wanted to see the outside of the house first.

It was an elegant, brick, Georgian home. She guessed there were at least five acres, with beautiful grass and landscaping down to the water's edge, and his private boat dock. Tied to the dock, under a protective awning, was a forty-foot, two-deck, red and white houseboat with a satellite dish on each end.

She walked through a nine-hole putting green, across the pool deck and into an 8x14-foot glassed-in sun room. This led her through open doors to what she guessed was a mastersuite. Later she discovered another mastersuite directly overhead on the second floor with its own balcony.

Throughout the house, she counted five bedrooms, four and one-half baths, custom-made closets, Pella Low E windows, and the gourmet kitchen where she had started. Looking around, as she reentered, she noticed the stainless steel Bosch appliances, two dishwashers and a six-burner Vulcan stove.

Alma found Brett on the patio, standing over a smoking grill, turning steaks and shrimp.

"Need some help, Chef?"

"You can toss the salad there on the bar. Looks like you need a refill on that glass, too."

"I think I'll switch to one of those Silver Bullets you're having. A good cold Coors might bring me back down to earth."

"Well, what do you think?"

"It's all gorgeous, Brett. How many square feet are there in the house?"

"A little over 5,000."

"I don't see how you could leave this place as much as you do. You have everything a person would want right here."

"I hate it. It's all the doings of my ex. The second one. I bought this charcoal grill, and the boat is nice when I can get my drinking buddies to show up for a weekend. The place is used mostly as a retreat for some of my business contacts. Impresses the hell out of a few CEO's from Pittsburg and Chicago."

"It's fabulous, Brett. I would love to visit again in the summer when we could take that ship out to sea."

"It's a houseboat, and this is a lake."

"But I agree. I don't think I would like to live here. I guess I'm still dreaming about my soon-to-be log cabin."

"I'm glad you are going to stay, Alma."

"I'm not sure I'm going to stay. I have loved my little vacation, and I would like to solve the mystery of Leroy, but I have never liked living in Buchanan County. I might still move to the beach."

"You're older now, Alma. All your dreams have been fulfilled."

"Then I must be dead. Brett, you drive down any road in the county and every flat spot, 50 foot wide, has a small house or trailer on it. If the spot of land is wide enough, there will be two houses, or twenty, packed side by side. Of course, you have the million-dollar house sitting between them if the owner can doze or blast out enough of the hillside. Oh, I forgot, there could also be a coal tipple or mining equipment shop hogging the space next door. Everything squeezed in beside the river or the road. Nothing on the mountainsides except the deep scars of strip mining, or roads cut for coal trucks to do their job."

"How many homes are there on the street you live on in Alexandria, Alma? What size lawn does your condo have? How many trees are there at the shopping mall in Seven Corners? How long do you sit in traffic to get to work in our Nation's Capital? How many homeless people take up the park benches when you want to enjoy your lunch outdoors? How many sirens or gunshots wake you in the middle of the night? What …?"

"Okay. Okay! I get your point, Brett. I guess I need to work on my vision. Something like 'the beauty lies in the eye of the beholder'."

He smiled as he served her up a plate of meat and fried potatoes to go with her salad and wine.

"I guess I'm just saying, Alma, that you and I can live wherever we want. Some of those people by the river can't. Some of them can, but choose where they are. They enjoy helping their neighbors, seeing them at an Old Primitive Baptist Church service with dinner on the ground and foot washing, fixing up an old car that your daddy might have driven, and maybe going to the lake on the weekend. I think most would rather eat at the Black Stallion Café, or one like it, in their work or hunting clothes than dress up for a fancy dinner of food with names they can't pronounce. It is rat race or laid back. Maybe other people prefer to chase their dreams, and dream for more, while some like contentment, satisfaction, and feeding their souls."

"I think you got a little of both down here, Brett. And I ain't eaten once on the ground or had my feet washed."

"Well, you just ain't been there on the right Sunday. Although, they seemed to have moved the eating on the ground inside."

Alma spent the night. She stayed three nights.

23

Log House

The snow was the best one yet. She had waded through about four inches of the beautiful white stuff to the wood piled up against the shed to add to her dry supply on the front porch. The electric heat would be enough to keep the house warm, but she wanted the feel and smell of the wood burning in her new fireplace stove. That Brett was so thoughtful.

She placed another stick of wood on the fire and leaned back on the couch with her father's files on her lap. The shot rang out, and a piece of glass from the window bounced off the papers in her hand. She rolled off the couch screaming, with papers flying, and crawled over and pulled the lamp cord from its outlet. She stayed on her hands and knees as she crawled her way to the kitchen and located her purse. The pistol was there and loaded.

When she opened the kitchen door, the white jeep picked up speed and turned the curve of the road.

She fired three shots, but she couldn't see any taillights after the first shot. Shivering, she thought from the cold, she went back inside and called the sheriff's office.

While she was waiting for Detective Rife to arrive, she dressed in warmer clothes and put on socks and her calf-high boots. She turned back on all the lights in the house and included the porch and back deck floodlights. She took her fluorescent lantern and walked out to the road.

The tire tracks in the new-fallen snow would be those of the jeep. She was careful not to disturb a crime scene. Just opposite the front window, now with a hole in it, she saw a small hole in the snow. She guessed the detective would find a bullet casing buried there. She walked down the road to the curve. Just before the road disappeared from view of the house, she found more holes in the blanket of new snow. Lying just slightly under the top layer, her lantern reflected off something red, which was probably a piece of the taillight. She smiled. Maybe her eagle eye was still sharp.

She had just gotten back to the house when Rife came charging up the road with his blue lights flashing. Thank goodness, he hadn't used the siren, or everyone in the hollow would be following him up to the house and trampling on any evidence available.

"Well, Detective Rife, it's about time. I don't suppose you could have avoided wiping out the fresh tire tracks of the getaway vehicle?"

"And how would you suggest I arrive to an emergency situation? Walk?"

"The emergency was about twenty minutes ago. After I shot his taillights out, he hurried on his way."

"What? You shot at an occupied vehicle? You could have killed someone!"

"Better him than me. The bastard shot into my house. That's an OCCUPIED house. There's a hole in my window, if you want to investigate, and I would guess a bullet in the wall on the other side of the room. But, before you go in, let me show you some possible evidence located out here in the road."

The detective had her hold her lantern close to the tire tracks in the snow that he hadn't traveled over, while he took several pictures. He also took pictures of the small holes in the snow before he dug out a 22-caliber shell casing and pieces of red glass. They went back inside the house and Alma showed him the hole in the window. Detective Rife bagged several pieces of the broken glass. Together, they found the small hole in the wall on the opposite side of the room near the ceiling. While the detective was taking pictures and digging out the bullet, she went into the kitchen and put on a pot of coffee.

After the officer had finished his investigation, they sat at the kitchen table and sipped on hot coffee as he completed a few notes on his pad.

"You're quite calm under the circumstances, Alma."

"I'm angrier than anything, Detective. I'll probably fall apart later. Why would somebody shoot into my house? Was he really trying to kill me?"

"I don't think so. If he'd wanted to shoot you, he would have done something to draw you into view.

I think he just wanted to scare you. For someone that's been in town for a short time, you seemed to have made an enemy, Alma. Have you got any ideas who might have done this?"

"Of course not! I'm a lovable, at least likable, person, Detective. I don't think I've gotten on the wrong side of anyone since I've been down here. Now, I don't know that I could say that about D.C. I don't think they would shoot me, though. It'd be more like burn me at the stake. Is Larkin still in prison?"

"I'm sure he is, but I'll check to be sure tomorrow. I might pay him a visit, anyway. You can get things done from behind bars even if you don't do them yourself."

"He's the only one I can think of that I might have upset. Most people just think I'm crazy for trying to find dead people. I guess with him, he might feel like I've trodden on his family name or something."

"Alma, do you want to go spend a night or two at the hotel? I can follow you to town and see that you are tucked in safely."

"No. I'll be fine right here. I suspect that jeep is not even in Buchanan County tonight."

"I can call Brett if you want."

"Now, Detective, you just go on home and get a good night's sleep. I want some results on this investigation, and soon. You may need your beauty rest come morning."

"Okay. Goodnight, Alma."

"Goodnight, Detective Rife. And thanks for the prompt attention."

He smiled and shook his head as he walked out the door and back to his vehicle. He was probably thinking of the scolding he got when it took him twenty minutes to drive from Grundy to get here.

She did finally go to sleep in the early morning hours with all the lights on and the pistol under the extra pillow near her head. She had finished the pot of coffee and watched the logs burn down in the fireplace. Maybe Larkin had someone come by to scare her off, but it wasn't going to work. She was here for the long haul. Whoever that was tonight, Alma was sure he'd never come back. He probably had to change his pants before he got out of the county.

It was near the end of January when Jeffrey Conners called.

"Who?"

"Jeffrey Conners, Ms. Woodson. I'm the contractor you hired last fall to build a log house in Little Garden."

"Oh, Jeffrey! I'm sorry. I had forgotten all about the house."

"You don't want it now? You paid a thousand dollars deposit when you signed the contract."

"Oh, no! I mean yes! I do want it. You just caught me off guard. With the holidays and everything that's going on around here, I just forgot about the house. Temporarily, I can assure you. Do you think we can get it built before next Christmas?"

"Maybe by the fourth of July, Ms. Woodson. That's why I'm calling. If everything is clear, and you're ready to go, I need to move some equipment in and build a road to the house site in the next couple of weeks. The logs for your house should be delivered on the twenty-first of February."

"That is wonderful, Jeffrey. And, if you call me Ms. Woodson one more time, I'm going to look for a new contractor."

"Sorry, Alma. I just wanted to make sure I was clear to go."

"Full steam ahead, Jeffrey. The property is legally mine. I bought out my brother and sisters before Christmas. I can't wait to get started. I may invite my aunts and Brett for the ground-breaking. What day did you say you would start?"

"I haven't set a date, Alma. I can give you a call a few days before, if you want. We're just building another house. It doesn't require a ceremony or anything. In fact, you don't have to be there."

"Oh, yes, I do. I intend to take pictures every step of the way."

"I'll call."

He did, and, on the first Monday in February, he pulled in with two dump trucks and trailers loaded with a dozer and excavator. Alma was ready with her camera. She didn't invite the aunts and Brett. That could wait for the completion and the ribbon cutting. She might even invite the press in for that.

Watching her house being built was an exciting time for Alma. She had bought houses before. She had never created and built one just for herself. She watched and directed. She took hundreds of pictures with her digital camera and had a new desktop and screen saver for her computer.

She sent pictures and details to Krista by e-mail and, occasionally updated the rest of her siblings.

One day, as she watched the big dozer push dirt and rock over into the hollow between the orchard and the now overgrown pasture to widen and level her backyard and parking area, she saw Rufus sitting on a log. He was mostly hidden by the trees. She smiled, but didn't attempt to approach him. She knew if she acknowledged him in any way he would simply disappear.

It was a good thing there wasn't much automobile traffic up the hollow. On February 21st, three tractor-trailer loads of logs blocked the road for half the day. Alma watched and took pictures as each truck backed up, with the help of the dozer, to the garden and unloaded the logs for her new house. The windows, doors, and other material would be trucked in later when Jeffrey was ready.

Alma was so thrilled with the event that she brought out a bottle of her best wine. She climbed up into the cab of each truck waiting to unload and shared a glass with the driver, as another one took their picture. When the unloading was completed, she insisted that Jeffrey and the dozer operator join her and the drivers in a group shot.

On Sunday, a few days after the logs arrived, Brett came over. He had hardly gotten out of the Hummer before she had his hand and was pulling him up to the garden to show all the progress.

"Wow! Jeffrey has been busy. I don't think you can continue to call this 'the garden'."

"It will always be the garden to us Woodsons. Let me show you these logs."

Alma showed him how each log had a number and a letter stamped on the end.

"That's to show you where each log goes. They all also have slots cut out near the ends so they fit together without using nails. Aren't they big logs, Brett? Jeffrey said you don't need insulation in the walls. I can believe that. Can't you?"

Brett just nodded and smiled. He had seen several log homes built, but he was happy that Alma was happy and excited.

They walked over all the graded area and the wide road Jeffrey had curved around the hillside. Brett approved, as he knew he would when he had recommended Conners. He did good work.

Brett spent the rest of Sunday with Alma. They went over the blueprints again. Over sandwiches and cold beers, she showed him the pictures she had taken and the slide show she had created on her computer.

When it appeared she had exhausted every detail about the house and was slowing down, she threw in the little piece about the shooting into her house. When he regained the color in his face, she showed him the bullet hole in her window and the wall. He pleaded with her to come live at the lake, or at least move into town where she would have others around until the house was built. She laughed it off. He really felt like she believed she had proven she could take care of herself and there was no more danger. Maybe she was right in this case, but, with Alma, would there be another?

Brett told her about his trip to Montana coming up tomorrow. He would be gone most of the week but would be by to see the progress on the house as soon as he got back.

Alma hated to see him go, but she had so much to do it would probably be best for both of them. Jeffrey was talking about tearing down the old house soon, to make room for fill dirt and sloping the ground back to the new house. She needed to pack up all she could in boxes and be ready to store them and move with short notice. She could get a room at the motel in Grundy until the house was ready.

Well, she had done that before.

On Wednesday while the crew was laying the first logs, with the help of a large crane, she decided to watch from a safer distance. She climbed up the hill to the edge of the woods and sat down on the same log where she had observed Rufus watching a few days before. It was a good view. She could see all the work going on, and up and down the hollow to the bends in the road.

About an hour later, he showed up. She didn't hear him. She just felt his presence.

"What do you think, Rufus?"

"I think you're putting another ugly scar into our beautiful mountains."

"There won't be a scar once I do the landscaping and plant some trees and bushes."

"And you had them cut down a bunch of nice trees when you had a perfectly good house. At least it was good enough for your folks."

"Rufus, it's obvious you and I are different. There's no way we could agree on this. Tell you what. In a few days, or weeks, the old house down there is going to be torn down. I'll put a red flag on the door when it is empty. You are welcome to take anything you want. And when it's on the ground, there ought to be enough good lumber to build you a mansion up there in the hills. You know, so it doesn't go to waste."

"I got all I need."

They sat quietly for a while. Just watching the work inch its way along.

Rufus finally asked her if she had found out anything about the men in the picture. Alma knew which picture he was referring to. She told him about her visits with Leroy's daughters. She told him about Jill and the two of them visiting Larkin in prison.

After several minutes of silence, during which Rufus hadn't responded to any of her visits, nor reacted to her entering a prison to talk to a convict, she told him about finding Betty Bracken's Bible and journal at the old home place at Deskins.

This got his attention.

"I know that place. House is about to fall down. Nobody's lived there for years."

"I know."

"Were there any revelations?'

"There was a whole book of Revelations in the Bible."

He looked her in the eyes and the corners of his mouth turned up. Not quite a smile.

"In the journal, Alma. Did you find anything to link Grady Bracken to Leroy?"

"Not really. The journal revealed him to be what Jill has already told us. He was an evil, mean man. But there were several pages missing, or torn out. I think Larkin might know something about that.

I hope to talk to him again. Maybe get Detective Rife to question him."

"Maybe you missed something."

"I don't see how. We searched through the whole house."

"Maybe there's something outside the house."

"Rufus, there's not much outside. A piece of a barn. The outhouse fell in while Brett was searching for the key."

"Think I might go over there and check it out for myself."

"I think you'll be wasting your time. If there is anything to discover, Larkin knows. We just need to squeeze him."

"Maybe. I don't have anything else to do."

"Okay. If you really want to search the place again, I'll pick you up tomorrow and we'll drive over."

"I don't need a babysitter."

"But you might need a witness if something turns up. I've got a feeling you wouldn't enjoy explaining details to the sheriff's department."

"All right. I'll meet you there. Around noon."

"That's about a twelve-mile hike, Rufus."

"Not the way I travel. Just over the ridge."

They watched the construction a few more minutes. When Rufus decided to leave, he simply got up from his seat on the log and walked up the hill and out of sight. Alma just smiled and shook her head. She guessed he had talked enough for one day.

Just about quitting time, Detective Rife arrived in an unmarked cruiser. He parked down at the road and looked up at the construction site, then leaned up against the hood of his car. Alma smiled as she made her way down the hill. Police work was confidential work she guessed.

"Hi, Detective. The hill too steep for you? I would have thought the police force was in better shape than that."

"Hello to you, too, Alma. I thought I would stop by and report about the shooting into your house. I guess I could have just pinned a copy to the house up there and everyone could weigh in."

"I was just kidding. I know you are in great shape. What did you find out? Did you catch the shooter?"

"Not yet. To tell you the truth, we don't have a lead to go on. I knew if I didn't report in, you would be downtown giving the Sheriff a lot of grief. For several weeks, we have checked all the repair shops and nobody has worked on a white Jeep, or, to be more specific, replaced any taillights. We have questioned all the auto parts stores and there have been no taillight covers sold for a jeep. We can't get a match on the bullet until we find the gun. The Sheriff has notified all the other police forces in adjoining counties that we are looking for a white Jeep with a broken passenger-side rear taillight. I'm sorry, but right now we are waiting for something to turn up."

"Well, don't worry about it, Detective. I'd almost forgotten about it myself. If Larkin had anything to do with it, he could have gotten the job done from Chicago, or somewhere, with all those prisoners up there from all over the country. I'm sure he won't be back."

"We checked the hospitals and clinics in the area. There was only one case of a gunshot wound. A grouse hunter shot his buddy up on Fletcher's Ridge, but he was treated and released."

"I didn't think Dick Cheney knew where Buchanan County was."

Rife smiled, but went right on as though he was getting used to her off-the-cuff remarks.

"I did question Larkin. He won't admit to knowing anything about a shooting or anyone driving a white jeep. I didn't mention your name. I didn't want to give him any ideas in case he hasn't thought about scaring you off."

"Thanks, Detective, for all you did. I don't think we have to worry about it, anymore. It may have been some drunken teenagers daring each other into dangerous acts. If it should happen again, I'll try to take out a tire, or two. Just kidding! Just kidding!"

"You'd better be kidding. If you are involved in another shooting, you'd better have a real good cause or the Sheriff might confiscate your weapon."

"I want you to know I had a good cause this time. I believe the Second Amendment gives me the right to defend myself. I also have a concealed gun permit. Now, if you don't have any more threats to make, would you like to go up and see the progress they have made on my new house?"

Rife smiled and rolled his eyes. This gal has been around the block a few times. He just hoped she didn't jump over to the criminal side.

"Not this time, Alma. I've got to get back. I may have to work a stakeout tonight."

"Oh, I would love to do that, sometime. Do you think you could take me along?"

"Not a chance. You'd probably not wait for the deal to go down. You'd just shoot everyone that showed up. Just kidding! Just kidding!"

She laughed anyway. It would probably be best if she stuck to nosing around and let the professionals handle the fireworks. She went back up to the house after he left and watched until the guys packed up their tools for the day.

24

The Cistern

The next day when Alma got to the old Bracken place, Rufus was already there, sitting on the door step in his shirtsleeves. Near the end of March, the mornings were still cold and she had on her hooded sweatshirt and a pair of cotton gloves. She had driven her car as far as she could and hiked the half mile on to the house.

"Have you found anything, yet?"

"Haven't looked."

"Well, let's get started."

They walked together through the house. When they got to the bedroom where Betty Bracken's things had been found, Rufus stopped her in the doorway.

"Let's not go in there. You've already searched this room and found the journal. I'd rather not add more footprints."

Alma noticed for the first time the footprints in the years-old dust and dirt on the floor. Three pairs of prints would surely be hers and Brett's and Jill's. There appeared to be more than that on the floor, but then again they had walked all over the room. She didn't remember anyone walking over to the window, though.

"Is that window open a tiny bit, Rufus?"

"I'd say about two inches. Why?"

"We had a key and came through the front door."

"Probably been that way for years."

"Maybe Brett checked it out before."

They walked outside. Rufus said he would check the barn while Alma looked around the yard and under the porch.

He heard her scream as he was leaving the barn. He broke into a run. As he rounded the corner of the house on the kitchen side, he heard her scream again. This time it sounded muffled, but continuous. He followed it to a concrete slab with broken boards covering an opening. Rufus removed the rest of the broken lid, or cap, and stuck his head down into the hole. There was enough light through the opening to see Alma sitting in about two feet of water screaming her head off.

"Alma! Alma, are you hurt?"

He had to raise his voice and ask again before she stopped screaming. With tears streaming down her cheeks, she held up her hands towards him.

"Please get me out of this hole, Rufus!"

"Can you stand up? Are you hurt?"

"I think I twisted or broke my ankle."

"Try to stand on your good foot. It's only about seven feet deep. If you hold up your arms, I think I can pull you out."

As she reached down into the water to help push herself to her feet, she suddenly jerked her hand free and grabbed for Rufus's hands.

He pulled her up until he could get his hands under her armpits and eased her back through the opening. He carried her to the first step of the kitchen porch and sat down beside her. He began to examine her ankle when he noticed she was sobbing and shaking.

"You'll be okay, Alma. I think it's just sprained a little."

"Rufus, there's …there's something down in that well."

"Like what?"

"Like sticks, or bones, or something."

"It's probably pieces of the boards you broke through. It's not a well. It's a cistern. A water cistern that used to catch the rainwater from the roof. The guttering has rusted away, and no water has run in there for some time."

"Rufus, I don't care about that. Those weren't broken boards I felt in the water. Whatever they are, they've been there for a long time. You've got to check it out. Please!"

"Okay, Alma. Let me borrow your scarf to wrap this foot first. If there is anything in the cistern, it's not going anywhere."

He retrieved her hooded sweatshirt and gloves from the edge of the porch where she had discarded them before she started her search around the house.

She gladly put them on. He took his time wrapping her ankle. More to calm her down than the good it would do. Maybe it would help with the swelling. When she began to get excited again, he told her if she didn't promise to stay calm and on the porch with her foot elevated, he wasn't going anywhere.

"I promise! I promise. Just go."

"I saw an old wooden ladder in the barn. I'll go fetch it and have a look. I'll also pull my socks and shoes off. I don't see why we both should get our feet wet. I expect I'll have to carry you back to your car."

"Just go, Rufus."

He finally did. He found an old ragged, dusty horse blanket in the barn and brought it back to cover her wet clothes and help keep her warm. He retrieved the ladder that had two rungs broken and pushed it down into the cistern. Carefully, he tested each step before he put his weight on it. When he eased his naked foot down into the water he shuddered. The long winter had left its chill.

When his fingers contacted something that indeed was in the water, he took hold and brought to the surface the leg bone and foot of a human skeleton. Rufus took a deep breath and released it back into the water. He slowly felt his way through the water until his fingers could outline what he knew was a human skull. Without disturbing anything more, he stepped back onto the ladder.

Alma watched him approach with his shoes in his hand. She knew by the look on his face that she was right. There was something down there.

"Well, Rufus! Don't just sit there putting on your socks. Tell me that was just a bunch of broken boards down there, then we can get the hell out of here."

"Do you have a signal on that cell phone?"

Alma clasped one hand over her mouth as she reached into her jacket with the other. She looked at the phone and nodded her head. Thank God, they were a little closer to Grundy and the county had used some of the coal tax to install more towers on the ridges along Route 460.

"Better call 911, or the sheriff's office. There are human remains at the bottom of that cistern."

Alma figured she was in shock. She wasn't crying or shaking. She just felt numb. She made the call, having the sheriff's office number in her contacts' list. She asked the deputy to put Sheriff Tabor on the phone. She told him about finding a human skeleton, gave her location, and told him he would need a four-wheeler of some kind to get into the Bracken place.

She sat beside Rufus and put her head on his shoulder. Unimaginable, considering all they had just gone through, they hardly said a word for the hour it took the sheriff, Detective Rife, and the county coroner to arrive in a Jeep Wrangler.

"Alma."

"Sheriff Tabor. You might want to look in that water cistern right over there."

She pointed to the cistern only yards away. Rufus didn't say a word. The detective and coroner walked in the direction she had indicated. The sheriff walked over and sat down on the edge of the porch.

"Alma, I'm guessing you and your friend here have a story to go along with this."

"This is Rufus. Legally known as Rayvar Jeeter."

The sheriff nodded his head towards Rufus, who didn't bother to get up from his seat for formal greetings.

"Rufus. I've heard of you, but I've never had the opportunity to meet you. I think you and my detective there may be acquainted. Which one of you found what you believe to be a body?"

Alma waited a second. It looked like Rufus was only going to respond if he was questioned directly.

"I was the one who fell through those rotten boards that covered the cistern. I didn't know it was there with all the leaves and stuff over it. I also didn't know what it was until Rufus pulled me out and explained. I hurt my ankle when I fell through. I discovered something in the water as I was trying to get out. Rufus went back down there and found the bones."

"Do you need medical treatment, Alma? I'm probably going to call in the State Police if the coroner confirms it's a body. They could bring along paramedics."

"Oh, no. I'm all right. Just a bit shaken."

Detective Rife and Coroner Jerry Smith, now with waders on, came back to join them.

"Sheriff, we're going to need some reinforcements in here. Their report is correct. Those are human remains down there."

"Okay, Jerry. I'll get hold of the State and have them bring in a forensic team. Ronnie, you know these two, so get the recorder and let's get a preliminary statement from them here. They can come in later, after we get with the State, and give a formal deposition. Alma probably would like to get home and take care of that foot."

"Right, Sheriff. How you doing, Rufus?"

Detective Rife walked over and shook hands with both of them. Rufus still didn't say anything.

Alma told them the whole story, starting with the picture her father had taken, which she had already shown them at their first meeting. The detective had more questions than the sheriff. He wanted to know why they happened to be here in the first place. What role did Rufus play in this discovery?

Although not complete, they seemed satisfied with her statement for now. Especially, after she explained about Jill being a relative of the Brackens, their visit with Larkin in prison, and their having a key to enter the house. Rufus finally spoke up and said he knew more about these mountains than anybody. He was just trying to help Alma find the missing pages to the journal, or evidence that Grady had anything to do with the missing black man.

"I don't think he's missing anymore, Rufus."

"What do you mean by that, Alma?" The sheriff asked.

"I think when you get through with DNA, and all that, you'll find out that we have found him."

"That possibility will be one of the first we examine."

"You will keep me posted, Sheriff, won't you?"

"Detective Rife will be heading up this investigation. I'll leave it to him to share what he can, without compromising the case."

"Detective?"

"Like the sheriff said, 'what I can'. Providing you understand confidentiality and don't go running your mouth to the press, or anything."

Alma promised.

The detective was going to stay and tape off the boundary until the State Police arrived and the remains could be removed. The sheriff offered to give them a lift back to her car. Rufus refused. Alma accepted, threw off the dirty blanket, and assured them all she could drive herself home. Thank goodness, it was her left ankle.

When she drove up to the house, she was relieved to see Brett amble down the hill from the construction site. Bless his heart; he seemed to always be there when she needed him the most.

"Good to see you, Brett."

"Well, I got through a couple of days early. I thought I would check in on your construction party."

"Construction is not the party right now. If you'll help me up to the house and fix me a double Scotch, I'll fill you in."

"Help you! What's wrong? You don't have any Scotch."

He opened her door for her. When she gingerly stood up and he saw the wrapped foot, he knew she really was hurt.

"What has happened to you, Alma?"

"Let's get up to the house, first. You can substitute Jack Daniels for the Scotch."

Brett picked her up and carried her into the house and into some dry clothes, although hers were about dried, now. He propped her up with pillows on the bed. He brought her a glass of Jack and water and sat down beside her.

With just a few interruptions, Alma told him how her last few days had gone. She had to start with her falling and twisting her ankle. He didn't learn until near the end that the fall was into a water cistern, containing a dead body.

"My God, Alma! It looks like I can't leave you for a minute. Why didn't you wait until I got back?"

"Little good that would have done. I think Rufus is just as capable of protecting me as you are. And he didn't do too good of a job. It was his idea to search for more of the journal. I thought it was a good idea. Now, I know it was. We just may have found Leroy. Me blundering into trouble is just par for the course."

"Thank goodness Rufus was there."

"Why, Brett, I don't think you're jealous anymore."

"I'm still going to pitch his ass into the creek for letting you get hurt."

Alma smiled and hugged him. It was so nice to have friends that cared.

She only had the one bad night. She had the nightmare with Brett's arms around her. He woke her at her first screams. With consoling whispers that it was just a dream and that everything was all right, and with soft caresses and fingers running through her hair, he soon had her calm enough to talk about it.

"Brett, it wasn't the Bracken place. I was walking around this house just looking at repairs I should make. Suddenly, this hand reached up through the ground and grabbed my ankle and pulled me down into this big hole. But, then, there was nobody there. Just a bright light and a round hole with drawings on the walls. All around me were pictures of men walking with a box in their hands and a round hat with a light on the bill. Their heads were all turned towards me, staring into my eyes. All, except one man. He was walking with his head down and no hat and he was reaching out to me."

"That was why you woke screaming and holding your ankle. I'm sure the pain in your foot made you dream someone was grabbing your ankle. And you have been working a lot on the new house and making plans to tear down this one. Dreams are crazy, sometimes."

"Brett, I think that one man with his head down and reaching for me was Leroy."

"Now, don't go reading something into a dream. Be glad the dream didn't have someone down in the hole with you, trying to cause you harm. Just pictures, that don't mean anything."

She smiled and gave him a peck on the cheek. She pulled his arms tighter around her. She would keep the thought to herself, but maybe the dream was telling her something. Maybe, Leroy was thanking her for finding him.

Three days later, Brett had to leave. His phone had been busy for the last 48 hours, and there was business he had to take care of. He insisted that Alma go to his place at the lake and stay until he could get back. He would have his secretary stay with her. Alma refused and told him she was okay where she was. Her foot was much better. She could almost jog up the hollow a ways. She wanted to finish boxing up her things and get ready for her new house. She would move into the hotel for a few days when they were ready to tear down her house. But, when the roof was on the log house and windows were installed, she intended to move a cot or small bed in, and they could just work around her.

25

Jill

After Brett left, she took a long shower, dressed in jeans and a pullover, and drove down to the Black Stallion for lunch. She ordered hamburgers, fries, and sodas to go for her and Aunt Paula. While she was waiting for her order, she had to fill in details to Lori about the dead body she and Rufus had found over at Deskins. At least Lori thought it was details. Alma only told her scant information about rumors the waitress had already heard. She didn't even attempt to correct the false information that was already circulating throughout the county.

Aunt Paula wasn't home. Her car was parked in the yard and the front door was unlocked, but Alma couldn't get an answer to her knock or her calls inside the house. She looked out back and up to the garden plot on the hillside. It was still too early in the spring to be messing around in a garden, but there weren't too many places she could search for her aunt. She placed the food on the kitchen table and walked up the road to Aunt Paula's nearest neighbor's house. She found the two women standing over a woodpile chatting away.

"Well, hi, Alma! I didn't know you were coming by today. I just walked up the road, and Shirley was restacking this firewood, so I thought I would give her a hand. Don't reckon she will need any more of this wood until next winter. For Christmas, Joe bought her an electric stove to cook on, but she's got to save this firewood for her Warm Morning stove in the living room when it turns cold again. Come on back to the house. I'll rustle us up some cornbread and beans for lunch. See you later, Shirley."

"Bye, Paula. Thanks."

When they walked into the house, Aunt Paula smiled and put her arm through Alma's in a small hug.

"You brought food. I can smell the fries from here. You know you didn't have to do that. I could've fixed us something in just a minute."

"I know, Aunt Paula. You are always doing the cooking. I wanted to surprise you. How long has it been since you ate a hamburger, fries, and a milkshake?"

"It ain't been as long as you think, kid. I sometimes splurge and go down to the Black Stallion and treat myself. I don't care as much for the fries since they quit cooking with grease."

"But you might live longer."

"I could ask you what you mean by 'longer', but let's not go there. Why do I have the pleasure of your company today? Brett leave town?"

"As a matter of fact, he did. But I wanted to visit a while and catch you up on my new house and things."

"I know about the new house. Let's get to the things."

Alma smiled. Aunt Paula always knew when there was something on your mind.

Over the next few hours, Alma told her aunt everything. She started with the house and meeting Rufus in the edge of the woods overlooking the job site. She even told her about the dream and how she was sure the body in the cistern would prove to be Leroy.

"You poor baby. I can't believe what you have been through in the past week, or so. Are you still having nightmares? How is your ankle?"

"I'm fine now, Aunt Paula. Just the one bad dream and I can out jog you up the road."

Her aunt seemed so worried about her. Often, during the story, Alma noticed her covering her face with her hands or listening with her mouth open.

"I'm really okay, Aunt Paula. No pain, sleeping well, and I think we are near the end of the mystery Dad left me. I just need to get the final word from Detective Rife that it's Leroy and find the nerve to break the news to his daughters. I also need to share some of this information with Jill. Maybe I'll go to church with you Sunday."

"That would be good, Alma. You bring Brett along."

"He's out of town on business. He tried to make me go live at his place at the lake, but I told him I had to visit with you. Besides, I make my own decisions and I wasn't going to the lake."

"Good for you. But, if you are going to church just to see Jill, I think you will be out of luck. I don't know what has happened to that girl, but she hasn't been to church in about two months. Right after you all went up to that Bracken place and found the Bible and journal."

"That's strange. I called her phone, but it has been disconnected. I also drove by her place and nobody was home. I figured I had just missed her. Do you know anyone who would be able to tell me if she is alright and how I could reach her?"

"You know she is divorced and living by herself? The only relative I know would be her cousin Hester Mullins, that's Jackson's daughter, and she lives up Young's Branch. She and Jill haven't been close for a few years, though."

"Divorced? I never heard about that."

"Yeah, at least that's what she told me. I feel so sorry for her. When she started coming to our church about two years ago, she was awfully shy. Finally, one Sunday she ate dinner with me. We moved out under a big old hickory tree to eat, and she just opened up. Told me about the divorce and how her husband had taken her two children and moved to Richmond. They would be grown by now and maybe have families of their own. She used to go to the Gospel Church of Jesus down near Grundy before she started at our church. She grew dissatisfied or fell out with that church over something. Didn't seem to want to talk about it for some reason. Just said she was so happy with our church and finally at peace with herself. Now, you got me worried about her. With her not showing up at church for the last few weeks, and you not being able to get hold of her."

"Don't start worrying yet, Aunt Paula. We don't know that anything is wrong. She could have just gone to visit some relatives, or something. Do her kids stay in touch with her?"

"I don't think so. Sounded like her ex-husband cut her off after they moved away."

"Well, I'll try to reach Hester next week and find out if everything is okay. I'll still go to church with you Sunday, if you will let me tag along."

"That would be great. Let's walk down to the store and get an ice cream. All this talk about missing people and dead people has got me down. An ice cream bar should get us on another track."

The next day she drove up the hollow of Young's Branch and found Hester Mullins. When she called Ronnie, he had been able to give her a 911 address for Hester. Only Hester wasn't a Mullins anymore. Ronnie informed Alma that she had married Josh 'Buster' Martin, had two girls, and was now a grandmother. A small fact that Jill had left out. Alma found her in the front yard digging up a flower bed and planting new bulbs. She had on a pair of bibs with the cuffs rolled up, a flannel shirt, and a green baseball hat with a picture of a tractor on it. Alma pulled to the side of the road instead of parking in the driveway.

"Hi! Sorry to bother you, but I'm looking for a Hester Martin . Would that be you?"

"It might. Who's asking?"

That was dumb. Alma should have known to identify herself first. This was Hester, she was sure, who looked quite like Jill, except a couple of years younger.

"Sorry about that. I'm Alma Woodson. My dad was Elmer Woodson, who lived over in Little Garden Creek, at Oakwood. I was hoping to find Jill Casey. My Aunt Paula Short told me her cousin lived over here."

"Hi. I'm Hester. I knew your dad and your Aunt Paula is one of my favorite people, even though I haven't seen her in a few years. Sorry to hear about your father. I'm afraid I can't help you out with Jill. She and I don't have a lot to say to each other anymore. I can tell you where she lives though."

"Thanks, Hester. I know where she lives over at Prater, but she wasn't home when I knocked on the door. Aunt Paula and I are kind of worried about her. She hasn't been to church, where she and Aunt Paula go, for a few weeks. My aunt says that's not like her to miss a Sunday."

"Oh, she was probably home if her car was in the drive. She just won't answer the door if she's not in the mood to talk to you. Would you like a cup of coffee, Alma? I just put a pot on before I came out here. We could sit on the porch awhile."

"That would be good, Hester."

Alma followed her up to the porch and took a seat in a weather-beaten Cracker Barrel rocker. A short time later, Hester brought them both a mug of coffee with a glass of milk and a sugar bowl on a small tray.

Alma took hers 'black' as she usually did. Also, because you never could tell about milk. She was sure the glass was clean, but some of these people bought milk from their neighbors. She wasn't about to drink anything that wasn't from a sealed container which came from the store.

"I would like to help you with Jill, but I can't reach her anymore. She left our church a couple of years ago and started going to that old-fashion church your aunt goes to. Now, she can go anywhere she wants, as we have freedom of religion in this country. And, I don't have anything against that church, and I adore your aunt, but Jill left with a chip on her shoulder. I'm afraid she turned into a religious fanatic several years ago."

"What do you mean by 'fanatic', Hester? We have found her to be shy but a humble, God-fearing Christian."

"Well, we thought so, too, until the last few years. Our church is very anti-abortion. Jill fell in with a group led by our pastor, and they even went to Washington, D.C., to join a rally protesting abortion."

"Some people would say that was a good cause."

"I know. I don't want abortion either, except to save the mother, or in case of rape or something. But she and the others were unyielding. They even talked about helping to close a clinic in Kentucky. She didn't come right out and say, but I think there was talk about bombing the clinic or killing the doctor. All she would say to me was that might be the only way to stop the murdering of babies."

"That doesn't sound like the Jill I know."

"She's changed, then. The last time we talked much, she was going off the deep end. She had two beautiful daughters who left with her ex-husband and are probably married now. She was a devil with them when they were teenagers. She wouldn't let them shave their legs, wear makeup, or go out on dates. She just about scalped her oldest when she got her ears pierced. That is what I mean by being fanatic. She thought she was a better Christian than the rest of us."

"I find this hard to believe, but please go on, Hester. It's just not the side Aunt Paula and I have been exposed to. In fact, Jill has been very helpful in an investigation I'm on that was left to me from my father."

"I can believe that. She is quite the con artist. I hate talking bad about her. She is blood kin. But it nearly killed me to watch how she treated her family. That is until they left. Then she devoted her time to the church. She was always a good worker, too. She works some in housekeeping at the hospital and subs as a cook at the school. She would do anything for you as long as she thought you were following Jesus. I think it was more following Jill's will than it was His."

"How can I get her to open up and talk to me about some of these things, Hester?"

"Just mention abortion and she'll be off. Or, you could offer to take her to your hairdresser or buy her a bag of makeup."

"I noticed she dressed homely, but I thought that was just for church."

"If you make any headway, Alma, please come back and fill me in, or bring Jill with you. Maybe we could all sit down and have a good talk and cry."

"I'll do that, Hester."

When she left Young's Branch, Alma decided to drive to Prater and try Jill's house again. She was totally confused and didn't know what to believe. Surely, Hester was just upset with Jill about something and wanted to damage her reputation for some reason. Jill had become her friend and had been a big help, especially with Larkin.

This time, Alma had some luck. Jill had just pulled into the driveway and was carrying bags of groceries into the house. Alma parked on the road and walked over. Jill had seen her coming but kept loading up her arms with bags.

"Can I give you a hand there, Jill?"

"That's okay. I think I have them all now. You can close the lid though."

Alma closed the trunk lid of the car and followed Jill up to the house. She held open the front door. Jill didn't invite her in, but she followed her into the kitchen and helped her unload the bags from her arms onto the kitchen table.

"Thanks, Alma. What are you doing over this way?"

"Checking up on you. Aunt Paula has been worried that you haven't shown up at church the past few Sundays. I also have some information I wanted to share with you. Have you been sick or anything? I tried your phone and came by, but nobody answered the door."

"I was probably in the shower and I must have just missed your call. As far as church, I can't make up my mind where I want to attend now. I'm thinking of going back to my old church."

"Oh, really? I thought you were so happy at Aunt Paula's church. This won't be good news to her. She will miss you terribly."

"I haven't decided for sure. What was the information you wanted to share? Have you found Leroy yet?"

"Maybe! Can we sit down for a minute?"

Jill had not offered her a seat. She seemed nervous that Alma was there.

"Sure. Have a seat at the table and I'll put on a pot of coffee. What do you mean maybe?"

"Well, you don't know Rufus, but he's a hermit who lives in the woods up the hollow from my house. I finally got him to trust me a little, and we talk sometimes. I told him about my search for Leroy and our finding Larkin's mother's Bible and the journal and stuff. He suggested we go back for another look at the Bracken place. Well, to make this short, I was lollygagging around outside of the house and fell through some rotten boards into a water cistern."

Jill dropped the glass coffee pot and it shattered on the floor.

"Jill, are you all right?"

"Yeah. Damn it, that was a new pot, too. I had just replaced my old percolator with a Mr.

Coffee. I'll grab a broom and dustpan and clean this up. You want a coke or something? I don't keep any alcohol in the house."

"A coke would be fine."

A minute later, Jill sat down at the table and they both sipped on their drinks.

"Sorry to interrupt your story, Alma. I just bumped that pot against the sink as I was filling it up with water. Quite clumsy of me. You had just fallen into a water cistern?"

"Oh, yeah. I turned my ankle when I fell in. I was fumbling around in about a couple feet of water, trying to stand up, when I found a dead body."

Jill's face turned pale and she leaned back in her chair.

"A dead body?"

"Well, it was just a skeleton, but it was human remains. Actually, Rufus went down and identified it. I just knew there was something in the water with me. Detective Rife and the coroner confirmed it was the remains of a human. The State Police took over and are running tests."

"Was it Leroy?"

"I'm sure it is, but the authorities won't say until they have all the results back."

"Well, Alma, it looks like you have solved the mystery your daddy left you. I'll bet Grady and his brothers put the body in there after they killed him. Too bad they are dead and there is nobody to hang over this."

"We'll see, Jill. At least I can tell Leroy's girls something. It's not good news, but it might help them get closure about their dad."

"Yeah. Well, keep me posted. I'll probably be at church this Sunday. I miss Aunt Paula, too."

Jill got up and dumped her coke can into the trash. Alma followed suit and started for the door. Jill didn't seem interested in prolonging the conversation. Alma wasn't sure if she had revealed too much information. Detective Rife had told her not to go running her mouth to the press, and she hadn't, but Jill had been a big part of her investigation and she deserved to know some of what was going on.

Alma did go to church with her Aunt Paula on Sunday. Jill was there, but came in after the service had started. They only had the opportunity to give her a hug and move over a little to give her a seat on the bench. The service lasted a little longer than usual. A young preacher had been ordained in yesterday's service and was given an opportunity to speak to the Sunday congregation.

Matthew Keen started off so low and humble that Alma had a hard time understanding what he was saying, although they were sitting only five rows back. Before it was over, anyone could have heard him out in the church yard. Alma couldn't tell if there was any punctuation in his sermon, because the only pause he made was in his desperate gasp for air as his words kept tumbling out. She was quite impressed, but not as moved as most of the congregation. Many of the men and women held handkerchiefs to their eyes, and several women were murmuring sounds that she couldn't understand. At the end Brother Keen asked for a song from Alma's cousin Jim Matney called "BEULAH LAND". This was odd to the faith's custom of lining a song with the members singing along, but Jim did a great job. Alma thought it ended the service well.

After filling their plates, they decided to take their food to a picnic table under a maple tree beside the church. Aunt Paula actually suggested it, as she was aware of Alma's hope to be able to talk to Jill in some privacy.

"Jill, I'm so glad you made it today."

"Me, too, Aunt Paula. I've missed this church more than I realized. I just got so down there for a few weeks. Maybe it was the winter weather, or Christmas without my kids, but I question a lot about my life and my purpose here."

"You have spent several Christmases now without your children. Didn't you tell me your ex-husband took them away when they were just teenagers?"

"Yes. But this year, I seemed to be alone more than ever."

"Oh, you poor dear. You should have come by and had dinner with Alma and me. Alma brought her friend Brett."

"Have you heard from Larkin since we visited him?"

"Of course not, Alma. Why, I'd be scared to death to talk to him alone. Do you think he had anything to do with the body you found at his place?"

"I doubt it. It seems he's been in prison a good while. I just wish he would tell what happened to the pages missing from his mother's journal."

"Oh, are there missing pages? How could you tell?"

"Well, the journal ended abruptly. I figured he, or someone at the hospital, had removed some of the pages. I'm probably wrong about that, though. She just may have been tired of writing it, or became interrupted, and never got back to finish it."

Alma suddenly had second thoughts about revealing too much of what she knew. It would be better to let things fall, or develop, as they may, instead of her feeding the fire.

"If you are finished with the journal, Alma, I would like to have it back and keep it with the rest of Aunt Betty's stuff. It and the Bible are really all we have of her and the family."

"Sure, Jill. I planned on returning it to you, anyway. Could I reread it one more time? There is a lot of the Appalachian way of life in her story. I think you will enjoy reading it."

"Well, I don't think any of us ever had it as rough as she tried to make out. I mean…well, you know I heard a lot of her tales growing up."

Alma thought she might be striking a nerve and decided to change the subject. Maybe Jill would like to tell what she thought about abortion.

"I'll bring the journal over to your house in a few days. Aunt Paula, did you ever hear whether they caught that man who killed the abortion doctor in Tennessee and hid out in the Smokey Mountains? Last I heard, they had hundreds of feds looking for him."

"I hope they never find him."

"Why, Jill! How can you say such a thing?" Aunt Paula had a shocked look on her face.

"They don't know if he killed the doctor, or not. Anyway, look at how many babies that doctor has killed. Don't you all think someone should have stopped him?"

"Abortion is legal in this country, Jill. Killing a doctor doing his job is murder."

"I don't care, Aunt Paula. Anyone who would kill a baby, unborn or not, doesn't deserve to live."

"Sorry I brought up the subject. Would you all like to get some dessert and a cup of coffee?"

"No, thanks, Alma. If you are ready, I think I would like to go home. I'm pretty worn out. Will we see you again next Sunday, Jill?"

"Sure. I think I'm back for good. Sometimes you just need some good old-fashion religion to set things right. I'll bring some of my potato salad next week."

They hugged each other and said farewell to several others still hanging around, or cleaning up, and loaded up in Alma's car and headed home.

On the way, Aunt Paula seemed unusually quiet.

"I'm sorry I brought up the abortion issue, Aunt Paula."

"That's okay, honey. I don't know what has happened to that girl. I ain't eating any potato salad that she brings."

Alma laughed. "I don't think she would poison the whole congregation, Aunt Paula."

"I know, dear. I understand that poor girl has been through a lot with losing her family and all, but she caught me by surprise with that kind of talk. I think she needs some friends. Maybe, we could invite her over to our places sometime."

"Maybe, Aunt Paula. Let's wait and see if she comes back to church regularly."

Alma decided not to tell her aunt about her conversation with Hester, just yet. By the time they arrived at her house, Aunt Paula was back to her optimistic, energetic self. She wanted Alma to go help her clean out the tool shed up near the garden. Alma made excuses to leave and finally got her aunt to promise to stretch out for a short nap before she got started on anything else for the day.

26

Detective Rife

The last Monday and Tuesday of April, Alma watched them put on the roof. Thank goodness April rains had held off. Overall, the work crew had favorable weather and once the roof was finished, they could work inside if it rained. She had overruled Jeffrey on the prefabricated ceiling that he insisted would do just fine. She had a log house and she wanted log rafters exposed. This had delayed the project for a couple of weeks, but now it was all coming together. The windows and doors would go in next week. Then, she could move in temporarily with a bed, a table over saw horses to store her personal items, a bucket, a bowl, and a mirror. Rufus might not need a mirror, but it was necessary for a woman.

Tomorrow, they would tear down the old house. She wasn't sure if she wanted to be around for that. She had already checked into the motel for a few days, so she might just sack out there with a good book.

Brett stopped by every few days to check on the progress. Or, so he said. She really didn't know what she would have done without him. He was so helpful and supportive in all the crazy stuff she got herself into. And fun, too. She wasn't sure if she was in love with him, but she knew it would break her heart if he never showed up again. Well, she would just leave the love part out of her thinking. That could lead to more complicated matters, like marriage, that neither of them wanted to consider.

She headed back for the motel. The next day was Wednesday. She had not forgotten about Max and his buddies meeting down at the Dairy Queen; she had just been a little busy. She turned in early and set the clock for 6:00 a.m. That would give her enough time to shower and get ready. At least she wouldn't have to deal with breakfast, although a bowl of cereal would be much better for her. If she was a regular at that ROMEO Club meeting, she would weigh three hundred pounds from eating all that sausage gravy and biscuits.

Alma took her seat in the same booth the next morning. She had finished her breakfast and was sipping coffee when Max came in. He gave her a wink as he sat down with the guys. The topic for today appeared to be politics. Specifically, the past Presidential election.

"Well, I sure as hell didn't vote for him."

"Would that be because he's a black man or because he's a Democrat, Larry?"

"Yeah, Larry, have you ever voted for somebody besides a Republican?"

"Well, I've not met a Democrat yet, running for national office, that weren't a flat-out liberal and a spendthrift."

"Carson, you're an educated man. Does 'spend' and 'thrift' go together?"

Carson just smiled and dropped his head. He wasn't about to bite into this bashing.

"Larry, I know you have voted for some local Democrats, like our sheriff. I think it's just all that spin the Republicans put out that's got you brainwashed. Don't you think the President might have saved us from going into a depression by getting that stimulus bill passed?"

Brody, Tommy, and Edward were united in ganging up on Larry. Carson and Max only butted in once in a while. Alma thought Max was probably keeping a lid on because he knew she was listening.

"Bailout, you mean. This country is going broke by the minute while the CEOs of all those banks he bailed out are walking off with millions of dollars. Even our grandchildren won't be able to pay us out of debt."

"Did you send back that stimulus check you got in the mail, Larry?"

"Hell, no! I bought myself a new flat-screen TV with that money."

"And we noticed you traded that old clunker you had for that new little Chevy out there. Pretty good deal, wasn't it?"

It went on for another hour. They let up a little on Larry and actually agreed with him on a few points. Alma thought, overall, they were well informed on national events and expressed a lot of common sense. Someone ought to tell the President to send a few of his advisors down to sit in on the ROMEO Club.

As the gathering was breaking up, Max went back to have his coffee cup refilled. He piddled around until all the guys had left, then walked over and sat down at her booth.

"It's been an interesting morning, Max."

"Ah, just shooting the bull. If any of us had enough sense to get in out of the rain, we'd probably done something with our lives besides digging coal out of the side of a mountain."

"I noticed you didn't have a lot to say. Was that because I was here, or is there something else on your mind?"

"Well, if you really want to know, I'm a little scared but mad as hell. I don't know why I'm bothering to tell you this. You can stop me whenever you want. I think they are going to come and get me anytime now. But I ain't going. I'm 87-and a-half years old. I've done what I've wanted to, and done a pretty good job of it, since I left home more than 70 years ago. I don't intend to let some smart-assed kids take me out of my house without a fight. Oh, I know what they *said*, that I could stay in my house as long as I wanted to and could take care of myself, but what they *say* and what they intend to *do* is another matter. That's why the trip to the store the other day got *detoured* to the 'home' for 'just a visit'. They said they *just* wanted to stop in and *visit* old Charlie again. But what it amounted to was they wanted the staff to have a chance to sweet-talk me, saying how old Charlie got a room to himself, a TV, meals cooked for him, and even snacks whenever he wanted one. Shit, Charlie doesn't even *know* he has a room or something to eat. He could just as easily be sitting on a log by the creek fishing for tadpoles."

"Are you talking about your kids, Max? You mean Sally and Kenny?"

"Yeah. This ain't the first time they have all but said I'm too old to be staying by myself. I go to see Charlie every once in a while, but lately they have wanted to take me by. Now, I don't mean they ain't good kids. They are. They have good intentions, I know. But they have all gone through hell once in a while in their lives, too. Take Kenny. He's on his third wife now. He's got five kids of his own. Two each by his first two wives and another with the current one. Think *he'd* let them tell him what to do? Hell, no! That's why he's been married three times. Well, he's *not* telling me what I've got to do, either. But Kenny is a good boy. He fixes my truck when it breaks down and plows my garden. Not that I couldn't do it *myself*, mind you. I just get tired easier now than I used to."

"Does Kenny think you can't live by yourself anymore?"

"Probably. That boy had a rough time after he graduated from high school. Oh, he was anxious to leave the nest, but then he hit the ground cause his wings weren't strong enough. It seemed like he was just going around in circles. Couldn't give him advice either cause he knew it all. Some folks today call it *rebellion* by teenagers. I think it's just *immaturity*. Until we fall down a few times, we don't know how to get up. After he got a little older, and married a time or two, he had a few scrapes and scars to know he didn't want to go that way again. When he got his first car and had to learn how to fix it cause he didn't have any money, he finally got on a straight line. *Now,* he does know something, and good mechanics earn good money. I think this new wife of his might be the one, too. They been working it out now for about ten years. I don't worry about him like I used to. But I don't want to *live* with him, either."

"Does Sally feel the same way?"

"Sally has tried to get me to move in with her and her family, too. She says she's a better cook than I am. I reckon that is true. She wants to take over paying my bills if I'll just give her 'power of attorney'. *Like* that's going to happen. I ain't seen a lawyer yet that I'd trust. Especially with *my* money. It wouldn't be long before what little I had would be his. I'll give you a little advice. Don't ever give up your checkbook. As long as you can hold onto that, *you've* got the power. I ain't gonna pay for a room at the 'home' either. I got more than a room in my old house, and I do just fine."

"Max, maybe you have gotten worked up over nothing. If your kids haven't come right out and said they wanted you to move into a home, maybe you have just read too much into them taking you by to see Charlie."

"Well, I've been sitting in this chair by the kitchen door overlooking the garden for two days now, and they ain't come. I've got the shotgun, 20 gauge, sitting in the corner where I can reach it real quick. *No*, it ain't for the kids, for goodness sakes! It's for them damn crows eating my corn in the garden. I got one the other day. Shot him right from my doorway. They are spooky birds. Always got a lookout. You can't hardly *ever* slip up on one. You got to shoot at them from cover. They remind me of thieves. One looking out and one a-stealing."

"Now, you got me a little scared. I don't reckon none of this is up to me, and I don't know if it's time for you to give up driving a car, but it wouldn't bother me if you gave up having guns around the house."

"I reckon if they were coming today, they would have been there before I left the house. It was almost 8:00. A body *ought* to have been up and going several hours by that time. I had my coffee and met the paperboy at six. I about scared the daylights out of him, though. I had stood behind the pine tree to get out of his way. I guess his headlights didn't hit on me. When he started to put the paper in the box, I reached out and took it out of his hand. I ain't gonna repeat what he said then. We talked awhile. Later, I apologized for scaring him."

Alma laughed. She could see he was settling down a little. She dug the pictures she had brought out of her purse and slid them across the table.

"Max, would you mind taking a look at these pictures and maybe enlighten me a little? Dad took this one of you guys, and you can have it if you want."

"Yeah, I remember when he would come in here. He took more than one picture. He wanted to do a newspaper story on us a few years ago, but some of the guys wouldn't go for that. This one here was made after the Red Jacket mine exploded. That was a sad time around here. My cousin was killed in that disaster."

"I'm sorry, Max. I've read about that accident. It was a tragic time for a lot of families."

"Hey, I know these guys, too. Well, all but the black guy. Grady, Jackson, and Thomas were a bad bunch. We never could figure why they never got locked up and the key thrown away. I guess they just never got caught with enough evidence. Any sheriff should have at least caught them selling moonshine. Who's the black man?"

"His name is Leroy Stuart. It took me a long time to find out his name. But, nobody seems to know what happened to him, or where he came from. Do you remember ever seeing this picture? Or, do you know anything about him?"

"No, Alma. I don't know anything about the black man, but I do remember your dad showing me that picture and asking me that very question. That was way back before we began to meet as a group. I know some of the others were approached by your father, also. It seems he just showed up for the picture, and then disappeared. Your daddy tried awfully hard to find out about him."

They talked on for a while. Alma tried to steer him away from worrying about his children moving him from his home to a 'home'.

"Max, I don't think your kids are worried about you living where you want to. You'll probably be there at your home doing housework, washing clothes, and fixing your own meals for another twenty years. Just don't go breaking any bones or busting your head in a wreck."

"Well, I just plan to stay away from doctors. I ain't having any more tests about my memory, either. Sally loses her keys all the time. I never do because I have a place for them, and I put everything in its place. I don't know why women carry such a big pocketbook. They are always laying their keys or phone down somewhere instead of putting them in that bag they are carrying on their shoulder."

"Max, you're a case. You just keep on straightening out those children and meeting every week with this ROMEO Club."

In the parking lot, she gave him a hug and a card with her name and phone number on it. He promised to call her if he needed reinforcements.

Alma still saw Rufus once in a while. She had to be sitting on his log overlooking the housing project or she would miss him. He would only stay a short time if she was there, with only a minimum of conversation. If she didn't go up to the edge of the woods, she would often spot him there for most of the day. He was a strange character, but she liked talking to him and being around him. It was talking to, and not with, because she did most of the talking. He knew what she knew about Leroy, so she kept him informed about the Bracken place and anything Detective Rife told her about the investigation.

Alma called Detective Rife about twice a week. She always got the same response. 'We haven't heard anything yet from the State. It takes time. I'll get back to you as soon as I know something.'

It was almost six weeks to the day after finding the remains in the cistern when the detective showed up at her new house. She was sitting on the edge of the wide porch swinging her legs to the beat of an Elvis song that Jeffrey's crew had playing on the boom box as they worked.

"Well, hello, Mr. Detective. I was wondering if I was going to ever hear from you again. You got any info for me? Or, did you just want to see my new house?"

"Hi, Alma. This is turning out great. I would never have imagined there was this much room up here. A perfect place for a house. The view's not bad either in the spring time."

"Thanks. It's not going to be just my house. I've decided to make it into a B&B. Want to book a room?"

"Not just yet. Can't see paying for a room when I got a whole house down the road a bit. As far as info, I got a little news for you."

"Want me to wave Rufus down here so you won't have to go over it twice? Oh, too late. He has vanished again. I guess he saw the law roll in, Ronnie. You don't mind me calling you Ronnie, do you? Detective Rife just sounds so formal."

"You can call me Barney, if you want. Don't faze me any."

"Now, why would I call you that?"

"You know, like Barney Fife, on TV. I get that a lot around the office."

"Oh, I don't watch that on TV. I just watch "Who Wants To Be A Millionaire" or "Dancing With The Stars". Or, maybe catch an exercise or food program once in a while."

"You don't watch the news?"

"Too depressing."

"Well, if you had, you might know we released the finding of human remains at the old Bracken place."

"Really! Did you release Leroy's name?"

"No name yet. And it's not Leroy, unless *he* is a *she*."

"A SHE? Are you sure? What would a *she* be doing up there in a cistern? I might believe that if we didn't know Betty died in the hospital over at Marion. But, all the *she's* are accounted for."

"Not this one. We have some more investigating to do. The State Police have a good set of dental plates to match up, and they found some DNA that doesn't match the body you found. That wasn't technically a skeleton you found. The body wasn't completely decomposed, although insects, worms, or rats had gotten rid of most of it. The overflow drain near the top had some veins growing down into the water, and we suspect, could have allowed access by some small animals. There were also some shreds of clothing underneath the body. I'm going to interview Larkin again to see if he can be squeezed for a little more information. He appears not to be a suspect, since he was in prison at the time."

"What time are you talking about?"

"The forensic people pinned the date of death a little over two years ago."

"Was there anyone living there, then?"

"Nope. The last time that house was occupied was more than a dozen years ago when Larkin moved out. I would say whoever murdered that woman knew it was abandoned and knew about the cistern."

"Maybe she wasn't murdered, Ronnie. What if she just fell through like I did, and banged her head, or something, and couldn't get out?"

"That's not what the evidence shows. The body was that of a young woman, approximately twenty years old, skull fracture with a blunt instrument, gunshot wound in the back of the head, and we think, moved at least several feet before being dumped into the cistern. Some of the rocks we overturned had evidence of blood underneath. Our next step is to ID the body."

"Oh, how horrible, Ronnie. There are some sick and cruel people in this world. Do you think she was related to the Brackens?"

"Don't know yet. But we will. It's hard to hide evidence, nowadays."

"I'm glad I didn't say anything to Leroy's girls. I was just sure we had found him, and I wanted to let them know."

"Alma, I'm going to put this to you as straight as I can. I don't want you to talk about this to anyone, except Rufus, and maybe Brett. I don't worry about Rufus communicating with anyone, and Brett is smart enough to know when to keep his mouth shut. Now, don't go getting your temper up.

I'm not saying you aren't smart. It's just you trust people a little too much sometimes."

"Well, it's a good thing you spelled that out, Mr. Detective. I thought I would announce it in church on Sunday."

"You know what I mean. Give us some time. When I can, I will fill you in on the investigation. But I don't want information out there to Leroy's girls, Jill, or even your Aunt Paula. And I thought you were going to call me Ronnie."

"Okay, Ronnie. I get where you're coming from. Jill and Hester are kin to the Brackens, but Aunt Paula can be trusted as much as anybody. But, I accept your limits. When do you plan on questioning Larkin? How about asking him where the missing pages to her journal are?"

"Probably tomorrow. Now I gotta run. Just remember, *mum* is the word."

"Yes, Sir!" Alma saluted the detective as he turned and walked to his car.

She watched from her front porch as Brett in his Hummer met the police cruiser in the road. They each pulled over a little on the narrow pavement and stopped to talk. Rife couldn't have told Brett much, because in just a minute he pulled out and drove up her new gravel road. She couldn't wait to get it paved, also, but she remembered all the other times she had been home when the whole road up the hollow was graveled.

She met him in the driveway and opened his door for him.

"Hi, Handsome. I've been thinking about you and hoped you would drop by."

"Well, he didn't haul you off to jail, so what charms did you spread around this time? I only have so much bail money to spare on troublemakers."

"I'll have you know I'm a valuable asset to the police force in this county. Without me, there would be no such thing as a cold case. They would just file a report and forget it. Before this is over with, I will probably be drawing a salary."

Brett laughed and grabbed her in his arms.

"I wouldn't be surprised. Ronnie said you would fill me in. But right now, I would like a cold beer and to check out your other job. How is the house coming?"

"We're getting there. I think I will move a small bed and a few things in the room upstairs in a few days."

She got him a Coors Light out of the cooler and herself a glass of red wine. Arm in arm, they strolled through and outside the house.

"How do you like the roof?"

"Good choice, again. You really have thought this through pretty good. How much fuss did Jeffrey put up about putting in log rafters?"

"The sucker charged me another three thousand dollars, that's what."

"The place doesn't look the same with the old house gone and the grade work going all the way to the road. It's turning into a beautiful place, Alma."

"Thanks." She squeezed his arm a little tighter. If Brett was pleased, then she had done it right.

"Have you thought about what you are going to call your bed-and-breakfast?"

"Hanging Inn."

"Hanging Inn? Where did that come from?"

"Well, Oakwood used to be called Hanger, right?"

"Yeah. So?"

"Don't you get it? Hanger. Hanging Inn. Makes perfect sense to me. If you are going to stay in Hanger, you might as well hang out at the Hanging Inn."

Brett laughed so hard he sloshed out some of his beer.

"It's marvelous, Alma! I would never have thought of that name, but I love it. Aren't you a little afraid it will scare off some of your customers?"

"Not since most of them will be tough old coal miners. Or, at least, men who have to appear tough enough to deal with coal miners."

"I think you have a point. The name will probably draw a lot of customers just out of curiosity. I suppose you will have pictures or articles up to inform people of the days of Hanger?"

"Of course. Dad left plenty of pictures and a few articles. When I get through, Buchanan County and all those that stay at the Hanging Inn will know we are the King of Coal. I hate it, Brett, but that's who we are, and this is where we are."

"I suppose you will be elected our next Coal Queen of the Appalachians."

She clasped her hands over her mouth.

"There is no such thing, is there, Brett? You don't really elect a Coal Queen, do you?"

"Not yet. But, I bet you could pull it off with your promotion of being King of Coal. Let's sit on the porch for a while, and you fill me in on Detective Rife's visit. Did he say how Leroy died?"

They sat on the only seat she had allowed on the porch, so far. A split log, with four legs pegged into holes on the rounded bottom, and with the wall as a backrest.

"It ain't Leroy, Brett."

The sun was sinking over the ridge as she finished her report. It was startling news to find out a woman had been killed and disposed of that way. Neither of them could imagine who committed such a crime, or why, especially in this area of the country. In Washington or Richmond, maybe, but not here.

"I think Ronnie is right. We should sit on this until more of the investigation is completed. I still would feel better if you moved in with me over at the lake. You could drive back over here every day if you wanted."

"No, Brett. I need to be here and keep Jeffrey straight. Besides, this murder, or accident, happened some time ago."

"It doesn't mean the killer, or killers, are not still around, Alma. What if they are and they find out you were the one who uncovered what they had believed was the perfect crime?"

"Now, don't you go trying to scare me, Brett Parker! You can stay over tonight, but don't think that kind of talk is going to get you a long-term residence. I say we get the first blaze going in that new fireplace and get some blankets and a pillow or two and sleep in front of the fire."

And they did, but Brett didn't have a smile on his face.

27

Krista

Alma decided the inside walls of her living quarters would be different from the rest of the log house. The dividing walls and rafters in the main house were also logs, or slabs of logs with the rounded side showing to give the appearance of real logs. In her rooms, including the large bath, she had them put in drywall. She was afraid she would get tired of looking at wood, even if beautiful, all the time.

Now, she was ready to paint her favorite colors in her private retreat. She chose soft beige for the wall opposite her bed where her dressing table would sit. The wall would also hold a 40-inch plasma TV. She would paint the wall behind her headboard a deep burgundy. The other walls, containing doors and large windows, would be off-white. All the closets in the house had cedar paneling because she liked the smell of cedar. Her bath had a large shower, a Jacuzzi tub, a basin with plenty of counter space, and lots of mirrors and bright lights.

Alma had never thought about all the advantages of designing your own house. Jeffrey said if she could get the painting done (which she insisted on), the house should be done in about two weeks. The landscaping and paving would take just a little longer.

Of course, Brett would show up just as she dipped her paintbrush into the pan. She had put on a pair of cutoff, faded blue jeans, since the weather had turned warm, and tied her hair back into a ponytail. Well, it was too late to do anything about it now. Today, she was a working woman. He shouldn't expect to see her beautiful all the time.

"Well, hi, Anne with an e. Don't you look lovely today?"

Alma laughed. Evidently, he had been to Green Gables on Prince Edward Island in Canada, or had read the book. She was impressed.

"Maybe when I finish this place, I'll write a book. How about 'Hanging out with Alma'?"

"Mind if I hang out a while? I could hold a ladder, or stir the paint, or just admire the view."

"I would enjoy the company, but don't you dare touch a paintbrush. This is my part of my creation."

"Don't you want to put on a smock or apron? You're going to get paint all over your clothes."

"That's why I'm wearing what I am, Brett. When I get through, I may frame these blue jean shorts and put them up in the main room over the fireplace."

He laughed, but thought that most likely she would burn them.

"Have you heard from Detective Rife lately?"

"No. I'm getting a little tired of waiting for him. I may call Brian in Washington in a few days and see if he can speed things up. Sometimes, I think the FBI and forensic people put a little place like Buchanan County on the back burner."

"Did you get to see Jill?"

"Yeah. She was at church last Sunday. She wants the journal back, Brett."

"When? Did you tell her about the missing pages?"

"Yes. She didn't seem all that surprised. She wondered how we knew that pages were missing. I tried to be vague and told her we were just guessing, since Betty had ended her story abruptly."

"Good. Don't you think we should stall about returning the journal? Ronnie might like to take a peek at it."

"Right. I told her I would like a few days to reread it. She agreed to let me keep it a while."

She didn't get a lot of painting done. Brett was a big help in keeping paint in the pan and holding the ladder if she needed him, but he also hinted at breaks. He brought her ice water and wine, ordered a carryout lunch from the Black Stallion, and insisted on timeout for lunch. By the time she called it quits, just before dark, she had only painted one wall and the trim over the doors and windows.

The next day, Brett was back early with ham biscuits and hot coffee. He had stayed in Grundy and met with two representatives selling longwall mining equipment until after midnight. Alma had already started, after retrieving her used paint brushes and rollers from the damp cloths she had wrapped them in last night. She didn't hesitate to stop and rewrap the items when she smelled the coffee.

About ten that morning, Detective Rife pulled into the driveway. They both eagerly put off the painting and pulled up a chair for everyone on the porch. With a fresh coffee in one hand, Ronnie pulled out his note pad with the other and began filling them in on the investigation.

"Alma, the body you found in the water cistern at Grady Bracken's place was a 17 year old female named Marlene Walker from Looney's Creek, below Grundy. She had been missing for almost three years, but nobody filed a missing person report because her parents thought she had run away with a boy from her church. Marlene's parents said she told them she was pregnant and was going to marry Radal Simpkins and move out of this 'hick' county. The boy's parents were equally deceived because, shortly afterward, they got a postcard from California saying he was fine and would be in touch later. Turns out Marlene had broken up with him, and he had driven to San Francisco and joined the National Guard. He now says Marlene was pregnant and he was trying to talk her into an abortion. When she refused, he fled. He was afraid to come home and face his family and Marlene and her family, so he joined the service. He just got out two months ago."

"Did he kill her?"

"Couldn't have. Records show he had been in the National Guard for several weeks, stationed in California, at the time of her death."

"Then who? Was she pregnant?"

"We don't know who, yet, Alma. The coroner says he couldn't determine if she was pregnant. When they sifted through all the water and debris in the bottom of the cistern, they didn't find anything like the remains of a fetus. He said that didn't necessarily mean she wasn't pregnant. Depending on stage of development and the time of decomposing, all evidence of pregnancy could have been lost."

"Oh, my God!" Alma covered her face with her paint-stained hands and cried.

"Ronnie, you got no leads as to who might have killed her?"

"No, Brett. Not yet. Like I said before, the evidence points to the possibility of the murderer being a woman. Marlene had been struck at the base of the skull with a flat object instead of on top of the head, indicating a shorter person. We think she was dragged over and dumped into the cistern instead of being carried. Some of the smaller stones have been disturbed and we found blood stains on some that had rolled over enough to be sheltered from the weather. Whoever did it was strong enough to remove the lid to the cistern and put it back in place and careful about covering up the rotten boards and cistern with broken limbs and leaves. Most of the rubbish Alma fell through came from a large oak tree several yards away from the cistern. But the cause of death was a single 22-caliber wound in the back of her head."

"Where did she go to church? You said she might have left with a boy from her church."

"It turns out she didn't, Alma. Let's see. I know I have that here somewhere. Here it is. Her church was located about halfway between Looney's Creek and Grundy and called the Gospel Church of Jesus. Mean anything to either of you?"

"Not me," Brett said.

"Alma?"

She had not said anything. She wondered if she should. She really didn't have anything but gossip.

"Alma?" Brett reached over to put his hand on her arm.

"I'm thinking, guys. I don't know if this is anything but gossip. I haven't told you about it yet, Brett, but I went to see Jill's cousin Hester Mullins Martin, that's Jackson Mullins' daughter, the other day. She and Jill used to go to that church. Hester still does."

Alma went on to tell them about her visit and conversation with Hester. She told them about Jill's reaction to the abortion murder in Tennessee. She and Brett filled Detective Rife in on the journal and the missing pages.

"What did Larkin say about the pages, Detective?"

"He said he didn't know anything about a journal and certainly nothing about any missing pages. He didn't seem to be hiding anything and admitted to tossing his mother's things into the corner of the closet. Alma, I doubt Larkin has read even a newspaper in the past twenty years. If he saw the journal, I doubt he even knew what it was or was interested in reading it."

They spent another hour talking over all the evidence known so far, brainstorming over different possibilities of who and why. Alma got the journal and gave it to the detective and told him about Jill's request to get it back. He promised to take good care of it, but if Jill should ask about it to just say he had taken the journal after having a conversation with Larkin.

This time she did go to Brett's house at the lake. She didn't want to be alone. Even though he would have stayed with her, she didn't want to spend tonight up in a quiet, dark hollow. Maybe tomorrow, or the next day, would be better.

When they got to the lake, the lights were on surrounding the driveway. It looked as if most of those in the house were burning brightly. Brett must have called ahead. They left their travel bags in the kitchen. He fixed her a glass of Jack and water and helped himself to a cold beer. They walked out to sit on the patio and look over the lake. A few minutes later, Alma asked if they could take their drinks down to the dock, where they would be closer to the water and could hear the fishing boats as they trolled up and down the lake.

The slow rocking of the dock underneath them and the sparkle of red and green running lights on the boats soon had her forgetting about cisterns and dead bodies. The whiskey probably helped, too.

Brett reached up into the rafters of the gazebo and brought down two small casting rods. He opened the small refrigerator, near the storage closet for life jackets and other boat accessories, and took out a small container of night crawlers. He offered her a fishing pole and started hooking a large worm onto his line.

"No, thanks. I'll just watch. I'm not about to touch one of those slimy worms for the largest fish in South Holston Lake."

"Okay, city girl. But, if I catch a nice big trout don't be asking to share it at dinner tonight."

She watched him tie a bobber on the line, so he could tell when a fish took the bait, and then toss hook, line, and sinker into the water. She saw the bobber floating back towards the edge of the dock they were sitting on.

After a few minutes, Brett asked her to hold the pole while he baited up the hook on the spare rod. He had no sooner turned his back before she saw the bobber disappear and the fishing rod in her hands bend towards the water.

"Brett! Brett! I think you caught something! Hurry! The line is all running off the spool."

"It's called a reel, Alma. Just turn the handle clockwise and reel it in. You may have caught your dinner after all."

Since he was making no headway in taking over, she frantically turned the crank on the reel as she held on for dear life. She backed up a step in case the fish, or whatever was on the line, was big enough to pull her into the lake. In a few minutes, she felt and saw the small sinker slide through the first eye of the rod. A small fat fish was dangling off the end of her line, just above the water. Quickly, she flung the end of the pole towards Brett and let the fish and rod fall at his feet. He just grinned at her.

"Alma one and Brett zero. Looks like I'd better get busy or I'm going to be skunked tonight. Do you want to keep it or throw it back?"

"Oh, throw it back! It's still alive. Watch the poor thing flop around. I bet it is screaming for its mommy."

"This probably is a mommy. You caught a pretty good-sized bluegill. Now, there's some crappie, and maybe white bass, that we can catch tonight. They're not bad eating once we fillet them, but I still prefer to catch a trout."

"I'm not eating anything that can look back at me. Why don't we just throw them all back?"

"We can. Does that mean you are going to fish?"

"Yes! If you will bait my hook. That was fun. But I'm still not going to touch one of those dirty, slimy worms."

Brett went back to the house and brought a bottle of wine and some cheese back to the dock. They fished, laughed, and teased each other until after midnight. Both of them forgot about the dark hollows and bad monsters that roam the world.

The next day, Brett drove them back to the Hanging Inn, after stopping in at Cracker Barrel for a big breakfast. This time, she let him join her in the painting. In two full days, they had the job completed. Alma was satisfied and happy. Now, she had to go shopping for furniture. Jeffrey said he was finished in the house, unless a pipe leaked or a bulb wouldn't burn. They would be finished with the yard and landscaping in another week. She could move in.

Brett gave her the name and location of several furniture stores in the Tri-Cities area. One was a large warehouse in Johnson City that offered wholesale prices to consumers as well as to retail outlets. She called Krista and begged her to join her for a few days. They had talked two or three times a week since Alma had moved back. Krista hadn't been to Buchanan County for several months, although Alma had spent a few long weekends in Roanoke. And she had not seen the new log house or the grade work after tearing down their old home place. Alma asked her to be her first official guest in her B&B. She didn't tell Krista that Brett didn't count as a guest.

When Krista agreed, Alma asked her to call when she got to Oakwood. They would meet at the Black Stallion Café for lunch, and she would follow Krista back to her new house. That almost proved to be a bad idea. Just after rounding the curve leading into full view of the house, Krista stopped dead in the middle of the road. Alma almost plowed into the rear of her car. Alma gave her a minute, and then lightly tooted her horn, so they could clear the road and move on up to the house. Krista did drive into the bottom of the driveway, but parked her car and got out.

"Alma, what have you done with our house? I can't believe it is no longer here."

Alma could see the sadness in her sister's face and the swelling of tears in her eyes. She walked over and put her arm around her shoulder.

"I'm sorry you miss the house, Krista. I did ask when I bought the place and all of you said I could do whatever I wanted. I even mentioned the possibility of tearing it down and rebuilding."

"Oh, I know, Sis. It's just such a shock to drive up and not even recognize where you grew up. Maybe you should have prepared me more. Maybe sent 'in-progress pictures'."

Krista was smiling now. She walked over the new pavement that was the lower parking area and used to be the foundation for their old house. Finally, she looked up the hill towards the garden. Again, her hands flew to an open mouth.

"Wow! Alma, it is beautiful! Even from down here, I love it. And you don't have to climb the footpath around the hill to get there. You have a curving driveway right into the garden."

"You want to drive or walk up?"

"Let's walk. I want to take in every inch."

They walked arm-in-arm up the driveway, around the house, and through what used to be the orchard to the new backyard and upper parking area. Stopping at every new twist and turn, Krista would point out what used to be there: the walnut tree, where they had stained their hands so bad hulling walnuts that Alma had worn gloves to school; the strawberry patch, where they had eaten more than they put in the pail or basket to carry back home; the apple tree, that had been Krista's favorite place to hide out and read a book; the huge boulder, which their mother had worried would break loose and come crashing down on their house; or the garden spot, that would one year yield corn and the next beans or sweet potatoes.

Once girls, and now women, they both wiped their eyes and gave each other a big hug.

"I'm sorry, Alma, for crying. It's all so lovely. I just see ghosts seeping out of the new landscaping. And look at that house! I can't wait to see the inside and sit on the veranda and look out over the hollow. You must have spent a million dollars on this project."

"Not quite. But I'm glad I was able to sell my house and condo in Washington. Right now, I don't owe a penny on this place, and I have a new business. Next year, I might want to sell it to you."

They both had smiles as they walked into the Hanging Inn.

28

The Rest of the Journal

Alma and Krista had spent a week buying furniture in Kingsport, Bristol, Johnston City, and all the way to Hickory, North Carolina. Now, she was sitting alone on her wide front porch waiting for the delivery trucks to arrive. Promises had been made that not only would the items be delivered today, but they would be assembled and set up per her instructions. She intended to watch every box opened and inspect every piece to verify she got what she paid for.

It wasn't the furniture trucks she saw coming up the road. The sheriff's car was probably none other than Detective Rife. She wondered if he had news or was just searching for some.

"Hi, Alma. You're up early. Looks like you are expecting someone."

"I am. My furniture should be here this morning. I guess it's a bit early for a truck to arrive from Tri-Cities. Speaking of early, I thought it was noon before the law could find their way to leave Grundy."

"Well, it will be noon before I meet with the State Police, but I wanted to see you before we go to arrest Jill."

Alma jumped out of her seat and spilled her coffee.

"Arrest Jill! For what?"

"For now, suspicion of murder. We are going to take her in for questioning, and we have a search warrant for her home."

"On what evidence? What proof do you have that she did anything? Just because she hated abortion doesn't prove she committed a crime, especially murder."

"Well, we have a little more than that, Alma. Enough to bring her in. Not only was she a member of Marlene's church, but we also have evidence she and Marlene were pretty close friends up until a few weeks before she disappeared. Witnesses say that they were last seen together arguing to the point of fighting. After that, nobody saw Marlene again. At least, she should have some answers for us."

"But arrest her! Why can't you just go ask her some questions?"

"Trust me, Alma. It's best if we get her in our environment and out of her comfort zone. If we can do this, and surprise her, she won't have time to get rid of any evidence she might have around or conjure up a story for her actions. Alma, there could be solid evidence that would prove she killed Marlene, or prove she is not the murderer. There were several pieces of evidence found in and around the cistern, but not the gun used in the murder. We think we can prove the link between them and Jill, once we have her in custody and search her house."

"Then I'm going with you."

"No, you are not. This is police business. I may have made a mistake to come here and inform you ahead of time. I guess I should have waited until after the fact, but I thought I owed you this much. I didn't want you to hear about her arrest from someone else. Without you, I don't suppose we would ever have found Marlene. But, I expect you to let us do our job without interference."

"You want me to just sit here while you go torture a poor girl over something I said?"

"Just sit here, yes. I have called Brett, and he's on his way to keep you company. And we don't torture, and it's not over just something you said. You just triggered a wider investigation. You could be a witness before this is over, so I can't tell you anything that might jeopardize any testimony you might give. I promise to fill you in on what I can, and tell you all when this is over. Fair enough?"

"I guess. So, Brett's going to be my jailer while you're having all the fun?"

"Something like that. You be a good girl."

Finally Ronnie Rife smiled, as he backed off the porch and headed for his car. He would have to keep a sharp eye out today. Alma Woodson had a habit of showing up in unexpected places.

The first furniture truck arrived before Brett got there. She was busy inspecting and giving instructions when he tapped her on the shoulder. She gave him a quick hug and turned to finish her directions to the young man unpacking a large crate. Then, she grabbed his hand and practically dragged him out to the back deck.

"Brett, you're not going to believe this! That detective is going to arrest Jill!"

"I know, Alma. It could be a temporary confinement depending on what they discover in the search and what she reveals in the questioning."

"It's all my fault. I should have kept my mouth shut."

Brett hugged her tightly and tried to assure her she had done the right thing.

"If Jill is innocent, then nothing is going to happen. Except, she might watch what she says about abortion and people deserving to die. Let's get busy and help get your furniture arranged. I'm sure Ronnie will be around later to fill us in."

Alma agreed. They worked like beavers until the last truck was empty and heading down the hollow. Brett had slipped out around noon and brought back burgers and fries from the Black Stallion Café for everyone. The delivery men were careful in their handling of the furniture and were experts in assembly. The only thing left for Alma to do after they left was to hang the paintings, pictures, and wall ornaments. The oriental rugs she had chosen were bright and colorful. She bounced from room to room in her excitement and inspected every detail. She only had Brett rearrange the recliners and sofa in front of the fireplace twice.

They decided to order takeout from the Café because both of them were too tired to cook or clean up to go out for dinner. Brett had Lori fix up a box for each of them with a 10 ounce steak, a house salad, and a baked potato. Alma brought out a bottle of her best red wine. They clinked their glasses together in a toast, over the granite top of her new serving bar.

After dinner, she put on some classical music and he built a roaring fire in the fireplace. A few minutes later, they were opening windows and doors to let some of the heat escape. Alma laughed and said it reminded her of President Reagan holding a fireside chat in the summertime, with the air conditioning on.

She brought out a large bottle of champagne and asked Brett to take a picture of her as she smashed it across the mantel of the fireplace. They were just sweeping up the glass and wiping up the liquid when the sheriff's car pulled into the driveway.

Alma met Detective Rife before he could close his car door.

"Have you released Jill, yet?"

"No, Alma."

"Have you charged her with the murder?"

"Yes, Alma."

"Did she admit it?"

"No, Alma."

"Well...."

"Alma, let's let the detective catch his breath. Why don't you invite him up to the house and offer him a cool drink and maybe a bite of something to eat?"

Alma looked away from the detective and took her hand off his arm. She hadn't realized she had grabbed hold of him.

"Of course, Brett. Ronnie, would you like a glass of wine and some Colby cheese?"

"A cold beer would be great. I think my work day is over with."

Alma got him a cold beer and a plate of cheese and crackers. When she got back to the porch, Ronnie and Brett were talking about the Braves game they had both watched on TV on Saturday. She handed the plate and drink to the officer and took a seat quietly over near the railing. Men! She would never understand them. Here they were, sitting on top of a murder case, and they wanted to talk baseball. A minute later, she butted in.

"I hate to break up this bonding you two are going through. But, Ronnie, can you enlighten us a little on your day's activities?"

Both guys laughed a little.

"Alma, Jill has been charged with the murder of Marlene Walker. She has a court-appointed lawyer and is being held without bail. We found a 22-caliber pistol hidden in her freezer. It was wedged between two large steaks that looked like they have been there for a while. I'm sure the bullet they removed from the victim's skull will match up with this gun."

"I could hire her a lawyer."

"You don't want to do that. You may end up being a witness against her. We found some other stuff, but the gun is probably enough to seal her fate. She talked pretty freely, against the advice of her lawyer. We learned she and Marlene were at first friends in the church, and then Marlene got pregnant. She and Marlene were strong anti-abortionists and had attended several sit-ins and demonstrations. After her boyfriend insisted on an abortion, and Marlene refused, he got mad and left. The next day,

Marlene changed her mind and told Jill she was going to do it, have the abortion. They argued about it, but Jill refuses to admit she killed her because of it. She did admit she had been to the Bracken place several times and did know about the cistern. At one point, she did say that whoever killed her should be given an award instead of being locked up."

"That is like admitting to murdering her, Ronnie."

She also admitted to being in the Bracken house the day before the three of you went there and found Betty Bracken's things. We pointed out to her that her footprints were in the dust between the window and the closet in the bedroom."

"But mine and Brett's footprints should have been in that room, also. We all three walked from the door to the closet."

"Only one set of footprints went to the window."

"And, she told me she had to work that day. I wanted to go right after we talked to Larkin, but she said she had to work and wanted to wait a day or two."

"Well, maybe the reason you found pages missing from the journal is because she got there ahead of you and tore them out. We found these tucked away in Betty's Bible that you said Jill had taken, after your visit to the old home place."

Detective Rife reached into his folded note book and retrieved several ragged-edge pages. He handed them to Alma.

"Jill told me to give them and the Bible to you. She said that you could keep the journal, unless Larkin came and asked for them."

Alma was speechless. She cuddled the pages in her hands, but didn't attempt to read the words written there. She hardly heard the conversation between the two men until the detective stood up and handed her the empty beer bottle and plate.

"Detective, I've been quite the fool. You've done a good job, and I believe you may have the right person behind bars. You won't get any more interference from me."

"On the contrary, Alma. I don't think any of this case would have been successful without you. I'm sure you will be hearing a lot more from the Commonwealth Attorney in the way of appreciation, once this is all over with. As for me and the Sheriff's office, thank you! Oh, one more thing, Alma. We found the white jeep with a broken taillight parked in the barn back of Jill's house. It had belonged to her ex-husband. She didn't drive it after that night she shot through your window. She swears she was just trying to scare you enough to make you go back to D.C. You evidently made her nervous and were getting too close."

They shook hands, but then Alma gave him a hug. As he drove away, she and Brett sat silently on the porch and watched the shadows cover the hollow.

After the darkness had enveloped all but the first stars of the evening, she got up and took Brett's hand and led him into the Great Room, as she now called it, and they took a seat on the sofa. Thank goodness, the fire had died out and the temperature was now tolerable. She turned on the light over their heads and looked at him. He nodded okay.

The last few pages were the ones Alma had hoped to find. The first mention of Leroy, even though nobody knew his name at the time, was when Grady had shown Betty the picture shortly before he had her committed to the Institute.

> *It was during one of his drunken rages. He threatened to do to me what he and his buddies had done to the black man. When I asked him what black man, he dug up a military metal ammunition box from under the back porch and showed me the picture. He told me how Elmer Woodson had taken the picture when they were building the railroad trestle going up Garden Creek and that the black guy shouldn't have been in Buchanan County, much less in the picture building a railroad when he wasn't even part of the crew. I was afraid to ask what they had done to the man, but I did.*
>
> *Grady laughed when he told me that he and Jackson Mullins and Thomas Wills had buried him in the concrete of the trestle support column. When I cried out and covered my head with my apron, he slapped me and told me that they had only done what any pure bred American would have done.*

HANGER

He said it was better than hanging him, which was what happened when black men assumed they could just move in wherever they pleased and take good jobs away from the white men and that it wasn't going to be that way in Buchanan County.

From that moment on, I have not spoken to my husband. I had nightmares for three straight nights after he showed me the picture. I now realize what an evil monster I had married. Because Larkin was so close to his dad and pretty much had the same personality, attitude, and beliefs, I didn't have much chance, or desire, to converse with him, either. It was only a few days later that Grady had someone from the Welfare Office come to the house to interview me. I didn't know at the time that he had gone to a judge to have me declared crazy and admitted to the Institute at Marion. The judge ordered an investigation and observation of me, and, without my cooperation the report stated I was unresponsive to human interaction and sat mostly in a chair wringing my hands and staring through a window. Within a month, I was free at last, locked up in the Southwestern Virginia Mental Health Institute.

Alma dropped the pages and leaned back into Brett's chest with tears streaming down her cheeks. He held her close and rocked her gently in his arms. For several minutes, neither of them spoke. That had been the last entry in Betty's diary. It was as though she had said all she wanted to say. Alma couldn't believe this had gone on in her own backyard. These people were honest, hard-working, loving, born-again Christians. How could such evil wolves like these men be living among the gentle sheep she knew? She wished Grady, Jackson, and Thomas were still living. She wouldn't try to have them arrested; she would just put a bullet through their heads, especially Grady. She wiped her eyes and looked up at Brett.

"What do we do now?"

"I don't know. What can you or anyone do? They are all dead."

"I don't care. They are still going to pay. Is it illegal to dig up bodies and hang them in a public square, or something?"

Brett hugged her again and smiled. "I think that might be illegal."

"Do you think they killed him before they buried him in that cement?"

"I choose to think so, Alma. There is no way to know, now."

"What do I tell Leslie and her sisters?"

"Pretty much the truth, but I think I would leave out some of the details. To know their dad was killed by prejudiced men, back in the days when segregation was the norm, might be easier for them to swallow than thinking he just ran away and abandoned the whole family. I don't think I would reveal how he died."

"You're right, Brett. I can hardly stomach those red-neck criminals' choice of murder, much less think of Leroy's family knowing how he died. Why didn't they just stick to making and running moonshine? And poor Betty. She only wanted to be a wife and a mother and have some kind of home to call her own. Why didn't someone shoot that bastard long before all this suffering took place?"

"Alma, Betty was not the only one to live that kind of life. Back during, and after, the Depression, there was little hope and a whole lot of drinking. Back here, things were less severe than in large cities. Most people in the mountains had a garden and a milk cow, and maybe a hog and they shared and bartered their way to better times. Some failed to manage what they had and just gave up. A lot of wives were left on their own to raise their family, and most, like Leslie's mother, made it work. Assault and battery and killings were not that uncommon. And certainly, not abandonment. Betty got the worst of the worst, and for a longer period of time, but she was not alone in an abusive relationship."

"I won't tell Leroy's children all I know, but I want them to know he was a good man and he loved them. I think Jill knew her dad and uncles were a rotten bunch. Maybe ignorant, but still rotten. I guess, in her case, the apple didn't fall far from the tree. I know now why I never got married. But, then again, I would have shot the son-of-a-bitch the first time he hit me."

"I know you would have, Alma. But, that's not why you never married. You just let me slip through your fingers, and it's taken a while to get back to me."

Alma laughed and gave him a big hug. "Don't flatter yourself, cowboy. I do truly love you for being here since I came back. You have made this place more than tolerable again. I see almost everything in a different light than I once did. Maybe, it's because of you."

29

Alma's Revelations

    The next morning she rolled over and looked at Brett. He was sleeping on his back, with his arms locked behind his head, and snoring slightly. A robin, sitting on a branch of the new dogwood tree just outside her window, was singing along.

    She slipped out of bed quietly, eased into the closet, and closed the door. She dressed in her jeans, a sweatshirt and tennis shoes and walked downstairs. She left him a note on the bar that she was going to see Rufus and would be back shortly. If he was going to fix breakfast, she would take a one-egg omelet, one slice of bacon extra crisp, one slice of toast lightly browned with butter on only one side, and a glass of V-8.

    Rufus was waiting for her, standing in his doorway wearing camouflage pants and a t-shirt. Before she asked, he handed her his cup of coffee.

She took it, walked over, and sat on the edge of the cot.

"Thanks for the coffee. I'm getting to the point I can't get going without some high octane. I've got some news. I started to say some good and some bad, but I guess it's all bad. The law has identified the body we found in the cistern at the old Bracken place. She was a 17 year old girl named Marlene Walker from down on Looney's Creek. She was pregnant, Rufus."

He didn't say anything, but changed his position on the log stool and reached for her coffee cup. He walked over to the wood stove and refilled the cup.

"I know you were going to ask who killed her, so I'll just tell you. It was Jill, Thomas Wills' daughter. I thought she had become my and Aunt Paula's friend. She was going to church with us sometimes. I guess you really don't know someone like you think you do."

"How and why?"

"How and why what? I swear Rufus; you are about the most talkative person I have ever known."

"How did she kill her and why?"

Alma explained in detail what she knew from Detective Rife's report. She expressed her appreciation for his interest, helping to discover the body, and persuading her to go take a second look at the Bracken place. She just couldn't understand why Jill would take the life of a mother and her baby just because she wanted to save the baby.

"It's her religion. What once was a thought becomes a fact, a belief, and then a religion. She is insane. Freedom of religion is for those who believe what we do. Kill all the infidels."

"I'm not sure I follow all that, Rufus. Maybe she was insane at the time she shot that bullet into Marlene, but I think she believed she was justified, and still does."

Alma brought out the picture of Leroy and, now she knew, his murderers. When she asked if he remembered her showing him the picture, he replied by naming all the men without turning it over to read their names. She explained about the journal and the detective finding the missing pages in the Bible Jill had taken from the Bracken place. She pretty much recited what Betty had written in her journal, including her hardships and abuse, and how Grady had described the killing of Leroy.

"Times are getting better. Grady, Jackson, and Thomas were not a lot different than Jill. They had their narrow beliefs and faith and were supported by groups of their kind. Television helped a lot in exposing the whole world to the thoughts and customs of others. But you know what, Alma? I think the Internet is the thing that may save us from killing off all mankind."

"You lose me, Rufus. What in the world does a hermit living in the woods of Buchanan County know about the Internet?"

"It allows us to communicate to the world. We no longer have to take as gospel what our king, president, or dictator says. If we want the truth, go seek it out. As far as what I know, I have books, thank you, and Jerry, the night security man at the library, lets me in the back door and into the computer lab, under directions from the librarian."

"How do you get to the library? It's all the way in Grundy. That must be more than a dozen miles."

"Not the way I travel. When are you going back to D.C.?"

"Back to Washington? Why?"

"You've settled your father's estate. Solved the mysteries. There's nothing left to stick your nose into."

Alma got up to leave. Or, to punch him in the nose.

"I just got my house built, and I will have a business up and running in no time. I intend to stay around at least long enough to see if I can learn to tolerate rednecks like you. By the way, I need someone to help around the place. Landscape work and so forth. I'll give you a place to live and regular food, if you think you could take a chance on becoming civilized again."

"Why would I do that? I've got some animals up here that are counting on me and I can count on them. I don't see that happening with the crowd you are running with."

She smiled and held out her arms.

"Can I give you a hug, Rufus? It might be a while before I see you again."

"Just one. And don't tell anybody."

When she walked in the door, she could smell the bacon and the coffee. Brett was at the bar with his coffee, reading a manual. He still had his robe on, but was barefooted. Her plate was covered, just opposite him. A twig from one of her holly trees was in a vase beside her glass of V-8 juice.

"How did Rufus take it?"

"Like Rufus takes everything. It probably made no difference whatsoever to him whether I came up to inform him of the latest developments, or not. I have a feeling he already knew, or would have shortly, regardless. I just hope my efforts are more appreciated by Leroy's daughters."

"When do you take on that chore?"

"Tomorrow. I want to close this chapter. I hate to be the one to tell them, but I think they have a right to know. I'm going to take Betty's journal for them to read."

"That should help a little. At least they will know that their father was not the only one to suffer from the hands of some evil men. Want me to go with you?"

"No, thanks. This is one thing I need to do by myself. I would appreciate it if you would meet me afterwards. Let's fly to Las Vegas, or somewhere, and get crazy."

"Deal!"

She called Dr. Pruitt that night and arranged the meeting for the next day at the same restaurant. Leslie didn't ask many questions, as though she knew this was about finally getting some answers.

She told them of the killing of Leroy by three evil, prejudiced, white men, the confession of the dying wife of one of those men, and that Leroy's body had never been recovered. Alma disclosed that, with the deaths of all the men and wives involved, those still living had little recourse for justice. Only now did anyone else know that Leroy had actually been murdered, instead of walking away and abandoning his family. She had not brought the journal, but she revealed all the gory details except the burial of Leroy. She watched as the tears flowed freely from Shirley and Tonya. Leslie and Kathy sat stony-eyed, clutching the napkins by their plates. Alma had stalled the conversation until after dinner had been served. She knew there would be no appetites once she told them what she knew.

The scene around the table was so much like the gathering of Alma's family after her father had died. There was a lot of crying, but also a lot of laughter, as each one of them remembered Leroy and the times when they were young, and he was their daddy. Shirley reminded them of how hysterical their mother would become when she retold how she had met Leroy floating down the Tug Fork River while she was trying to catch a catfish for dinner. There seemed to be little doubt now of the love that had been in their family. Tonya told of the Christmas when their daddy came home with a pocketbook for each of the girls and one for their mother. Instead of wrapping them, he had placed one inside another as he had picked out the size of the purse based on the age of the girl. When he gave their mother hers, she kept pulling out smaller purses with one of his daughter's name on it.

After about an hour, Alma knew it was time for her to bail out and let the sisters have precious time alone. She gave each of them a hug. Leslie hung on for an extra squeeze.

Alma walked out and called Brett on his cell phone. He gave her the address to the Pikeville airport and told her to plug it into her GPS.

The plane was sitting on the runway and the engine was running.

The flight to Las Vegas took them a little over five hours. Alma cried on Brett's shoulder most of the way. Well, she didn't really cry. She just vented about Leroy's daughters, Rufus, Jill, her aunts, and the ROMEO Club. She still couldn't believe she had been taken in so by Jill. It wasn't like she was a gullible old woman from the city.

"I was born and raised in the Appalachian Mountains and know all about the rednecks, moonshiners, and tobacco-spitting, horseshoe-pitching drunks that hang out on the riverbanks and any flat space they could call a ballpark. I have never been afraid of any of them, but I would have been afraid of Jill, if I had really known who she was."

"I don't think some of your relatives would appreciate you calling them rednecks."

"Well, some of them were. I think most of them have grown out of it, though. Thank goodness, most of MY relatives are all like my aunts. Sweet, caring, moral souls."

"Are you implying my relatives aren't? I don't know of any of my kin that made or sold moonshine. And I don't ever remember any of them chewing tobacco."

"Of course not, Brett. Your mother was just as sweet as Aunt Ellie. I bet she would have knocked some heads together, though, if she caught you smoking a cigarette."

"She did, once. It wasn't a cigarette, it was a cigar. She didn't actually catch me smoking. She smelled it on my clothes. I tried to blame it on Harold Shortridge and said it was secondhand smoke, but she didn't buy that. She called Harold's mom and we both got cracked on the head."

"Do you know what Aunt Ellie still calls me?"

"Alma Louise. I've heard her at church and during Christmas, but I was afraid to repeat it."

"You are a smart man, Brett. I've always hated that name. Only my family knows my full name, and they also know to only call me Alma. But Aunt Ellie is so sweet when she says it, I can't confront her."

"What's wrong with Alma Louise? I like it. Alma means 'maiden', you know?"

"Stop it right now, Brett Parker! That name sounds like a hick. Makes me think I should be starring on the "Hee-Haw" show, or something. This is the only part of the country that parents call their kids by first and middle names. In some countries, people only have one name. I think I could vote for that."

"It might be a little confusing in a room full of 'Almas'."

Alma laughed. The rest of the flight was more lighthearted. They sipped on wine and talked a little about her plans for the 'Hanging Inn'. She told him that when they got back, she was going to hold an open house and invite the ROMEO men to be her first guests. Free of charge, of course. If any more of them were like Max, they would probably refuse and declare it was just a trap to get them into a 'home'.

Brett had his pilot fly them over the Grand Canyon National Park. Alma pointed out the mule trail going down the side of the canyon and told him about the time she actually rode down the Bright Angel Trail on one of those beasts to the Colorado River.

They flew over Lake Mead and into McCarran International Airport. Brett had booked them into the MGM Grand Hotel, so they got the hotel limo to take them down Las Vegas Boulevard South to the main entrance of the hotel. Brett checked in while she stayed with the luggage and the bellhop. When they reached their suite, Alma checked it out as Brett plopped down on the long sofa and kicked off his shoes.

"Brett, I can't find the cord to pull these drapes back."

"Try the remote on the table. Or, there should be a button on the wall."

"Wow! I've stayed in Las Vegas before but never at the MGM. This view is magnificent!"

"This is the living quarters. Go upstairs and check out the bedroom and bath."

Alma was gone for several minutes. When she came back, she was wearing a soft, white, long robe and a big smile.

"There's only one huge bed up there, Brett. I guess you'll have to take this sofa."

"Guess again. I paid for these rooms, and I intend to spread these weary bones out on a nice soft mattress covered in silk. A nice, soft, silky lady beside me would be nice. Maybe I should have checked with the bellhop to see if one was available. By the way, are you wearing anything under that robe?"

She threw a cushion at him and opened the robe to display her traveling clothes.

"Had you going there for a minute, didn't I? You've got to go upstairs and take a look. Besides the large bedroom with the king-size bed, there's a recliner and a dressing table and mirror. The bathroom is bigger than my kitchen. With mirrors and lights everywhere. And between the bathroom and bedroom is a hot tub big enough to hold all my guests at the inn, with mirrors all around."

"Maybe we can try that out tonight with soft music, a good glass of wine, and sweet-smelling candles burning."

"You ain't getting me in that Jacuzzi, with all those mirrors, at my age. What's not sagging is bulging. Maybe twenty years ago, you and I both could have strutted in front of mirrors that big with nothing on but a smile. But, not now. Of course, that beer gut on you is kinda cute."

"When you get back from the casino floor tonight with your feet and legs hurting, you'll be glad to sink into the bubbles and let the hot water ease your pain away."

"We'll see. What are we going to do first?"

"I thought we might walk up to Caesar's Palace and have dinner at the Restaurant Guy Savoy.

They have the best Artichoke and Black Truffle Soup, and I think you will like either the marinated Tuna or Red Snapper. Are you hungry?"

"Starved!"

They spent the next three hours strolling up Las Vegas Boulevard, eating a delicious meal, enjoying several glasses of wine, and then trying to burn up some of those calories hiking on up the street to the Treasure Island Hotel and Casino to view the pirate ship and the bubbling water fountains.

By the time they got back to their hotel, they were perfectly happy to sit down at a blackjack table and play a few hands. Brett lost a thousand dollars and Alma won three hundred. He called it beginner's luck. She admitted he had to advise her on almost every hand. He told her that was why he lost, because he couldn't concentrate on his hand.

When they finally called it a night and went back to their suite, Brett filled the hot tub and lit several candles. He smiled as she made no protest or complained about age or body fat. He thought she had forgotten about the lights and mirrors until she flipped off the lights as he helped her out of her clothes and into the tub. They were both a little woozy and giggly, as they settled in up to their chins with another glass of wine in their hands.

The conversation was light as they enjoyed the soothing classical music through Bose speakers, but Brett had to defend his skills as a gambler. When he noticed her eyelids drooping, he eased out of the tub and held her robe for her. He left her toweling off her hair and turned down the covers on the bed. By the time he returned from brushing his teeth, she was sound asleep in her robe on top of the bedding.

During the next four nights, they enjoyed the Sahara, Mandalay Bay, Excalibur, and all the night life only Las Vegas could offer. Every night, they took in a live performance at one of the famous hotels and tried to help the economy by squandering a few thousand dollars. They even sat in on a wedding in a lovely wedding chapel, where the couple was married by 'Elvis'. Brett had bounced his eyebrows at her as though he was considering such an event, but she punched him in the ribs with her elbow as she shook her head.

After the fourth night, Alma said she had enough of the good life. She wanted to get back home and feel like a real person.

"Would you like to fly back to D.C. and check in on old friends before you hide away in the mountains?"

"No. Right now, I don't care if I see another city for a while. My friends are all in Buchanan County now. I really do miss speaking with Krista and my aunts at least once a week. I actually like going to church, and I may become a regular at the Dairy Queen on Wednesday mornings. Am I getting old, Brett? Have I lost my adventurous ways? Why am I content to settle down in the Appalachian Mountains and slave for some traveling coal salesmen and try to save a hermit like Rufus?"

"Everything that goes around comes around, Alma. You have made your circle. You have been on a wild, crazy, and wonderful ride. With maturity and age, some values change. I think we both have ridden in the fast lane long enough. We can now slow down and enjoy people for who they are instead of what they can bring to the table. It started for me about five years ago. Now, I truly look for ways to invest in worthy causes and people instead of having them invest in me."

"Is that what those trips to Montana and Chicago and Pittsburg are all about?"

"No. But they helped to build that new wing on a hospital, or a new building on the campus of a local college, or even a new high-tech football field for a high school located in some coal mining community that has always played on a rocky or muddy field."

And he had, too. Alma remembered passing one of those fields on her way to Grundy. Harold had said it cost over a million dollars and had artificial turf, new bleachers, and an electronic scoreboard. She was more impressed with the new dormitory at Virginia Tech. She couldn't understand why anyone would need a million-dollar field to play ball on, but then Brett was a famous jock in these parts.

30

Open House

The flight back to Tri-Cities Airport was shorter than the flight out. Maybe part of the reason was she was so tired and exhausted with all the partying and she slept a good portion of the way. She also spent some time thinking about the opening for the Hanging Inn. Would the old guys show up if she extended an invitation? She planned to use it as an advertisement ploy and get a good write-up in the Bluefield paper. Maybe, it would hit the AP and be printed in cities like Chicago and Pittsburg where a lot of her potential customers might come from. But most of all, she wanted to do something nice for the club. All those old men had lost their wives, and most of their families lived their own lives and only checked in once in a while.

Brett had out his laptop and was catching up on some business and emails, but if she had asked, he would have told her he was just giving her some time to recover and think about the days ahead. Well, that was what she was doing. She got out her notepad and a pen and began jotting down her thoughts on the opening week.

Lori had agreed to leave the Black Stallion and come to work for her. She would make Lori the general manager of the Hanging Inn. She would pay her a salary comparable to the managers of the nicest resorts in the state. This was Brett's idea. At first, she had balked and said she wasn't paying any nosy waitress more than the minimum wage. He was quick to point out that someone would come along and do to her just what she was doing to the Black Stallion, and she would lose one of the most honest and trustworthy persons he had ever known. Besides, was she in this for the short or long term? Alma would have the opportunity to train Lori just the way she wanted the Inn to be run. In the beginning, that might include maid service and cooking, if she was willing to pay enough and show appreciation for a job well done. Alma had reconsidered and was confident that Lori would be there as long as Alma would be.

She offered, also, to build Lori a nice bedroom in the basement of the Inn that would be a lot nicer than that two-bedroom trailer she lived in, but Lori refused. She was happy in the mobile home stuck up in the hollow of Young's Branch. And her husband Cory wouldn't consider Alma's offer, anyway. He worked in the coal mines down at Harman and was perfectly satisfied to squirrel hunt the hills behind their home and spend a couple of weekends a month camping out at South Holston Lake, or some riverbank. Brett suggested she try to hire Cory to do the maintenance and landscaping around the inn. If she had a happy couple working for her, she might have caretakers for the rest of her life.

Well, somewhere down the road that might be a possibility, but right now she couldn't see trying to match, or beat, the pay Cory was getting at the mines. She still had hopes that Rufus could be persuaded to come out of the hills and live a civilized life.

She jotted down some thoughts about food and drinks she needed to stock. From witnessing the breakfast scene at the Dairy Queen, she would definitely need a large coffee pot. She wondered if she could get by with having an RN visiting while they were there, if they showed up. She bet none of them had their blood pressure taken on a regular basis. Checking for diabetes and high cholesterol should be easy enough if she could find a way to get them to cooperate. Well, she could always see how it was going and get rid of anything that might upset them, or make them leave.

Brett had the pilot land at Pikeville so Alma could pick up her car. He wanted her to go to the lake with him, but she insisted on going home. It seemed odd to be calling Oakwood home, but she was getting to like the sound of it. Brett said he would come spend next Friday night for Open House and help out with the older gents if Alma got them to agree to spend the night. She thanked him for a wonderful week in fun city. Brett watched her drive off after he had given her a big hug and kiss. Then, he got back in the plane for the short jump over to Tri-Cities Airport.

The next morning, Alma was awakened with loud banging on her front door. She scrambled out of bed and tucked the pistol from the nightstand drawer into her robe pocket before she eased downstairs. She peeped through the window and saw Lori's white jeep, with the top off, sitting in her driveway. She opened the door to the smiling waitress and stepped aside to let her in.

"Good morning, Alma. You said to be here at 8:00. I'm five minutes early."

"I don't care what I said. You could have at least taken a seat on the porch until I woke up and had myself a cup of coffee. By the way, don't people around here ring doorbells? You scared the hell out of me pounding on that door."

"Sleeping in past 8:00 in the morning is no way to start out running an inn or any other business. I figured if you didn't hear me pull up in that noisy jeep, you wouldn't hear a little bell. Just show me where the coffee pot and coffee are located, and go make yourself comfortable on the veranda. I'll bring you a hot cup in just a few minutes."

Alma did just that. The first thing she was going to do was give that girl a key. This was her home. If she wanted to sleep in, she would.

Shortly after she had settled in the rocker on the porch, enjoying the breeze blowing up the hollow, Lori showed up with a tray containing two steaming cups of coffee, a sugar bowl, cream pitcher, and a notepad.

"Here you go, Ms. Alma. If you had any scones or sweet breads, I would have brought you one to go with your coffee."

"Just drop that 'Ms. Alma' crap, Lori. This is probably the first time in your life you have gotten up before me. I don't expect you to serve me coffee or anything else unless I break a leg, or something. Add some of those things on the grocery list, and maybe a couple dozen donuts. A trip to Food City is going to be the first thing we do. There's hardly enough in the house to feed me, much less houseguests."

"Yes, Ms… I'll start a list right now, Alma."

"On the list, add a half-dozen keys to be made for the front door. I intend to give you one today so you won't break down the door. I also need to find a registered nurse."

"Oh, that one's easy. My sister Hazel is a registered nurse and works in Dr. Sampson's office. Are you sick, or something?"

"No. My first guests, I hope, will be six men in their eighties, or near that. I want someone dressed in civilian clothes helping me around the kitchen, who can also take blood pressure and check for diabetes and high cholesterol without them knowing they are being tested. Do you think your sister can do that?"

"She can test them, but I don't know how you are going to do that without knocking them out."

"Leave that to me. How about giving your sister a call to see if she would be willing to participate and arrive a little early, so we can go over the plan? Tell her there will be a free meal included, in addition to her charges."

They spent the next hour going over details about Lori's new job. Alma was surprised to find her agreeing to all her demands in running the Inn and suggesting a few procedures of her own. Alma promised to hire a maid, housekeeper, and a cook as soon as the inn was up and running with enough reservations to make it promising. But until then, she and Lori were the staff at Hanging Inn.

Wednesday morning Alma showed up early at the Dairy Queen. She wasn't taking any chances on a phone call. She wanted this invitation to be face-to-face. With her cup of coffee and a sausage biscuit, she took a seat at the table where the ROMEO Club usually sat. When Larry showed up and stopped a few feet away, just staring at her, she knew this was the straw that could break and destroy her plans. If she could land Larry, then the rest would jump into her net.

"Good morning, Larry. Would you mind if I joined you for a few minutes this morning? I really, really, need the advice of a man who has been around the horn before. Someone that knows how this county runs, and can keep me from stumbling over my own two feet before I learn how to stand."

Alma managed to express her saddest eyes with her winning, captivating smile.

"You're Elmer Woodson's daughter, right? You've been in here before and cooked Max a meal after he wrecked his truck?"

"Yes. I'm Alma Woodson. Dad left me a mess of paperwork to straighten out. And that Brett Parker has talked me into a business deal that could bankrupt me if I don't get off to a solid start. I really need the advice you, and maybe your buddies, could give me on how to survive in Buchanan County."

"Well, I can't speak for the others, but if my two cents worth can help Elmer's little girl out, I reckon I can afford a few minutes. You're in Max's seat, but I guess he won't mind sitting down there on the end."

"I can move down to the other table. I didn't know you had specific seats."

"Oh, no! I think you are fine right where you are. This boring group should be happy to have a new face at the table. There comes Brody and Tommy now."

The two men got their orders at the counter and headed towards their seats. Just as Larry had done, they stopped short of the table and stared at Alma.

"Sit down, boys. She don't bite. This is Elmer Woodson's daughter, Alma. She wants to fill us in on a situation she is in and see if any of you boneheads can help her out."

The guys sat down and started in on their biscuits and gravy, with a mumble now and then about the weather or what was growing in their gardens. Carson came through the door and, before he got his order, Ed followed. Finally, Max showed up. Max didn't stop to place an order. He saw Alma as he came through the door and came back to the table.

"Max, I'm sorry I got your seat. I offered to move, and Larry told me to stay put. I'll be happy to move if you want me to."

"No, of course not. I'm just surprised to see you here. Did Big Mouth here invite you to sit in on a bunch of bragging old jackasses? I'll warn you now, most of us don't have a clue what's going on. We just come in to kill some time and get pumped up on high-octane coffee. Of course Brody can't cook, so we watch him eat his biggest meal of the day."

"I can so cook. Yesterday morning, I boiled three eggs and fried a slab of country ham."

"Sit down, boys, and dig in to your breakfast. Alma wants to share something with us, and I, for one, am thankful to have a beautiful face and a fresh topic to enjoy. Alma, why don't you fill us in with what's on your mind?"

Larry pushed back his empty gravy box, and picked up his coffee, and leaned back in his chair as though he was the chairman of this group.

"Well, first of all, I have to confess I already know all of you because I have been eavesdropping for a few weeks now."

"We all know that. Why do you think we cleaned up our language a little bit?"

Everyone laughed, or smiled, and nodded their heads at Larry's remark. Alma had thought that only Max had caught her.

"Anyway, apologizing for that, I told Lori, she's a waitress up at the Black Stallion Café, that if I ever needed some advice I was going to crash your meeting here and just ask straight out for your opinion."

"Well, ask away. Our two-cents worth is worth about that."

"You all probably know Brett Parker. He was a classmate of mine at Garden High School a few years ago. We ran into each other again when I came back here from Washington, D.C., to settle my father's estate. I know I should have known better, but I let him, along with my sister, talk me into retiring from a perfectly good job with the federal government and moving back here and starting my own business. It's taken about a year, but I've had the old home place, here in Oakwood, torn down and built a new bed-and-breakfast inn. Now it's time to open the business, and I'm scared to death I've made a mistake."

"That sounds like Brett, don't you agree, Ed? Where there's a chance to make a buck, you'll find Brett Parker."

"Yeah, Brody, but Brett doesn't make many mistakes. If he says it's a good deal, then I'd put my money on him."

"Did you let him in on a percentage, Alma?"

"No, Tommy. He pretty much guaranteed it though. He said if it didn't make a profit in five years, he would buy it from me."

"Then, I say you got yourself a gold mine, Alma. I think we'll all agree you should go for it."

"Well, that's not the only problem. I'm glad you all think I should go ahead with it, but I have never done something like this before. What I really need is a trial run. I need some guinea pigs. That's where you come in. Now, before you say no, hear me out. I would like to invite all of you to be my first guests Friday night. I will serve some wine, beer, soft drinks, or coffee with cheese and finger sandwiches around five or six o'clock. You can lounge around in the great room, or on the porch or deck, until you want to go to bed. You will wake up to the best breakfast you've had since you lost your wives. All you have to bring is your shaving kit and some pajamas. And, it's all free. I just need your opinion if I'm doing it right and what I should change before I start charging some poor stranger for a night's lodging."

"I don't sleep in pajamies."

"I haven't slept in nobody's bed but my own since Ethel died."

"I haven't drunk a beer in twenty years. I don't think I ever tasted wine."

"Come on, guys! This is Elmer's daughter asking for a favor. I think poor old Elmer would roll over in his grave if you just flat out said no to his little girl."

Alma could tell that Larry was getting a kick out of all the excuses, but he seemed willing to join her side. Max hadn't said a word. Brody wasn't going to let him off the hook.

"What'd you say, Max? I'll do whatever you do."

"I'm going to do it. I don't know how long it's been since I slept on new sheets, and I want to see what she's done to Elmer's place. You don't have to sleep in pajamas, Carson. You can stay in your bibs until you go to bed and sleep in your birthday suit for all anybody cares. And she said she would have coffee for all you rednecks that have never tasted the finer things in life. As far as never sleeping in somebody else's bed, you're going to be sleeping in a strange bed for a long time, before long. So, let's do something for the 'Gipper'. If Elmer was there, he would probably take our picture and have it in the Bluefield paper the next morning."

With Carson and Tommy grumbling a little, they finally all agreed they would show up Friday evening between four and six o'clock. Alma smiled. She got up and walked around to each one and gave them a big hug. She even gave Max a peck on the cheek. Then, she took her leave.

It took Alma and Lori the next two days to get ready for the guests. When Brett showed up around noon on Friday, everything was ready. They had large trays of vegetables and dip, fried mushrooms, olives, Colby cheese wedges, peanut butter celery sticks, mixed nuts, quarter sandwiches, and small country ham biscuits. Alma had Lori add a plate of miniature chocolate and sugar coated donuts beside the coffee pot. There was a small table, covered with a white crocheted cloth that Alma's mother had made, with white and red wine and wine glasses sitting in the corner beside the dining table. A cooler of iced-down, assorted beer was on the floor next to the wine.

"Can I just move in? I'll sell my house at the lake and rent a room here for the rest of my life."

"Oh, Brett, do you think it will do? I'm so nervous. I have one of Aunt Paula's breakfasts lined up for in the morning, including chocolate gravy and blackberry jam."

"They'll love it! This will be one of those things that will get stretched out of shape and told over and over down at the Dairy Queen. I'll take some pictures. If you get their permission, you can later display portraits of your first guests over the fireplace."

They all showed up about five o'clock. Alma almost laughed out loud as she watched them crawl out of Brody's Cadillac. All six of them had ridden together. It reminded Alma of the '60's when the teenagers tried to see how many people they could stuff in a Volkswagen. None of them had a piece of luggage, but they all carried a bulging paper bag. Someone must have loaned Carson a pair of pajamas.

Brett didn't get out of his seat in the rocker, but he greeted each one of them by name. He quickly put them at ease with a wisecrack about Brody's car and asked 'if they were afraid Alma didn't have enough parking for all of them to drive, or was Brody the only one to know the way to Elmer Woodson's place'. He added he had already picked out the nicest room in the Inn, and they had better be good to Alma or she might make them sleep in the basement.

"Brett, cut it out! Don't pay any attention to him, boys. He's just jealous he has to pay for his room tonight. Come on in. I'll show you where you are going to sleep. Then, just make yourself at home. We're not serving dinner tonight, but there are plenty of things to snack on or drink. Everyone serves himself and eats wherever he wishes. The sofas and recliners are around the fireplace. We have seats out here on the porch or the back deck, and a few in the yard under the trees."

They followed her silently in single file, with Max in the lead. She thought about saying this wasn't first grade, and she wasn't their teacher, but she decided to get this first step out of the way and let them settle in as they would. She showed each of them their room, the bath, great room, kitchen and dining area. She pointed out the food and drinks and invited them to help themselves.

Larry was the only one to get a beer. All the others got a cup of coffee, some with cream and sugar. Max picked up a couple of chocolate donuts. They stood around holding their drinks and looking over the place. Alma was getting nervous. She started easing back to the front porch to join Brett. They followed.

"Well, what do you think, Larry? I know you have an opinion of what Alma's done to her old home place."

"It's nice, Brett. It just don't look like it used to. I mean, it don't look like it belongs in Buchanan County. I always thought Elmer had a nice comfortable place back up here in the hollow, but this must have cost a million dollars, or something."

"About half that, Larry. One couldn't very well open a bed and breakfast in the old house. She had to do a lot of grading to make room for the inn and enough parking for the guests. I don't think everyone is going to gang up and arrive in a fancy Cadillac."

"I like it. I can't believe how pretty it is up here on the hill. Elmer had his garden and orchard up here. I can remember sitting on his front porch down there by the road and choking on the dust from the dirt road when the coal trucks went by."

"Yeah, Tommy, them were the good old days. Now, the road is paved and the mines have closed, and the only traffic Alma sees are the three or four neighbors still living up the hollow. Pretty peaceful, huh?"

Everyone sat on the porch for the rest of the evening. Some went back for drinks or snacks once in a while. Alma was pleased when one or two went for a walk to the back of the property and checked out an apple tree or pointed out where something had been located when they had visited her dad years ago. She knew they were okay for the night when they started picking on Larry and Brett joined in, until Larry returned the punches with a tale on him.

Just after dark, she noticed two had gone inside, for what she thought was a refill on their coffee, and didn't return. A little later, she and Brett were alone on the porch. She asked him if they were alright. Should she go check on them? When he told her it was their bedtime, she glanced at her watch and saw it wasn't yet 9:00. She went in to get two glasses of wine, and, sure enough, she could hear snoring from the bedrooms. At least they hadn't been so uncomfortable, or so scared they weren't in their own beds, that they couldn't fall asleep.

She had planned breakfast for 8:00 the next morning, but when she got up at 6:00 she heard talking and laughing downstairs. She showered and dressed, then greeted each of them as she passed on her way to the kitchen.

"Fresh coffee will be ready in a few minutes. I didn't know you guys were such early risers. I don't recall you getting to the Dairy Queen before seven or eight o'clock."

"That's okay, Alma. We usually had a couple of cups at home before we went to the restaurant. You take your time."

About 7:00, Lori and her sister Hazel pulled in. Alma had the coffee about ready, but she wanted to wait to serve it until Hazel could check their blood pressure and test their sugar and cholesterol. She knew it should be done before they had anything to eat or drink. Knowing this bunch, half of them would load their coffee down with three or four spoonfuls of sugar. As soon as the girls got in, she let them in on her plan.

Brett finally got up. They could hear his laughter above the others as the stories got lively. The ladies rattled pots and pans and tried not to listen in, but had to turn their heads at different times while preparing breakfast.

"Yeah, Larry, tell Brett about the time you almost got arrested over at the Breaks."

"Ed, I didn't get arrested. It was all a mistake."

"I'll tell you, Brett. Larry was on a senior citizen outing about a month ago over at the Breaks Interstate Park. They were all walking towards one of the overlooks when he felt the urge come on. So, he takes a little detour up one of the trails. He's there hiding behind a tree, taking a leak, when this younger lady comes by and sees him."

"She didn't see nothing!"

"Anyway, she goes down to the parking lot where a Park Ranger is sitting in his truck and reports Larry. The Ranger goes with her back up the trail and arrests him for exposing himself in public."

"He didn't arrest me, Ed. He just stopped me to ask questions and clear up the matter."

"Well, he would have arrested you if you hadn't claimed the lady couldn't have seen anything. You said you were behind a tree. She admitted she didn't see anything, she just knew what you were doing. Brett, Larry told the officer that he was nearly eighty years old and, when a person gets that old, he has to go when he has to go. He also told him the woman couldn't have seen anything because he was holding it in his hand, and he couldn't see it."

"I guess he's just built that tool shed a little too big, huh?"

Everybody broke up. Brett was the loudest. Alma and her help were doubled over the counter. Lori dropped the cantaloupe she was peeling onto the floor.

Alma walked over to the group of men and plopped down in one of the recliners.

"Guys, you're going to have to knock this chatter back a little bit. It's not because I've got two young ladies over there that have probably heard worst; it's because we can't get anything done. Hey, Hazel, could you come over here and check my sugar?"

As Hazel was gathering up her testing unit and the blood pressure cuff, Alma explained to anyone listening.

"I promised Aunt Ellie I would check before I ate anything each morning after she told me that my grandmother was diabetic at an early age, and it wouldn't hurt to just keep an eye open."

"Let me check your blood pressure, too, while I'm sticking your finger. With all that laughing, you may have to put your feet up and calm down a little bit."

"Now, Hazel, I'm not going to have you check me all over in front of these men unless they do it, too."

"Well, how about it, boys? Any of you brave enough to have your finger stuck and your blood pressure taken to impress little old Alma here?"

Brett, being in on the plan, jumped in first.

"I'll do it. I tell you what, let's have a contest here. The one with the lowest blood pressure gets to be first in line for breakfast. Are you next, Max?"

"Yeah. I have my blood pressure checked every time I go to Wal-Mart. Nothing to it."

In about twenty minutes, Hazel had obtained a drop of blood and checked blood pressures on all of them. She explained to Alma, later, that if anything was out of normal range she would have to persuade them to go see a doctor and have blood drawn for full lab results. Nobody tested high except Tommy. He explained he was already taking blood pressure pills and medication for Type 2 diabetes and was seeing a doctor monthly for his Black Lung disease and for his oxygen supplies. The rest of the guys appeared to be in good shape, for the shape they were in.

The men spent about ninety minutes eating breakfast and sitting around sipping coffee and telling Alma what a great place she had here. The only real suggestion they had was from Max, who said she ought to take the large-screen television out of the Great Room and limit TV to the bedrooms. All of them agreed with him that the best part of their stay was the fellowship they had on the porch the evening before and then again before and during breakfast. Alma agreed, thanked Max for his suggestion, and promised it would be done.

    Alma didn't plan on making it a practice, but she hugged each of them and thanked them for coming. She told them if they ever got kicked out of their homes for telling dirty jokes, or anything, to just come to the Hanging Inn and hang out with her. Carson told her he would burn his house down before he let anyone kick him out. She didn't doubt it.

31

Finally

Brett stayed and helped clean up. After the beds were changed and the bathrooms cleaned, Alma gave Lori the rest of the day off. Hazel wouldn't take payment for her services, claiming it was the highlight of her career.

That afternoon, Alma and Brett took a long walk up the hollow and she showed him where Rufus lived. Of course he wasn't home. She told Brett they wouldn't enter his shack because she was certain they were being watched. They looked around a little. Brett seemed to be impressed with the location Rufus had picked out. He had Alma climb on his back and he carried her back down the steep hill, as Rufus had done the day after she thought he had shot her.

The two of them had dinner that evening on the back deck. He grilled the steaks, and she mixed the salad and fried the potatoes. They had fresh fruit left over from breakfast. She brought out a bottle of red wine. A slight wind was blowing through the trees and they could see and hear the birds as they went about feeding the young in their nests. A fox squirrel chattered at them from the tall branch of a hickory tree just beyond the rear parking lot. Alma loved her new place. It was so beautiful and peaceful and nothing like she remembered.

After dark, they took the cover off the hot tub and turned off all the lights. She even had a switch to turn off the street light on the power pole at the front entrance. You had to look straight up, but the stars were so bright when there was total darkness, before the moon came out. She had Brett point out the different constellations to her, again. She could still only pick out the Big Dipper, after he had so patiently named them for her before.

After several minutes, and their necks were cramping, he handed her a glass of wine. After she had taken a few sips, he took it and placed it on the side of the tub. He took her hand, and she felt his foot slide up the back side of her leg. Seconds passed before he coughed gently into the wind and she heard him take a deep breath.

"Alma, I want to ask you something, and I want you to promise to count to one hundred before you answer me. Promise?"

"No, I'm not going to sell you the Hanging Inn."

"Be serious. Promise?"

"Okay, Brett. I promise I'll count to a hundred. Do I have to count out loud?"

"No."

She waited, but he didn't say anything. Just as she was getting nervous, he blurted it out.

"Will you marry me, Alma?"

Then he got scared. Her head disappeared under the water. He swore he could have counted to a hundred before she bobbed back up.

"I think, now, that I've loved you from way back in high school, Alma. After these past few months, and especially after watching you with those old fools last night and this morning, I just don't think I want to live my life the way I have for the next fifty years. I want you by my side, as my wife. I won't ask you to give up the Hanging Inn, or anything. I'll work with you on anything you want to take on. I'll fully retire if you say yes."

"If you'll shut up and let me answer your question, Mr. Parker. What took you so damn long? YES! YES! I would love to marry you, Brett."

She leaped into his arms and they both went underwater. When they came up, she was straddling him with her arms around his neck and their lips locked in a passionate kiss. Neither seemed to want to let go. Just as the full moon broke over the eastern ridge, he took her back under the water. This time, they both came back up gasping for breath, but still locked in each other's arms.

Brett reached around her, unfolded his towel, and took out the ring he had bought two months ago. He, again, took her hand and placed it on the ring finger of her left hand. She couldn't see it very well in the dark, but she felt it with her fingers as if she was reading Braille. He watched as she slowly climbed out of the tub and made her way through the sliding door to the dining area. She turned on a light, even though she was stark naked. His heart skipped a beat as he watched her lower her head, with tears streaming down her cheeks, while clutching the ring in both hands between her breasts.

She dried her eyes with the back of her hands, turned off the light, and marched back to the tub. She climbed in and sat between his legs with her back to him. She leaned her head back into his chest and clasped his arms around her waist.

"When did you decide I might be the one for you?"

"I think Cupid shot his arrow at the Black Stallion right after you came back home. I bought the ring two months ago. I don't take rejection very well, so I waited."

"Why tonight?"

"Every day, every moment, I've spent with you these past months have made my time away from you a little more miserable. After watching you with the ROMEO Club, I realized even more how much love and compassion you still have to share. After two months of backing off, I decided I would never have a better opportunity to get you in a love-sharing mood than now. Since you said yes, then I want to sell out, fully retire, and make you and me top priority. If you had said no, then I planned to buy a couple of other interests and double my work schedule. Alma, I would be a miserable and disconsolate creature if you had said no."

"I thought you would never ask after we both said we didn't want to consider marriage. I'd never met the one, and you'd never met the right one."

"Until now. The others were opportunities to get married and settle down. I felt from day one that they could work out and then they might not. With you, it's neither a question mark, a maybe, nor a possibility. You own my heart and soul. Handle them with care, or I'll be another desperate old fool eating Wednesday morning breakfasts at the Dairy Queen."

She laughed and poked him in the ribs with her elbow.

"They aren't old fools. They are like sweet raisins left on the vine. You would be honored to be one of them, but it's not your time. Do you have a date in mind?"

"How about tomorrow?"

"Now, you are an old fool. This will be my first marriage and my greatest moment. I plan to make it unforgettable. You don't have to spend a penny of your money, but I want to get with Krista and plan every detail. I'll need at least a month."

"You pick a date and a place and I'll be there. I've got a credit card in my wallet with your name on it, and that goes with the ring. I want this wedding and honeymoon to be on me. You buy the moon, and I'll rent a spaceship."

"Oh, it has to be here! I can't imagine being married anywhere but Buchanan County, with all my relatives and friends here. And where would be nicer, or more appropriate, than the Hanging Inn? It's our baby. Your idea and my creativity. How about a month from today? On the anniversary of our engagement?"

"Okay. You and Krista get it all arranged. That will give me time to set in motion the disposition of my business arrangements and assets. From now on, all the trusts or philanthropy decisions will be in both our names. How about turning around, and maybe we could consummate our engagement?"

Alma smiled. She had felt the passion growing behind her. So she did. And they did.

Wedding planning was a whirlwind. Krista practically moved in with Alma. Thank goodness, Lori was happy to take over the management of the Inn. Reservations were already full for the next two months, thanks to Brett's word-of-mouth and the article the ROMEO Club had given permission to be printed in the "Bluefield Daily Telegraph". Alma hired two more women to help Lori and a laid-off coal miner to do maintenance. She also made Lori the bookkeeper and gave her power-of-attorney to write and sign checks for the Inn. She and Krista were then free to concentrate solely on the wedding.

"Alma, this is the biggest rock I have ever seen. What size diamond is this? Are all of these stones on the band really diamonds? How much do you think he paid for a ring this gorgeous?"

"Give it back, Krista. I only took it off for you to get a closer look. I think the big diamond is maybe a carat and those 21 smaller ones maybe about a quarter-carat. I didn't ask him how much he paid, but I'm sure it was in the thousands. I'm almost afraid to wear it out in public. But ain't it beautiful, Krista?"

"It's more than beautiful. Now, we have to get the rest of this wedding organized. I don't know where we are going to find a dress to match that ring. There's the cake, flowers, food, wine, guest list, music, and so much more to plan for in such a short amount of time. You know, Alma, most of this wedding is going to have to be imported to Buchanan County. This should be the biggest wedding this county has ever seen. Are you sure you want to have it here at the Hanging Inn?"

"You had better slow down and back off the 'big' stuff Krista. Of course I'm going to have my wedding here. And Brett agrees. You have got to start thinking 'normal, regular, average, and small' or I'm going to have to look for another wedding planner."

"Oh, Alma, I want to go all out. You have to at least consider a wedding dress that won't embarrass that ring."

"We'll look, but I won't let you pressure me into something unreal."

First, they went on the Internet and searched for wedding cakes, wedding dresses, and drinks, especially wine that would be appropriate for an elegant, but small, wedding.

"I like this cake, Alma. It's a fondant cake with sugar-paste clematis, dark chocolate vine design running down the side, and pink sugar balls on top. It's also got a little statue of a bride and groom on top."

"Yeah! Look at the suggested price per slice - $14. And it's way too huge. Remember Krista, there will probably be less than twenty guests here."

"How about flowers? You want all white, or red, or an assortment? Do you want just roses, or peonies and gardenias and hydrangeas? "

"How about Indian Paint Brush, red roses, and dogwood?" Alma looked at her sister out of the corner of her eye. Krista's hands on her hips revealed she had caught the sarcasm.

"Well, if you're going to do that, you might as well throw in some redbud."

They looked at wedding dresses next. Alma really liked one they found in Jodi's Fashions on 18th Ave. in Brooklyn, New York City. It was a luxury A-line Strapless Court Trains Lace Organza wedding dress. She was having trouble with the nearly one thousand dollar price tag.

"I'm going to call Tri-Cities Airport and see if we can get a flight tomorrow morning to New York. Okay, Alma?"

"Okay, but make it round-trip and we're only going to shop for no more than two days. Promise, Krista?"

"I promise. We don't have much more time than that, anyway. I think we can get it done in two days."

When Brett came in that evening, after giving both girls a hug and accepting congratulations from Krista, he and Alma decided on a walk up the hollow so he could stretch his legs, after a day in conferences with his brother and attorneys. They really just wanted to get away from the energized Krista and Lori as they packed a traveling bag for tomorrow's trip.

"So the mountain gals are off to the city tomorrow?"

"I guess, Brett. I'm not sure I should have let Krista talk me into that. She's been on the Internet all afternoon looking at wedding stuff. Now, she thinks we have to go all the way to New York City to find me THE wedding dress."

"I think that's an excellent idea, Alma. If you have time, please do this the way you want. I don't want to wait to get married, but I want you to have everything just the way you might dream it to be. The sky is the limit, as far as I'm concerned."

"Don't be silly, Brett. I want a nice wedding, but I don't care about wasting money, even if it is your money. This is Buchanan County. I don't think some of the folks we're going to be inviting would feel comfortable if it gets too big and fancy."

"You're the one being silly. These folks read fashion magazines and watch the Travel Channel and award shows on TV and have seen the best of the best. They would give their eye teeth to be part of an out-of-this-world wedding. Just ask your aunts."

Alma had to laugh. She could just picture her two aunts, all dressed up in their best, coming to a fancy wedding and enjoying every minute of it. But, she couldn't see either one of them going out and spending another dollar on a fancy dress they would only wear one time.

"Okay, Brett. We'll see what we can do, but we'll be back in two days, three at the most. I've got too much to do to be going crazy in New York with a crazy sister."

"Take your time and show Krista around the city a little. Take her to a show on Broadway. I've got to leave tomorrow, also. I'm flying to Pittsburg, then Chicago, and on to Montana to tie up some loose ends. By the time our wedding is over, I'll be free as a bird to take a month, or longer, honeymoon. Where do you want to go?"

"I don't know. How about you?"

"I want this to be your choice. It's hard for me to pick a place you haven't been. Maybe you could pick a place you really enjoyed and we could go there again."

"No. I want our honeymoon to be somewhere just for us. Have you been to Australia?"

"Once. My brother and I went to the Outback to hike and to check on investing in a diamond mine in the Kimberley."

"Really! I've read where Western Australia is the world's biggest producer of natural diamonds. Did you buy a diamond mine?"

"Yeah, that's where that rock you're wearing came from. No, just kidding. We decided the black diamond is all we needed to concentrate on."

"Shoot, I would love to own a diamond mine. I've never been to Australia. Let's go cruise the South Pacific on our honeymoon. We could visit Tahiti, maybe New Zealand, and stop in Sydney. If the temptation is great enough, we could hike into the Outback. Maybe, at least, go see a diamond mine. What do you think?"

"South Pacific, here we come! You'd better give Lori a crash course in managing this place for a while and have Krista as a backup. We could be gone several weeks."

"Oh, I forgot about the Hanging Inn. We can't possibly leave for more than a week, Brett. I'm just getting it off the ground. Maybe we could go over to the Breaks Interstate Park for a few days.

Then, if something goes wrong, Lori could get in touch with me."

He laughed and pushed her towards the bank of the creek.

"Lori will do fine. In any case, I've asked Charlie if he'll check in once in a while. You can give both Lori and Krista his number in case they need anything."

"You know, Brett, I've never met Charlie. He graduated about five years before we did, and I never really knew him."

"Well, you're going to know him. He's my best man. He now heads up all the family business. From now on, I only give him advice when he asks for it. He promised to keep a check coming my way."

They had come to the end of the road, so they turned around and headed back down the hollow. Alma wondered if they were making a big mistake. Would Brett regret giving up control of all he had worked so hard for and marrying her? Would she miss the independence she had guarded so carefully over the years? She took his arm and leaned her head on his shoulder, as they meandered back towards home. Lost in their own thoughts, they both knew it was now or never.

The next morning, Alma and Krista left before daylight to get to Tri-Cities Airport for the 7:00 flight to New York. After checking in, they had over an hour's wait, thanks to 9-11, so they headed to the vending area for a cup of coffee, and maybe a sweet roll of some kind.

"Alma, I've been thinking of the drinks for the reception. I know we'll have coffee and bottled water for our aunts and some of the older people, but I don't know what wine or champagne to serve."

"I think you'll want to pick one white and one red wine, Krista. You don't want a sweet white wine, or a big Barolo, or a red Zinfandel. I'd say a Sauvignon Blanc or a dry Riesling and a Chardonnay or White Burgundy from France. For the red pick a Pinot Noir. As for the champagne for the toast, I'd go instead with a Prosecco or a Cava."

"My gosh, Alma, you have totally lost me. I guess you'll have to be in charge of the wine."

"Oh, just tell Brett he's in charge. He'll turn it over to Charlie, and everyone will be happy."

"Whew! Thanks. I'll do just that."

Brett had said to treat Krista to New York City, so Alma had the taxi drop them off at the Mandarin Oriental. She wanted a view from high above Central Park or overlooking the Hudson River. When they checked into their 34th floor room, Alma pulled back the drapes of the floor-to-ceiling windows and just stood back and enjoyed the look on Krista's face. She wondered, with the king-size beds and spacious powder rooms, if she would be able to get Krista out of the hotel to do any shopping.

That afternoon, they saw the strapless wedding dress in Jodi's and looked at several bridesmaids' dresses. Alma liked the brush train chiffon woven satin evening dress but, again, wasn't sure about the $900 price tag. She wouldn't let Krista pressure her into getting the dresses and said they would sleep on it and maybe come back tomorrow.

They dined that night at the Time Warner Center and sipped wine for an extra hour as they discussed the wedding and New York City.

"I think you should have gotten the wedding dress and the bridesmaids' dresses, Alma."

"You know what I'm thinking. I think I'll have everyone dress like the actors in West Side Story. All the girls will have full skirts or dresses, and the guys will have tight pants or jeans, with white T-shirts or collared shirts with the collars turned up. I'll have Brett and the boys in the wedding party slick back their hair and the girls will all get perms or sleep in rollers the night before. We'll inform the guests of our theme and encourage them to dress accordingly."

"You're drunk, Alma. I can just see Aunt Paula with her hair curled up and wearing a full tailed skirt with ten petticoats underneath. If she drinks some of that fancy wine you're planning on having, she'll probably lose her teeth in the wine glass."

"No, I'm not kidding, Krista. We're going to the first Broadway show tomorrow of West Side Story. Then, you can give me your honest opinion."

"I'm telling you now. We're going back to buy those dresses. Then, you can take me to a show. Nobody will be able to find those kinds of clothes in time for the wedding, anyway."

"Then, they can all wear peg-legged jeans and white T-shirts. The ladies can wear whatever skirt or dress they want, as long as they have a tight-fitting blouse and an open sweater. You just wait until you see the show."

The next day, they went to the Broadway show. Both girls had seen the movie in the early 1960's - Alma shortly after moving to D.C. and Krista while she was still in high school, at the old Lynwood Theater. Nothing compared to the Broadway musical. They sat spellbound in their seats as the theater emptied. They walked arm-in-arm several blocks back towards their hotel.

Finally, Krista came to her senses.

"Let's do it, Alma. I want to dress up like we did in the good old days. I want to hear that music again. I'll bet you and Brett could still pull off a dance or two like they did on that stage. Just think, you graduated from Garden High School about the time the movie got nominated for a Tony Award for Best Musical. Do you think if I stuff my bra, I could look just a little like Natalie Wood?"

Alma laughed. She was sure that Brett would look better than Richard Beymer had in the movie.

"We'll do it. Tomorrow, I'm going to show you the city. Then, we're flying home and getting this West Side Story wedding on the road.

The next day they toured the Empire State Building, Rockefeller Center, the Statue of Liberty, Ellis Island, and the Metropolitan Museum of Art. They collapsed in their bed before the sun went down.

Alma detoured from Tri-Cities Airport to drop Krista off at her home in Roanoke. Krista wanted a day to catch up with some housework and fill Jack in on the plans. Her husband didn't mind the time she was putting in with Alma. With Janice out of state and William up to his neck in his business, Jack was glad to see the two sisters bonding again. He had always doubted Alma ever coming back home again.

When Alma pulled into the driveway at the Hanging Inn, she was surprised to see no cars in the parking lot except Lori's and a sheriff's car. It was late in the evening, so, surely, at least some of the guests had arrived. When she had called Lori last night, she said they were full and everything was going just fine. Lori met her at the door.

"What's wrong, Lori? There are no cars in the parking lot. Did you have a bomb scare, or something? Why is there a sheriff's car in the driveway?"

"Slow down, Alma. That's Detective Rife's car. Ronnie is in the Great Room and said he needed to talk with you. I'll tell you about the guests, later."

"Hi, Detective. Have you scared all my guests away? There's not been a criminal spend a night here since we opened. Oh, I bet it's about Jill. Do you have news about her? She didn't escape, or anything?"

"Sit down a minute, Alma. You always have asked too many questions."

Alma sat down on the hearth of the fireplace. She looked the detective in the eyes for a minute, and then she buried her head in her hands. She didn't want to see the truth. She didn't want to hear it, either.

"Alma, there's been an accident. A plane crashed in the Rockies, just east of Montana. Alma, I'm so sorry, but Brett and his pilots are dead."

Alma's later years

32
Alma Looks Back

Alma had allowed Krista and Lori to give her an eightieth-birthday party last year, but she wasn't having any of that this year. She might let them try again if she made it to ninety. She spread the files and pictures out on the bed and began to place them into piles. The ones from her dad's files were now old and fragile. She smiled. Pretty much like herself - old and brittle.

She picked up the one of the three white men and the black man in the middle. She could still name the men in the picture without turning it over to read the back. The big guy on the left was Grady Bracken and he had a son named Larkin. She reckoned Larkin had finally gotten out of prison a while ago, but she hadn't heard anything about him for more than twenty years. The man in the middle of the back row was Jackson Mullins and he had a good girl named Hester. If Hester hadn't helped her out, they would have never figured out who killed the poor girl in the cistern up at Grady's place. The man on the right was Thomas Wills. Thomas' daughter Jill had fooled both her and her Aunt Paula completely. They had actually liked the young woman and couldn't believe she was a murderer. The black man in the middle, with Grady's big hand on his shoulder, was Leroy Stuart. He had four beautiful daughters who had made wonderful lives for themselves after Leroy had been buried, possibly alive, in the concrete of a railroad trestle just a mile down the road from the Inn, by the three white men.

Alma looked at the picture a few seconds longer, and then placed it on top of an old diary that had faded in color and was ragged around the edges. She would read the account of Larkin's mother's hardships again, but not just now. She would still seek revenge for her if she could. Maybe, if Larkin was still alive and out of prison, she could find him and pull out his fingernails one by one, or something.

She dumped the folder with pictures and notes from her early days working for the government. She liked the one of her with President Reagan and Nancy. She remembered the time the Secret Service had asked her to look after the President's daughter for a few minutes, while the President and First Lady visited with some foreign dignitaries. She smiled as she remembered losing Patti in the hallway as she let her run and play. It took ten Secret Service men to round up the little girl before the President and his wife returned.

She turned over the picture of her and Neil Armstrong to see if she had written the names on the back. One day, her nieces and nephews might run across some of the pictures and not know who they were. Heck, some of them might not know who she is. She hardly ever saw any of her family, anymore. Krista would check in about once a month, but she never brought her kids or grandchildren. Well, anyway, if they wanted to know, she would have at least recorded the names of the people in the pictures. The last time she had seen Neil was before she had retired from working for the State Department. She had run into him at that famous Redskins quarterback's restaurant out near Seven Corners. Now, what was that quarterback's name?

Alma pulled her cell phone out of her pocket when she felt it vibrate. She always had the ring turned off because she liked to check and see who was calling before she answered. If it rang when others were around, they would know she had gotten a call and didn't bother to answer her phone. This time it was Lori, and she knew what she wanted. It was time for dinner. If she didn't answer, then Lori would just come up and pound on her door.

"Yes, Lori."

"Alma, it's time for dinner. Would you like me to bring up a tray, or do you wish to join us in the dining area?"

"I'm coming down. Ain't it a little late to be eating?"

"Same time as always. Five o'clock."

"Well, my clock says about a quarter after. Anyway, I'm coming on down."

She hung up without saying goodbye. After all these years, Lori wouldn't know what to say if she offered a greeting or a farewell. Alma knew she ought to be nicer to Lori and her husband Cory. They may very well be the only reason she wasn't in a nursing home or assisted living somewhere. Cory had come to work for her at the Hanging Inn about a year after she had opened the bed-and-breakfast. Lori had been there from the start. Those two actually ran the place now, even though Alma was the owner. She really only lived here now like a guest, but that didn't stop her from issuing orders and making demands on how to run the place and how to treat the other guests. Of course, Lori promptly disregarded everything she said.

    Alma got her cane and walked downstairs. She could still handle the stairs without the cane, but she would need it after dinner for her walk up the hollow. She had stubbornly refused to have anything to aid her in getting around, until she had fallen two years ago against the bathtub and broken a bone in her upper thigh. It had only been a hairline fracture, but it sure hurt like hell. After leaning on Cory for almost a month, she had agreed to get a cane. Now, it was part of her and it helped in her walk.

    "Cory and I are having pork chops with our vegetables, Alma. Do you want me to add one to your plate?"

    "Of course not, Lori. You know I gave up meat a few years ago. I'll just have some of those carrots and green beans and sweet potatoes, with a glass of milk. Maybe I'll have a small bowl of pinto beans with cornbread, too."

    "What have you been doing today, Alma? I haven't seen you since breakfast."

"Well, I've been busy. I'm organizing my files and cleaning out some of that stuff in my desk. I can't stand being unorganized and having a mess where you can't find something when you need it."

She saw Lori look over at Cory and smile. She knew what they were thinking. They had heard all this before. She guessed she had used the organizing bit a little too much. Well, it was true. She didn't often throw away anything, but she did go through it all and would sometimes place things in a more detailed folder, or add a note of reminder.

"I think I will have my dinner on the back deck. Cory, would you be so kind as to carry my tray out to the table by my chair?"

"I'll be happy to, Alma. I thought you only used the cane to go for walks up the hollow."

"Well, that's exactly what I'm going to do right after dinner."

She could hear them through the partially opened window by her chair as she ate her vegetables. Lori liked to run the air conditioning in the summer, but Alma insisted on fresh air after the heat of the day had passed, with open windows and sliding screen doors for cross ventilation.

"I think I'm going to offer to help her organize her files the next time she wants to work on them. I think I could finish that job she's been working on for the past ten years in about thirty minutes."

"Now you be quiet, Cory. She's not just organizing, she's remembering. I know how it was last summer when I cleaned out my old sock drawer and ran across pictures of the kids when they were little and in school. You just can't pick up a picture and put it somewhere. You have to take time to remember the good old days."

Alma picked up her plate and moved over to another chair and side table. Sometimes it was best not to hear what someone else was thinking.

She looked out to the old parking lot, where a few fruit trees had been growing in the past. The parking lot was still there, but now there were another twenty bedrooms built over the top of it on tall, stilt like, steel posts. She had built herself an additional bedroom and master bath on the first level of the inn, for when the time came she could no longer climb the stairs. For now, Lori and Cory used it when they were too busy to spend the night in their home. Climbing the stairs was something she wanted to do as long as she could. She knew the exercise was good for her, as well as the daily walk up the hollow when the weather would allow it.

The demand for more lodging had increased with the new Pharmacy School that had been built out of her old high school. Now, there were hundreds of graduate students attending the renovated building she had so anxiously wanted to vacate. They had built an additional building on the baseball field, for administration, classroom, and labs with the same outside architectural design as the old Garden High School. Where the elementary school had once been across Garden Creek, there was now an overflow parking lot with a new bridge to the adjoining parking lot of the school.

She was proud of the Appalachian College of Pharmacy, although she hated that Garden High

School no longer existed. The school board had consolidated Garden and Whitewood High Schools and built the new Twin Valley High School over at Whitewood. Although she didn't object to the consolidation, she didn't think it made any sense to locate the new school across the mountain, where it made it so hard for other schools to get to, instead of along the only four-lane highway in Buchanan County.

She finished what she wanted of her meal and left the plate and glass on the table. If Lori hadn't picked them up by the time she got back from her walk, then she would take them in and put them in the dishwasher. She eased down the handicap ramp with her cane, holding to the handrail. The hardest part of her walk was the climb back up the driveway. But she knew, as long as she could make it up the hill, she was still a good ways away from the assisted-living thing Krista kept bringing up.

Alma didn't go as far as she used to. She still tried to make it up to the forks of the road where Rufus's trail had snaked along through the weeds. It was all grown up now. The crazy fool had killed himself. No, she knew it wasn't suicide but he had killed himself nevertheless. Being over seventy-years old and climbing up in an old, handmade deer stand was the same as committing suicide. He had fallen about twelve feet out of the stand when one of the rotten boards had broken. He landed and hit his head on some rocks below. Nobody found him for a week. Then, the county buried him without a formal funeral before most people knew he was dead. She had let the Sheriff and members of the Board of Supervisors hear about that. After making several excuses, like he had no family with his ex-wife dying several years before and no kids, they apologized for their actions and said it wouldn't happen again. She wouldn't let it lie until they wrote it into their policy and procedure manual.

She stopped several times to catch her breath and let her legs revive, and to reminisce about earlier walks up this hollow. Some memories she pushed aside and concentrated on the ones when Rufus would suddenly appear and walk with her for a while. He had shown up often right after she and Krista had spent that fabulous week in New York. Rufus would tag along until she turned to walk back and usually stayed with her until they came within sight of the inn. Sometimes, he would take her arm or put his hand on her shoulder as they walked. He hardly ever said anything, but, if he found her mood going downhill, he would point out a bird or ground squirrel, or some wildflower that he would venture up, or over, the hillside to pick for her.

She wondered if his shack was still standing. Probably not, after all these years. Hunters or ginseng gatherers had most likely ransacked the place, taking his guns and anything of value, which couldn't have been much. Rufus's life must have been lonely, but she never heard him complain about anything except to be left alone. His war injury probably had something to do with his relationship with his wife and their sexual compatibility; them having no kids, and him leaving her so quickly after returning from the war. Alma was glad the wife had moved on, married, and had children of her own.

Men and their egos. She shook her head and walked back to the inn.

"Alma, the Hospital Board called to ask if you wanted a ride to the Board meeting tomorrow evening, at 5:00. I told the secretary you would call them back, if you did."

"Thanks, Lori. Why would I want them to pick me up? I've always driven myself, before. I guess, just because I'm about to have another birthday, they think I can't drive. Well, the day I can't drive myself to those stupid meetings is the day I resign."

She stomped off to her room. She always took another shower after her walk and put on her nightgown and robe. The water felt good, and it was a pleasure to feel clean and refreshed as she sat in the glider on the front porch listening to the evening sounds and watching the sun go down. She couldn't actually see the sun setting, because it moved out of sight here in the hollow just after mid-day, but she often got a pretty colored sky when the clouds hovered just over the ridge tops along Route 460. Also, this was the time of day when the guests started drifting back in. They would usually stop and take a seat to chat a while.

Most of her guests were there for the long term. She had about six that paid in advance for a whole year. They didn't want to take a chance of losing their room or not getting one. Two of the longwall mining equipment salesmen stayed at the Hanging Inn only three or four nights a week, but would pay for a month in advance so they would be guaranteed a room. The same was true of a few of the wealthier pharmacy school students, although most of her guests from there were the parents, or State or Federal officials checking on the school. She didn't do any advertising, and didn't need to. The Hanging Inn's reputation had gotten around.

"Hi, Marshal. Did'ya make a pile of money today?"

"Hello, Alma. I did okay. I sold one longwall machine and two roofbolters. That ought to make my wife happy when I get home."

They all stopped calling her Ms. Woodson when she threatened not to rent them a room. She knew it was traditional and a credit to their upbringing to call old people Miss, Mrs., or even Ms., but even though she was now old, and not just older, she just plain liked to be called by her first name. She smiled at the recollection of how she hated the name Alma Louise when she was a teenager.

"Are you heading home tomorrow?"

"Yeah. I'm flying out of Tri-Cities about noon. But don't you be giving my room away. I've got five more companies to call on next week."

"Don't worry, Marshal. If I recall correctly, you've paid up until the end of the year. I really don't see why you don't let me rent the room when you're not here, and I could refund you some of your money."

"No way! The company thinks I'm getting a real deal the way it is. I guess, by some of the expenses they pay out when I go to Pittsburg or Chicago, it is a good deal. I'll probably spend more time here and in West Virginia now that the underground mining has picked back up. Putting a stop to that mountain-top-removal mining has been a big boost to us. The Federal government did us a big favor."

"I'm glad to see it stopped, too, Marshal. I remember when I first came back here. The strip mines and the tops of mountains scraped off looked horrible. Now the hardwood trees are coming back. The work done on land reclamation has been a blessing."

"Yeah, it was the right thing to do. I never thought the coal companies would lose that fight. I guess the regulations to keep the streams and the cost to refurbish the land was too expensive. Anyway, they're mining more coal than ever and most of the deep shafts are located below Dismal Creek and closer to the West Virginia and Kentucky borders. You've seen a lot of changes here in Buchanan County, haven't you, Alma? Did you ever think you would see the mines and tipples camouflaged behind a forest of pine trees?"

"Yeah, I've seen a bunch. The pine trees help a lot with the dust, too. You are too young to remember the Red Jacket mine explosion, Marshal, but that happened about the time I was born. Lots of men have lost their lives in coal mines. I guess the only good thing you can say about surface mining is very few have gotten killed riding a dozer or monster trucks. But a few have, when a boulder rolled down the side of the mountain into a bedroom. The men seem to like the work inside, and I reckon they have provided a lot of energy for America and kept electric bills down. I'm glad they have gone back underground since the government set such high safety regulations. Knock on wood, but there have only been a few accidental deaths in the past ten years."

"It seems like the county is known now for the educational opportunities, as much as it is for its coal reserves."

"How about that! Who would have thought you could get a pharmacy degree or become a lawyer in Buchanan County? There's also a new nursing and physician assistant's school at our hospital now."

"Yeah, I know. My daughter is planning to enroll there next year. I heard you are mainly responsible for that school."

"I might have had a little to do with it. I serve on the boards of all three schools. Maybe not for long, though. They think I'm getting too old to drive to their meetings."

Marshal laughed. He knew Ms. Woodson could afford her own car and driver, if she wanted one. And he didn't think any of the board members would have the nerve to suggest she was too old, unless they were tired of serving and wanted to move out of the county.

"Well, Marshal, I've had my glass of wine, and old people who have to make a board meeting tomorrow must get their sleep. I think I'll turn in."

"Goodnight, Alma. I'll see you next week."

She handed him the rest of the almost-full bottle and a clean glass, and made her way inside, without the aid of the cane.

33

Railroad Right-of-Way

"I thought you were going to take Alma to Norfolk today. She told me last week she would be gone for three or four days and if I could spare you, she needed a driver."

"Change of plans. She's organizing today."

It was kind of a joke between them, but both Lori and Cory knew better than to let Alma overhear them, or they would be out looking for a job. She was plenty capable of kicking them out and running the whole show by herself. At least, until she could get new and respectable help.

"It seems now the Norfolk Southern Corporation is sending a representative here next week. I think Alma still has a lot of pull."

"No doubt about that. Well, you'd better get started planting those blight-resistant chestnut trees she ordered, in the woods up above her orchard. She's determined to bring back the chestnut trees her daddy talked about."

Alma did indeed have pictures from her father's file of the magnificent trees and articles he had saved from when they all got wiped out. But today, she was going through pictures she had put aside years ago. Pictures of Brett Parker.

She took the stack of pictures she had taken over the one year she had really known him to her rocker over by the window. Maybe she could look at them now. He had done so much for her and most of the other residents of Buchanan County. Now, she thought it might be time to go back and remember the good times and be thankful to him for rescuing her from the jaws of the Nation's Capital.

The first picture was the one she took when they were riding Brett's 4-wheelers on the strip job, with him chasing a fox along the highwall. *Sorry Brett, but you would have to find another place to ride your toys, now. Most of the strip mine roads have been filled in or slid in and the highwalls can be transversed again.* She smiled, thinking of the day she outshot him, and wondered if he ever confessed the fact to his men friends.

She had taken several pictures of him getting into, or out of, his big Hummer. The giant vehicle looked like a tank, but actually rode pretty good.

She held on to the next one with trembling fingers. It was the photo taken at Christmas at Aunt Ellie's house. The two of them, Brett and Aunt Ellie, were both holding on to the bowl of chocolate gravy. Alma couldn't tell if her aunt was passing it to him or he was returning an empty bowl. Her good, sweet, precious Aunt Ellie had only lived three years after this picture was taken. Well, she had gotten to know the real Brett Parker that Christmas.

She only briefly looked at the next several pictures. Most of them had been taken at South Holston Lake - at his house, on his boat, or fishing from the dock. He actually had taken one of her catching her first big fish, and one of her and a good-sized crappie.

When she came to the one with him, Aunt Ellie, Aunt Paula, and Jill having lunch at church under the big oak tree, she had to lay the pictures on the bed and walk out on the deck and breathe some fresh air. Today was pretty much like that day had been. The sun was bright. A slight breeze was blowing, enough to make the ladies wearing hats or bonnets hold on to them. The flowers planted under the eaves of the church were in full bloom, much like the daylilies she was now looking at, bordering the path leading up to her orchard.

She waved at Cory as he straightened up and wiped his brow. So, he was finally getting around to planting her chestnut trees. She would never see them become timber, but she would love to think she had a hand in their return.

Jill got out of prison a few years ago. Alma didn't know if she was a changed woman or not, but she had not come back to Buchanan County. Detective Rife said she moved to New Orleans and, last he heard, worked part-time cleaning a hotel in the party city. He thought maybe her religion had changed a bit in prison. The choices one makes in life can lead to such great rewards and satisfaction, or to devastating failure and heartbreak.

Alma always felt she had mostly chosen the right roads to travel, and the rewards had been wonderful. Now, she wasn't so sure. Losing Brett had made her feel more alone than ever, and she had to work at finding satisfaction in her life. Well, there were still good deeds that could be done, and she certainly didn't need to go down this pity road.

She went back inside and picked up the pictures again. Aunt Paula had always been such an elegant lady. Except maybe when you caught her working in her garden, minus her false teeth. She looked closely at the dress her aunt was wearing. She was sure it was one the talented woman had made for herself. All of the women back then made the clothes the family wore. A tear slid down her cheek as Alma recalled the night; only a year after she had told her aunt she was finally getting married, she got the call from the hospital that her Aunt Paula had suffered a major heart attack. In a little over two years, she had lost both her aunts.

Alma looked at a picture of Brett in his cowboy hat and boots. He wasn't one to dress up, but you could catch him quite often looking sharp in his western attire. She was sure this was his dress-up look when he flew into Montana. Whenever she talked about her aunts getting old, or the fact that she and Brett were now senior citizens, he would insist on changing the subject, saying that, as long as they stayed healthy and active, they would die with their boots on. She had no doubt he did.

Alma leaned back on the bed and held the picture close to her chest. She had almost not made it back then. Detective Rife and Krista stayed with her almost constantly for two months after she got the news of the plane crash. The day after the funeral, Charlie came by the Inn and spent the whole day with her, and they talked about Brett. Charlie shared the life of the energetic and, sometimes, mischievous little boy, who she almost knew, as he was growing up. She shared the days of two people reaching retirement age and acting like two teenagers falling in love for the first time. They laughed a little, cried a lot, and sometimes got downright angry. She had never known Charlie, but, after that, although he never became her brother-in-law, he did become her 'brother'.

    About six months later, Charlie had called and asked her to meet with him and the Parker family lawyer. She hesitated. He pleaded with her that it was what Brett had wanted and she might want to hear what his plans had been. The only plans she had been interested in included her, and Brett had dashed all of them into a mountainside in the Rockies. She finally agreed to meet with them. She thought there might be some insight she could shed on Brett's latest dreams, of things that could be done for the people of Buchanan County. Like the daycare center for seniors at his old home place, that was very busy.

    She never asked for it, she never wanted it, and she never spent a penny of the twenty-five million dollars on herself. Part of the fortune he had left her in his will was in Parker Corporation preferred stock that kept funneling cash into the BretAlou Foundation she established. Charlie was the President of BretAlou. He could have contested the will and won, but he never considered doing so.

He loved his only brother and felt Brett was in sound mind when he made her one of his benefactors. Charlie and the Parker Corporation had still inherited the majority of Brett's fortune.

Alma dug through some more of the pictures and picked up several showing the different building stages of the medical wing to the hospital. Even though BretAlou had initiated the building of a teaching hospital wing with a five-million-dollar donation and helped raise the remaining funds needed, she declined the offer of naming it in honor of her or the Parker family. Instead, she wanted it to be called the Appalachian Medical School, just like the Appalachian School of Law and the Appalachian College of Pharmacy.

It was nearly midnight when Alma gathered up the remaining pictures and filed them away again. Some of the last ones she looked at were of the condos and townhouses she had built along the banks of the Levisa River and Garden Creek, where shacks and trailers had once stood. She didn't own a room in any of the buildings. As soon as a townhouse or condo was sold to a hard-working coal miner, often financed by BretAlou, she would start the plans to build others. As she laid her head on the pillow and pulled the blanket up around her chin, her thoughts turned to maybe her last big project. She only had to get the railroad to go along.

Krista drove into the driveway while Alma was sitting on the porch with her morning coffee. She had a bag with her, so Alma assumed she might be staying a few days. That could be good or bad.

She loved her now 'only' sibling more than anything but sometimes they just got on each other's nerves. Krista was ten years younger than Alma and thought she had to take care of them both. It reminded Alma of Max and how he worried about his children committing him to a nursing home. Krista would bring up a retirement or assistant-living place over at Abingdon once in a while, but she didn't push it. She once said she would move into assisted-living with Alma, since she also was alone. Her husband Jack had died five years ago, and her children had long ago moved out and had families of their own. Alma had told her the only assistance Krista needed was to get off her butt, do a little exercise, and make a contribution somewhere. She never heard anymore about it.

"Good morning, Alma."

"Good morning. You moving in?"

"Well, I can turn around and go home, if you want me to."

"Don't be silly. I was just kidding. You can stay as long as you want. Come on up and get yourself a cup of coffee."

Krista dropped her bag inside the door and went into the kitchen and poured a cup of coffee. She took the pot out on the porch and refreshed Alma's cup. After she returned the pot, she pulled her chair up close to the railing, placed her feet on top, and practically laid down in the seat.

"What bedroom do you want me to take?"

"Take the master bedroom on the main level. Lori and Cory have no reason to stay over, and I'm not ready to start using it yet. Why don't you just move in here, Krista? You don't have any reason to drive back to Roanoke anymore. All your children have moved away. You're about like me. The only close kin we have are each other."

"I can't do that. I've got all mine and Jack's stuff up there, and you don't have anywhere to store anything. When I come here, all I usually get is a tiny bedroom. Besides, there's my church."

"Hell, you don't go to church except at Christmas and Easter, now that Jack's gone. If you'll move down here, you can go with me every Saturday and Sunday to a real church. I know Aunt Paula would be proud to look down and see you sitting there."

"What about my stuff?"

"I'll move downstairs into that room you'll sleep in tonight, and you can have my room. It's large. I'll close off two bedrooms upstairs for you to store all the rest of your STUFF. You ought to get rid of most of that, anyway."

"I'll think about it. You going to sit here all day, or do you want to drive over to Abingdon and take in a play at the Barter Theatre?"

"I can't today. I've got a board meeting this afternoon. I'm just getting charged up."

"Guess what I got in the mail this week, Alma?"

"With all your excitement, I'd say it was the same as I got - a check from the gas and oil company."

"How about that? After all these years of fighting them every step of the way, they finally are forced to release our money from the escrow accounts. I can't believe they were able to steal our gas rights like they did our parents' coal rights."

"Well, actually, Krista, our grandparents sold the rights to the coal on our land. The trick they tried to play on us was claiming that it included the rights to the gas. It's taken a lot of years, with the courts and the government getting involved, to get us a royalty on the vast profits the companies made on gas they took, that rightly belonged to us."

"Well, it's a little late for me to enjoy most of it, but my kids and grandchildren will be happy. What are you going to do with your share?"

"It'll all go into the BretAlou Foundation. I'm just happy that the other families can finally benefit from all they have suffered trying to survive in this county."

They smiled at each other and clinked their coffee cups together in a toast to a big 'W' on the small people's side of the scoreboard.

On Wednesday of the next week, the representative of Norfolk Southern Railroads showed up. He booked a room for three days. Alma didn't even think about providing a room free of charge. If she got what she wanted, then she might consider writing it off at the end of the week.

She first met with Mr. H. Herbert Smithfield after breakfast on Thursday, on the back deck of the Inn. Lori set up a small table with two roll-away armchairs and a separate table with coffee, wine, and pastries. H. Herbert had spent the remainder of the evening before with the Congressman for the ninth district of Virginia, surveying the railroad property in the eastern part of Buchanan County. As Alma approached the table where he was sitting, he immediately rose to greet her. She extended her hand and said, "Hello. Please call me Alma. I own the Hanging Inn. I believe we have an appointment."

He smiled. "Then call me Herb. I'm representing the Norfolk Southern Corporation located in Norfolk, Virginia. You have an unusual, but very beautiful, place here."

"Thank you. Would you like a refill on that coffee, or something to eat, before we get started?"

"No, thanks. I helped myself to coffee and was just appreciating the peace and quiet of the mountains and the lovely singing of the birds."

As Alma filled her cup with steaming coffee and pulled up her chair, he busied himself with his briefcase and pulled out several folders and a laptop computer.

"If you're ready, Ms. Woods... Alma," he smiled at his slip, "we'll get started. We have received all your petitions and documentations and your very unusual proposal. The lawyers, of which I am one, and engineers have reviewed your entire proposal, and met with the board of Norfolk and Southern several times over the past year. I must admit that we, the lawyers and engineers, fervently objected to any consideration being given to your proposal. We felt selling, or giving up any of the railroad's property, would be detrimental to our interests. We believe there is a possibility that in the future, energy resources will be in such demand that recent actions and regulations could reverse themselves and opportunities again would be in our favor. However, the Board and President of Norfolk Southern agree with you."

Alma pumped her fist in the air and screamed out a hallelujah loud enough to bring Lori running out to the deck.

"Oh, go away, Lori. We're fine. I just got carried away with some good news this fine gentleman bestowed upon me. Wait, you can bring us a bottle of our best champagne and a couple of glasses."

"I've read your proposal over several times, Alma, but I'm still curious why you want this particular property and if you have any detailed plans."

"Herb, how familiar are you with Buchanan County and its history?"

"Not very familiar. Your Congressman, Mr. Kirk, took me on a short tour yesterday. I'm from the Eastern Shore and have seldom been past Roanoke in Virginia."

"I'm not surprised. Most of our own elected representatives never consider Southwest Virginia as part of the state. They think everything ends at Roanoke. Most of the counties down here are probably closer to the capitals of West Virginia and Kentucky than they are to Richmond. Buchanan County has the most valuable resource in the state, but also the most neglected and deprived people in the country. Only recently, have the educational opportunities been available to residents of the Appalachian Mountains. The Community College System finally gave us a chance. Travel our roads and taste our water where the public water systems have yet to be provided. A lot of our now-paved roads are just one lane."

"Yes, I noticed this road up to the Hanging Inn is very narrow and would be considered one-lane."

"I've kept the well my parents had, and I use the water occasionally to wash an automobile. I sometimes spring it on a guest from the city or Eastern Shore. It's perfectly safe to drink and has been tested. I'll have Lori bring you a glass, if you want to taste water my brother and sisters and I grew up with?"

"No, thanks. I'll take your word for it."

"Well, it has a sulfur odor and a lot of iron in it. We carried water from the creek to wash clothes when I was young. The well water would leave a reddish stain in the sinks and tubs that we had to scrub off with soda and a toothbrush about once a week."

"Thank God for the Flanagan Lake over near Haysi. Congressman Kirk tells me it furnishes fresh mountain water to several counties. How about the railroad land? In your proposal, you brought up the need for development. Do you have something specific in mind?"

"Herb, as you drove around with our Congressman, how many acres of flat level land did you notice in any given mile?"

"Well, thinking back, I don't rightly remember seeing an acre of level land except where a school, a ball field, or maybe a large business like a hospital or a shaft mine existed."

"Right! The Federal Government and the Army Corps of Engineers had to dig out half a mountain to make a few acres of level land to move Grundy. Maybe, if we had more suitable land, there would be more than one town in the whole county. An acre of level land in Buchanan County is worth almost as much as the coal underneath it. Herb, the Appalachian people have been ripped off all their lives. We made it through the Depression with little farms and living off the land. Our ancestors, having little money or none at all, sold the coal rights for a fraction of what they should have been paid. Later, their mountains and farms were destroyed for the right-of-way to the coal lying underneath what they thought was theirs. In recent years, with the help of the government, they have lost again when the gas companies were required to put the royalties they should have received into escrow accounts until the courts figured out who owns the gas - the land owner or the coal owner. Imagine a family in these mountains having to hire a lawyer to fight a coal company and sue to get what is rightfully theirs. Thankfully, our representatives passed legislation that finally lets a family get the royalties they deserve."

"I agree, Alma, to everything you have said. But the railroad paid a fair price for the right-of-way through these mountains, which was essential if coal was going to become a major energy source."

"Right. My point is the railroad took a good chunk of our land. Now, there are places the railroad is not being used. I think you should let that valuable land go back to the community for the greater good. I don't think a train has traveled up the Levisa River beyond the coke ovens in the past ten years. Since the shaft mines and the loading docks have closed down here in the Garden Creek, Oakwood, and Keen Mountain areas, there is no need for the railroad. But there is a great need for the land."

"For what?"

"Well, the land up at Keen Mountain that the shaft mine and railroad occupied for years could now be used for a civic center so the people here didn't have to travel to the Tri-Cities, or to Roanoke, to see a performance or have a convention. There is a lot of talent in these mountains, but they have to leave to fulfill any dreams or ambitions. My BretAlou Foundation would like to build a ten-story apartment building in the triangle between your railroad tracks, next to the Pharmacy School. I can't add any more rooms here at the Hanging Inn, and there are very few places to rent for the students at the Law School and the Medical School down at Grundy. With available land and some development, we could open another nice motel and some modern restaurants in this part of Buchanan County."

"Well Alma, you've sold the Norfolk Southern Corporation, and now you've sold me. If you are willing to sign some papers, I'm authorized to sell to the BretAlou Foundation all the railroad land along Route 460 and Garden Creek, east of Dismal Creek."

"I think that is just great! I'm afraid, if the price is too high, I will have to ask for a contingency to get the Board's approval to raise any additional funds necessary."

"Is one dollar too high?"

"For all the right-of-way you just mentioned?"

"That's right. Norfolk Southern Corporation wants to be a good neighbor. They have decided to donate the land to your Foundation, but it will be an easier settlement if they sell the land to you and provide the deeds per sale. That requires an exchange of legal tender to satisfy the sale."

Alma walked over to the table and poured both of them a glass of the champagne Lori had brought out in a large bucket of ice. She took several deep breaths to prevent herself from hyperventilating. No dream of hers this big was supposed to come true.

"Mr. Smithfield, I will have to go to my room to get the Foundation's checkbook and as soon as I sign those papers, we are going to have ourselves a toast."

"That will be fine, Ms. Woodson. I must say you drive a hard bargain."

He was smiling as she walked away. She had to use her cane to make her return to the deck. With all the trembling going on inside her body, she didn't know if she could hold the pen to sign the contract.

When it was all signed, and she had handed over the check, they raised their glasses and clinked them together before drinking the toast.

"Now, Herb, when can your railroad start taking up all that track?"

"After our talk today, I can see why you would be in a hurry. It will take several months to remove the rails and crossties, and maybe up to a year to include the trestles and concrete pillars. If you want us to grade the road bed and fill and level portions of the land, the corporation has agreed to do that, also. But, it may take a little longer, depending on what is required."

"You can do all that, and it will be a welcome contribution. Could I request permission to oversee the removal of one particular pillar supporting the trestle going across Garden Creek? I would appreciate the permission, but I would rather not have questions as to my reason. After it is all said and done, I will explain."

"I don't see why that will be a problem. I don't understand, but I can wait for an explanation. I'll be sure to inform the foreman-in-charge of your wishes. He will notify you when the removal will take place."

"One more thing, Herb. Would you spend an extra day here and let me show you around? That Congressman just doesn't really know the back roads of Buchanan County."

"I was hoping you would ask. If you're ready, I'll buy your lunch at the restaurant of your choosing. Then we can get started."

34

Leroy

Within six months, the railroad had taken up the entire track from Keen Mountain and Garden Creek to nearly a mile east of Dismal Creek. Alma spent the long, cold and snowy winter huddled close to the fireplace of the Hanging Inn. It wasn't that she was idle. She had met with Jeffrey Conners' son several times to finalize the plans for the new apartment building. She had received approval from the Planning Commission and was one step away from the go-ahead for her construction project. She didn't expect any problems with the Board of Supervisors. And, a couple of Supervisors had already complimented her on her foresight in the need of housing in Buchanan County.

      Herbert called about once a month to check on the progress and Alma's satisfaction. He told her the grade work would probably not start until spring, after the ground had thawed out and dried up a little. He would let her know the timetable to take down the concrete pillars, but he suspected that could start a little earlier, if she needed to get her project moving.

She waited until March to call him back to say she was ready to start the removal of the pillars, so she could contract the building of a flood wall on Garden Creek and begin the fill to raise the site above flood stage. He promised her the work would start within the month.

Charlie called her and asked if she would go with him to visit the Parker Senior Center. She had been so happy that Charlie completed the project Brett had started at their old home place. She gladly said she would love to go with him. When they arrived unannounced, the Director of the Center took them on a tour and they had lunch in the cafeteria. Both Charlie and Alma were impressed with the management of the place. What had started out as a daycare for seniors had developed into a full assisted-living complex. What Charlie wanted Alma and his director to tell him was how badly they needed to expand into a nursing home.

"Charlie, I think that would be great. I know we have the need for one. Nowadays, families don't have the time to care for an elderly member, with both husband and wife working outside the home. Also, a lot of people are living much longer. You don't see many like the ROMEO Club members living by themselves anymore. I know Max and them took younger men into their club there near the end, and they still get together every Wednesday morning, but some of them don't live by themselves like Max and his group did."

"Then you agree, Alma that I should go ahead with the expansion? I will have to remove part of the hillside and build a wall beside the creek to have the room."

"I say go for it. What do you think, Ruby?"

"I would be so pleased if you could do that, Charlie. I have several day visitors that probably could move in now. I know our policy is that all day visitors have to be able to care for themselves, such as feeding and using the restroom facilities, but I just can't turn some of them away. A Nursing Home is badly needed, Charlie."

"Good. Let's get started. With what Alma's doing, we should about even out the housing need in this county."

On Saturday, the 17th of March, Roscoe Breeding, the railroad foreman in charge of the demolition crew, met with her at the construction site.

"I understand from Mr. Smithfield that you want to have a say in how we get rid of these concrete pillars and the trestles."

"Well, you have already removed the rails, and I don't care how you dismantle the iron works of the trestles. I just want to watch over the destruction of that one particular pillar. I want you to take it down from the top with maybe a jackhammer, or some chiseling device, a chip at a time."

"Are you crazy, lady? Ms. Woodson, that could take weeks and cost piles of money. I don't think Mr. Smithfield had that in mind when he said to follow your instructions."

"Well, Roscoe, I am probably crazy, and have been since I moved back to this county. But, if you want to give Mr. Smithfield a call, then go ahead. Or, if you want, you can have a room at the Hanging Inn for tonight, and I'll tell you a tale that will make you want to take that pillar down with a sharp knife and a brush."

Roscoe didn't seem to want to place a call to Mr. Smithfield, at least not until he had heard the whole story from Alma. He accepted her invitation to spend the night at her inn.

That evening, she poured him a glass of wine and sat in the chair beside him by the crackling fire. She started her story with the picture her father had taken all those years ago. She pointed out Leroy and told what she knew of Grady Bracken, Jackson Mullins, and Thomas Wills. She told Roscoe of the mystery her dad had left her, how she had tracked down the question mark in the picture to be Leroy, and how she had found his four girls.

About midnight, when they were on their second bottle of wine, she gave him Betty's journal and told him about Larkin and Jill.

"I'm going to bed now, Roscoe. You go ahead and read that journal. In the morning, if you want to call Herbert and tell him you intend to take down that pillar your way, then make the call. I don't think we'll have to take off but a few feet of that crown, and then you can blast the rest into the creek. Breakfast will be between six and nine o'clock. Goodnight, Roscoe."

"Goodnight, Ms. Woodson. I think you can rest pretty easy tonight. From what you have already told me, I think we'll do it your way."

On Monday morning, Alma drove Brett's Hummer, which Charlie had insisted she keep, down to the destruction site and sat in the vehicle on the overflow bridge. The old vehicle had been kept in her garage, and with Cory's help, treated with tender-loving care all these years.

With the labor going on only a hundred yards away, she could see that Roscoe had the men being extra careful in their detail work. Not only were they using cutting and chipping tools, but he also had them sift the material through a screen before they dumped it into a huge bin. Evidently, Roscoe had told the crew what they were looking for.

After about an hour, another vehicle pulled up behind her. Shortly, the former detective, Ronnie Rife, opened the passenger door of the Hummer and asked if he could join her in her vigil.

"Of course, Detective, hop on in here. We have a ringside seat. How did you know I was here? What do you think is going on?"

"Oh, the whole county knows by now that you have stolen the railroad's property for your own personal gain. After all, the railroad crews have been taking up their tracks for months now. When the Sheriff told me you were demolishing the trestles and piers and had applied for a permit to build a flood wall, I figured I'd better come up here and keep an eye on you."

"I won't make a penny off this deal, Ronnie. I'm just trying to help provide affordable housing for the college students. The rent will be cheaper than what a lot of people are paying to live in some of these trailers. Right now, I'm just watching them tear down one of the pillars that supported the trestle crossing Garden Creek."

"And looking for Leroy's bones."

"Now, how did you come to that conclusion? I think you're getting a little senile in your old age. How old are you now? About ninety, I would guess. And I thought you gave up detective work a long time ago."

"I'm still about the same age you are, so don't push it too high. Over the years, the new sheriffs in town have always kept me informed. You never know when a cold case gets hot again and you need to confer with someone who was there. It wasn't hard to figure out what you were up to when I heard they were taking down the concrete pillars, and I got up here and saw they weren't blasting them into the creek, but chipping out bits as a dentist would drill on a tooth. Remember, I was active back when you discovered who Leroy was and when you found the diary."

"I'm glad you're here, Detective. It wouldn't seem right to be investigating again, without you by my side. Anyway, if we find any bones or fragments of bones, I'll need someone with police connections to do CSI procedures on them."

"I'll be glad to help. You have dug up one of the most fascinating mysteries in the history of Buchanan County. I would love to see it through to

'Case Closed'. You do know that you are fast becoming one of Buchanan County's legends?"

"You mean history, Detective. Anything I or BretAlou have done for this county is on record. So, it's facts, not legend."

"Some of the stuff I hear is beyond believable facts. It could be rumors and exaggerated gossip, but it's becoming legendary."

"Like what?"

"Like you came back here as a CIA or FBI agent and uncovered a murder that happened back during the Depression."

"Fact. Except for the part of the agent."

"That you solved the murder of Marlene and had Jill sent to prison. Then went to bat for her, and she escaped the death penalty."

"Mostly facts."

"That you have made millions of dollars from the Hanging Inn and the coal and gas royalties that you cheated your brother and sisters out of."

"Ouch! That hurts. False. Not a bit of it true. The coal rights were sold long before Dad bought this land. The gas royalties are just now being released from escrow accounts, and Krista and the grandchildren are getting an equal share. The Inn makes a small profit each year. I don't think I want to hear any more about legends or history that I may be a part of."

"That guy in the white hardhat is heading our way."

"Oh my gosh, Ronnie. Do you think they have already found something?"

"We'll soon find out."

When she got back to the inn, Alma found Krista stretched out in the hammock, reading a book.

"Get up from there, Krista. Go pack a bag, then get on the phone and make us some reservations for flights to Atlanta, Houston, and Charlotte, North Carolina. Tomorrow, at the latest."

Krista jumped up and closed her book.

"What in the world are you talking about, Alma? What has happened?"

"They found Leroy. This time, I am sure. Detective Rife is taking the bone fragments to the lab in Richmond himself to positively identify him. He said he would have the results tonight, or tomorrow. It seemed like he has a personal friend working there. We have to get word to Leroy's daughters."

"Do you even know where they live after all this time?"

"I just told you. I get a Christmas card from them every year. Now, let's get moving. I may need some help packing. I'm shaking like a leaf."

"Can't you just call them? I don't know if you're up to that much traveling."

"Don't be a nerd, Krista. Of course, I can't just call them. This is news they've waited their whole lives for. Where is their daddy? Now that we know, we have to be there to hold their hand as they find out."

And she was. It took three days to get the news to all the girls. It took Detective Rife an extra day to confirm the DNA match to that of Leroy's daughters, which Alma had retrieved back when they thought they had found Leroy in the cistern. When Alma and Krista reached Leslie in Chapel Hill, North Carolina, she traveled with them, by car, to tell her sister Shirley, now living in Charlotte. The two sisters joined Alma and Krista to fly to Atlanta, where Tonya joined them for the flight to Houston to tell the last sister, Kathy.

    Krista watched her sister sleep on the flight home. Alma looked so peaceful. Occasionally, a smile would cross her lips, and a tear would drip from the corner of her eye. Krista looked out the window of the plane at the white clouds floating underneath them and up into the depths of the Carolina blue sky. She could imagine a smile or tear on their father's face, also. Leroy could finally rest in peace.

ABOUT THE AUTHOR

Vic Edwards

is the author of *Hanger*, his first novel. He graduated from Radford University and taught school in Giles County for 25 years. He and his wife Sue are now retired from teaching and live in Bristol, Virginia. They have three children and six grandchildren.

vicedwards@bvunet.net

Made in the USA
Charleston, SC
25 November 2011